Toil Under The Sun

by
R. Phillip Ritter

Bloomington, IN   authorHOUSE   Milton Keynes, UK

AuthorHouse™
1663 Liberty Drive, Suite 200
Bloomington, IN 47403
www.authorhouse.com
Phone: 1-800-839-8640

AuthorHouse™ *UK Ltd.*
500 Avebury Boulevard
Central Milton Keynes, MK9 2BE
www.authorhouse.co.uk
Phone: 08001974150

This book is a work of fiction. People, places, events, and situations are the product of the author's imagination. Any resemblance to actual persons, living or dead, or historical events, is purely coincidental.

© 2006 R. Phillip Ritter. All rights reserved.

No part of this book may be reproduced, stored in a retrieval system, or transmitted by any means without the written permission of the author.

First published by AuthorHouse 11/9/2006

ISBN: 1-4259-1987-1 (e)
ISBN: 1-4259-2010-1 (sc)

Library of Congress Control Number: 2006902342

Printed in the United States of America
Bloomington, Indiana

This book is printed on acid-free paper.

This book is dedicated to

Richard P. Ritter, Sr.

who served as a lieutenant with the U.S. Army in the Philippines and Korea

Reviewed by

Kristine Larsen Ritter
and by
Carole Healy, Cynthia Johnson, Doug Larsen, Cathy Muse,
and Sybil Ritter

Cover Design by
Kristine Larsen Ritter

All is vanity.

What do people gain from all the toil

at which they toil under the sun?

A generation goes, and a generation comes,

but the earth remains forever.

Ecclesiastes 1:2-4

Prologue

Remembering a dream, February 2003

    I am an old man now, and yet I still think of the dreams that haunted my youth many years ago. One dream in particular tormented me more than the rest: the one of the little boy sitting in an old tree. I believe this singular vision came to me during periods of troubled sleep. I do not remember the exact patterns of the dream, but it did appear several times on consecutive nights. Once it even came to me during a late Saturday afternoon nap while an October wind raged against the big picture window in my parents' living room. Unlike my other dreams, I always remembered every detail long after the bright morning sun or fierce autumn storm or bitter winter gale had finally awakened me; and it always played out in the same purposeful way, without meaningful difference, with no memorable variation from beginning to end. I am telling you about my dream now because it is crucial for you to understand this one thing. This is more important than anything else you may know or learn about me. I believe this is true because I did not really care about my own life until I finally understood the dream. At that moment, when I awoke to smell the pungent sea air and hear the squawking gulls hovering above and feel the soothing rumble of the ship's engines, my restless mind at long last found peace.

    As far back as I can remember, even before the first grade, I have always dreamed. My earliest dreams were not all that interesting. As a matter of fact, most of them were actually pretty boring. But when I neared the end of elementary school the dreams became more unusual, as well as more memorable. The specific dream I am about to share with you first appeared on a humid night, early in the summer before my first year of junior high school. I remember this because the dream followed the tumultuous day I first began to question why I had been brought into the world. No—there was something more than that: it was the day I first began questioning my very existence. This same day was further defined by a remarkably violent thunderstorm, a cloudburst that did not release its final torrent of warm rain until hours after I awoke from the dream. I will never forget the jagged flashes of light on the poster-cluttered walls of my small bedroom, the fragrant smell of rain drifting through the open casement window, and the relentless pounding of drops on the wood shingle roof above my bed. When I sat up, sweat-soaked sheets clinging to my shivering legs, I struggled to breath and tried to scream to my parents. The dream had frightened me more than anything ever had before. Ironically, it had begun calmly enough, with no anticipation of the rage to come. But let me tell you about the dream itself, and you can judge this for yourself.

The dream always began on a clear, peaceful night with me flying around in the sky, high above a forest of dark trees that spread endlessly in every direction. Although I would have preferred otherwise, I did not fly gracefully like a soaring eagle. Instead, I forced myself through the air by franticly dog-paddling my arms and bicycle-kicking my legs. The faster I paddled and kicked, the higher I flew above the ground. If my feet or hands slowed even slightly I began sinking down into the darkness below. As far back as I can remember, I never flew this way in any other dream. I always moved jerkily through the cool night sky, apparently lost, until a sphere of softly glowing blue light appeared far off in the distance, the smooth top of the sphere barely visible above the trees. I hovered momentarily to study the light, keeping my feet and hands going so that I wouldn't fall to the ground, then always turned and headed for it. I never did anything else: I always flew toward the light.

When I neared the light, I slowed my arms and legs a little and began a smooth descent into the forest. The trees never had individual shape from above, but when I moved past the first branches they snaked crookedly around and above me, black and gnarled, nearly closing off any view of the sky above as I dropped closer to the ground. After descending slowly through the clutter of branches, surprisingly without touching a single one, my bare feet squeaked when they touched a thick layer of damp moss on the forest floor. I wiggled my toes into the moss; they squeaked again.

Without any hesitation, not even to squeak my toes one last time, I began searching for the blue light. At first I could never find it, no matter where or how I explored. Before long, maybe twenty minutes at most, a familiar sound of wind chimes, muffled by distance and the dank forest air, attracted my focus until I recognized a faint hint of blue light reflecting off a few of the glistening branches. I began walking toward the reflections, not easily at first, because the moss-covered ground that had once squeaked under my toes now pulled at the bottoms of my feet with an unpleasant sucking sound, resisting my efforts to move quickly toward the light. This frustrated me; still I trudged on for hundreds of steps, moving barely a few inches with each torturous stride. I grew more and more exhausted, and at the moment I thought I would never reach my destination the blue light unexpectedly began advancing toward me.

Now this is the part of the dream that still troubles me to this day. Although I struggled to walk, resisted at each step by the increasingly sticky moss, the blue light moved closer nonetheless, faster and faster, until it suddenly engulfed me, crackling ominously all around. The blue light blinded me at first, but as my eyes adjusted and my sight slowly returned, there at the very center of the light sat a little boy in an old tree; high up on a thick branch, his slender arms clutching the rough bark of the trunk, the glowing light appearing to emanate from inside of him. I squinted to try to recognize the little boy; I could never see his face clearly enough. I even tried to cup my hands tightly around the sides of my eyes to shield them from the light, but still could not see the boy's face enough to make him out.

I stopped trying to walk because the moss prevented me from approaching closer to the little boy. So I rested, and while I paused I again felt the coolness of the moss against my feet and heard the wind chimes, still oddly muffled and distant. To my surprise, the wind chimes sounded no closer than when I had first listened to them. If anything, they seemed even farther away. I looked up to the sky as I listened, and for the first time noticed the full moon floating unhurriedly past a ragged opening in a cluster of tall trees. The moon shined brightly at first, brighter than the blue light—then a wisp of dark cloud slid across its face, and then another, and another, until the wisps formed together into an expanding mass of dark clouds that nearly covered the moon and blocked most of its light. As these clouds continued to gather and darken the moon, I felt an icy breeze curl up around my neck and then across my cheek, releasing an instinctive shiver down the middle of my back. The shiver intensified and spread out across my legs and arms, and then a new and stronger gust fluttered the thin fabric of my shirt. Only seconds later, I felt the first icy snowflake settle and melt on the top of my ear. I turned away from the small boy and toward the snowflake, just before another one landed on my nose.

When I turned back to face the old tree, countless snowflakes, crusty and razor-edged, now swirled around inside the dome of blue light, mysteriously contained by the luminous outer surface of the sphere. The wind intensified too, and as it quickened the little boy trembled when a frosty gust cut across his bare legs and arms. He turned his face away as shards of snow stung his smooth cheeks, but the wind detected his movement and instantly changed direction, stinging his face again. He closed his eyes to protect them against the driving flakes. He pulled himself more tightly against the tree's rough surface to resist the now pounding wind by digging his fingers into the deeply furrowed bark. I did not believe it at first; when I squinted my eyes into tiny slits and cupped my hands around the sides of my face to see more clearly through the storm, I could see that it was true: blood flowed from the little boy's hands, his fingers and palms savagely wounded by the jagged edges of bark; blood streamed down his arms in thin rivulets and dripped off his elbows into lumpy puddles on his shuddering legs and the swaying branch that held him high above the ground.

Frightened by this horrific scene, I strained again to run toward the tree to help the little boy; the moss still clung tenaciously to my feet and restrained me from any forward movement. I screamed at the boy, hoping to offer him any encouragement that I could; no sound came out. I twisted my body and waved my arms to signal to him that he was not alone, but the boy, his face still turned away from the raging storm, could not see me. I yearned desperately to help the little boy, and yet I did not know how. Then, as I felt a crushing hopelessness tear at my heart, two misty shadows floated between the twisted branches beyond the old tree. The shadows moved methodically around the tree until they stepped into the blue light, revealing themselves as a man and woman, both gaunt and stooped with age. I strained my eyes to see who they were, but like before with the little boy, could not recognize them. They stopped underneath the boy and began calling to him, beckoning him to come down from the tree. He glanced at them, first the man and then the woman, and quickly looked away. The old man and woman began waving their arms and screaming at the little boy, just as I had, pleading with him to come down from the tree; he ignored them and, pulling himself even tighter against the rough tree, refused to come down.

The storm intensified and, concealed by the raging wind and snow, the old tree and the little boy who sat in it and the old man and woman vanished from my sight. Then, for reasons I did not understand, I pulled one foot back and the moss quietly released me. Startled, I continued stepping back, easily, no longer hindered by the sticky moss, until I reached the edge of the sphere and there felt an unexpected warmth. I turned into the warmth and walked effortlessly through the bright surface of the sphere. As the blue light faded behind me, I stepped into the glorious sunlight and felt a rush of cool air and saw visions of rolling hills spotted with fragrant green trees. I closed my eyes for a moment and breathed in the sweet-smelling air; and then, when I turned to look back, the dream ended in a shroud of regret. The dream always ended this way. Always.

Chapter 1

Inland from the Oregon Coast, July 1931

A child is born into new life, a brown-haired boy with delicate features. The child is delivered by a grizzled, elderly doctor in a windowless room, deep inside an aging brick-clad hospital. The doctor is assisted by a young nurse who began working at the hospital a few months earlier. After an arduous and unpleasant pregnancy, the child arrives without difficulty beneath a ceaselessly buzzing fluorescent light fixture, the light of the fixture vibrating pale green off the glassy ceramic tile floor and wainscots. The child will never know this: before he has lived two months, his adolescent mother will turn sixteen.

The young mother conceived the child on a blustery October night almost nine months ago. Later, when she is many years older, she will still remember the time of day, five minutes before midnight, with surprising clarity. She will also recall the blurred motion of torn curtains gracefully buoyed by the gentle push of a cool night breeze through an open bedroom window. She conceived the child that night with a man four years older. She loved the man, or thought she did, and she believed that he loved her. He had told her of his love many times; each time she convinced herself to trust his words. This was not difficult for her, because she had felt alone and unloved before meeting the man, and he had given her at least the promise of love. Because of this anticipation she felt better when they were together. He stayed with her until she missed her period. When she told this to the man, his casual indifference surprised her. Then he left; quietly, early in the morning darkness, without saying goodbye to her or leaving a note. For a few weeks she expected him to come back. He never did. When she finally accepted that he would never come back, she felt alone and unloved once again.

Her parents named her Sarah, after a great grandmother who had emigrated from England for an unremembered reason. Sarah stayed in the departed man's small, dingy apartment for nearly a week, until the landlord—an obese, self-important man—arrived to collect the rent. He listened to Sarah beg for nearly a minute before escorting her and a few meager possessions out of the building into the modest street that fronted the main entry doors. She stood there, listening to the echo of the slammed doors, her feet straddling a jagged crack near the edge of the uneven sidewalk, long enough to pull on a threadbare jacket, then walked down the street three blocks before veering into a narrow alley. Hungry and dehydrated when she had left the apartment, four more days of wandering with no food and only random sips of water did not improve her condition. Sarah probably would not have survived much longer, but she was lucky and found a part time job washing dishes at a small restaurant a few blocks from the waterfront. She had been hanging around in the alley at the back of the kitchen looking for scraps of discarded food when Jake, the owner of the small restaurant, stepped through the rear door for a smoke and found her. His chest ached when he first saw the ragged young girl fishing through his dumpster; he offered her a meal and then a job.

Jake gave Sarah an advance in pay so that she could buy food and rent a small room in a boarding house that he helped her find. Jake and the woman who owned the house attended the same church. Although not close friends, they were connected by a common desire to help others whenever practicable. After three months, Jake noticed Sarah's expanding belly. He promoted her to assistant waitress and gave her a small raise. He told her that she deserved the promotion and pay increase because of her reliability and hard work. She thanked him, but did not use the extra money to buy food or clothing or to move into a bigger room at the boarding house. Instead, she carefully saved her profit in a small wooden box she had found in the room, probably forgotten by a previous tenant. She kept the box safely hidden under her bed.

With the passage of another four weeks, Sarah's pregnancy became obvious to everyone; even Mathew, the young waiter from South Dakota who usually didn't recognize anything taking place around him unless it either exploded or caught fire. With confirmation of the child, Jake's already natural tendency to worry about Sarah broadened. Often, especially when she finished work late in the evening, Jake would stop her as she prepared to leave.

"Hey Sarah…are you finished for the day?"

Sarah untied her food-smudged apron and tossed it into a hamper by the swinging kitchen doors. "Yes, Jake. I took care of all my receipts, cleaned my serving area, filled the salt and pepper shakers, set the tables for breakfast, and now I'm heading home. Is there anything else you need me to do before I leave? I could stay a few minutes longer."

Jake squeezed his chin and glanced down at his watch, pretending to consider her question. "No, no. I think that should just about do it for the night. Anyway, Mathew is still here if I need anything. I was going to say that I do have some leftover food in the back that will just go to waste if someone doesn't eat it. Would you mind having a bite before you go? You know how I hate wasting food."

Sarah smiled, turning her head slightly to conceal the smile. Jake had made this offer several times before, always accompanied by the same mock concern about wasting food, but Sarah had never accepted. "Sure Jake. I think I will stay and have something to eat tonight. I *am* pretty hungry, and a little tired too. I don't know if I'd have the energy to get anything to eat otherwise."

While Sarah ate, Jake sat at the table and told stories about his life. When she neared the end of the mashed potatoes and gravy, he asked, "Did I ever tell you about my wife? I don't think I did, but please stop me if you've already heard this. I don't want to bore you any more than necessary."

Sarah swallowed a partially chewed green bean, forcing it down with some milk, then balanced her fork on the rim of the plate. "No, Jake. I don't think you did."

Jake turned his head and gazed through the big storefront window into the street. "Yeah, Kay was a dear lady. We met at a church social a few weeks before Christmas; got married almost a year later. My parents weren't too happy about it because we were so young. I think dad was ready to go along with it, but mom thought we should wait a few years. We didn't wait. We were in love, so we ran away and got married anyway."

Sarah picked up her fork and licked it. "How old were you?"

"Uh, pretty young, but older than you. We had a lot of good times together. Took a dandy trip to Arizona once—to see the Grand Canyon. Yeah, that was a dandy trip. I remember we both got sunburned; we didn't mind too much. Even took a side trip to Flagstaff. Had a good time there too. We decided to have a kid on that trip."

Sarah had not heard Jake talk of any children before. "You had a child?"

Jake turned back to the table and fidgeted with the corner of a napkin. "Well, no, we didn't. We certainly tried, harder than you can probably imagine, but we never did have a child. We even went to see the doctor, a couple of times. He said there was nothing he could do about it. Kay was pretty miserable after that. I got pretty upset myself, but I think it hit her a lot harder than me. She really wanted to be a mother."

"What happened after that?"

Jake's voice softened. "I guess we just went on with our lives. Kay never seemed the same after that. We drove down to Flagstaff again a few years later, but it just wasn't the same. The years went by and we both got older. About 10 years ago Kay got sick and died. The doctors said she had pneumonia and that they couldn't do anything about it. It made me really angry at first, but I don't blame them now. I don't think anyone could have done anything about it."

Sarah finished her dinner and stood up to leave. She couldn't think of anything more to ask, and didn't know what else to do. "I guess I should be going now. It's late, and I've still got a long walk to the boarding house. Thanks for dinner. I really appreciate it."

Jake did not stand up. "Oh, sure Sarah. Glad you could stay and eat something. You know how I feel about wasting food. Let me have Mathew walk you home. I don't like the idea of you walking alone this late at night."

"Oh, Jake. You worry too much. I'll be fine. I've done it before."

"I know you have, but Mathew won't mind." Jake slid a thumb and finger into his mouth and whistled so loudly that Sarah winced. "Hey Mathew. How about walking Sarah to the boarding house? I'll finish up your chores for you."

Mathew tossed a damp rag onto one of the tables and trotted over. "You want me to walk Sarah home, Jake?"

"Yeah, that's what I said isn't it, so get going. And Sarah, no complaints from you either. Mathew's going to walk you home, and that's that."

One night, a few weeks later, while Sarah ate her dinner of leftover food and Jake talked about the restaurant business, he asked her about the baby for the first time. She hesitated at first, then told him the entire story: about the man she had loved, the awful night he left her alone, about the landlord coming to collect the rent; then she began sobbing. Jake listened with deep sympathy before asking if she had made any plans for the baby. She admitted that she had no idea of what to do. She explained that she hoped to have the baby at a hospital, but didn't think she'd have enough money to pay for it. She worried about her child growing up poor. She wanted desperately for her child to have a decent life, a better life than she did. Jake told her calmly that he knew a doctor at the hospital in the next town, and promised to talk to him. Although Sarah thanked him, she did not believe anything would come of it.

After several more evenings of dinner and casual conversation, Jake told Sarah that he had talked to the doctor, the one he had told her about, and that all the necessary arrangements had been made for her to have her baby at the hospital. He had also questioned the doctor about cost, and had been assured that she would have enough money to pay for it out of her savings—when the time came. Jake explained too that he had mentioned her situation at church last Sunday. One of the church members had approached him during coffee hour after the service. She told him about a childless couple she knew—friends of hers who lived in a small town down the coast—who had been trying unsuccessfully to adopt a child for over two years. For some reason they had been unable to have children of their own. Jake's church friend thought the couple would make fine parents for Sarah's child. Jake had met them once before, and agreed. At first Sarah resisted the idea of giving her child to strangers. She had never considered such a possibility. She had devoted all of her energy to imagining her child growing up with her in spontaneous privation.

Jake tried to comfort her so that she felt better about the idea. "It's just something for you to think about," he said. "You know Sarah, you don't have to do it if you don't want to. My friend said they would make good parents, and I'm inclined to agree with her. Besides, they live in a small town down south, near the ocean. It sounds like it would be a great place to grow up. But you don't have to make any decisions right now. All you have to do is think about it." Jake studied Sarah's passive face for a positive response.

She lowered her eyes to conceal an unexpected sadness. "I don't know, Jake. I don't know if I can give my baby away to strangers. I mean, it's my child after all. I know I don't have much to offer, and it would be a hard life, but at least we'd be together. Maybe I could even go back to school and get a better job. I mean, not to say this isn't a good job. I mean—well, you know what I mean."

Jake listened pensively. He knew this would be a difficult decision for Sarah. He still encouraged her to make the best choice for her child. "It's your decision, Sarah, not mine. But I think you're going to have a hard time raising a child without any skills or education. Raising a kid isn't any picnic, you know. And with no husband around to help, you'll have to work doubly hard. I think you ought to give this idea a real chance. I think it might be the best way to go for everyone. Why don't you sleep on it before deciding anything?"

Sarah's mind began swirling with contentious thoughts. She wanted to keep her baby as well as give it the best possible life at the same time, but didn't see how she could achieve both. She questioned her own motives for keeping the child, and then wondered if they were mostly selfish. She finished dinner with her eyes down before finally looking up at Jake. "Alright, I'll sleep on it. I'm too tired to decide anything right now anyway." She pushed her chair away from the table and wobbled when she stood up. "I should probably start walking home now, before it starts to rain. It smelled like it might rain a little while ago."

Jake stood up too and helped Sarah get her jacket on. He whistled. "Hey Mathew. Grab your coat. I'd like you to walk Sarah home. Do you mind?"

Mathew removed his apron with a flourish as he weaved artfully between the tables and chairs. "No problem boss. I'm ready to go right now."

Jake waved to Sarah and Mathew as they stepped off the curb in front of the restaurant, but they had already turned and didn't see him. Sarah thought about Jake's suggestion while they walked through the musty streets. Her heart and mind fought a cruel battle: one yearning to keep the child to cherish it with a mother's love, the other promising to give it away to a better life. She raced back and forth between images of the child living with her in love and poverty, or of the child growing up with strangers who had the resources to give it a far better life. She did not know what to do. As they neared the boarding house, she had a premonition that her child would be a boy. "I think I'll name him Darrell," she whispered to herself.

Mathew overheard her hushed comment, although he did not recognize any of the words. "Did you say something to me, Sarah?"

Sarah had nearly forgotten that Mathew was walking next to her. His question startled her. "No Mathew. I'm just talking to myself. I do that sometimes."

This response disappointed Mathew. "Oh. I thought you were saying something to me."

"No Mathew. Sorry."

Mathew feigned a cheerful attitude. "No problem at all. I just thought maybe you wanted to talk, that's all."

When they arrived at the stone walk that led to the front porch of the boarding house, Mathew told Sarah to have a good evening, then quickly walked away. As she stood on the front porch watching him vanish down the street, a flash of lightening broke across the sky to the west. A distant rumble of thunder soon echoed against the tall trees surrounding the old boarding house. A few minutes later it began raining. Sarah held her hands beyond the protective edge of the porch roof and felt the cool drops on her fingers and palms. By the time she pulled back the blanket on her bed, the gentle rain had turned into a storm. Sarah and her child did not sleep well that night as they listened to the distant thunder and swaying trees through the open bedroom window. The storm had not abated when she finally drifted into an uneasy slumber.

♦ ♦ ♦

A small town in Southwest Oregon, August 1948

It had become an old pattern, one they had practiced over and over again until they could perform their roles flawlessly. The son, separated from birth by seventeen tumultuous years, would leave with friends after a hurried dinner, usually unfinished. His destination and intentions for the evening would be obscured by carefully selected words crafted into elusive sentences that sounded reasonable at first but later provided very little useful information. There would be a discussion of an expected return time, with expansive promises and predictable counter threats of grave consequences. The parents would hope for a better conclusion to the evening so that there might be peace in the house. The son would stride briskly through the front door, slinging his jacket casually over a shoulder as he walked away to hop into the car of one of his friends, an expression of false maturity beaming across his youthful face. The parents and son would wave to each other in a desperate attempt to appear reconciled. Then the parents would wait; nervously; expectantly; anticipating the gladness of promises fulfilled. And the son would be late again—very late. And a subtle smell of alcohol would permeate his breath. And the parents and the son would repeat the old pattern of destructive confrontation and accusations. Tonight would begin no differently.

John waved cynically with a brusque, backhanded snap of his free hand while his busy hand crushed a folded newspaper into a misshapen wad. Headlights flashed across his eyes as the car backed up the driveway, blinding him momentarily. He watched a floating image of the headlights fade away while his vision readjusted to the room light. He squeezed the newspaper again and spoke to Martha out of the side of his mouth. "Well, I sure hope he makes it back on time tonight. I've just about had it with his bullshit."

Although Martha agreed with John's assessment, she feared his vulgar language predicted an approaching disintegration. "John, he hasn't always been late. He's made it back before midnight several times."

John turned away from the big picture window and squinted at Martha. "Yeah, like maybe two or three times. And it's been so long I can't remember when those two or three times happened. Mostly he's been late. And he probably only made it back on time because whoever was driving him around all night couldn't stay out any longer. I really doubt he made it because he decided to. That's why I think this is a bunch of absolute bullshit."

"You don't have to swear about it. You don't even know if there's any reason to get upset yet. Why don't we just relax and read for awhile?"

"Well, I'm already pissed off, and I feel like swearing. It makes me feel better."

"It doesn't look like you feel any better. He's not late yet, so there's no reason to get worked up about it. I think we just need to sit in the living room and calm down. All that bad language is not going to help you feel better."

"Damn it, Martha!—it does make me feel better."

"I'm not going to argue with you. You can stay here by yourself and swear all you want. I'm going to sit in the living room and read so that I don't have to listen to you."

"Fine. I'll stop swearing and sit in the living room—but I'm not going to enjoy it."

John was born in the winter of 1903, two weeks before Orville and Wilbur Wright achieved the first sustained flight of an airplane at Kitty Hawk. He grew from a small child to a young boy in a farming community in northern Iowa. His oldest memory of the town was very peculiar. He remembered walking barefoot along a tree-lined road on a humid summer day, and an old woman standing at the edge of the lawn in front of her house handed him an ice cube. He didn't know why she gave it to him, or how she had managed to keep it from melting in the intense heat, but he did take it from her wrinkled hand, and then sucked it to nothing as he continued his walk. Sometimes he wondered if this had really happened, then he remembered the taste of the ice and the touch of the old woman's hand. His parents moved west soon after the ice cube incident, about the time he had managed to accumulate a few close friends. During his high school years he worked in a local cannery during the summer. He worked full time at the cannery after high school, and when he had accumulated enough money he attended college in Ames, Iowa. The money ran out during the first semester of his sophomore year. Fortunately, before bankruptcy had ended his college education, he met Martha in the school library. She worked in the reference section three days a week as a librarian's assistant. She worked there because she hoped to become a student some day. She married John two years after they met. They struggled to conceive a child for three more years, reaching a point of desperation more than once. Sometimes, when they were trying too hard and feeling more and more the impossibility of it, John thought back about the time he met Martha and questioned if it really should have happened. Maybe his feelings for her had been a mistake; maybe they should never have met; maybe he shouldn't have spent so much time in the library.

John's eyes jumped randomly across the same words for the third time after quickly glancing back down to the musty pages of the enormous dictionary. The words hadn't made much sense the first two times; this additional reading proved equally meaningless. He paused for a long time at a semicolon before allowing his eyes to creep up again over the top of the book binding. This time they found an empty chair, and panic instantly twisted his stomach. *Where'd she go? Maybe she finished whatever she was working on and left the library for the night. Maybe she moved to a different table. Maybe she—*

"Excuse me." She stood next to him, within an easy arm's reach.

John hesitated before cautiously turning his head toward the sound of her voice. He used this slight delay to relax his face into an indifferent expression and to think of a witty reply. He focused on her lips while he spoke, avoiding her eyes. "Uh, you mean me?" *Did she know he'd been looking at her? Had she come over her to tell him to knock it off? Darn it! He should have studied in the dorm tonight.*

"Yes, I do. Are you finished with the dictionary? I'd like to look up a word." She tilted her head down to look into his eyes, but he turned away.

"The dictionary?" He squeezed both hands and wrinkled one of the fragile pages, right at the word *discomfit*. "Sure. I, I'm, I think I'm finished."

"Are you sure? I can wait if you need more time."

"I'm sure." He stood awkwardly, almost tripping over the chair leg when it caught a rough spot on the hardwood floor. "Here. You can use this chair. No reason to carry this huge book back to where you're sitting." His stomach tightened again. He couldn't possibly be stupid enough to say what he'd just said, could he? Why not just tell her he'd been watching her most of the evening.

She smiled. "No, that's fine. Why don't you just look up the word for me? Then I can be on my way."

"Sure, I could do that." He slumped down into the chair. The chair leg slid across the rough spot and squeaked. "What word were you thinking of?" He began thumbing aimlessly through the pages.

"I'm looking for the spelling and definition of the word ĭ-grē′-jəs. Can you look that up for me? I need it for a report I'm working on."

"Uh, sure. I can do that." John quickly pressed his thumb against the black I-J tab and opened the dictionary to the wrong section.

She leaned over his shoulder, nearly touching his back. "I think it begins with an 'e.'"

"It does? That's strange. It doesn't sound like an 'e.'" John thought he had a pretty decent vocabulary, but he'd never heard of this word before.

"Yeah, it's spelled e-g-r-e-g-i...." She stopped and lowered her eyes before saying the final three letters. "Well, actually, I'm not sure how to spell it. That's why I came over here to look it up."

Thankful that he had not been caught, John did not notice that she already knew how to spell the word. He hurriedly turned to the correct page and found it near the lower right-hand corner. "Here it is. Egregious. It says conspicuously bad or offensive. Egregiously, adverb. Egregiousness, noun. It comes from Latin. Imagine that. Never heard of it."

"Oh, me neither. I only heard it recently, during a meeting; the person who used it didn't explain what it meant, so I thought I should look it up." She folded her hands below the black leather belt on her dress and raised her eyes again.

Having successfully found the strange word, and feeling more relaxed now, John bungled into his next question. "My name's John. How about you?"

"How about my name? Is that what you mean?"

"Yeah, that's what I mean. What's your name?"

"It's Martha."

John reached out his hand. "Glad to meet you Martha."

Martha did the same, and, touching his hand with a gentle firmness, said, "Nice to meet you too, John. Maybe I'll see you again some time."

"Again?"

"In the library, I mean. Maybe I'll see you in the library again."

"Oh, yeah. You probably will. I come here all the time, and I've still got almost three years to go before I get my degree."

The thick hour hand nearly touched the black two on the kitchen wall clock. Martha moved erratically between the living and dining rooms, with an occasional side trip into the bedroom. John stood motionless; his eyes searched for automobile headlights in the darkness beyond the streaked picture window. He appeared subdued and relaxed: in truth his anger amplified with each passing minute. His calm appearance belied the profound turmoil swirling around inside. He had become skilled at sustaining these extended periods of mock calmness through years of disciplined practice, yet sometimes the anger exceeded even his ability to control it and boiled over unexpectedly. He had never hit or pushed anyone (he had thought about it a few times), but occasionally he said hurtful things that he later regretted. Although he usually apologized, it often took several weeks to find the right words. The heart attack that would almost kill him in less than two years would be the unfortunate physical manifestation of these buried emotions—along with a few other things.

Martha stopped pacing halfway across the living room and began talking anxiously to the back of John's head. "Do you think I should go out and look for him?" The head did not answer. "What if he's hurt? Maybe he's been in an accident and he's lying in a ditch somewhere. I think I should go out and look for him. I can't just sit here and do nothing."

Always logical, John replied unhurriedly with carefully measured words. "First of all, you're not sitting. Secondly, I don't see any reason why you should go out looking for him at this time of night. Your chances of finding him in the dark are pretty much zero. Plus he'll probably show up about ten minutes after you leave." John spoke with the calmest voice he could muster, and his anger plunged a little deeper.

Any patience Martha might have saved for John's predictable logic evaporated at his sarcastic remark about sitting. She turned and walked into the entry and began pulling on her coat and boots. "You can stay here and stare out the window if you want. I'm going to go look for him. He might be hurt and I'm not going to wait here all night for the police to show up and tell me so."

A little jab creased the lining of John's stomach. "Suit yourself, but it probably won't do any good. Like I said, he'll probably come home right after you leave."

Martha's hand had just touched the doorknob when headlights flashed near the mailbox at the top of the driveway. The car paused for almost five minutes before moving slowly down the rutted driveway toward the house. John watched the headlights bump up and down at each rut and pothole. The car stopped near the front porch light for another three minutes. His son finally opened the passenger door and tumbled out. With palpable sarcasm in his voice, John announced: "Well, it looks like he's made it safely home at long last. I guess we had nothing to worry about after all." Too agitated and relieved at the same time to care about the sarcasm, Martha removed her hand from the knob and stepped back from the door. Then, when the car turned and headed up the driveway, John noted with clear resentment, "Hey, look at that. That kid drives a better car than I do. I don't get it. Why does that kid drive a better car than me? Where's he get the damn money anyway? I just don't get it."

As Martha hung her coat neatly on a polished oak dowel near the front door, the night she and John named their new son flashed into her thoughts. They had both suggested several possibilities during the long drive home after picking him up at the hospital, but could not agree on any of them. Upon reaching an impasse the next day, they checked out a book of names from the local library and studied it both together and separately for two days more. With further negotiation they agreed that the name should express some meaning special to both of them. After discarding all of the distant relatives and close friends and not so close friends, as well as a few names they had never heard anyone called by, they chose Timothy, which means *blessed of God*. With this decision consummated, Martha insisted that everyone call him Timothy; not Tim or Timmy or Tims or Tim Tim or Timmy Wimmy or any other possible moniker variant. At first John teased her that she couldn't control her son's nicknames; however, by the time he reached first grade, everyone, including his friends, called him only Timothy.

Timothy lifted up on the front door when he opened it so that the hinges didn't squeak too much, and stepped soundlessly into the entry. He unzipped his jacket and then casually noticed his father standing by the big picture window in a favorite bathrobe and his mother dressed in heavy boots. He quickly affected concern; in truth he felt no concern at all. He had successfully handled similar situations many times before. All he had to do was stay calm and feign deep repentance for his tardiness. This approach had worked very well several times before, and he expected it to work again this morning. He began the process with an appropriately light comment. "Sorry I'm so late. Guess I lost track of time. What are you guys still doing up?"

John had already reached that special point where he could no longer maintain his fiction of calmness. Anticipating Martha's response, his voice crackled with hostility. "What the hell do you think you're doing coming home after damn two in the morning?" John's use of the words "hell" and "damn" signaled to Martha that he had reached a genuinely uncontrollable rage; she stepped in front of Timothy to shield him from the impending onslaught. She prepared to say something in his defense when she sniffed a faint aroma of alcohol. She turned and moved closer to Timothy and sniffed again to be sure. She knew he had been drinking, but she asked him anyway. "Timothy, have you been drinking again?"

Timothy had not anticipated his father's angry explosion or his mother's accusatory question. When he entered the house he had actually hoped to avoid detection altogether. Now he would have to talk his way out of an unexpected mess, and with no time to think of a clever response. He decided to try a simple lie that had worked several times before. "No, of course not. Why would I want to do that? I've got school work to do in the morning."

John didn't need to smell Timothy's breath for himself. He knew that Martha hated these confrontations and would not have asked the question unless she had really smelled alcohol. He stepped closer before speaking. "So…not only do you stroll in here hours past the agreed time, but you've also been drinking again." John changed his mind and decided to smell Timothy's breath anyway—to dramatize his bitterness. He nudged Martha aside, grabbed Timothy roughly by the shoulders, pulled him close, and snorting his face like a rabid hound confirmed Martha's suspicion. "Why, you little bastard, you *have* been drinking again, haven't you! And not only have you been drinking again; you're also a damn liar too. You know what, I'm not going to put up with this crap in my house anymore. I'll tell you what you little shit…you get out of my damn house before I…I…damn it…get out…get the hell out of here." John rotated his grip to the back of Timothy's shirt and, almost tripping on a throw rug in the hallway, wrestled him to the front door. Timothy only croaked out a few muddled sounds when he tried to say something. Tears filled his eyes and rolled down his cheeks when John forced him through the door. As they struggled beneath the porch light, Timothy lunged, tearing himself away from his father's bitter grasp, and began marching up the driveway. He turned to say something, but then couldn't think of anything to say. He spun away and continued marching until he passed the familiar mailbox and disappeared down the road.

Stunned by the angry scene that had just played out in her home, Martha's lips trembled. "John, how could you say such hurtful things? How could you throw him out of the house like that." She yanked her jacket off the polished oak dowel, nearly snapping the brittle wood, and started toward the front door to go after Timothy.

John held her arm—a little too firmly—when she tried to pass him. His anger had not diminished. "Let him go. He'll come back in a few hours. He just needs some time to cool off."

Martha glared at John. "Why did you say those things? What were you thinking?" John glared back without responding. He released her arm, then twisted abruptly and walked into the bedroom without saying good night. He could think of no good reason to continue this useless conversation, and he needed to get some sleep.

Chapter 2

A pastoral road weaves the Oregon night, July 1931

Martha pressed the newly wrinkled infant against her chest and carefully rested her cheek on the child's head. The boy's eyes had not yet opened and he squirmed incessantly, but to Martha he had instantly become the most beautiful thing she had ever held in her entire life. John glanced over at the new baby briefly every few minutes because the darkness and winding road demanded most of his attention. The last thing he needed was to drive off a curve into a big spruce tree or smack a deer or crash into some idiot who wasn't paying close enough attention to oncoming traffic. They still had over 50 miles to go, and a long day of paperwork and waiting and then more paperwork and meetings and constant anticipation and all the rest had tired him more than he thought possible. Martha sat quietly in the passenger seat while he drove, not moving much except for a subtle rocking motion, enjoying the child that she had so desperately sought for almost three years. Now that she held the child in her arms, and even though he wiggled ceaselessly, she at last enjoyed a remarkable peace.

John's left eyelid fluttered when he squinted into the intense cone of light projected by the car's headlights. As he carefully navigated each curve, the light pulsed rapidly against the thick trees pressing against the edge of the road. He began to worry in earnest now about the possibility of a deer leaping out onto the road and smashing violently into the front of the car. This troublesome thought sparked memories of a story his dad had told him when he was a young boy. The story began with his dad and mom driving somewhere in the middle of Georgia, before his birth. His dad never explained what they were doing there, and he never asked. The trip had been uneventful until this point; then a big hog suddenly appeared in the middle of the road. Hogs don't leap; therefore, his dad reasoned, it must have been just standing there. The road had been constructed too narrow for his dad to swerve around the beast, so he clenched the steering wheel with both hands and stepped down hard on the brake pedal. He only succeeded in plowing straight into the unfortunate animal and then dragging it down the road about a hundred feet, leaving a gruesome trail of splattered blood, chunks of flesh, and even a few bone fragments. The entire front of the car caved in at impact, and probably killed the hog instantly. His parents waited hours in the dark before a passing farmer driving a flatbed truck loaded with wood crates picked them up. It took several hours more to get the car towed to a nearby town. A tobacco-chewing attendant dressed in greasy coveralls greeted them when they drove up to the gas station. After they explained what had happened, he responded with great surprise: "Why did'n y'all bring the hog with ya? We could'a et it!" John remembered laughing at his dad's unintentional punch line. He also remembered this particular story so well because his dad had shared so few with him.

"Martha, remember that story I told you about when my parents ran into a big hog in Georgia? It's a great story. Do you remember it?" John kept his eyes centered on the road. He anticipated the deer at any moment.

"He sure squirms a lot," Martha responded, using John's unrelated question as an opportunity to discuss something she thought more important. "Do you think he's alright? I don't think he's slept at all since we left the hospital. Seems like he should've fallen asleep by now, at least for a little while."

"Uh, yeah. He's probably fine. I would guess all babies squirm a lot after they're born. It probably means he's really healthy. I wouldn't worry about it." John, always keen about not worrying about anything, tried to move the discussion back to his original question. "Anyway, do you remember that story?"

Annoyed at John's lack of concern, Martha pretended to have not heard the original question. "What story is that?"

"The one about the big hog in Georgia; the one my dad ran into in the car; then when they finally got towed to the gas station, the attendant was disappointed that they didn't bring it with them, because they could have eaten it for dinner."

"Yes, I remember the story. I think you told it to me a few years ago. I remember the part about the big hog. You know, I'm still worried. I'm not sure it's right that he wiggles around so much. Maybe we should go back to the hospital and check with one of the doctors."

"Well,"—when John began a sentence with "Well," it meant that he wasn't quite sure what to say, and starting with "Well," following by a thoughtful pause, gave him a moment to think— "I…I really don't think I'd worry about it, plus we're more than half-way home. It would be silly to drive all the way back to the hospital when we've gone this far. Why don't you feed him some milk? Babies like milk. Maybe it'll help him sleep." *Damn it. Doesn't she have something better to do with her time than worry about stupid stuff like that? And driving all the way back to the hospital—what the hell is that all about? That's got to be one of the silliest ideas I've heard in a long time.* He leaned forward slightly and glared aggressively at the snaky road ahead to imply to Martha that any further conversation could be dangerous.

"I fed him some milk half an hour ago. I don't think he's hungry. Something else must be wrong. Maybe he has a tummy ache. Maybe I should try to burp him. I don't think he's burped yet." Martha pulled a soft cloth over her left shoulder and wedged the infant into the correct burping position. She patted him gently between the shoulder blades about a dozen times, and nothing happened—except more wiggling. Martha's sense of peace, so satisfying only an hour ago, began slipping away. She accepted that she wasn't an expert on baby behavior, yet still sensed that something wasn't quite right. "Do you mind turning up the heat? Maybe he's cold."

John clenched the steering wheel, causing the car to drift to the right. "Damn it Martha, it's roasting in here and he's already wrapped in two or three blankets. He'll die of sunstroke if I turn the heat up any more. If you want to know the truth, what I should do is open the damn window and let in some fresh air before we all suffocate." Martha stared straight ahead and did not make a sound. John waited for her to say something for more than five minutes before turning up the heat.

Martha relaxed when John reached across the dashboard and slid the heater knob over about a quarter inch; unfortunately, too much time had passed for her to offer him any thanks. Her thoughts had also jumped to another important topic. "Have you thought anymore about a name?"

"A name? No, not really. I didn't think you liked my last suggestion, so I stopped worrying about it."

Martha giggled. "Your last suggestion? You mean, Mortimer?"

"Yeah, Mortimer. What's so funny about Mortimer?"

Martha sniffed back a little snort and tried unsuccessfully to stifle another chuckle. "Just listen to the sound of it. Moooor-tiiiii-muuuuur. How would you like to be named Moooor-tiiiii-muuuuur?"

"Have you got a better idea then?"

"Yeah. How about Clancy? I've always liked that name. I think it sounds very sophisticated. Don't you?"

John made no attempt to repress his own snort and laughed heavily. "Clancy? Clancy!? Are you kidding me? You give him that name, and he'll get beat up on the school playground every day of his life. I'd bet money it."

"Well, that may be so, but it's certainly a lot better than Moooor-tiiiii-muuuuur."

After this failure to decide upon a name, the remainder of the drive home was punctuated by empty conversation and suffused with growing tension. Martha repeatedly adjusted position in response to her baby's continued squirming. John distracted himself by playing with the rear view mirror from time to time or by readjusting the heater in an effort to appear helpful. He now regretted his earlier outburst about the car heater. He just wanted to get home and go to bed without further confrontation. His stupid remarks had only succeeded in imbuing the drive with a real sense of endlessness.

When they finally rolled down the dirt driveway to the house, they were both beyond simple exhaustion. Martha opened the car door, nearly stumbled as she stepped out, then trudged relentlessly to the front door. She spoke to John, without turning her head, before reaching the porch. "Bring all the stuff into the house. I'm going to try to put him to bed."

John leaned passively against the side of the car. His first thought was that "all the stuff" could damn well wait in the car until morning, but after the car heater incident, he knew implicitly that this would only exacerbate an already exacerbated situation. He had learned this word in college and, although he never spoke it out loud, liked to think the word in situations like this. He straightened up, pressed his hands against the back of his head, sucked in a deep breath of cool air, and with grim resolve forced his weary feet and legs to move around to the back of the car. He opened the trunk and began grabbing "all the stuff" to carry it into the house. After he had piled the first load of "all the stuff" on the living room floor in front of the couch, he heard Martha in the bedroom trying to convince "Mortimer" or "Clancy" or whatever the hell his name might be, to go to sleep—apparently without much success. In addition to squirming, the baby had now begun whining in a shrill, annoying manner. "This is going to be a long night," he mumbled to himself as he shambled out of the house. He carried the last of "all the stuff" into the living room a few minutes later. After kicking off his shoes and dropping his clothes on the floor, John fell into bed for what would become a long night of restlessness.

The baby slept for brief periods a few times; mostly he squirmed and sobbed and gurgled and cried. Martha and John took turns trying to feed him, trying to burp him, and trying to hold him while walking around the bedroom. At about 4:30 am, during John's turn, he actually walked through every room and hallway in the house, talking to the baby like a real estate agent. John began to think that he might have lost his mind when he showed the broom closet to the baby. "You know, Mortimer, this broom closet would make a really great bedroom for you. Look—it's just your size, and as a special bonus it's really far away from our bedroom so we can't hear you cry. It could be quiet for both of us. We'd have to rearrange the mops and brooms and furniture polish a little, but just think how perfect it could be for both of us. I can get you into here with only a small down payment, say that little gizmo you're sucking on. So Mortimer, what do ya say?"

By the time John's alarm clock went off at 6:30 am, he and Martha were both emptied of any remaining strength. Martha's elbows and shoulders throbbed as she held the baby and shuffled in ragged circles at the foot of the bed. John stared blankly at the wall, struggled to pull on his slippers, and thought about how painful it was going to be to work that day. He felt like a dog's upchucked breakfast and dreaded the idea, but took pride in being a good employee and believed he had no choice. Martha also had a long day ahead: her new baby's restlessness would continue without remission. At that moment they both felt too tired to think of the days ahead, and did not imagine that this pattern would go on for another three weeks before things improved. Just in time too—John and Martha were both very strong-willed, but when things finally got better, they had both reached a state of sober desperation. Even Martha began wondering why she had ached so for a child. She soon admitted to herself that this did not look anything like the blissful experience she had envisioned.

♦ ♦ ♦

From Oregon to Tarawa, August 1948

Timothy had walked along this road many times before: first as a young child on his way to play with friends on a cool winter day after Christmas, then to school when late spring faded into early summer, and now to nowhere in particular as the crisp night air stung the inside of his nose. A dark ocean swelled into brief view after he ascended a gentle rise in the road, then receded when the road turned inland a little and dove behind a long copse of trees. He walked briskly with assertive strides, moving down the road as quickly as possible, hands shoved deeply into the leather-trimmed pockets slashed across the sides of his jacket. He felt an uneasy hollowness inside; a familiar sensation at first, then unfamiliar because he couldn't connect the feeling with a specific event or place. The hollowness encouraged him to think about how he had wondered much of his young life if he really belonged—in this town, in this home, with these parents—and now that his father had tossed him aside, he knew that he did not. He had run away several other times during the last two years, but always came home after a few hours. His record had been six hours. This time would be different. This time, he promised himself, he would never go back.

The first hint of morning sun brightened the sky above the eastern tree line after some twelve miles of persistent trudging. He stopped to rest against a weathered fence post and watched the sun break over the rolling mountains. A tangled strand of barbed wire scraped along the side of his leg when he bent down to remove a stone from his shoe, then sprung back to its original position when he straightened up. He remembered watching the sunrise before, but this time it looked different. A few cars passed by, probably on the way to work, and he decided to stick his thumb out. Three more cars drove by without slowing before an old farmer driving a faded pickup truck pulled over and rolled down a dust-streaked window.

"Where ya going, young man?" the farmer asked, a wad of chewing tobacco bulging his left cheek. He spat through the window with practiced accuracy after finishing his question.

"Uh, to the next town I guess."

The farmer eyed him suspiciously; then quickly spat again, almost hitting Timothy on the foot. "You're a little young to be walking around out here in the middle of the night, aren't ya? Shouldn't ya be at home?"

Although he'd been walking for many hours, he had not taken even a few seconds to consider the possibility that someone might ask him this question. He thought the farmer would drive him straight to the local police station and turn him in if he told the truth. "I'm on the way to visit my dad. He lives in the next town. I haven't seen him in a really long time. Can you give me a ride?"

The farmer studied him carefully, then spat yet another brown gob through the window. Timothy tried not to look at it as it zinged by his leg. "Well, I suppose that makes sense. Go ahead and hop in the back. I'm headed in that direction anyway, so I can get ya mostly there. Save ya the trouble of walking at least." Timothy smiled, walked around to the back of the truck, and lifted himself over the tailgate. He found a reasonably comfortable seat on a bale of hay. As the truck lurched forward and began picking up speed, sunlight broke fully over the hills and flooded the road with warmth. Timothy shifted his position on the bale so that he could feel the sun on his face.

His clothes picked up a delicate scent of manure long before they reached the next town. After stopping to let him off, the farmer waved to him, the transmission slipped into gear, and the faded pickup truck lurched away. The morning sun had warmed the air considerably by this time, and Timothy felt a little more comfortable than during his long night walk. He spent the day exploring the unfamiliar town, attempting to appear inconspicuous, mostly trying to figure out where he could sleep without getting into trouble with the police. A knot of hunger twinged inside his stomach before noon. He discovered a few wadded-up dollar bills in his pants pocket. After smoothing them out, he bought some candy and a bottle of Coca Cola at the local grocery store. At dusk he returned to a small park with trees and benches near the middle of town, across the street from the fire station. Exhausted by lack of rest and food, he slid underneath one of the benches and tried to sleep. The temperature dropped 15 degrees by midnight; he mostly shivered until sunrise. He chastised himself repeatedly throughout the night for not grabbing a heavier jacket. A hat and gloves would have been nice too.

The next morning, he spent the last of his money to buy an apple and a small bottle of milk. His hunger, only briefly allayed by this meager snack, returned completely an hour later. When his normal times for lunch and dinner passed, he found it difficult to think of anything but food. The temperature dropped again that night, lower than the previous night, and he slept fitfully under the same park bench. He had nothing to eat for another day, and began to regret the many times he had complained about his mom's meals. He considered stealing food from the grocery store where he had purchased the apple, then worried that he would be taken home by the police if caught: he decided to starve instead.

Several streetlights flashed on as dusk transitioned into evening. By chance, he wandered into a damp alley a few blocks from the fire station and found himself standing in front of a dumpster, near the back door to a restaurant. The idea of eating garbage from a dumpster nauseated him, but the insistent ache in his stomach now dominated his mind more strongly than the filmy vomit taste at the back of his tongue. He stood in the shadows of the alley and stared at the dumpster for a long time, waiting for the right moment. He had just reached out to open the lid and begin fishing around for something to eat when an old man in a grease-stained apron appeared at the back door. After blinding him with a flashlight, the old man invited him into the restaurant to eat something. The old man asked Timothy if they had met before. Timothy told him this was not possible. Timothy thought it odd that some stranger would give him free food, but he was too hungry to argue about it.

He wandered the streets and alleys of the town for another two days and again felt the torment of an empty stomach. On that second night, the fifth day since he had left home, he hiked down to the waterfront and stood at the edge of a narrow pier that raised up level with the street on blackened wood pilings. Hungry, tired, and cold, he stood there, unable to enjoy the view of ocean and small boats and drifting clouds. He looked down to rub his eyes and glimpsed a flicker of light through a crack in the pier's weathered deck. Dropping down to his hands and knees, he turned his face and pressed an eye close to the crack. The light flickered stronger, but he still could not identify it. He stood up and walked about a hundred feet along the waterfront road to a stairway that angled steeply down to the beach. He skipped down the wooden treads until he reached a wave-battered platform, then jumped down onto the rocks and sand below. He squinted back down the beach to where the pier connected with the road and could see a small flickering campfire. He walked instinctively toward the flame, slipping from time to time on slime-covered rocks. When he approached to within about fifty feet, he could see a man sitting near the fire.

Timothy walked thirty feet closer and stopped, his arms clenched tightly around each other. The man wore a torn raincoat and a dark wool watch cap. Timothy smelled food cooking on the fire and could hear something sizzling next to the fire. The man appeared startled at first and sat up suddenly, but then relaxed. After deciding that Timothy looked miserable and harmless, the man spoke to him in a friendly voice.

"You want something to eat young man? I caught a nice fish today and just finished cooking it up. It's a salmon. I think it must have weighed at least 12 pounds before I gutted it. It put up a great fight. You can have some if you want. There's more than enough for both of us."

Timothy listened to this invitation with justifiable disbelief. For the second time this week, someone he had never met before had offered him food just as he neared (what he believed to be) the edge of starvation. He tried unsuccessfully to conceal his eagerness. "Sure mister, I'd love something to eat. I haven't eaten in quite a while."

The man grinned and pulled a metal plate out of a bag. He held the plate next to the salmon, still hissing next to the fire, and flaked off some of the succulent fish with a fork. He held out the heavy plate and Timothy stumbled forward to take it. The salmon, glazed with brown sugar and butter, had a unique flavor Timothy had never tasted before; he devoured it with a few quick bites. When he finished, the man slid a few more large chunks of fish meat onto the plate. Timothy noticed the man's left hand: thin and withered, and drooping loosely at the end of the raincoat sleeve, it did not seem to have much strength or mobility.

"I've got some coffee too. You want a cup of coffee?"

"Sure, a cup of coffee would be great. I'm actually pretty cold. Maybe some coffee would help warm me up a little."

The man groped around inside the same bag until he found a metal cup, then poured some hot coffee into it. "Be careful not to burn your lips. These metal cups can get pretty hot." He gave the cup to Timothy with his good hand.

"Thanks." Timothy blew over the rim of the cup before carefully sipping some of the coffee. "What's wrong with your hand?"

The man pulled the raincoat sleeve down over his bony wrist. "Maybe we should introduce ourselves. My name's Seth. What's yours?"

"Timothy."

"How old are you, Timothy?"

"Seventeen, but I'll be eighteen in a few months."

"Is that so. I got hurt in the war."

"The war?"

"Yeah. The war in the Pacific."

Timothy considered this declaration before asking his next question. He'd studied World War II in school; he didn't remember anyone mentioning the War in the Pacific. Maybe he had skipped class that day. "How'd you get hurt?"

"Got shot."

"Got shot? Who shot you?" Timothy leaned forward a little.

"A Jap sniper. Tarawa. November…1943." Seth surprised himself when these words spilled out. He hadn't said a word about this to anyone since it happened, a period of nearly five years. Yet for reasons he did not understand, he felt comfortable talking to this young stranger who had appeared mysteriously out of the darkness. Maybe he admired Timothy's curiosity. At one time he had lost most of his.

"What's Tarawa? Never heard of it."

This amused Seth. Probably most people had never heard of it. "It's an atoll in the Gilbert Islands where a lot of men died. Tarawa is a special place." Seth spoke with a wisp of sadness in his voice. Bitterness had once consumed him; the bitterness had turned to simple grief during the last several years, a grief that had just begun to release him.

He tossed a gnarled chunk of driftwood into the fire with his good hand and a storm of sparks swirled up and evaporated into the cool night air. And then he told his story to Timothy.

"I was in the first wave. We actually landed on Betio, one of Tarawa's islands. That's where the Japs had built an airstrip. Betio was actually pretty small. I don't think any part of it was more than three hundred yards from the water. And it was flat, really flat." Seth paused to stir the fire with a crooked stick. The fire crackled with renewed heat when the glowing coals rubbed against each other. Then he sat very still and stared into the flames. When he resumed his story, he spoke more softly.

"The Navy blasted the hell out of that island. I thought the damn thing would be blown to pieces—saving us a lot of trouble—but when the shelling stopped the island looked pretty much the same." Seth picked up his cup of coffee and cradled it in his hands.

"We climbed down the side of the ship around 0400. I got my rifle tangled in the cargo netting on the way down and the Marine above me stepped on my hand. I remembered swearing at him, but I don't think he heard me. We were in the Higgins boat by 0420. Some of the Marines climbed from the Higgins boats into amphtracs."

Timothy had never heard these terms before. "What's a Higgins boat? And what's an amphtrac?" He slid closer to the fire until his toes almost touched the glowing rim of hot coals.

Seth looked into Timothy's eyes for the first time since the beginning of his story. "A Higgins boat is a landing craft. An amphtrac is sort of half boat and half tank: it has tracks and a propeller. About twenty Marines and all their gear can fit into one." He sipped some coffee, and his eyes returned to the fire.

"We headed for the lagoon side of the island, with the amphtracs in front. When we got about three thousand yards from shore the Japs opened up on us with heavy artillery. Big shells splashed all around us. At about two thousand yards bullets from long-range machine guns started slamming into the front of the boat and whistling overhead. At about three hundred yards, the length of three football fields, we hit the reef. We were supposed to go over it, but the tide was too low and we got stuck. We sat there not going anywhere. While we were trying to figure out what to do, the Japs sighted in on us and opened up with everything they had: artillery, machine guns, mortars, rifle fire—everything. One of the mortar rounds landed right next to the boat and knocked a bunch of us to the deck. I landed on top of a skinny corporal from Missoula—funny I remember that." As Seth spoke of these events, buried images began forming in his mind. They appeared fuzzy at first, but when he continued the story of that distant autumn morning, the images sharpened and intensified.

"We finally figured out that we wouldn't last much longer if we stayed in the boat, so they started lowering the ramp. The damn thing got stuck on the reef too and only made it part way down, but not far enough for us to climb over it. We stood there for a few seconds, staring at the top of the ramp, and then one of the officers ordered us to go over the sides. That was quite a trick, loaded down with all that gear. Some of the guys landed on the coral and managed to stand up; other guys disappeared under water after they jumped over the side—I never saw what happened to them. I finally got over the side and fell into the water; it came up to my armpits. The ones who made it started moving through the water toward the beach. It was slow going, especially when I had to move around floating clumps of dead Marines. I don't know what happened to any of them; they were just all stuck together. Men were falling all around me, but somehow I kept moving forward without getting hit. I don't know why. I guess I was just lucky."

A pair of seagulls, fighting over an eroded fish carcass somewhere beyond the pier, squawked angrily at each other. A wave crashed and surged up the beach toward the fire; countless foam bubbles fizzed as they broke against sand and rock. The fire snapped. Neither Timothy nor Seth heard these sounds as the Marines in the story moved forward to the beach.

"I saw a long pier sticking out to my left, so I started wading over to it. When I got close to the pier, an amphtrac blew up right in front of me. Chunks of metal and body parts landed all around me. A dozen other Marines had made it to the pier too, but nobody from my unit. I looked out over the beach and saw that some of the Marines had moved across the sand and were crouching behind a long seawall. The beach was littered with bodies, and bodies floated in the surf and out into the sea. I ducked behind one of the pilings and waited. After a few minutes the Japs sighted us under the pier and started raking us with machine gun fire. Then mortars started landing closer too, and I knew I couldn't stay there. I started moving from piling to piling toward the beach with some of the other Marines. We were nearly there when the guy in front of me got spun around by a sniper's bullet: he fell face up with blood spurting from his chest. He looked dead to me, so I stepped over him and ran toward the seawall. Bullets pounded the sand in front of me and around my feet. I finally made it to the seawall and dived to the ground. A mortar round exploded behind me. I just kept my head down, afraid to look up. I stayed that way for a long time."

The fire had cooled down a little. Afraid to interrupt the story, Timothy reached over slowly, picked up a small chunk of driftwood, and carefully set it on the edge of the fire. The fire hissed a little, and a few sparks floated up on the heated air, but Seth did not appear to notice. No longer staring into the fire, he gazed right through Timothy and out into the moon-sparkled sea.

"I finally sat up against the seawall and looked back toward the reef. I couldn't believe my eyes. There were dead Marines all over the beach; some in big mounds; some scattered around by themselves. The water had turned red where it lapped up on the sand. The next wave was coming in and Jap artillery began pounding along the entire reef. One of the Higgins boats suddenly exploded just as the ramp hit the water. I think everyone on board must have been killed. Somehow Marines kept coming ashore. Most of them were gunned down, but some made it to the seawall. An amphtrac plowed up the beach and headed right at me. A bunch of us rolled out of the way just before it punched a big hole through the sea wall. The Japs hit it with heavy machine gun fire, but it kept moving forward. I sat there for I don't know how long, watching the amphtrac, not hearing the explosions and bullets and screaming men around me, not knowing what to do. I finally looked up; a young lieutenant stood right above me, shouting something. Even though he wasn't from my unit, I finally heard him."

"Let's go Marines! Get off your damn asses and follow that amphtrac." The young lieutenant moved along the seawall and screamed this over and over again until he had everyone's attention. He motioned up and down the seawall to the thirty or so Marines hovering behind its protective ledge. Seth had felt relatively safe behind the seawall, and could even rest a little; now he had to move into the open again. The lieutenant gestured by throwing an invisible baseball into the jungle and the Marines moved forward through the hole in the seawall, attempting to stay close behind the lumbering amphtrac. Machine gun fire raced along the top of the amphtrac until it reached the following men. Several were knocked down, but the rest kept moving forward. The amphtrac rolled through a small clearing that gave view to the Japanese airstrip. It was strangely quiet for a few moments, and then artillery shells began landing all around. The Marines dived to the ground and scratched for cover.

The young lieutenant found a radio and screamed into the handset for reinforcements, but seawater dribbled out of the base; after crackling for a few seconds, it went dead. He crawled from man to man, looking for another radio, and finally found one strapped to a dead Marine. Both the radio and the Marine were riddled with shrapnel. The lieutenant swore and slammed his fist into the radio. Amazingly, they had actually made it to the airstrip and no one knew about it. He decided that one of the Marines had to go back and tell someone. The young lieutenant looked around and noticed Seth pressed against a ridge of sand at the base of a small tree. He crawled over to Seth and began yelling instructions at him.

"I need you to go back to the beach. We've got to get reinforcements to hold this position much longer." A mortar round exploded nearby; the young lieutenant covered his ears and grimaced. "Tell them we've established a defensive position at the edge of the airstrip. They'll know what to do. Now run—and don't be long! We're dying out here." The lieutenant slapped Seth on his back and rolled over to leave.

Seth listened to the lieutenant's instructions, and decided that he actually liked the idea of returning to the seawall. It was sure a lot safer than this place. He waited for the machine guns to start moving the other way, then forced himself up and began running toward the hole in the seawall. He darted smoothly around bodies and trees and debris along a path that led back to the beach. The hole in the seawall came into view as the explosive shock of another mortar round threw him to the ground. Blood trickled from his nose and down across his bristled lip. Once again he forced himself up, but he ran more slowly now. A Jap sniper, camouflaged high up in a tree, picked him up and began leading him in his sights, waiting for the right moment. Seth tumbled awkwardly to the hole and the protection of the seawall when the sniper squeezed the trigger. The sniper's bullet arced smoothly through the humid air, traveling thousands of feet per second, racing to intercept its target. The bullet cut easily through Seth's sweat-soaked shirt, just above his left shoulder blade, and passed cleanly though his body in a fraction of a second. Seth slumped to the ground. He raised his head and looked through the hole in the seawall and out to sea. The Higgins boats still exploded on the coral reef. Marines were still being slaughtered as they waded through the water and onto the beach and across the sand. He watched the frightful scene for a few more seconds before blacking out.

When the story ended, Seth moved his eyes to the fire and stared through the swirling flames into the damp sand beyond. He sat like that for a long time, not moving or talking. Timothy sat motionless too; thinking; imagining; dreaming: he dreamed of dying on the beaches of Tarawa.

Chapter 3

First grade reader, autumn 1937

Tiny chairs arranged leg to leg along a flawlessly constructed circumference, the circle of first graders appeared to slowly implode as his turn to read approached. He looked up from his book and out over the little round faces. The circle shuddered with another throbbing contraction, and the faces appeared to shrink too. But the first grade reader, the thin little book that lay open across his frail legs, the book that he pretended to understand, the book that he now loathed in direct proportion to the sweat dripping from his hands—it grew larger and heavier with each ominous tick of the black-framed wall clock. He shook his head in disbelief. The book always looked so tiny over on the table next to the big playground windows. And yet when it rested on top of his legs while he sat in the circle of children, its great weight nearly crushed him into the floor. He peered down at the open pages again, hoping that by some unexpected miracle the letters and words might unscramble today. Maybe something would change if he scrunched his eyes more, or concentrated harder, or held the book very still. But nothing worked. The inky words looked the same as they did yesterday, and the day before that, and the week before that: completely meaningless.

He decided to use a trick that had worked the other day. Although it did not solve the fundamental problem, it provided an alternative far better than stammering incoherently in front of the other children. The trick was simple. He would listen carefully and at the same time memorize the words read by the child just before him. He would then look down at the little book and repeat the words, not perfectly, but close enough to convince everyone that he could read. After one of the children pointed out his error, he would apologize for losing his place in the story and the teacher would move on to the next child. Today he sat next to Jenny. She had red hair tied into a ponytail above each ear and could read without hardly trying. He listened intently while she took her turn. Jenny swung her feet back and forth under the chair and read with a childish expressiveness. When she finished, she laid the book down on her lap and smiled contently. Timothy breathed deeply before repeating Jenny's words. He even mimicked Jenny's points of emphasis and syllabic accents. He had repeated almost three sentences when Miss Hennessey asked him to stop. She removed her glasses and looked out through the big playground windows; she remembered that this had happened before.

Miss Hennessey had graduated in 1929 from a small college in eastern Washington. She asked to teach the first grade when the principal, Mr. Gazelski, offered her a job, and then he assigned her to the fourth grade instead. She asked him the same question at the end of six consecutive years; each time he assigned her to the fourth grade. After the sixth year she decided to keep her mouth shut. To her surprise, he moved her to the second grade. At the end of last year, Mr. Gazelski decided that she could teach, and he finally gave her a first grade class. With this personal goal accomplished, Miss Hennessey thought she had achieved her true purpose in life. But her true purpose had no specific connection to the first grade, as she thought. Her true purpose was instead to teach children to read, especially children who struggled to read. And not just to read, but to love reading as she did. She did not understand this important distinction when Mr. Gazelski called her into his office and told her that she would be moving to the first grade. She would grow to appreciate it in the coming years.

Paradoxically, Miss Hennessey had been a poor reader as a child. Although she had demonstrated precociousness in many ways, reading had not been one of the ways. Instead, reading quickly became a painful struggle in elementary school, and then remained only slightly less painful through the tangled days of junior high. At some point, and she couldn't remember exactly when or why, she decided to become a better reader. This led to an expanding and increasingly passionate—some of her closest friends would say compulsive—study of writing, composition, poetry, literature, grammar, style, usage, and the rest. She focused on English in high school, and then became an English major in college. So although her love of reading, and special talent to teach this same love to young children, may have been won with intense personal dedication to overcome a fundamental deficit that had been genetically preordained, many would say that it was a gift. But gift or not, Miss Hennessey felt a special love for children who struggled to read.

"Timothy, did you notice that you're reading the same thing Jenny just read?" Miss Hennessey replaced her glasses and then studied Timothy through thick lenses that distorted her eyes and the sides of her face into unreasonably small images. She began wearing glasses in the second grade. Her vision worsened each year, to the dismay of her parents, forcing the lenses in every new pair of glasses to thicken. Her changing eyes finally stabilized in high school, but not before the lenses had achieved an unglamorous weight.

"Uh, no, I didn't Miss Hennessey. I thought I was s'posed to read that part." He had to lie or she might make him read the next part, the part he should have read, the part he did not even know where to find. The book resumed pressing into his legs while he waited for her response. He glanced down at the book to reassure himself that the words stilled jumbled around on the page, and they did. His faith that this would ever change died a little more. He shifted his thoughts to something more productive—where could he hide during recess.

Miss Hennessey studied him for about 10 seconds, although it felt like 10 minutes to Timothy. This was the second, or maybe the third time he had lost his place in the story and inadvertently read the same thing as the child before him. She studied him a little more while he squirmed around in his little chair, and sensed that something was not right. Finally, after what now seemed like twenty hours to Timothy, she said, "Alright Timothy. That'll be fine." She asked the next child to read without saying another word to him.

The children read a little longer, one after another, without any embarrassing pauses or failures, without accidentally reading the same thing as the child before, and then the morning recess bell rang. Timothy, relieved that the reading group had finally ended, began looking forward to what now could be a pleasurable recess. He had just taken his first step toward the classroom door when Miss Hennessey called his name. "Timothy, I'd like to see you during recess. Would you please wait at your desk?" He knew he had no choice; he wondered why she asked him like he had something to say about it. After arriving at his desk, he tried to think about what he must have done or said to get into this much trouble. He sat at his desk and watched glumly while classmates poured through the classroom door into the hallway.

After the last child raced out of the room, Miss Hennessey moved some things around on her desk before walking over and sitting in one of the tiny chairs next to Timothy. She pulled at her ear and thought of the questions she wanted to ask him. She began ominously: "Do you enjoy reading, Timothy?" After making this simple inquiry, she leaned forward and smiled, lifting the rear legs of the little chair off the floor.

Timothy's throat tightened. Miss Hennessy's malicious question slapped him across the face. He would have to choose his answer carefully to stay out of trouble. "Yes, Miss Hennessey. I like to read. It's one of my favorite things." He might have gone a little too far with that last part, but he didn't want these questions to go on forever, and he thought a strong answer would end the discussion sooner. Maybe he could even salvage a few minutes of recess.

"I see. What kind of things do you like to read?" Miss Hennessey thought back over the last several weeks. She couldn't remember ever hearing Timothy actually read something accurately. She wondered how she had missed this. Maybe she had focused too much attention on the children who read easily and didn't require much coaching. She thought to herself that she should be more observant in the future.

"Well, almost anything." Timothy knew this could be a potentially dangerous response, but these questions were getting trickier and he didn't have a lot of time to think. He decided to try a diversionary tactic to give himself more time. "What kind'a things do you like to read, Miss Hennessey?" This question appeared to surprise her—just what he had hoped for.

"Well, uh, almost anything, I guess, just like you."

Darn. She answered that one without even thinking. Quick—ask another question before she does. "What'cha reading now?" *That should keep her busy for a few minutes.*

"Why, I'm reading *Look Homeward, Angel* by Thomas Wolfe. It's a book I've been wanting to read for a long time. I've heard it's very good." Miss Hennessey leaned back in the tiny chair. She removed her glasses again and carefully considered her next question. "What are you reading now?"

Timothy swallowed hard and squirmed some more in his chair. He wasn't reading anything, and he didn't know the names of any books either, but he had to say something to protect his earlier lie. Unfortunately, before he could organize his thoughts, he blurted out: "Uh, well, uh, I, I'm reading *Look Howard Angel* too!"

Miss Hennessey smiled; Timothy did not notice the smile. "Really, Timothy. Why, that is impressive. How do you like it?"

Too late to amend his impulsive answer. His only choice now was to move forward and hope that he could somehow hold this mess together. "Well, it's really good. I really like it." Possibly laying it on a little thick, but he began thinking this might really work. Miss Hennessey laughed quietly, convincing him that she actually believed his absurd lie.

"This is really quite amazing, Timothy. We are both reading the same book at the same time. Who would have thought that was possible? You know, I have an idea. What do you think about this? Since we both love to read the same kinds of books, maybe we should read together, every day, just the two of us. What would you think about that, Timothy?" Miss Hennessey had no intention of pointing out his obvious lies and inconsistencies. She simply hoped to convince him to read with her, allowing at least the possibility of teaching him to read without the other children around to poke fun at him when he stumbled. She quickly added an important clarification to her offer. "Of course, there's no reason to read *Look Homeward, Angel* together, since we are reading it separately. We should read something different, maybe one of the books I have here in the classroom. What do you think of that idea, Timothy?" She smiled more broadly this time.

Timothy thought about this. That wouldn't be so bad. He liked Miss Hennessey, and he knew he couldn't get out of this without doing something. She would probably get bored with him in a few weeks anyway. "I guess that would be OK. Can I go to recess now?"

"Sure Timothy, you can go to recess now. There's still a little time left."

Timothy bounced up from the tiny chair and bolted toward the classroom door, accelerating as he maneuvered around several desks and chairs.

"Timothy, walk in the classroom!"

Almost knocking over a coat rack when he slid to an abrupt stop just short of the door, Timothy looked back at Miss Hennessey with a mischievous smile, then began walking briskly. He pushed though the door and into the empty hallway. When the door latched behind him, he broke into a run again. At the end of the hallway he burst through the big double doors into the bright morning sun. He raced away from the building until he reached the center of the playground where screaming children, each doing something different, each unaware of his sudden presence, surrounded him with noise and motion. He no longer thought of what had just happened with Miss Hennessey. He closed his eyes and felt the warmth of the sun on his dirty face. Happy that he didn't need to hide, he quickly forgot about his agreement with Miss Hennessey to read every day. Miss Hennessey would not forget.

♦ ♦ ♦

Paladins on the Union Pacific, September 1948

Rivulets of water streaked across the window; and mimicking random bolts of lightning above the distant ocean's smoothly curving rim, met the sharp edge of aluminum at the perimeter of the glass in small explosions that vaporized in the catching wind. A long, bending sliver of light, the day's remaining breath fading with each sky-illuminating bolt, bristled behind trees racing along the bands of gleaming steel. The lightning bolts, spectacularly visible against the graying sky, diminished underneath the loud, rhythmic whirring of the spinning wheels. A gentle swaying motion joined the vibration of the steel wheels, the two forces coupled by the physics of motion and sound. The swaying pulled to one side, and the seething locomotive appeared at the edge of the window, then became fully visible when a flash of the day's fading glow reflected for an instant off some piece of shiny metal. And at that moment, as the last light of the day faded, the engine and its long line of trailing silver cars dissolved into the darkness of approaching night.

Humphrey leaned forward in his seat and watched a rain drop etch a jagged trail across the window. When the drop reached the aluminum frame at the edge of the glass, it clung for a moment before the wind blew it off. Even though he had never traveled on a train before, he liked everything about it: he liked the way he felt inside the passenger car, safe from the raging storm outside; he liked the drops of water when they raced across the window, driven haphazardly across the polished plate by the tremendous speed of the train; he liked the conductor's luminous tenor voice as it heralded each new stop; and he liked the gentle swaying of the passenger car. The motion reminded him of his father's fishing boat when it rolled against the peaceful waves on a clear day. A few times he thought he could almost smell the sea, despite the rain-streaked window that separated him from it. Humphrey studied flashes of the ocean between sporadic clumps of trees, and he imagined lighting strikes miles away on the stormy sea where frigid water, treacherous and black, churned above infinite depths and frightful creatures. Then he shivered when he imagined himself trapped in his father's fishing boat in this imagined storm.

The gentle swaying soon lulled Humphrey into a fragmented sleep. He slept for about an hour, but the sleep did not refresh him. When he awoke, he felt the familiar nausea that usually remained after he slept longer than 20 minutes but less than a full night. After he rubbed his eyes to restore his vision, he noticed the flickering lights of an approaching town. The train slowed when it moved into the town, the clanging wheels echoing off fences and buildings that were too close to the polished tracks. Humphrey watched fences and buildings and loading docks and a water tower move by the window, then pulled a worn leather case from his travel bag. He unsnapped a leather flap and gently removed a small wooden chessboard. He lifted the top of the board to reveal 32 miniature metal chess pieces, each exquisitely cast. After dumping them into his open hand, he replaced the lid and set up the pieces. He opened his bag again and pulled out a book of historic chess games. He carefully opened it to a marked page and began playing though one of the games. By the fifth move he had lost all awareness of his surroundings.

A young man, one of dozens on the train, watched Humphrey set up the little chess set and begin playing an invisible opponent. The young man studied this curious activity for several minutes before deciding that he had to investigate. He stood up, and, shoving his hands up to the arched ceiling of the car, pretended to stretch before casually stepping across the narrow aisle. Humphrey, oblivious to the young man now standing nearby, continued moving chess pieces as illustrated in the book. The young man rested his hands on the padded back of Humphrey's seat and leaned closer. He could now hear Humphrey muttering to himself.

"Mind if I ask what you're doing?"

Humphrey twisted his neck and looked up at the young man looming above him. "What's that?" he asked, having heard the sound of the words but not the words themselves.

"I said, do you mind if I ask what you're doing?"

Humphrey thought about how he should answer this question as the train rattled through a track switch. "Well, I think you just did."

This snippy answer surprised the young man. "Did what?"

"You asked me if you could ask what I was doing. Isn't that what you asked?"

Another odd reply. The young man quickly evaluated whether Humphrey was a sarcastic asshole or an inept square. He finally decided that Humphrey didn't look like the sarcastic type. "You know, now that you mention it, I guess I did. Mind if I sit down?"

The young man looked strong, and dangerous too, so Humphrey decided he couldn't stop him from sitting down. "It's a free country. Go ahead."

The young man plopped into the seat across from Humphrey, facing the rear of the train. He bent forward to study the little chess set more closely, blocking the light with his head. "So…what exactly are you doing here?"

Eager to resume his game, Humphrey had little interest in talking to this presumptuous stranger. He raised his eyes from the board. The young man appeared friendly enough, even if he still looked a little dangerous. Probably best to talk to him, and then maybe he will go away. "I'm playing though a famous chess game. It's written in this book. See."

The young man glanced over the worn pages of the book; he did not recognize the unfamiliar annotations and symbols. "You know, I've always wanted to learn to play chess. I would have asked my dad to teach me, but we never got along very well, especially during the last couple of years. Anyway, it seemed like we were never both in the mood to play a game at the same time."

Humphrey now regretted that he had acknowledged the young man's right to sit in front of him—teaching the young man to play chess could take hours. "Well...I don't know. Chess is a really complicated game, and I'm not a very good teacher. Maybe some other time."

This instantly annoyed the young man. "Like when? You will never see me again. It's now or never, and I think now's a good time. And I bet you're a lot better teacher than you think. Anyway, was there something else you had to do?"

Humphrey stared down at the little chess set. He purchased it six years ago with money saved from his paper route. He ordered it from a catalog because he could not find one in town. His mom had helped him fill out the order form on a Friday afternoon after school. It took forever, nearly two months, for the chess set to arrive. He remembered his delight when he opened it up and set up the pieces for the first time. Since then he had played hundreds of games, nearly all of them by himself. And he had cared for the little chess set with impressive devotion. It looked almost as new as when he had first opened up the package. He winced at the thought that some stranger might fondle his board and pieces.

"Well, I guess we could spend a few minutes learning some of the basics. I don't see much point in doing more than that since you're a beginner."

"Hey, that's great. Now tell me, what's the main thing I should know about chess. I mean, is there one thing that's more important than anything else?"

What a strange question, Humphrey thought—then he realized he didn't have any idea if one thing might be more important than anything else. "Well, uh, I'm not sure I know. I'll have to think about that one. Maybe we should start by just learning how to set up the pieces. Then we can look at the names of the pieces and how each one moves. Does that sound alright."

"You're the teacher. Sounds fine to me."

Humphrey didn't want to admit it to himself, but he liked being called a teacher. No one had ever called him that before. He cleared the remaining pieces and set the board neatly on top of his legs. Without looking up, he explained, "The first thing you need to know is the orientation of the board. The white square always goes in the lower right-hand corner." He touched the square for emphasis. "You got that?"

The young man squeezed his chin and squinted at the single white square. "Yeah, that's easy. All I've got to do is remember 'white-right.' Nothing to it."

This simple statement impressed Humphrey. He had never thought of it that way before. "That's pretty good. White-right. I'll have to remember that one myself. Now, let's go over the names of the pieces and set the board up. The first piece you need to know about is the pawn. There are eight of them, and they line up on the second row like this." Humphrey set each of the white pawns accurately in the center of every square on the second row.

"Second row, pawns. That should be easy to remember too. They're short so the other pieces can see over them. If they were on the first row, they wouldn't be able to see what they're supposed to do."

Humphrey continued without comment, although he had never heard that one either. "The next piece is called a rook, but I like to call it a castle instead. There are two of them and they go on the corner squares. They actually look like little towers with battlements on top."

The young man picked up one of the dark castles and twirled it back and forth between his thumb and fingers while he examined it. "Castle. That should be easy to remember too, because it does look like a castle."

Humphrey picked up one of the knights, but before he could say its name the young man interrupted him. "I know the name of this one. It's called a knight, even if it does look like a little horse."

Humphrey held the piece close to his face. "That's what everyone else calls it. I like to call it a Paladin."

This puzzled the young man. He knew the piece was called a knight. He had never heard anyone call it a Paladin. "What's a Paladin? Never heard that one before."

"I like to call it a Paladin because that's what my dad called it. My dad said that the Paladins were the knights who guarded Charlemagne. There were twelve of them, and they were the most loyal and courageous knights in the land."

"Charlemagne? Don't remember anyone mentioning him in school. What'd he do?"

Humphrey set the knight on the black square next to the castle and adjusted it until it was accurately centered. "Actually, I don't know a lot about him either. He was some sort of king who lived over a thousand years ago. I think he was really famous." Humphrey picked up the remaining knight and admired it as well. "I do know that Orlando was the most famous Paladin. He was Charlemagne's most loyal knight, and so brave that he actually killed a giant with a sword."

"Orlando killed a giant?"

"Yeah, he did—with a sword. My dad told me some other stuff about Orlando, but I can't remember much of it. The main thing to remember is that, just like Orlando, the Paladin's most important job is to guard the king—even if he has to sacrifice himself to do it."

The young man began setting up the black pawns on his side of the board. "And how exactly does the knight—I mean Paladin—go about guarding the king?"

"We'll get into that in a few minutes. First we need to go over the rest of the pieces, and then a few basics." Humphrey talked about the bishop and the king and the queen, and the way each of the pieces moved on the board, and how to castle the king, and then how to start the game. He told the young man that he should move the Paladins before the bishops, that he shouldn't move the same piece twice during the first ten moves of a game, and that he should try to control the center. Then he showed him a good opening that worked pretty well for both sides and they played a game. The young man made quite a few mistakes, but by the time they started the fourth game the mistakes began to diminish. Humphrey also realized at this point that he was enjoying himself. He had to admit that he liked this better than playing alone, even if the young man talked almost every move.

They had reached the middle of the seventh game when the train slowed, ran for a long time at reduced speed, then decelerated to a lurching stop. The young man continued to study the board beyond the stop, his face twisted with intensity. He found the relationship of the chess pieces, and the meaning of the relationships, deeply interesting. He had lost six games in a row, but that didn't matter. He had learned something new with each loss. Humphrey looked outside when he felt the train slow. The rain had let up during the middle of game three. He peered through the rain-streaked glass and read the words "San Diego" on a faded sign next to the tracks. Time to get off the train.

"Sorry, but I've gotta go. It's been nice playing chess with you." Humphrey picked up the board and carefully stored the pieces. He slid the chess set gently into the leather case and packed it into his travel bag.

The young man responded, "Thanks for the chess lesson. I always wanted to learn how to play chess. Maybe I'll even win a game some day."

"I'm sure you will. Maybe we'll even play again sometime." Humphrey quickly shoved his arms into his jacket and stepped into the aisle.

"I don't think so, but that's OK. I enjoyed the games, even if I did lose every time."

"I wouldn't say that. I think you may have started to work me into a difficult position in that last game."

The young man smiled. He knew Humphrey had clobbered him in the last game too. "Thanks. I was just playing like you taught me."

Humphrey smiled too. "Thanks." Humphrey picked up his bag, walked down the aisle, and stepped off the train. A stream of young men, very close to his age, moved across the platform toward the Spanish style railway station. A large sign with the words "Santa Fe" ran along the ridge of the building's main roof. Humphrey joined the stream. He walked though the building and out through a pair of large swinging doors at the main entry. Several buses waited on the curb, each with a Marine Corps Sergeant standing by the folding bus door. Humphrey picked out a bus with a dented fender and got on. He moved down the aisle, crowded with other young men, and picked out an empty seat. Several minutes passed before he became aware that someone was standing next to him. He looked up; the young man from the train, the one he had taught to play chess, leaned over him.

"Hi. Remember me? We played chess a few minutes ago. I was about to beat your ass in that last game. Mind if I sit down?"

"Sure. It's a free country. Go ahead."

The young man threw a small bag into the overhead rack and sat down next to Humphrey. The Marine Corps Sergeant stood next to the driver now, studying the young faces crowded into the bus. The sergeant asked a stocky youth in the front seat if he had a cigarette. The youth pulled a pack of cigarettes from his jacket pocket, shook it to make sure there were smokes remaining, and handed the pack to the sergeant. The sergeant had a broken nose and cauliflower ears, and didn't look like someone you wanted to mess with. The sergeant pulled out a cigarette, tapped it briskly on the steel pipe at the edge of the seat, lit it, sucked in a breath of smoke, and then put the pack in his pocket. He grinned and said, "You won't be needing these where you're going, son."

The young man watched the sergeant take the cigarettes and then turned back to Humphrey. "Hey, I never got your name."

Humphrey paused for a moment: he was not fond of his name. "It's Humphrey."

The young man smiled, and then broke into a broad grin. "Humphrey! That's pretty good. Which parent inflicted that name on you?"

"My mom. She had a great grandfather named Humphrey, and she liked the name. It must have been a good name in those days."

"Yeah, I guess that could be. Maybe you should use your middle name instead. What's your middle name?

"Uh, it's worse."

"It's worse? What is it?"

Humphrey paused again. "It's Roland."

"Good grief, Humphrey! It *is* worse! Who gave you that middle name?"

"My father."

"I think we should stay with Humphrey. It's actually not such a bad name when you get used to it." The young man fought hard to control his intense amusement.

"What's your name?" Humphrey asked, trying to take the focus off his own name. Maybe the young man had also been given an embarrassing name.

"Why, it's Timothy."

The folding bus doors slammed, the parking break released with a prolonged squeal, and the bus shook when it rolled forward. They were on their way.

Chapter 4
The tree fort, April 1941

Timothy eyed down the length of a two-by-four. The rough end of the stud pressed against his nose, leaving a temporary pattern of small red dots. He didn't know exactly why he should do this, but he had seen his dad go through the same ritual many times and figured it must be important. He tossed the warped stud onto an expanding pile near his left foot and picked up another, eyeing down its length in the same manner. *This is going to take a while*, he thought to himself. John had torn down an old shed behind the house last weekend, and after finishing the unpleasant job had suggested to Timothy that he build something with the demolished materials. "You know, Timothy," he had said, "you should take these materials and build a tree house or something." Timothy didn't think much of the idea at first; it somehow became more intriguing to him during the passing week. And so, here he stood; sorting through a lumpy pile of wood and shingles and nails and other debris, trying not to step on anything sharp, searching for useful materials to build a tree house.

To help move the project along, his dad had given him a big red coffee can over half full of used 16-penny nails, a claw hammer with a sturdy wooden handle, a warped but still functional crosscut saw, and a broken crowbar streaked with rust. Although the crowbar didn't actually work as intended because the chiseled end had a chip missing, it could still be used for whacking on things when necessary. When he gave him the tools, John had said, "I'm just loaning you these tools to build the tree house. Be sure to return them when you're done. And be careful not to lose any of them or leave them out in the rain." In truth, John had no further use for any of the worn-out tools. He just wanted to teach Timothy to be accountable and thought this might be a good way to do it.

The day had turned warm since breakfast, warmer than usual for this time of year, certainly warmer than last weekend, and Timothy began sweating as he strained to lift several slabs of asphalt shingles off the pile. A bead of sweat rolled down the side of his forehead and splattered through his eyelashes, stinging his eye. He dropped a ragged chunk of shingles and rubbed his eye with a dirty hand, but it didn't help much. A gentle breeze rustled the leaves of the trees near his house, causing a soft fluttering sound that Timothy liked. A few puffy clouds floated above. The gentle breeze pushed the clouds high across the sky, casting strangely shaped and soft-edged shadows that moved gracefully over the ground. Timothy thought the clouds made the day more remarkable; he preferred them to the emptiness of a crystal blue sky. He had never really cared for days with clear, sunny skies—not that there were all that many of them during the year—but when they did occur, he usually longed for a few clouds. Days without clouds were just too simple and monotonous. He rubbed his eye again before prying some more shingles out of the pile.

Phijit sat patiently near the edge of the demolished shed, moving his head from side to side and up and down as he followed each of Timothy's motions with intense interest. His tail drummed vigorously against the damp ground, signaling his hope that Timothy would throw a small chunk of wood for him to retrieve. His wet nose traced a smooth pattern in the air, following Timothy when he bent down to pick up a shingle. Part Border collie and part something else—most likely more than several something elses—Phijit became a member of the family when John and Martha got a call from the local veterinarian about two years ago. The vet had found him behind the clinic in a cardboard box, abandoned and near death, and John and Martha had agreed to adopt him. The vet told Timothy that Phijit's ancestors were reindeer-herding dogs brought to Scotland by the Vikings, and that they were bred with Scottish sheep dogs to make the Border collie. Timothy thought it was pretty neat that his dog had descended from the Vikings. He remembered pictures of the elegant, sleek Viking ships from a book at school. He didn't know much about Scotland, except that the men who lived there wore funny dresses.

By early afternoon, Timothy had accumulated a large pile of studs and rafters and shingles and other indescribable materials that were destined to become part of his tree house. No, he thought, house wasn't the right word. He would not build a house; he would build a fort instead, something magnificent and secure where he could hide from attackers. After making this important decision, he attempted to visualize a tree fort built of wood studs and rafters and asphalt shingles, but instead saw stone walls with battlements and slender stone turrets with narrow, vertical slits topped with toothed stonework. This persistent image would not help him build a tree fort with the materials he had to work with. Even if he did have a bunch of stones, which he did not, how would he get them up in a tree? He tried to think of something different, something made of wood, and the stone turrets kept gushing into his thoughts. And then, to make things worse, he began seeing a drawbridge spanning a wide moat filled with putrid, slime-covered water and fire-breathing monsters. The possibility of building this image was almost certainly minimal, especially given the current availability of heavy construction equipment. But then, he thought if he actually could dig a moat there wouldn't be much problem filling it up with water; that would take care of itself. The putrid slime and fire-breathing monsters, on the other hand, could present more difficult challenges. He decided to ignore these lurid mental images when the castle's defenders began pouring boiling oil over the stone battlements onto hundreds of attacking Vikings. He also glimpsed a couple of reindeer-herding dogs yapping just beyond the edge of the moat; he ignored them too.

"Well, Phijit, I think it's time to scout out a good place for the tree fort. We have to find the right spot before we can move this stuff and start building, so let's get going." Phijit tilted his head to better understand Timothy's words. He also drummed his tail a little harder. "Of course, you wouldn't understand that, would you, because you've never built a tree fort before." Timothy didn't stop to think that he'd never built one either as he headed toward the spruce grove behind the house. At first he walked briskly, but then picked up his pace to a jog before breaking into a full run. The ground rose more steeply and became softer underfoot when Timothy and Phijit neared the uneven perimeter of the grove. Phijit raced ahead of Timothy then came back, and then raced ahead again, barking sharply each time he passed by. They finally stepped underneath the overhanging branches at the grove's outer edge and were instantly bathed in cool, speckled shadows. Timothy slowed to a patient walk and Phijit raced by him again. Timothy looked up through the branches, and while admiring the trees began walking unknowingly in a loose circle. This was not the first time he had visited the grove, yet somehow he had never before appreciated the astonishing tallness of the spruce trees. He completed the circle before resuming his search for a place to build the tree fort. Phijit had calmed down by this time, and stayed closer to Timothy as they walked deeper into the grove.

"You know, Phijit, we shouldn't go too far, 'cause we've got to haul all that wood to the place we pick. Maybe we should head back and take a look at some of the trees we already walked by." Phijit barked in apparent agreement and sprinted away when they turned back. Timothy soon hiked up to a group of three matching spruces and stopped. The trees were spaced about 10 feet apart and formed a near equilateral triangle. He studied the trees for a long time, and after careful consideration decided he could build a good platform between them, beginning with a board on each side. The spruce trio would make the perfect place for his tree fort. "OK Phijit, I think this is the spot. Let's go get the wood and tools and anything else we might need." Phijit cocked his head and barked, and they ran out of the cool shadows of the spruce grove, down the gentle slope, and past the demolished shed to his house.

Balancing near the top of a ladder leaned against the roof eave, John watched Timothy and Phijit run down the hill as he cleaned spruce needles and black gunk out of a gutter. They disappeared behind the house for a few seconds, then suddenly appeared around the corner before darting by the foot of the ladder. Fearing that he might get knocked off the ladder, John grabbed the gutter with both hands and braced his feet when they ran by. "Hey you two. What's going on here? What's the big hurry?"

Timothy stopped abruptly just beyond the foot of the ladder, breathing excitedly. Phijit overran him and then raced back to sit attentively at Timothy's side, his incessantly drumming tail pounding on the ground in an annoyingly consistent rhythm. "We're building a tree fort and I need the wagon to move the stuff I picked out and we've got to get going before the day runs out so I haven't got much time."

It pleased John that Timothy had taken his advice about building something with the shed materials, but he tried not to show it. "A tree fort, huh. Where ya building it?"

"In the spruce grove up on the hill. It's a great spot. I gotta go."

John had just started his sentence when Timothy darted away with Phijit jumping and barking and running all around him. "Be care—" Too late: gone. John wanted to talk to his son about the tree fort. Maybe later, he thought to himself. He wiped both hands on his shirt and then resumed digging spruce needles out of the gutter.

Timothy and Phijit raced around the back of the house to the spot where his mom kept the wagon. The wagon formed a lumpy shape under an old canvas tarp, streaked with water from a brief morning shower. Timothy grabbed a damp corner and dragged the tarp off, slipping as he fell backwards. He found the wagon handle half-buried in mud; with Phijit's help he quickly dug it out with his fingers. Santa Claus gave Timothy the wagon over two years ago (at least that's what his mom and dad told him). It had polished slatted wood sides that folded down to make loading easier, and large rubber wheels that bounced erratically when he pulled the wagon too fast. He once used it to pull Phijit around the yard when he was a puppy; now Phijit would not stay in the wagon for more than a few seconds. The wagon wheels squeaked when he rolled them over the muddy ground to the pile of tree fort construction materials. In a few minutes he had his tools and the first load of wood studs balanced awkwardly across the top of the wagon and began trudging up the gently sloping green hill toward the spruce grove with Phijit leading the way. They arrived ten minutes later with all of the tools and most of the studs. After unloading the wagon next to the spruce trio, they ran back to the pile, the wagon wheels bouncing behind. The air began to cool as the afternoon lengthened, and clouds thickened and spread across the graying sky. After five trips, Timothy decided they had enough materials to officially begin construction.

Timothy and Phijit gazed up at the magnificent spruce trio, thinking hard about how and where they should begin. Timothy envisioned the platform as high as possible above the ground. At the same time he knew there might be limitations to what he and Phijit could accomplish with a hammer, bent saw, and rusted crowbar. After thoughtfully considering his options, he fished through the can of nails and twisted out several rusty spikes. One of them was remarkably crooked, so he whacked it with the side of the hammer to straighten it out a little. He used the crosscut saw to cut off a chunk of two-by-four stud, about one-foot long. He centered it on the closest tree, about a foot off the ground, and pounded the spike in. He stepped on the board to test its strength. It remained level until he slid his foot a few inches to the left of the spike. He fell to the ground; the two-by-four spun around like a propeller and whacked the side of his knee. He jumped around a few times, then carefully leveled the step and drove in a second nail to stabilize it. Timothy sawed off three more one-foot lengths of stud and nailed each of them up the side of the tree about a foot apart. He thought they looked pretty straight when he finished. Now he needed a long board to span across two of the spruce trees. None of the individual rafters were long enough, so he scabbed a couple of two-by-eights together using a handful of galvanized 16-penny nails. The nail points poked through the other side of the opposite board; he hammered them down until they bent deeply into the surface of the wood. The resulting beam didn't look exactly straight, but Timothy thought it should be good enough for the task at hand.

With his hands on his hips, he stood silently and admired the irregular pattern of nails that held the two boards together. He realized that he now faced a new and more complex challenge: how were he and Phijit supposed to get this ungainly thing up in the air? And even if they did figure out how to do that, how then were they supposed to hold it up and attach it to the big spruce trees at the same time? He crossed his arms and, supporting his chin with a thumb and his nose with a bent index finger, stood very still while he considered this dilemma. Timothy had seen his dad do this when things were not going well. He didn't know exactly how it was supposed to help, but to his surprise, it worked: he got an idea just by pushing against his chin and nose. He would need a long piece of rope to make the idea work. Back to the house, with Phijit running ahead and then back again and then ahead again while barking continuously. John had nearly finished cleaning out the last gutter when they arrived at the foot of the wood ladder for the second time.

"Dad, dad, I need some rope! Do you know where I can get some?"

John peered down from the top of his ladder for the second time. A black smear of gutter gunk glistened across his forehead. "Uh, yeah. There's some rope in the garage, under the workbench. Don't lose it or leave it in the rain. And dinner's in an hour. Don't be late!"

"Thanks dad! I won't."

Timothy found the rope where John said it would be. He raced back to the spruce trio with the rope coiled around his shoulder. Panting heavily, he tossed the rope over a low branch with a looping side arm motion, tied it to the end of the beam, and pulled the beam up to the level where he had decided to build the platform. He climbed up the new two-by-four ladder and nailed one end of the beam to the tree with one 16-penny nail so that it could rotate. He sawed four one-foot lengths of stud and nailed them up the next tree—a little better this time because now he knew how to do it—then repeated the process at the other end of the beam. By dinnertime he had built all three sides of the triangular frame that would support the main platform of his tree fort. He had also pounded about three-dozen nails at the end of each board to securely fasten them to the spruce trio. When they had finished, Timothy and Phijit sat for a moment and admired their impressive work. "You know Phijit, we're a real team, aren't we. I didn't think we'd get this far in a single day. We're amazing!" Phijit looked up and tilted his head from side to side and appeared to grin with satisfaction.

The night passed without dreams and the morning arrived slowly, cooler and darker than the day before. It rained briefly around 4:00 am, and the damp smell of it still imbued the air at sunrise. Clouds spread across the sky more abundantly by breakfast, and running together at shredded edges mimicked a fine watercolor painting. Timothy and Phijit got up earlier than usual. Both were eager to work on the tree fort again. Timothy had actually slept very little during the night because of his excitement. He finally fell asleep by 4:00 a.m., so he missed the rain. Phijit slept fine, even though his legs jerked in a running motion many times during the night. After eating a hasty breakfast of cereal and juice, they raced through the kitchen door and around the side of the house and up the gentle hill to the cool grove and the awaiting spruce trio.

"Here we are again, Phijit. What do you think we should start with today?" Phijit pretended to understand Timothy's question. "I see. You know Phijit, I think you're right. Let's start building the floor. I'll get the nails. You get some boards."

Phijit didn't exactly help very much with the boards, but Timothy found some good nails near the bottom of the coffee can, and some decent boards too, and began hauling them up the two-by-four ladder and setting them in place over the top of the beams. He had finished a corner of the floor when the thundering crackle of a distant lightning flash arrived at the spruce trio. Timothy and Phijit looked up for a moment, but could not tell which direction the thunder had come from. "Mmmm, looks like it might rain, Phijit. We'd better work a little faster. I'd like to get most of this floor done before we stop today."

Timothy worked a little faster and another crash of sound echoed around the trees. He hauled another board up to the platform, set it in place, pounded the nails through the board into the beam below, then repeated the process. Sometimes he had to use the claw hammer to pull out a bent-over nail. He tried to straighten the nail out as much as possible with the hammer before pounding it in again, but he didn't have a lot of time. The rain finally began falling into the spruce grove, slowly at first in small scattered droplets, then more rapidly, and water began glistening on the finished portions of the deck. Timothy hurried his pace even more as the droplets grew in size and splashed around him. He decided to get at least a couple more boards on before quitting for the day. He pulled up one of the longest boards and moved it into place. He groped around for the hammer and could not find it. He stood up and yelled to Phijit: "Phijit, have you seen the hammer? I thought I left it right here." He spun around suddenly, looking for the hammer behind him. Another clap of thunder arrived at the moment he slipped. He waved both arms to catch his balance, but the slip had gone too far. He twisted down, and the edge of the platform smashed square across his pelvis, knocking his breath out. He continued spinning around as he fell over the beam. He crashed into the ground face-down and then did not move. The rain began falling with more intensity.

John paced around the kitchen with his hands in his pockets. Rain had pounded the roof and run down the windows for over an hour now, and Timothy still had not returned from the spruce grove. He could wait no longer. He pulled on a hooded rain jacket, slammed the kitchen door open, and jogged briskly up the gentle hill. He entered the coolness of the damp spruce grove and began searching. He did not know where to look for the tree fort, but thought it shouldn't be too hard to find it. After searching for a long time, he saw Phijit lying next to Timothy's motionless body below three soaring spruce trees. At first he paused; then he broke into a run and rushed to Timothy's side. John knelt down and gently turned him over. Timothy opened his eyes and looked into his dad's bleary face.

"Timothy, are you alright? What the hell happened?" John worked hard to maintain a calm sound in his voice.

Timothy did not know what had happened. He remembered looking for the hammer before slipping and falling off the platform and instantly colliding with the ground. He must have blacked out after that, because everything else looked fuzzy. A dull ache pulsed above his nose and over the top of his head. "I, I don't know. I don't feel very good. I think I might'a hurt myself." The right side of his face was swollen and bruised, and a deep cut had opened up across the top of his nose. Blood smeared over both eyebrows and across his left cheek. He could barely open his left eye, and his right eye had puffed shut. Although he didn't know it then, he also had a hideous bruise across the front of his pelvis where he had hit the sharp edge of the platform before spinning over the side.

John studied him briefly, and concealing his emotions with practiced skill convinced himself that Timothy would be all right. "I think you'll live. Let's get you back to the house before this storm gets any worse." He didn't say anything more, and remained unusually calm while he helped his son up. They did not speak to each other as they walked out of the spruce grove and down the gentle hill to the warmth and safety of the house.

◆ ◆ ◆

Cold weather training, January 1950

Inside, where darkness filled the tent and pushed against the thin canvas walls, stalactites of icy breath formed along the sagging ridge line. The darkness concealed the frozen drips and intensified the perception of cold, already sufficient in and of itself. It was cold beneath the tent too, and hard. The soil, frozen crystalline weeks earlier, worked cooperatively with the dense air to magnify the intensity of the cold. During the ephemeral days, the low sun afforded some warmth when it peered through the trees—if you were lucky enough to stand in it. Yet gray clouds often concealed the sun, preventing the warmth from reaching the ground and those who searched for it. Then you had to keep moving: if you stopped, the cold enveloped you and flowed through the seams of your clothing and around the edges of buttoned flaps and over the top of upturned collars until it found your naked skin. The cold then seeped through your skin until it lived inside of you. After that, no amount of jumping around or arm slapping or standing in the sun's meager warmth could force the cold out again. At night, the cold could be kept out by pulling the sleeping bag's drawstring tightly around your face, leaving an opening barely sufficient to breath through. But then you had to remember to avoid breathing inside the bag, difficult to do when you slept, because if you did, your breath's latent moisture condensed in the insulated folds and linings and created frozen paths that the cold used to penetrate the bag. The insatiable cold then found you again, and your only hope would be for sun in the morning. If an overcast sky or mountains or trees blocked the sun, you lived in misery until the next night, when darkness and misery increased. Then, as you again shivered uncontrollably in your frosted bag, you longed for the overcast sky.

Humphrey discovered a natural truth in less than one day: when you are cold at night, and cannot sleep because of it, time slows to the horrifying pace of a beguiling nightmare. Your mind soon becomes insidiously unsettled and you begin thinking in ways both fascinating and disturbing at the same time. And when the cold and your disquieting thoughts begin working together, the possibility of peaceful sleep, and the stillness it could bring your troubled mind, becomes utterly hopeless. Any alternative soon appears more desirable than this endless suffering—even crawling out of the frosted bag with its marginal warmth, staggering into the blackness outside the inadequate protection of the canvas tent, and standing on the frozen ground to take a piss.

"Timothy, are you awake?" Humphrey waited patiently for a response before reaching outside of his bag and jabbing Timothy on the side. "Timothy, are you awake? I can't sleep."

Timothy jerked, then grunted though sleep-swollen lips. "Huh, uh, what?"

"I said, are you awake?"

Timothy coughed and rolled onto his back. "Not now you damn fool. What's the big idea waking me up?"

"I'm cold and I can't sleep. Do you mind talking for a while? Maybe it'll help me go to sleep. I was thinking that I could either go outside and take a piss or talk; I decided to talk."

Timothy grunted and let out a deep breath. "You should've taken a piss."

"Do you think tomorrow's going to be hard? The sergeant said we're going to cross over a stream on ropes. I hope the ropes aren't too high. I'm not good with heights."

Timothy twisted his head around until the bones in his neck cracked. "No, I don't think it'll be hard. I used to climb on ropes all the time when I was a kid. I even built a tree fort once that had a long rope strung between the fort and a big spruce tree. I used to climb along that rope all the time. It's easy."

"You weren't wearing a pack with an M-1 strung over your back when you did that."

Timothy considered this difference. "Well, that's true, but I'm a lot bigger now, so I think it'll be about the same."

Humphrey changed the topic. "Remember that time in boot camp when we lifted the bread and jelly from the mess hall. That was pretty good, wasn't it."

Timothy had forgotten about the bread and jelly incident. "Yeah, that was pretty funny. We planned that little maneuver for days. I squeezed that loaf of bread down flat until I could hide it under my shirt, and you stuck the jar of jelly in your pants. We had a real feast that night after lights out. Yeah, that was pretty good. We should do that again sometime."

"Yeah, we should. Boy, I wish I had some of that bread and jelly right now. I can still remember how good it tasted. I thought it was the best thing in the whole world that night." Humphrey sucked on his tongue as he remembered the jelly taste.

"Yeah, it was pretty good. I think it tasted so good because we had to work so hard to get it. Say, I have an idea. Why don't you open some C-rations and pretend like it's bread and jelly. One of the guys said he heard they were left over from the Civil War, but I told him I didn't know there were any Marines in the Civil War."

"What was left over from the Civil War?"

"The C-rations."

"I don't think there were any C-rations in the Civil War. They're probably left over from World War II. They'd be frozen anyway."

"So would the bread and jelly, if you had any."

"Yeah, I guess you're right."

They talked for another 20 minutes until Humphrey drifted into an uneasy sleep. Timothy thought about the bread and jelly for a while, then rolled onto his side and closed his eyes. They both slept for another hour before the sergeant arrived at the front of the tent and yanked the flap open.

Sergeant Johnson's baritone voice boomed inside the tiny tent. "Time to saddle up, sleepy heads. We got work to do, and the day's a wasting!" The sergeant often used this expression, especially before 6:00 am in the morning.

Timothy slithered out of his sleeping bag and immediately felt the freezing air prickle his exposed skin. He dressed quickly and crawled out of the tent on his hands and knees. He stood in front of the tent stamping his feet against the hard-packed snow in a useless attempt to generate some warmth. His eyes searched above the trees for the sun but found only streaky gray clouds—there would be no warmth to stand in today, he thought to himself. Humphrey emerged from the tent a few minutes later, without his boots on. After a delirious night without much sleep, his incoherent mind had forgotten this final but critical component of gear. He stared down at his lumpy sock toes, not quite sure what to do.

Timothy looked at Humphrey's feet too. "Humphrey, you forgot to put your damn boots on. Your feet are going to freeze. Get back in the tent and put your boots on before the sergeant sees you standing there like a big dope." Humphrey continued staring at his toes, appearing to not quite understand, before crawling clumsily back into the tent without responding. He found his boots under one of the sleeping bags. It took some effort to brush the crusted snow from his socks before he could pull the boots on. His hands, already stiff and aching from the cold, struggled to tie the frozen boot laces. He emerged from the tent again, this time fully dressed.

After an abridged breakfast of warm coffee and frozen C-rations partially heated in boiling water, the platoon packed up their gear and moved out. They hiked over a mile through trees sagging with fresh snow until they came to a noisy, rushing stream with crusted ice along the edges. Two thick ropes stretched across the stream, one high and one low, spanning about 30 feet from side-to-side. The bottom rope hung in a taut catenary about fifteen feet above the water's surface. The churning stream made a deceivingly pleasant sound in the frozen quiet of the forest, broken only occasionally by a chattering squirrel or an agitated bird. Timothy thought about the spruce grove behind his house when he heard the squirrel.

Humphrey interrupted his reverie. "Timothy, did I ever tell you that I'm not very good with heights?" Boot camp had consisted mostly of marching and pushups and cleaning things and learning to shoot and more marching and then more cleaning. Humphrey had never been ordered to do anything this high off the ground before, especially above a freezing river.

Even though Humphrey had mentioned this fact in the tent, Timothy acted surprised. "Shoot, Humphrey. It's gotta be no more than fifteen feet above the stream. If you ask me, that's hardly off the ground at all."

This observation did not comfort Humphrey. "Well, it may look hardly off the ground to you, but a six-foot stepladder is more than I can usually manage, and that's on solid ground."

Timothy tried to visualize Humphrey falling off a six-foot stepladder. "You aren't kidding, are you?"

"No, I'm not kidding."

"Good grief, Humphrey. Why'd you enlist in the Marine Corps if you're so afraid of heights?" Timothy held a hand over his mouth to conceal an erupting snigger.

"Hey, I didn't enlist in the Air Force, did I? I enlisted in the Marines because I thought we'd be staying on the ground. If I'd known we were going to walk across some damn ropes strung a mile above a raging river, I might've changed my mind!"

"Don't exaggerate. It'll just make things worse."

When he had completed his unappreciated counsel, an idea emerged in Timothy's mind that he thought might help. He immediately looked around for the necessary prop. About twenty feet away, he spotted a small stump about ten inches in diameter. Timothy walked over to the stump and stepped up onto it. Several of the other Marines watched him with both curiosity and restrained amusement. He then began a presentation designed to propel Humphrey effortlessly across the river.

Timothy removed his helmet and pointed at the side of his head. "Humphrey…fear of heights is all in your head. This stump is only a few feet off the ground, so it's easy for me to stand on it and keep my balance. I can even jump up and down if I want to, and spin around too." Timothy jumped twice on each foot before executing an acceptably graceful pirouette. This impressed everyone because he still had his pack on. "Now imagine that I'm not standing on this stump near the ground, but instead that I'm standing a hundred feet up in the air at the top of a tall tree. Let me ask you—what would be the difference? I should be able to jump up and down and spin around just the same, right?" Timothy jumped a few more times then spun around again. "See, it's just mind over matter. If I can do this on a stump close to the ground, then I should be able to do the same thing a hundred feet up in the air. There's absolutely no difference!" Timothy began a final pirouette to drive his point home. When he returned to his starting position, his toe caught a chunk of bark and he fell backwards off the stump. He hit the ground hard before quickly rolling over to his hands and knees. He stayed that way until his breath returned. Several Marines laughed and made coarse jokes. Timothy stood up and brushed frozen leaves off his hands and knees. "Well Humphrey, you get the idea." He repositioned both pack straps before picking up his helmet. "I've got another idea. Let's just stick together and I'll help you get across the damn stream. Just make sure you don't look down."

Sergeant Johnson lined up the Marines to cross the stream; Timothy and Humphrey moved to the end of the line to delay their turn as much as possible. When each Marine traversed the ropes successfully, Humphrey became more and more agitated as his turn approached. He struggled to think of an excuse to get out of this. Within a few unfairly short minutes, the sergeant ordered him to step onto the rope. Humphrey balked.

Sergeant Johnson allowed himself a near second of compassion, then boomed, "Private, you get yourself up on that damn rope and cross this damn stream before I grab you by your balls and throw you across." Getting thrown across the river sounded pretty good to Humphrey, but he knew that even the sergeant didn't have enough strength to toss him all the way to the other side.

Timothy offered immediate encouragement. "Go ahead, Humphrey. I'm right behind you. I'll help you get across."

Humphrey slid his foot along the lower rope, grabbed the rope overhead and, after gaining some balance, began shuffling out over the water. Timothy waited until Humphrey had moved about five feet before following. They were moving pretty well until Humphrey reached the center of the stream. He glanced down into the blurred water and stopped moving. Then he began shaking. Timothy moved up a little closer.

"Come on Humphrey. You're almost across! Just a little further and you'll be there. Don't stop now."

Humphrey tried to look back, and began shaking more aggressively. The bottom rope suddenly swayed back and forth, gently at first, then with increasing amplitude. The upper rope swayed violently in the opposite direction. Humphrey held on for three sways before his feet snapped off the bottom rope. He held on to the top rope for a few seconds more, but could not support his own weight plus the gear that loaded him down. When his hands released the rope, he tumbled toward the stream. The bottom rope slapped him hard across the face as he spun by and jerked his helmet off. His feet hit the water at a small angle and he knifed in, disappearing instantly below the surface. His following helmet floated briefly before the swirling water flipped it over and sucked it down.

Timothy still clung to the twitching rope as he watched Humphrey go in. He squeezed the upper rope hard and tried to decide what to do. "Shit, Humphrey. I guess were both going to get wet today." Timothy sucked in a deep breath and let go. The water felt a lot colder than he expected.

Chapter 5
Don't eat the applesauce, October 1941

An effective vaccine for rubella, still decades away, would have protected the young woman during her second month of pregnancy. The virus infected her while she shopped downtown at her favorite store. She had been searching through racks of clothing for a new blouse when the virus found her. At first the symptoms were mild, of almost no concern at all. She did have the typical rose-colored rash, as well as a slight fever and mild sore throat, but nothing that she would have characterized as serious. The rash began innocently enough on her face, but then spread rapidly down to her chest, arms and abdomen, and ultimately to her shapely legs. When her husband noticed the extent of the rash, he immediately insisted that she see the family doctor. The doctor examined her briefly, asked a few questions, then told her that she had the German measles. He also told her that it would go away on its own. As he predicted, the rash vanished in three days and she soon looked and felt like nothing had happened at all.

Seven months later, the young woman gave birth to her first child. She saw only perfection when she cradled her precious boy and stroked his downy head. Her husband beamed with pride when he held his new son for the first time. They called him Jonathan, the boy's name they had chosen months earlier. They had picked out Jennifer for a girl, a name they would never use. But when they returned home, and a little more time had passed, the infant boy did not act as they thought he should. When the young woman bent over the smooth wooden side rail of the crib and lifted her child out, he refused to cuddle when she pulled him close to her breast. Instead, he stiffened like a gnarled chunk of driftwood as if to resist the cuddling. He did the same with his father.

As Jonathan grew older other behaviors appeared, strange behaviors that were even more troubling. He never smiled, even when his mother praised him with a soothing voice or his father surprised him with a silly face. He did not appear to make eye contact with anyone, including his parents. When he played with the wooden alphabet blocks his doting aunt had given him for Christmas, he arranged them repeatedly in the same consistent, meaningless pattern. Once he did this from the end of breakfast to the beginning of lunch. When his father tried to show him how to spell a few simple words with the blocks, he quickly rearranged them into the same meaningless pattern. After suffering through too many failed spelling lessons, his father became discouraged and stopped trying. When Jonathan should have been old enough to make his first friends, he made none. He preferred to play alone, although the things he did when alone hardly looked normal to his parents. Sometimes he burst into a rage for no discernable reason, hitting violently at unseen phantoms in the air around him, or biting at his wrists and arms, or rolling on his back and kicking at the floor with his heels. Once he banged his head against the wall seven or eight times, raising a neat row of glistening lumps along his swollen hairline. As Jonathan's rages increased in frequency, his parents learned to quickly hold him down so that he wouldn't hurt himself or break something. After experimenting with a number of different techniques, the human straitjacket—nestling him in crossed legs while holding his opposite hands from behind—proved to be the most successful. Sometimes they had to hold him for an hour or more before he calmed down enough to be safely released. A few times, when he had pushed one or both of them to the limit of physical or emotional exhaustion, they took turns and held him in 20-minute shifts.

 Jonathan did not attend the local elementary school until he reached the age of eight. By that time, the savagery of his rages had diminished, and the rages themselves emerged less often. The school principal placed him in a special class with children who had been classified mentally retarded by the school district psychologist. But his apparent retardation came with an interesting twist—he had a stunning artistic gift that sometimes poured out during the quiet times between rages. Because his parents had never given him anything to draw with—they were too afraid that he would jam a crayon up his nose or stab himself in the eye with a pencil or pen—no one noticed the gift until Jonathan started school. After two months of mostly sitting like a stone and refusing to socialize or speak with any of the other children, he found a number two pencil and a half-used pad of paper while sitting stoically in the corner of the room. He picked up the pencil and rolled it in his hands for a long time. Then he drew a nearly flawless image of his left shoe, including the frayed threads holding the seams of the canvas top together. His teacher found the wadded up drawing in the same corner at the end of the day, hours after the children had gone home. She had no idea who had made the wonderful drawing, but she figured it out a week later when she recognized Jonathon's shoe. She did not know what to think at first. He behaved like a complete lump most of the time, devoid of any thought or emotion. Could he really have done this?

She encouraged him to draw again, but whenever she sat him up with paper and pencil laid neatly on top of the student desk, he did nothing except rock back and forth, not making eye contact or talking or drawing or doing anything at all. He seemed detached and completely disinterested. She told him that she thought he had great potential to become an artist, but he did not appear to hear anything she said. She put different objects in front of him and invited him to draw—flowers and an apple and a coffee cup and a model airplane—but he did not appear to see them. She even pinned the drawing of his shoe up on the wall next to her desk and then showed it to him. He stared vacantly when she pointed at the shoe on his foot then compared it to the shoe on the wall then pointed at his foot again. She finally assumed that someone else must have made the drawing, and gave up.

More than a week passed—a meaningless period of time for Jonathan filled with muddy thoughts and dark visions. He sat quietly near his preferred corner after lunch; unresponsive to the other children, unwilling to play or talk, apparently indifferent to his surroundings. But his eyes had fixed on a small bronze statue of a cowboy riding a wildly bucking horse. The horse snorted through flared nostrils and the twisting cowboy whipped a coiled rope briskly through the air. Jonathon studied the sculpture for a long time, analyzing every shadow and line. Then he found a pad of paper and a number two pencil, where his teacher had left them, and began. He drew the statue in a curious way, not beginning with smooth ovals and lines to establish size, relationships, and proportions. Instead, he just began at the left, where the horse's upturned nose thrust into the air, and worked his way to the right, expressing every detail when its time came to be expressed. If the statue had been reversed, he would have started at the horse's tail. When he finished, about two hours later, he dropped the drawing on the floor and walked over it on his way to the other side of the room, where he arranged some alphabet blocks into one of the meaningless pattern he knew so well. His teacher found the new drawing at the end of the day, just like before, but this time she knew instantly who had done it. She pinned it on the wall next to the shoe.

Jonathan improved a little over the next few years, but around the age of twelve began the annoying habit of repeating what others had just said. He actually became surprisingly good at it, and could sometimes repeat dozens of words accurately. No one, however, interpreted his mechanical reiterations as communication, nor did they find this bothersome habit an invitation to friendship. He had a new teacher at this time as well, a young man named Mr. Flynn who had worked for the past five years with mentally retarded children at an elementary school in New York. After meeting with Jonathan for the first time, and listening to him repeat all of his words, Mr. Flynn set a personal goal to teach Jonathan as many basic living skills as possible before the end of the year, beginning with eating lunch by himself. Instead of joining the other teachers for lunch in the staff lounge, Mr. Flynn started going to lunch with Jonathan at the school cafeteria. They did this for several weeks, and Jonathan actually began learning how to select a tray and silverware, walk along the lunch line without touching any of the food, and pay for his lunch at the cash register at the end of the long stainless steel serving counter. Jonathan still required a bit of guidance, including help counting his money, but Mr. Flynn became more heartened by the obvious progress at the end of each new lunch hour.

Less than a month away, Thanksgiving quickly approached and autumn rains surged across the flat roofs of the school, drumming pleasantly complex patterns that Timothy enjoyed listening to. Although he had never taken the time to figure out why, he liked the cool rains better than the oppressively beating sun. The sound and smell of rain filled him with a comfortable gloominess that felt right to him. Not that it made him happy, exactly—it just felt right. But today, with the darkening rains driven against the school windows by an increasingly savage storm, he also felt the subtle edge of rage that sometimes crept into his mind when the gloominess grew beyond his ability to control it. He did not know where the rage came from or why it existed, but over time he had learned to feel restlessly comfortable while it squirmed around in some unknown crevice of his brain. He walked into the cafeteria with his eyes focused directly in front of his feet and tried not to think about it too much. He amused himself for a moment with the notion that he felt hunger instead of rage, although he knew this couldn't be true because of the huge breakfast his Mom had forced him to eat that morning. Timothy did not notice Mr. Flynn and Jonathan when they stepped into the serving line behind him.

Mr. Flynn's voice swelled with enthusiasm as he talked Jonathan through each important step of correctly procuring a nutritious school lunch. "OK Jonathan, let's get a tray and some silverware. Oh yeah, and a napkin too—don't forget the napkin. Remember how we did it yesterday?" Jonathan, without talking or making eye contact with Mr. Flynn, robotically picked up the various items as instructed. He had some trouble with the napkin, but finally got a finger around it. "Good job, Jonathan. Now…let's move on down the serving line and see what's on the menu today. I bet it's something good! Oh look, Jonathan—they're serving tuna casserole and apple sauce today, your favorites!"

After receiving a lump of tuna casserole, Jonathan stared blankly into a stainless steel bin overflowing with a rippled mound of applesauce. He then began speaking in the second person, a habit that Mr. Flynn had been unable to break. "You, you don't want the applesauce. You hate the applesauce."

"You mean, 'I don't want any applesauce,' right Jonathan?"

At that moment, a heavy woman wearing a massive white apron and a black hairnet slapped a huge gob of applesauce down on Jonathan's tray. His eyes flared in instant horrification and his hands began trembling as they struggled to hold the tray level.

"You d, d, don't like the apple sauce. You d, don't, like it!"

Mr. Flynn tried to calm Jonathan by pointing out the health value of applesauce. "Well, it's really good for you Jonathan. It's got lots of vitamins. Why don't you just try a little?"

Jonathan became more agitated when the applesauce flowed across his tray and begin seeping beneath the tuna casserole. "N, N, No! You don't like it. Take it off! Take it off, now!" Alarmed by Jonathan's unexpected outburst, the heavy woman reached across the serving counter with a big stainless steel spoon and attempted to scrape the applesauce off the tray. "N, no, t, take it off. You don't want any. Take it all off!"

The heavy woman squirmed her face in confusion. "I'm sorry honey, but that's the best I can do. Would you like a little more tuna casserole instead?"

Not the right question. Jonathan lost any remnant of control and, after pausing to build up sufficient energy, flung his tray sideways, hitting Timothy in the back. As apple sauce and tuna casserole dripped down the back of Timothy's jacket, Jonathan began hitting the air around him, and after several wild jabs connected with Timothy's head, striking him squarely on the right ear.

Timothy heard an explosion of bells just inside his skull; the rage inside broke loose like a surging flood, taking complete control of his actions. He swore, then spun around and hit Jonathan square in the face, breaking his nose. Jonathan covered his face with both hands, blood pouring out between the fingers. Timothy pounded the back of the bloody hands, breaking Jonathan's left thumb and right index finger. Timothy began winding up to hit Jonathan again when Mr. Flynn forced himself between the two boys and grabbed Timothy by the wrists. Timothy tried to kick Mr. Flynn in the knee but missed. Mr. Flynn forced him down to the ground and sat on him; then began screaming for help. Jonathan slumped against the cold edge of the stainless steel serving counter and sobbed. Blood dripped down his neck and soaked the front of the shirt his Dad had given him for his birthday. Jonathan pulled both hands away from his face and studied the blood smeared across his wrists and forearms. He would not draw again for a long time.

♦ ♦ ♦

Troop ships across the Pacific, July 1950

Humphrey listened to the uneven vibrations of the troop ship's engines, and thought about the many times he had motored far out into the surging waves in his father's 52-foot fishing boat. His father, William, had fished the seas off the Pacific coastline for over three decades before a ruptured disc forced him to forsake his lifelong passion. He often took Humphrey with him, usually in a vain effort to encourage an interest in his beloved profession. Sadly, and to William's grave disappointment, Humphrey never cared much for fishing. He didn't mind going out on the boat during calm seas, but he loathed rough weather with nearly the same intensity that his father loved fishing. Unfortunately, and often to Humphrey's dismay, his father's exuberance for fishing appeared to increase when the waves crashed over the bow and flooded across the decks and tossed the boat around. Although Humphrey never told his father, these storms at sea terrified him beyond what he could bear. But William never took him to sea again after discovering this innate fear during a monstrous storm about eight miles off the Oregon coast. The men did not fish during this storm; and, for the first time, Humphrey glimpsed panic in their eyes.

The men worked two-hour watches while winds and rains raged and swirled and battered the helpless vessel. William manned the helm most of the night, grabbing an hour of precious sleep only once when he could no longer keep his exhausted eyes focused on the towering waves beyond the salt-streaked glass of the wheel house. At one point the anchor broke loose and began hammering the bow, causing a frightful slapping sound to echo throughout the boat. Neil, one of the youngest men, volunteered to go over the side in a skiff to secure it. He worked his way along the pitching hull of the fishing boat while two of the older men strained to control the lurching dinghy with brine-crusted lines. The small skiff smashed against the side of the larger boat over a dozen times before Neil secured the anchor. One time a plunging wave almost tossed him over the gunwale into the inky water. After pulling Neil back onto the fishing boat, and cutting the swamped skiff loose, William found Humphrey cowering below decks, sobbing uncontrollably as each new wave surged against the staggering boat. He studied Humphrey long enough to judge him a coward, then returned to the wheelhouse to renew his battle against the relentless storm, his heart drenched in shame. Everyone thanked God and hugged when they returned safely to the harbor the next day, late in the afternoon. Humphrey's mom waved from the old dock when they came into sight, tears flowing down her face. William never asked Humphrey to go fishing again.

After he walked off his father's fishing boat that terrible afternoon, Humphrey vowed quietly to himself that he would never go to sea again. But now he had managed to get himself on another vessel, and out to sea once more, and into yet another monstrous storm. The size of this ship did dwarf his father's fishing boat, he chuckled cynically to himself, but the size of the storm also dwarfed any that he could remember, including the storm that had ended his fishing career. At least he had hundreds of other guys with him to share the experience, even if they were stacked together like sardines in one on those little metal cans where you peel back the lid with a slotted key. As he thought about the sardine can, Humphrey estimated that he had about 11 inches or so from the end of his nose to the bottom of the next bunk, just enough room to turn over without scraping his knees, if he kept his legs straight. And although he struggled to conceal his fear of the storm, he still considered himself luckier than many of these guys—he hadn't become deathly ill and puked his guts out. This, he rationalized, had turned out to be one of the few advantages of growing up with a father who owned a fishing boat.

Timothy lounged placidly in the bunk across the narrow aisle, reading a *Life Magazine* he had borrowed from one of the officers. He realized after a few dozen pages that reading the magazine while the ship heaved around so much made him queasy, and he decided to stop. He rolled the magazine into a tight cylinder and attempted to spiral it like a football as he threw it across the aisle into Humphrey's bunk. It opened with a noisy flutter before landing on Humphrey's leg. "Hey Humphrey; how come you never get sick? Almost every guy I know is puking their damn guts out except you. Why don't you try reading that magazine for a while and see if you can still keep your dinner down. If you can't read the words, just look at the pictures."

Humphrey glared at Timothy in mock contempt. "I'm not interested in reading a magazine right now, especially one with pictures, but I'll play you a game of chess if you're looking for something to do."

Timothy curled his lip in a puckish smile. "Well, I don't know if I'm interested in losing any more this week. How many times have you beaten me anyway? Two thousand? Three thousand? I know it's in the thousands anyway."

"We've only played seven games this week; and as a matter of fact, one of them ended up a draw."

"Yeah, right. You call it a draw, but I think you offered it because you were just tired of playing any more. By the way, what day is it? I think I lost track of time while I was reading that magazine. You'd better give me the year too. This damn storm has really screwed me up."

Humphrey pulled out a small, wrinkled card calendar that he carried around in his shirt pocket. "It's Monday, July 31, 1950."

Timothy frowned. "Damn. The last day of July. How long have we been on this stupid boat anyway? I'm surprised we haven't killed each other by now."

"I'd say about two weeks. Yeah, that's right, about two weeks. And it's actually a ship, not a boat. Boats are small: ships are big." Humphrey had circled the embarkation date in pencil on the little calendar the day the ship had left San Diego. He shoved the card calendar back into his pocket just as Gunnery Sergeant Talbot appeared at the far end of the aisle. When the Gunny began walking toward him, Humphrey noted that he had the straightest back he had ever seen. The Gunny also had a peculiar way of looking at you that instantly made you wonder what you'd screwed up this time, even if you hadn't done anything wrong at all. His eyes would move first until they had locked on to yours, then his head would slowly turn until it caught up with the eyes. Then you waited in fear. Gunny Talbot checked each of his Marines, one at a time, as he moved down the crowded aisle.

Timothy had bounced around in an excessively good mood all day, for no reason that Humphrey could discern, so he asked a smart-ass question when the Gunny reached his bunk. "Hey Gunny. Where'd you say we're going again? I think I forgot."

Gunny Talbot stopped abruptly and turned sharply. The ship shuddered again as it plowed through another big wave, but he maintained perfect balance against the rolling deck. Timothy later promoted a rumor around the ship that Gunny Talbot had sewn horseshoe magnets into the soles of his boots.

"What'd you ask me, private?"

"I said, where'd you say we were going again? I forgot. Sir!"

Gunny Talbot's eyes narrowed. "We're going to Pusan. We'll be there in a few days, so make sure your gear is in order. We have to walk off this ship ready to fight. Every Marine is going to have to do his job if we're going to have any chance of getting out of this one."

"Pusan? I thought we were going to Japan. Shoot—I've been looking forward to it. I've always wanted to see Japan. How come we're not going to Japan?" Humphrey had never heard Timothy say he wanted to go to Japan; he didn't know if this was true or not. Timothy often joked like this when in a good mood, and didn't talk much when in a foul mood, so Humphrey usually found it easy to tell the difference.

"We just got diverted; we're not going to Japan anymore; we're going directly to Pusan. You'll love it. I heard it's a damn paradise." Gunny Talbot turned sharply again and weaved briskly down the aisle, narrowly missing each of the rifle butts and sea bags and feet and knees and other body parts sticking out from the bunks. He paused briefly at the end of the row of bunks beneath an obnoxious yellow light before disappearing around the corner.

The Gunny's little speech did not convince Timothy that he wouldn't mind missing Japan, assuming that he really did want to see it. "Yes sir! I'm sure I'll love it. I can hardly wait. But I wanted to see Japan. And where the hell is Pusan?"

This blatant audacity astonished Humphrey: Timothy clearly possessed an uncanny gift for sensing the edges of human vexation. Of course, occasionally he crossed over one of those edges, but usually he demonstrated a genius for walking right up to this invisible boundary and dancing along it, usually in both directions before he finished whatever he had to say. "You know Timothy, I'm amazed the Gunny hasn't locked you up in the brig yet. He must have an awfully good sense of humor to put up with all the silly questions you ask."

"Why would he want to do that? You heard him. They're going to need every Marine to get out of this one. That includes me. Uh…and you too, Humphrey. Let's just hope we don't have to take the high ground. I wouldn't want to have to rescue you in the middle of some battle because you're swooning from altitude sickness. Damn, I was really excited about going to Japan. Where the hell *is* Pusan, anyway?"

Humphrey ignored Timothy's irksome little joke. He didn't see why his fear of heights should be so funny. But the joke didn't really bother him all that much either. He had become sufficiently tolerant of Timothy's acrid sense of humor during the last few months because it usually indicated a good mood. When Timothy wasn't in a good mood, his jokes were infrequent and, if expressed at all, dull. Humphrey had therefore decided that he preferred the acrid sense of humor, even though it could be very annoying.

The storm eased during the night, bringing a calmer morning with scattered sunlight and streaky gray clouds, but the tensions of so many men living together on a ship for so long did not. Timothy's mood changed too with the easing of the storm, almost like his mood preferred the rain and wind. Humphrey had noticed this strange conversion before. He had never met anyone before whose moods appeared to swing in contradiction to the weather.

They had both returned from a substantial breakfast of nothing particularly recognizable or edible and were relaxing in their bunks again. Timothy flipped through the wrinkled pages of the same *Life Magazine*. Humphrey played through another famous chess game with his small wooden chessboard and little metal chess pieces. He had played through this same game the week before, but liked it so much that he had decided to play through it again.

Finally bored with the magazine, and depressed by the improving weather, Timothy resorted to griping to pass the time. "Hey Humphrey, what would you call that white stuff the cook served us for breakfast this morning? I ate a whole bunch of it and I still don't know what to call it. Do you think I'll get sick, or maybe even die from eating so much? I mean, if I couldn't even tell what it was, maybe I shouldn't have eaten so much. Maybe I shouldn't have eaten any of it. Did you eat any? Do you think I'll die?"

Humphrey had little interest in supporting Timothy's griping, so he gave a decisive answer that he hoped would end the discussion. "I think it was some sort of chopped potatoes with some sort of white sauce. At least that's what it looked like. And no, I don't think you'll die—at least not here on the ship."

"I'm not so sure. On the other hand, it doesn't make any sense that they would be trying to kill us here on the boat—I mean ship. That wouldn't make any sense at all. I mean, if they killed us on the ship by feeding us that white stuff, there wouldn't be anyone around to get killed after we get off in Pusan, wherever the hell that is."

All this talk of death worried Humphrey. He had tried not to think about dying, but Timothy kept bringing the subject up. He had nearly worked up the courage to tell Timothy to knock it off when another Marine walked between their bunks and leaned in close to Timothy's head. A skinny Marine who complained a lot, he had obviously come to do some more complaining. Humphrey knew that the skinny Marine had chosen a poor time to approach Timothy, given the improving weather and Timothy's eroding mood. He thought he should warn the skinny Marine, then decided it wouldn't change anything. Humphrey simply rolled onto his side, propped his head on his hand, and prepared to enjoy the show. Maybe a little entertainment would distract him from Timothy's morbid obsession with death.

"Timothy, did you take my socks? I hung my socks up to dry on the side of my bunk, and now I can't find them. One of the guys told me he thought he saw you take them." The skinny Marine twisted his face into different shapes as he spoke.

Timothy casually lowered the *Life Magazine*, then stretched both arms out and yawned. "I didn't touch your stupid socks. Hell, I didn't even know you wore socks."

"Yeah, yeah. Very funny. Well, I think you took my socks, and I want them back. So hand 'em over—right now."

Timothy's face tightened. Humphrey knew that he should worry when he saw this face. He decided to offer the skinny Marine some urgent advice. "I wouldn't go there. Why don't you ask someone else if they've seen your socks? I don't think Timothy knows where they are."

Angry that he could not hang his socks up to dry without someone stealing them, the skinny Marine turned abruptly and scowled at Humphrey. "Hey, did I ask for your opinion?" He snapped back to Timothy. "OK, Timothy; what's it going to be? Are you going to give me my socks, or am I going to have to look through your stuff and find them myself?"

In an instant, Timothy pivoted out of his bunk and leaned into the skinny Marine, nearly touching his birdlike nose. Then, as Timothy's eyes narrowed, he sucked in a raspy breath and exhaled with a snort.

Humphrey intensified his plea. "I wouldn't accuse Timothy of stealing your socks if I were you. I think it would be best if you just backed away slowly and asked someone else. Maybe you could even—"

The skinny Marine barked at Humphrey without turning his head. "Hey, butt-off Humphrey. If I need your help, I'll ask for it." When he finished his retort he pushed against Timothy's chest and renewed his accusation. "Time's up, Timothy. Give me my damn socks, right now. I know you've got them, so stop the bullshit and hand 'em over!"

Timothy responded in mid-sentence, somewhere between the words *the* and *bullshit*. "No one accuses me..." and that's when he threw a punch, landing it just above the skinny Marine's solar plexus, popping him backwards until he fell against Humphrey, almost knocking both of them over, "...of stealing any damn socks."

The sudden attack stunned the skinny Marine momentarily, but he quickly rebounded to throw a counter punch. Then they clinched like a couple of angry boxers and began pounding each other with short jabs and looping uppercuts. They pushed back and forth; the skinny Marine slipped and they both collapsed to the deck. Timothy quickly leveraged his leg under the edge of the lower bunk until he rolled over and sat on top of the skinny Marine, then hit him twice in the face. The second punch split the skinny Marine's lip, splattering blood across his cheek. Humphrey thought he should do something, but also knew that Timothy became nearly uncontrollable when he exploded like this: any attempt to physically intervene could be very risky, if not suicidal. While Humphrey considered his options, other Marines gathered around and yelled profane encouragements. But several of them soon realized that Timothy had gone berserk and grabbed his arms and pulled him off the skinny Marine. It took four of them to do it. Timothy still flailed and kicked as they pushed him against the side of the bunk. Then two men lifted the skinny Marine off the blood-flecked deck and carried him to the infirmary. He never asked Timothy about the socks again.

Chapter 6

Fishing the pristine river, June 1942

The river flowed deeper where it curved beneath the old concrete bridge. In the cool shadow of the bridge the edges of the river were rocky and difficult to traverse. But just beyond the bridge, west toward the rising valley, the river's course flattened and spread onto more gentle terrain that one could walk with ease. Easterly from the bridge the river did not widen for a good distance, probably a quarter of a mile or more. The river flowed more quickly here before it slowed to a gentle pace and spread easily into more complex patterns around small bushy islets and constantly warping mud flats. Where the river deepened, the surface surged smoothly and the dark waters did not reflect much sunlight. In the shallow places, where water sucked and churned above smooth rocks that tried desperately to transmit their shapes to the surface, the sunlight shimmered in myriad tiny explosions sparkling with motion. The intensity of the sparkles diminished when the sun moved closer to the distant peaks rising up beyond the smooth valley to the west, but the sparkles still glowed nonetheless.

Buttressed by the concrete bridge above the deepest part of the river, a gravel-surfaced road led cars and trucks northwesterly toward several small towns and beyond there to yet smaller towns. To the southeast, the road veered directly south before traversing the lumpy western shore of a large, shapeless lake. The road then weaved through dense pine forests to more small towns and beyond the forests to real cities. But the cities sprawled far away; far enough away to be soon forgotten by anyone who walked along the pristine river, listened to the smoothly flowing water, and watched the afternoon sun sparkle in the churning water above the shallow rocks.

John stood at the edge of the river now, fussing with the drawstring on a small canvas bag. Martha had fabricated the bag for him only a few weeks ago, and the stiff canvas resisted the string's movement through the folded and sewn edge. After swearing a few times, John opened the bag and carefully removed a small fly reel and stainless steel folding box filled with artificial flies. He had bought this equipment a few months earlier, along with a decent fly rod recommended by the owner of the local hardware store, as well as a book on the art of fly-fishing. Filled with excitement after these purchases, he had practiced casting on the gently sloping lawn behind the house almost every night in preparation for this trip. These practice sessions had actually gone pretty well, considering that he taught himself how to cast by studying a series of intricate line drawings that spanned nine pages in the fly-fishing book. But although he had successfully learned the sequential parts of the cast, he struggled with the timing and integration of the parts: something the book could not teach him. In particular, he tended to start the forward cast too soon, before the backcast had finished and the line had drifted into a proper hook. This habit often resulted in a disastrous tangle of line, or worse, snapping off the fly. The problem persisted for weeks until one Friday evening when a neighbor, returning from a day of carpentry work at a construction site a few miles away, stopped at the road above the house and noticed John practicing. The carpenter liked to be called Benjamin, and he turned out to be an avid and experienced fly fisherman. After silently admiring John's persistence, Benjamin offered to give him a lesson in the fading light. Benjamin held John's rod hand and guided it several times through the proper timing of the entire motion, and for the first time John felt the beauty of a well-executed cast. At that moment, when the line unrolled smoothly and laid out in front of him with an elegance he had not experienced before, he could not wait to get to the river and cast into real water. And now, after much anticipation, John stood at the river's edge, selecting an untried fly from his new stainless steel fly box, eager to make the first real cast of his life.

Timothy stood nearby, flinging smooth rocks over the surface of the river. He had an awkward throwing motion, but occasionally one of the rocks landed correctly and skipped once or twice, encouraging him to try again. He had just picked up a really big rock when John called him over.

"Timothy—come over and take a look at this." John had managed to assemble the slender fly rod without breaking it and had also snaked some line through the ferrules. As he prepared to tie a fly onto the end of the delicate leader, he tried to remember if he'd picked out the correct one or not. The owner of the hardware store had called it a "Royal Coachman," but John couldn't remember anything else about it. He decided that he had no idea if it would catch any fish or not, but he liked the look of the wings and the little red belt, so he decided to use it. If it didn't work, he could always try one of the other flies, even though he didn't know if they would work either. With a grunt, Timothy heaved the big rock into the river. The rock ruptured the water's surface with a resonant "kerplunk," then dove straight to the bottom. Timothy had hoped it would skip. He shuffled over to John's side with his head down, despondent because the big rock had not skipped at least once.

"Let me show you how to tie a fly on. This is the knot they showed me at the hardware store. It's also in the book I read. I forget the name of it, but it's kind of complicated." John fumbled with the unreasonably slender leader as he tried to loop it multiple times around itself to form the knot. At one point he almost had it, then the end slipped through all the little loops he had worked so hard to form and the whole thing fell apart. "Well shoot, I almost had it." He resolutely started the knot again; when he got to about the same point as before, the loops slipped away again. "Tell you what, Timothy. Why don't you go skip some more rocks, and I'll call you when I've got this thing figured out." This suited Timothy, who didn't understand why he had to watch a knot tying demonstration anyway. He soon found several good skipping rocks and began flinging them against the smooth surface of the river. After a few more tries, and without swearing even once, John had the knot tied almost perfectly. "Timothy, I've got the knot tied. Come over and try a cast." This suggestion to "try" a cast troubled Timothy. He had already been forced to try a few casts behind the house, and had nearly ripped his ear off every time.

John handed Timothy a baseball cap. "Here. Put this baseball cap on backwards. It'll protect your ears when the fly goes by your head." Timothy pulled the cap over the top of his head and turned the bill around to cover his ears.

"Dad, are you sure this is a good idea? I didn't do so good in the backyard." Timothy worried that the razor sharp fly hook could still somehow get around the bill and slice into his ear. He reached back and nervously adjusted the baseball cap again.

"Sure it is. It'll be fun. Now wiggle the rod back and forth to let some line out. That's good. Now…pull the line off the water…gently…gently." Timothy jerked the fly line off the water and the fly zinged by his head. He ducked, and the line curved into a misshaped figure eight before snapping back on itself and grabbing onto a bush by the edge of the river. Not realizing this, he yanked the rod forward with all his strength, causing the line to tighten around the slender branches and green leaves of the bush. Somewhere deep inside the bush, the Royal Coachman hung from the end of the tangled leader and fluttered helplessly.

John rubbed his eyes. "Not all that bad for the first cast of the day." Then he massaged the back of his neck. "Why don't you go get the spin rod out of the car and do a little fishing with that? The lures are in the green tackle box, on the floor in front of the back seat. I'll stay here and untangle this mess." Timothy darted away like a squirrel chasing after a rolling acorn, thankful to get away from the nasty little zinging fly that tried to rip his ear off whenever he attempted casting. The spin rod would be much safer, and far less arcane. He ran by the tent where Martha scurried around setting up for dinner. She spotted him in her peripheral vision and yelled at him when he galloped by.

"How's the fishing, Timothy?" Her head bobbed up and down as she watched him leap over a fallen log.

"It's great, Mom," and he vanished behind the car. He found the spin rod and box of lures on the floor in front of the back seat—just where John had said they would be—and after skipping away from the car and then returning to slam the car door shut, hurried back to the stream. He navigated through a broad thicket of bushes and young pines to the concrete bridge, then traversed the slick rocks along the river until he crossed the jagged edge of the bridge's shadow and stood in the full warmth of the afternoon sun. He stopped there, closed his eyes, felt the sun's pleasant warmth on his upturned face, and listened to the river's satisfying gurgle. He stood motionless for twenty seconds or so, and then became impatient to fish. He pried opened the box of lures and cautiously rooted through the eclectic contents to avoid getting cut, or worse yet, hooked. He found three lures that he liked. One of the lures had stainless steel rings and a tiny propeller. He attached the propeller lure to the snap swivel at the end of the fishing line and prepared to cast, but then thought that it might work even better if he used all three lures at the same time. He dug two more rusty snap swivels out of the bottom of the tackle box and used them to attach the other two lures to the end of the line as well. He thought this new "tri-lure" contraption looked both impressive and beautiful, even if it felt a lot heavier than usual—and because it offered a bristling array of nine hooks instead of only three, surely would improve his chances of catching a nice fish.

He moved closer to the edge of the river, slowly coiled his torso and pulled both arms around as far as they would go, then flung the tri-lure toward the opposite shore with an explosive snap. The reel hissed as the tri-lure shot out over the river, and because of the contraption's improved weight it didn't land in the center of the river like Timothy had expected—it just kept on going. Timothy watched helplessly as the tri-lure crossed the entire width of the river and dived into the thick bushes on the other side. The tri-lure's exceptional performance pleased him; however, when he tried to reel it in, he discovered that the line had tangled itself in the bushes. Now he had to decide between two bad choices: he could pull really hard and hope that the tri-lure released itself without breaking the line, or he could go fetch his errant contraption by crossing the river without hip waders or any other protection from the frigid water. Timothy tried several strong pulls on the line before deciding he would have to cross the river to untangle the tri-lure.

A few hundred yards beyond the other side of the concrete bridge, John struggled with different problems. He discovered very quickly that casting into moving water required more skill than casting onto the grass behind the house. His first three casts were downstream; when he pulled the line in he had to fight the current, which made the fly leap out of the water in a wildly unpredictable manner. He turned around and tried some casts upstream instead. At first this appeared to work better, until the rushing current piled the loose line up against his legs, then around his legs, then into a tangled mess behind his legs. He did not remember seeing this diagram in the book. It took a lot of complicated work to get the line back onto the reel where it belonged. Then the wind gusted and blew his backcast into a shape that didn't look like any of the diagrams in the book either which caused the forward cast to get caught in a snag. John began thinking that he should limit his fishing to calm days behind the house. He made one more cast downstream; and then, with the line still out, decided to walk upstream to another spot that he hoped would offer better chances for success. He had walked about a hundred feet when a fish swallowed the fly on the end of the trailing leader. John took about ten more steps before he felt a tug on his rod. He carefully pulled in the line and netted the fish, a small grayling. He didn't remember seeing a diagram like this in the book either, but regardless of his actual technique, he had finally caught a damn fish.

After successfully retrieving his line from the bushes, and with new knowledge of the tri-lure's full capabilities, Timothy could now cast into the center of the river almost every time. The river had soaked his jeans above the crotch during the unfortunate crossing; the warm afternoon sun provided some comfort. He flung the tri-lure out over the water again and listened to it make the same pleasant "kerplunk" as a skipping rock, then reeled it in slowly, jerking the rod every few seconds to make the tri-lure look more inviting to any passing fish. He worked his way back toward the bridge, then under the bridge and across the rocks, then to the edge of the bridge, and finally to the end of the shadow from the late afternoon sun. He decided to make a long cast, more down the length of the river than across it, to see just how far the tri-lure could travel unobstructed by riverbank bushes. He wound up again and whipped the rod across his body with every bit of strength he could muster, and once again the line flew off the reel with a metallic hissing sound. He was amazed by how far the tri-lure flew before slicing into the water. He admired his toss for a few moments and, as he prepared to begin reeling, felt a strong tug on the line. Timothy pulled the rod tip up and the line tugged again. He began pulling up and reeling down, like John had taught him, and when he had pulled in about 20 feet of line a huge—at least it looked huge from a distance—rainbow trout exploded through the water's surface and floated gracefully in the air before twisting back into the river. The trout had the sharp barbs of the little propeller lure hooked perfectly through its upper lip.

John fished several other parts of the river, trying desperately to catch something using the legitimate technique he had learned from the book. It didn't seem right to have caught the grayling the way he did; he had kept it anyway because the unfortunate little fish had swallowed the fly deep inside its throat and would not have survived if John had released it. Thankfully, he had only one more confrontation with the ubiquitous bushes. And although he had caught only the one little fish, he did finally have to admit to himself that his fly-casting technique had greatly improved. After a long afternoon and hundreds of casts, he had even learned to use the wind and flow of the river to his advantage. He began to enjoy the challenge of using the river's current and a brief gust of wind to encourage the little fly to land where he wanted and how he wanted. But it had been a long day, especially with the early morning drive, so he decided to make one last cast before returning to the campsite where Martha could make a dinner of grayling and whatever else she had brought for the trip. He thought there might be at least four or five bites in the little fish; maybe a few more if the bites weren't too big.

As John approached the campsite, he could hear Martha and Timothy chattering away about something. Martha turned around and looked up when she heard John's footsteps. "John—come and see the big fish Timothy caught!"

John quickened his pace, eager to see the fish—especially its size. Maybe Timothy had caught another grayling so there would be at least eight bites. He walked up to the ring of campfire rocks and suddenly stopped. Martha held a large rainbow trout up in the air, its scales and fins luminous in the slanting sunlight.

"Look at this, John. Have you ever seen anything more beautiful in your whole life! And Timothy caught it all by himself, over by the bridge. I can't get over how huge it is!" John had never seen Timothy smile with such enthusiasm. Come to think of it, he hadn't seen Timothy smile much at all in recent months. John quietly admired the fish and felt pride for Timothy's achievement, although he couldn't quite bring himself to say anything out loud.

"So, what'ya catch it on?" John asked this question with practiced restraint.

"I caught it on this." Timothy held up the magnificent tri-lure contraption in his hand. The little propeller caught a breeze and flashed in the fading sunlight.

"That's quite a lure, son. Did you think this up yourself?" John studied the tri-lure with obvious interest. After the purity of fly-fishing, the downright sloppiness of the tri-lure distressed him. John struggled to justify the obvious success of the tri-lure with fairness in the universe.

"Yup, I did."

"Well, I'll be damned. I guess we're going to have fish tonight." John would show Martha and Timothy the little grayling later. Right now, he just wanted to change into some dry socks and take a short rest before dinner.

♦ ♦ ♦

At the tip of South Korea, August 1950

Loaded down with overstuffed duffle bags, sloshing canteens, canvas bandoliers filled with ammunition, M-1 rifles, sharpened bayonets, and other accouterments of battle, Timothy and Humphrey trudged heavily down the gangplank toward the dock below. After three weeks at sea they were both thankful to get off the rolling troop ship and onto firm ground. They were also thankful for the possibility of better food, although this gratitude would soon prove premature. Timothy remained disappointed that he had missed Japan; he also appeared pleased to see that Pusan was a major city, not some ragged little Podunk at the water's edge as he had expected, even if the dock did swarm with a crushing horde of people.

Timothy tipped his helmet up, wiped the sweat off his forehead, and stepped off the end of the gangplank. "Hey Humphrey, where do you think all these people came from? Do you think they all live here? I've never seen this many people in one place in my entire life."

Humphrey arrived at Timothy's side in time to hear the last few words of his question. "What about one place in your entire life? You'll have to talk louder. I can barely hear you above all this noise."

Timothy raised his voice and turned his head. "I said, have you ever seen this many people in one place in your entire life. Do you think they all live here?"

Humphrey looked around for the first time. Crowds of people surged along the dock in both directions. He also noticed that almost everyone carried something in their hands or on top of their heads. A young woman carried a small blackened teapot in her hand and balanced what looked like a wadded up chunk of old carpet on top of her head. "I don't know. There sure are a lot of them, and they all look like they're going somewhere. If they all live here, it must get pretty damn crowded when everyone goes to work in the morning."

"Well, I don't care if it's crowded if we get a chance to look around before heading out. Looks like a pretty interesting place to me. Maybe it'll make up for missing Japan."

Humphrey had never really believed Timothy's claim that he had wanted to see Japan. "Did you really want to see Japan? I never heard you talk about Japan until after the Gunny told us we weren't going to stop there."

Timothy acted surprised. "Yeah, of course I did. I really wanted to see Japan. I read about it in a *National Geographic* once, and ever since I wanted to go there."

"You read *National Geographic*?"

Timothy grinned. "Yeah, I do—every chance I get."

Although Timothy hoped there would be some interesting things to do and see, Pusan would suffer the same fate as Japan. Unfortunately, and to Timothy's renewed disappointment, the Marines stayed in Pusan only one brief night. At dawn the next day, before the sun had warmed the cool night air, they moved by train forty miles to the west where they bivouacked near the southernmost limit of the Pusan Perimeter.

The line that would be called the Pusan Perimeter began near the 38th Parallel shortly before dawn on June 25, 1950 when seven infantry divisions and one armored division of the North Korean People's Army crossed into South Korea. The advancing line swept away all resistance in its path and crossed like an insidious shadow over the South Korean capital city of Seoul in a mere three days. The line rolled south nearly one hundred miles during the last week of June and the first two weeks of July, as reeling U.S. Army and Republic of Korea forces fought a desperate delaying action while enduring heavy casualties. By the first day of August, the line—which now stretched from P'ohang on the east coast then fifty miles west to around Taegu in the interior then seventy miles south to the coastal Chinju-Masan region—encircled a fragile vestige of the peninsula, a meager ten percent of the former Republic of Korea. At the focus of this encirclement, the port city of Pusan, now choked with millions of people fleeing the collapsing line, provided the final haven for an ever-growing swarm of refugees.

Toil Under The Sun

The train, after veering sharply to the northeast, stopped again, this time for more than a few minutes. Humphrey, sleeping soundly for the first time in two weeks, was jolted awake by the squealing of steel wheels against steel rails as dozens of brakes forced the train to a shuddering stop. He had pulled the fabric-covered brim of his helmet down over his nose to keep the light out; when he raised it again to peer through the window, a momentary flash of sun blinded his sleep-dilated eyes. He squinted to see why the train had stopped again, but felt too groggy from his meager nap to make any sense of the blurred images on the other side of the dusty glass. He turned his head away from the glare of the window and saw Timothy sitting up stiffly. The noise of the wheels and brakes must have awakened him too.

Humphrey rubbed his eyes and muttered through swollen lips. "How come you're still awake? We've hardly slept in two weeks."

"You know something Humphrey? We gotta stop taking these damn trains. It seems like only bad things happen when we take the train. First, there was the train to boot camp. Then the train from Pusan to the front where we get shot at almost every day for two weeks. And just when things seemed to be settling down a little, they put us on another damn train to who knows where. All I can say is, it's probably no place good."

Humphrey yawned and stretched his arms out while he listened to Timothy's insipid analysis. "You've got a point there. Looks like the train's going to sit here for a few minutes. Looks like some of the guys are getting off too. Maybe we should get off and walk around a little, while we have the chance."

Timothy leaned over and tried to glance down the tracks; he bumped his forehead on the glass before he could see anything. "Yeah, that's fine with me. I could use a little walk. I haven't walked nearly enough in the last two weeks. Maybe we'll even get to walk around without someone shooting at us. That would be a nice change of pace."

This comment annoyed Humphrey almost immediately. "We wouldn't get shot at so much if you'd stay put and quit running around like a damn idiot. You know those guys shoot at anything that moves."

"What—you think I should slink along the ground like you do? Anyway, how're we supposed to know where they're hiding unless they stick their heads up to shoot at us?"

"Well, you could just stay down and wait for one of their damn idiots to get up and run around like you do; then we could shoot at him instead. That would be a lot safer."

Humphrey cracked his back when he stood, then followed Timothy down the aisle to the end of the car, almost tripping over the butt of a Browning Automatic Rifle that had slipped out past the edge of seats. They stepped outside onto a rigid steel platform at the end of the car, then walked down creaky steel steps to the warm ground that edged the sloping bed of crushed rock beneath the rails. Scrubby brush grew knee high several feet beyond the lower edge of the crushed rock, then swept away into a expansive field recently yellowed by the hot sun. Humphrey soon felt the warmth of the ground through the soles of his boots. Although he didn't realize it at the time, he would remember this warmth with intense nostalgia in less than four months. Now, the surplus heat just added to his discomfort. As Humphrey prepared to complain about the heat, he noticed that the train had stopped just beyond a small village.

A group of Marines had gathered a few cars up the tracks, so Timothy and Humphrey walked over to see what they were doing. The Marines displayed many different stages of dress. A few—with helmets, ammo belts, canteens, and rifles slung over a shoulder—looked ready for an imminent attack on the train. Others dressed more randomly, with helmets missing or shirttails pulled out or no shirt at all. One Marine displayed a little of each, with the added eccentricity of a missing boot. Humphrey chuckled at the ragged holes in the heal and big toe of the exposed sock. The focus of the gathering turned out to be two young Korean boys. Humphrey guessed their ages at five and seven. He guessed they were brothers too, but then again, Koreans all looked alike to him: they might not be brothers at all. Maybe they didn't even know each other. But then again, they both wore the same clothes—white long-legged shorts and white short-sleeved shirts. But then again, almost everyone dressed like this in Korea, so that didn't necessarily mean anything either. Humphrey and Timothy walked up behind the young boys as one of the Marines offered them each a

Toil Under The Sun

candy bar. The two boys chattered away at the Marines in little voices; unfortunately, no one in the group spoke enough Korean to understand more than a word or two.

Humphrey decided that he wanted to give the boys some candy too. "Hey Timothy, you got any candy left?"

"No, I ate it all."

"You ate it all? Are you sure?"

"That's what I said, isn't it? I finished off the last of the candy this morning. Why don't you give 'em a C-ration instead? I'm sure they'll be your friends for life after they finish it. Anyway, what happened to your candy?"

"I gave it to you."

The train whistle shrilled up and down the track, signaling time to leave. Several of the Marines finished loading the young boys down with candy before boarding the train. No one gave them any C-rations, although Timothy continued to hound Humphrey to give them a couple of cans. The train moved forward with a quick series of evenly spaced jerks before rolling ahead with smoothly increasing speed. Ten minutes later, the train sped onto an old steel trestle bridge and then slowed when it began crossing the wide banks of the Naktong River. Timothy, who had traded places with Humphrey—Humphrey was trying to sleep again and didn't want the sun shining in his eyes this time—peered though the grimy window glass down to the river below. He could not see as well as he wanted to. He clenched the end of his sleeve with his fingers and carefully wiped a neat oval of clean glass large enough to look through with both eyes. When he had finished, the window grime formed a messy smudge on the back of his sleeve; he would not have cared if he had noticed it.

Timothy could now survey the river easily by pressing his left cheek and nose against the glass. As the train rattled across the midpoint of the bridge and approached the opposite riverbank, Timothy noticed two small shapes at the water's far edge. Although the train had slowed to cross the river, it moved persistently and would soon roll beyond the edge of the river. As the shapes approached, they became people, then a man and small boy, and then clearly a father and son. They were doing something, but Timothy could not quite see what it was. It seemed to him that whatever they were doing, they were enjoying themselves. He thought he could see them smiling and laughing, although he couldn't be sure because they were still very small. He suddenly yearned to know what they were doing and why he imagined they were so happy, but only seconds remained until the now accelerating train would rush beyond the edge of the river and the father and son would vanish forever. He sat almost directly above them now, and, looking west down the meandering length of the river into the late afternoon sun, he squinted as the water around them sparkled briefly and then changed into a deep, mottled gray. At this moment, when the light of the diminishing afternoon sun reflected off the smoothly flowing surface of the Naktong River, Timothy realized what the father and son were doing and why they seemed so happy: they were fishing together.

Chapter 7
Mister Stinky, April 1943

Grade school had been neither pleasant nor unpleasant. Certainly he could remember a few good times, and more than a few times that were not so good; but when he thought about it, and he did not think about it often, the last few years had passed tolerably. The most important thing, however, had become his successful progression to the sixth grade and, after nearly eight months of dedicated persistence, the end of it had finally come into his youthful view. He thought about the approaching summer days, now only weeks away. He knew summer would soon arrive because the vertical red line on the rusting metal thermometer hanging on the wall near the back door of his house—he checked it every morning before walking to school—had started to rise persistently. The rains had weakened too: this also provided a reliable sign of the shifting seasons. Although he looked forward to summer, he really didn't mind the rain. He actually liked it more and more with each passing year. When lightning snapped brilliantly across the clouds far beyond the spruce grove, and thunder rumbled over the house a few seconds later, and wind gusted and swirled until the trees vibrated with strain, that's when he liked the rain best. A detached and pleasurable warmth lived deep inside him when he sat by the big picture window in the living room watching the raindrops collide against the glass and flood down over the windowsill. He enjoyed the sound of raindrops splattering on the roof above. He liked the musty smell of the rain. He liked the eerie sound of wind in the trees. He liked the steel-gray clouds. He liked almost everything about the rain. But it wasn't raining today; it was what most people would call a nice day, and he found it a little boring.

He lived a sufficient distance from the town where an abundance of space still bordered the house, and could play without much concern that someone would notice him or care much about what he did. He thrived in the space because things didn't close in around him and he could play alone when he wanted to. He especially cherished the towering spruce grove that flourished a few hundred yards from the house. It offered him a different kind of space where he could walk and play and talk amongst the gently swaying trees fully isolated from the world. He had walked to the spruce grove earlier in the morning, just when the low sunlight had begun warming the treetops, to construct a few minor modifications to his tree fort and to check on Phijit's grave. Phijit remained one of the few exceptions to his enduring desire for seclusion. He had never objected when Phijit ran by his side, and sometimes thought that Phijit had possibly been his best friend ever. He cried after the truck killed Phijit, but not until two full days had passed. He remembered being surprised by his emotions; he also remembered feeling intense embarrassment after regaining control of himself.

It was over a mile from his house to the first row of dwellings that defined the edge of town, and at least another half-mile to the grade school. He had seldom walked into the town in the past, except to go to school or to run an occasional errand for his mom or dad, but recently he had made a new friend, an event both remarkable and, in a mysterious way, expected. More remarkable though, were the many children who had sought after his friendship in the past: whether he liked it or not, he had the misfortune of being the kind of person other people wanted to know; equally remarkable, he had little awareness of this. He spent year after year of grade school piling up missed opportunities for good friendships, although he had little awareness of this either.

He cradled a small, black leather book and a box of shiny pencils in the hooked fingers of his hand and walked along the uneven side of the dirt road to town. The book had a peculiar purpose because the pages were not filled with words and pictures—they were simply, blank. His mom purchased the book at the local bookstore after he had shown an interest in drawing. His dad hadn't acted particularly happy about the book when his mom brought it home because he thought the price too extravagant for a book without any words in it; in the end he grudgingly condoned it, without actually saying that he did. A few weeks later his dad gave him some special artist pencils, purchased during a business trip in the next town. He used the artist pencils to fill almost half of the little leather book with drawings, some of them surprisingly good. An atmospheric drawing of his tree fort, shrouded in smudgy mist,

Toil Under The Sun

flowed across two of the pages. There was an elevation drawing of the side of his dad's car, complete with shading to represent the side panels. An austere line drawing of the shed behind his house showed a wood ladder leaned up against it, the same one his dad used to clean out the gutters. He had attempted a landscape on one of the pages, with the spruce grove on a distant horizon line and the gentle hill sloping up to it in the foreground, but had never finished it because he couldn't figure out how to draw the grass. A drawing of his shoe, the one with a broken lace, nearly filled an entire page from edge to edge. He had even finished a drawing of Phijit, although that had been a hard one to complete because Phijit never sat still for more than a few seconds at a time. He decided that next time he would draw from a photograph instead of the actual subject.

He walked by the first house that began this side of the town—a small structure with asphalt shingle roofing, a modest covered porch with painted wood posts, and a carport that appeared to lean against the side of the house for lateral support. Trees and shrubs and flowers of many varieties, fragrant and strangely comforting, surrounded the house on all sides. Meticulously clean garden tools had been stacked evenly along the side of the carport. He thought an old man lived in the house, but he didn't know for sure because it had been quite a while since he had seen him working in the front yard. The next house looked almost the same, except someone had forgotten to build the carport. He thought a young family lived in this house because he remembered seeing small children in diapers running back and forth through a whirling sprinkler in the center of the front lawn. He didn't know their names or where they came from or what they did, and it had been months since he had seen the children, so he couldn't be absolutely sure they still lived there either. Maybe they had moved to some other small town, or a bigger house in this town.

A slender gray cat lived in the third house. At first the cat had acted skittish when he walked by the house on his way to school. When he tried to approach the cat it would dart away, usually to a ventilation well that led to the crawl space under the house. Over time the cat became more trusting, and eventually waited for him on his way to and from school. The gray cat waited for him now, at the ragged fringe of lawn that defined the boundary between the front yard and the dirt road.

He stopped and stroked the cat behind the ears, spoke some soothing words, and then moved on. The gray cat would probably be sitting in the same spot when he returned home; there would be an opportunity to pet him again.

His new friend lived a few front yards beyond the gray cat. After walking this short distance, he hesitated at the edge of the road before walking up to the front door. He did not wonder if his friend was home—he knew that he would be. His friend almost always stayed home, unless attending school or visiting the doctor or accompanying his parents on an occasional ride in the family car. His friend didn't go outside of the house very often. It just depended on how he felt at the time. Sometimes he had to stay at home and could not go to school. Once he didn't go to school for a long time, for reasons that were never fully explained or understood. Now things seemed better, and he attended school almost every day.

He walked up to the front door and banged on the metal frame of the screen door with the heel of his free hand. A woman, not much older than his own mom, opened a wood door and looked at him through the screen. The screen door had a little tear in it down near the bottom corner. His friend's father had intended to repair the tear last summer, but had never gotten around to it.

The woman's face brightened when she saw him standing on the porch. "Why Timothy, what are you doing here today?"

"I came to see if Jonathan wants to draw. I brought my book and some pencils." Timothy held up his little leather book in one hand and the box of artist pencils in the other to make sure Jonathan's mom could see them clearly.

"Well, I think he might. Why don't we go see what he's doing?" This seemed like a natural thing to say, although she already knew what he was doing. She stepped aside and pushed the screen door wide open with her outstretched hand so Timothy could come in. The corroded spring at the top of the door creaked when it reached its limit. He stepped from the bight sunshine of the dusty porch into the cool shadows of the house. He knew where to find Jonathan, and walked directly down a short connecting hall to an arched opening that led into the living room. He discovered Jonathan sitting cross-legged in his usual spot by the picture window, playing with some wooden alphabet blocks. He was older now, and could arrange the blocks in dozens of meaningless patterns instead of just two or three. However, the miracle of his early arrangements remained. Though meaningless to anyone who stood beyond the boundary of Jonathan's private world, the patterns were nonetheless exceptionally consistent. And some of them were beautifully complex as well—they just didn't mean anything to anyone except Jonathan. Timothy walked across the worn living room rug without making a sound and kneeled down at Jonathon's side.

"Hi Jonathan. How's it going today?" Jonathon did not respond to Timothy's question and continued arranging his blocks. He grabbed a blue "R" and shoved it next to a red "Z" with a slight click. Timothy noticed that some of the letters had been placed upside down or sideways. "You know, Jonathan, you're going to wear those blocks out if you're not careful. Maybe you should do something else for a while." Timothy chuckled quietly to himself, knowing full well that Jonathan probably didn't even begin to understand his private joke. He didn't mind. Jonathan's mom said it was good to talk to him, even if he didn't seem to pay any attention. "School went pretty good this week. How'd it go for you? I thought it went pretty good." Timothy didn't really believe this, but he thought he should talk positively about school when he visited Jonathan.

Jonathan's hand froze on a block, and he looked up and fixed his eyes about six inches to the right of Timothy's head. "School went good for you. School went good." Jonathan had the habit of saying "you" when he meant "me"—Timothy had learned to understand this and knew what he meant. These simple words pleased Timothy. Sometimes Jonathan didn't respond for a long time, and occasionally not at all.

"Yeah, I guess it went good for me too. Did you do any drawings this week? I did a couple of new ones. Would you like to see them?" Timothy moved closer to Jonathan and opened the little leather book. "Look at this, Jonathan. It's a drawing of my baseball glove. What do you think? Do you like it?" Jonathan appeared a little more interested now, and actually looked at the drawing. He rocked back and forth while he studied it.

"Drawing good. You like drawing."

"Well, it's not as good as one of your drawings, but I think it's pretty good for me. Have you got any drawings to show me?" Jonathan continued rocking back and forth; he sustained this for several minutes without responding. "Well, maybe I'll just look around and see if there are any new drawings." Timothy walked into the kitchen and found Jonathan's mom cleaning a hummingbird feeder in the sink. He asked her if Jonathan had done any new drawings since his last visit. She led him back to the living room and pointed at a pile of drawings stacked neatly on the coffee table in front of the sofa. Timothy slid the pile off the table, sat next to Jonathan again, and began viewing the drawings, one at a time. There were 16 in all, so it took a long time to go through them. Timothy thought they were beautiful, and more extraordinary than he could ever hope to achieve.

"Wow, Jonathan! These are really good. This one is the best shoe drawing you've ever done, much better than your last one." Jonathan seemed to enjoy drawing his shoes, but unlike the dependable patterns of the wooden alphabet blocks, they were never the same because the angle of view and quality of light were never the same. "Would you like to do a drawing right now? I brought my artist pencils. You could try one, if you like. If your mom says it's OK, I could even leave one here for you to use. Do you think you'd like that?" Jonathan didn't say anything and continued rocking. Timothy opened his little book to a fresh page, selected a pencil with a good point, and began looking around for something to draw.

"What would you like to draw, Jonathan? Maybe we should try something instead of your shoe. What do you think about that?" Jonathan stared ahead and did not answer. He just rocked smoothly back and forth, looking as if he might start arranging the alphabet blocks again at any moment. Timothy decided to use a trick that had worked before. "I know, Jonathan—where's Mister Stinky? Has he been here today? Maybe Mister Stinky would like to draw with us. I bet he would—that is, if we can find him." Timothy set the book and pencil down on the floor and began searching around the living room. He looked below the coffee table in front of the couch, then fished around underneath and behind both of the couch cushions, then waved his hand behind the couch. "Well Jonathan, Mr. Stinky's not where I thought he'd be. Maybe he's under your dad's easy chair." Timothy hopped across the living room and dived to his stomach. He poked his head under the easy chair. "No, he's not here either. Are you sure he still lives in the living room? Maybe he's moved into the dining room. I know, maybe he's hiding in the bookcase." Timothy stood up and walked over to the bookcase. He found a small bulldog hand puppet leaning against the encyclopedias. He slid Mister Stinky onto his left hand and then hid him behind his back. He cleared his throat and prepared to speak in Mister Stinky's high-pitched puppet voice.

Suddenly, Mr. Stinky floated in the air in front of Timothy. "Hi, Jonathan. It's me, Mister Stinky. I've been taking a nap by the encyclopedias. How's it going? Look's like you're going to do some drawing. Mind if I watch?"

Jonathan stopped rocking and slowly turned his head. Mister Stinky waved at him when they made eye to eye, or in this case, button to eye contact. Mister Stinky had gained Jonathan's attention in a way that no one else could.

"Hey, Jonathan. Do you mind if I give you a kiss?" Mister Stinky gave Jonathan a kiss on his nose. This evoked a small but unusual smile from Jonathan. "How would you like to draw a picture? Look, I have an artist pencil that Timothy gave me. He said you could have it if it's OK with your mom. What do you think? Would you like to draw a picture? We could even draw another picture of your shoe if you'd like to." Mister Stinky cuddled the artist pencil in his furry paws, and Jonathan reached out and took it from him. He studied the artist pencil by rolling it around in his hands and on the floor a few times, and then picked up a piece of paper. He started drawing a picture of Mr. Stinky. Timothy held the hand puppet very still, as still as he could, while Jonathan worked. When Jonathan had finished the drawing, he dropped the pencil and began rocking again. Mister Stinky quickly floated through the air so that he could look at the drawing, and began speaking again in the familiar high-pitched voice. "Wow, Jonathan. That's really good. It looks just like me, not that I know what I look like, because I've got these button eyes and it's hard to see in the mirror." Jonathan suddenly grabbed Mister Stinky, pulling him off Timothy's hand, and hugged the bulldog hand puppet tightly against his chest.

"Like Mister Stinky. You like him a lot." He rocked again and cuddled the little bulldog hand puppet under his chin.

"Yeah, I think Mister Stinky likes you a lot too, Jonathan. Well, now it's my turn to draw. Maybe I should try a picture of Mister Stinky too." Timothy opened the little leather book again and picked out a pencil with a good point and started. He struggled with his drawing because Jonathan covered parts of Mister Stinky with his arms and kept rocking back and forth. With effort, and some creative interpretation, he completed a respectable drawing of the hand puppet. "Well I don't know, Jonathan. It's not as good as your drawing, but it's pretty good. What do you think?" Timothy held the leather book up so that Jonathan could view the drawing; he didn't seem to notice or care.

Timothy stayed a few more hours and did some more drawing. Jonathan just sat quietly and rocked with Mister Stinky. The day had reached late afternoon when Timothy left. Jonathan's mom thanked him for spending time with her son before she closed the screen door with the tear down near the bottom corner. Although the air had cooled a little with the declining sun, it remained comfortably warm. Timothy stopped to visit the gray cat again. He sat down on the side of the dirt road and the gray cat crawled into his lap. He petted the cat until it purred noisily, then stood up to continue his journey home. When he reached the last house at the edge town, the old man stood out front watering the flower bed that rimmed the front of the little white house. This at least confirmed that the old man still lived there. Timothy could smell the water in the air. It reminded him of an impending rainstorm.

♦ ♦ ♦

A walk in the Korean night, August 1950

After a long train ride without much sleep, Gunny Talbot was pissed—not because of the train ride itself, because of something else. His rifle company should have been boarding trucks hours ago for transport to the assembly area; instead, after waiting until late in the afternoon, the trucks never showed up. Then, after asking one of the officers a few questions, he found out that the trucks that were supposed to carry his infantry company to the front had been diverted to move an artillery battalion instead. This really pissed him off. Then he began worrying that this poor beginning might be an omen of events to come. This gloomy possibility pissed him off even more than the errant trucks.

He stood rigidly in front of his rifle company with an austere scowl pressed neatly into his face. He spoke to his men in a blatantly sarcastic tone. "Listen up. Looks like the trucks that were supposed to take us to the assembly area didn't show up. Seems they got diverted to move some lazy-ass artillery battalion. This really pissed me off at first, but you know what, the more I thought about it, the more I began to realize that my company of Marines doesn't need to ride into combat in any damn trucks. As a matter of fact, I'm glad another unit stole our trucks. Therefore, gentlemen, we're going to take a little nature hike. Time to saddle-up and get the hell out of here."

Timothy, to no one's surprise, had to ask a question. "How far is this little nature hike anyway? I mean, anyway sir."

Gunny Talbot still seethed with too much latent anger about the trucks to take offense to the question. "I'd say no more than twenty miles. Maybe a little less if we're lucky."

Timothy's eyes widened. "Twenty miles! It'll be dark when we get there! Are you sure we shouldn't wait for more trucks?"

"There aren't any more trucks. Are you afraid of the dark or something?"

"No sir. It's not me I'm worried about. I'm concerned about Humphrey here. He starts acting really peculiar when the sun goes down."

No one laughed, or even chuckled a little, faced with the reality of walking twenty miles in the dark to a battlefield. Humphrey didn't think the part about him acting peculiar at night was very funny either, but he expected this sort of humor from Timothy and didn't say anything. Although there had been some good-natured complaining about it, the train ride hadn't been all that bad compared to what they were about to do. At least it had been relatively cool when the wind moved through the cars. You could also take a nap if the train noise didn't bother you too much. Now, the hot afternoon air mixed with the dust of the road to create an unpleasant stickiness, and it would probably get worse until the sun went down. Without the trucks they also had to carry all of their gear. Even with all of this, they formed up and began a march that would take them twenty miles into the fading western light.

Timothy adjusted the position of his rifle sling against his collarbone and stepped into line behind Humphrey. The road did not appear to have too many bumps or potholes; maybe this wouldn't be too bad after all. Timothy began talking a few minutes after they stepped off. "Humphrey, what are you thinking of doing when you get back home?"

Humphrey struggled to adjust the straps of his pack and to find a comfortable stride for the long walk ahead at the same time, so he did not put a lot of thought into his answer. "When I get back home? I don't know. I guess I hadn't really thought about it, especially at this particular moment."

Timothy pushed his question in a different way. "There must be something you want to do when you get home. I can't believe you haven't thought about it."

Humphrey completed seven or eight steps before responding. "Well, I certainly don't want to work on the fishing boat with my dad. I think that's what he hoped I'd do some day. It's not what I want."

Timothy waited for more; when Humphrey did not continue, he asked his question again. "So you don't want to work on the fishing boat with your dad. I can understand that. What is it that you do want to do? There must be something."

Prompted by Timothy's insistence, Humphrey considered this question more thoughtfully for the first time. He *had* thought about something that he wanted to do, but because he believed it might be impossible, he had never taken the idea very seriously, or told anyone about it. He told Timothy about it now. "I thought about going to college once or twice, but it's awfully expensive. I'm not sure I could ever afford it. I know my parents can't afford it. They have enough trouble paying their own bills. I'd have to figure out how to pay for it by myself if I ever decided to go."

"College, huh. Why would you want to go to college?" Timothy had never enjoyed school very much; going to college struck him as a questionable idea. The last thing he wanted to do was continue the misery of school for another four years.

Humphrey continued his struggle to find a comfortable stride. He almost had it at one point before tripping on a rock. "I don't know. To make something of myself, I guess. That would probably be the main reason for going."

"To make something of yourself? What do you mean by that?" Timothy coughed into his fist to dislodge some of the road dust.

"You know, to make something of myself, like a doctor or a scientist or something." Humphrey hadn't really figured out why he would go to college. He just had this general notion that he could make something out of himself if he did.

The rifle company marched through a small village, one of several they would pass before the day ended. An old man with a long white beard watched sadly from the doorway of his tiny house while young children danced alongside the column of advancing men. One of the youngest boys pretended to march. Several of the Marines stepped away from the column to give candy to the children. Gunny Talbot pretended to ignore what they were doing. During the last weeks, the old man in the doorway had watched countless refugees walking east with their meager belongings. Now he watched Marines walking west toward the enemy that had created the refugees. He thought nothing good would come from any of it.

"You want to be a doctor?"

"I don't know. That's just one possibility. I said I hadn't really thought about it very much. Maybe I'll go to college first, then figure out what I'm doing after I get there."

"I suppose you could do it that way, but it sounds backwards to me. Where would you go to college? Have you thought about that?"

"No I haven't. I guess I'd want to go someplace that's as far away from home as possible. I wouldn't want to live too close to home. Well, maybe it would be good to live close enough to visit my parents once in a while. But I wouldn't want to be so close that it was too easy to visit."

This surprised Timothy. "You'd want to visit your parents? Why would you want to do that? Aren't you glad to be out on you own?"

"Sure I am, but they are my parents. We haven't always agreed with each other, especially my dad, but we're a family and always will be. What I mean is, it would be good to go to college, but I'd still want to see my parents from time to time. Wouldn't you?"

Timothy struggled to understand this, then moved on. "What I really wanted to know is, did you have a particular college in mind? I wasn't talking about the distance." Timothy found himself interested in Humphrey's idea about going to college. He had never thought of going to college himself, but who really knew what might happen after he returned from Korea.

"Not really. It would have to be something I could afford. I imagine I'd have to get a job at some point. I'd also have to work some to save enough money before I went."

Timothy did not ask another question after Humphrey said this, so they both walked quietly for a while. The Marines marched for another hour before Gunny Talbot ordered them to take a break. The men moved off the road and dispersed. Humphrey found a comfortable position against a large rock and dozed for a few precious minutes. The bottom rim of the late afternoon sun touched the low hills and sharply angled ridges to the west, and the air began cooling with the fading light. Another group of refugees moved past the Marines in the general direction of Pusan. They were probably several families who had stayed together for some modest security. One man pulled a small cart piled with what looked like household goods. They all looked very tired.

Gunny Talbot strode along the edge of the road above the meandering line of resting men, ordering them back into line at intervals. "Time to saddle up. We've still got a long way to go. Everyone up. Let's get moving. Time to move out." He grabbed and shook a few of the men who slept through his commands. The Marines were on the march again within a few minutes. After a few more minutes had passed Timothy felt like talking again.

"Can you study art in college?"

Humphrey had never heard Timothy mention an interest in art. "Are you serious? What kind of art?"

"What kind of art?" I don't know. Just…art; like pencil drawings—that kind of art."

"Pencil drawings? Well, I suppose. But I'm not sure you can study just pencil drawing. You'd probably have to do other things too."

"Like what kinds of other things?"

"Well, uh, like painting and sculpture I guess. Stuff like that."

Timothy considered the reasonableness of having to study other things besides just pencil drawing. It did make some sense that you couldn't spend four years doing only pencil drawings. That could actually get pretty boring. It might even be fun to try his hand at painting. Sculpture might not be too bad either. "Are you sure about that?"

"No, I'm not sure. I'm just making this up as I go. I just can't imagine you can study art in college and just do pencil drawings. That's all."

"Painting and sculpture too? I guess that wouldn't be too bad. Maybe it would actually be kind of fun."

"You'd probably have to take history and English too. Also math, and maybe some sort of science."

This perturbed Timothy. "You're kidding! Why would I have to take all of that stuff if I'm there to study art? That doesn't make any sense at all."

"Because it's college, that's why; and you're supposed to be well rounded and know a lot of different stuff after you graduate."

"I see. Well, I guess the history makes sense, especially if it's art history. But what does math have to do with art? I don't get that."

"It probably doesn't have anything to do with art. Like I just said, it makes you well rounded."

"Seems like a stupid concept to me. What if I don't give a shit about being well rounded? What if all I want to do is study pencil drawing?"

"You know, you don't have to go to college if you don't like it. You can do something else instead."

"Like what?"

"I don't know. You should be the one telling me. You're the one who doesn't want to take math. You could do something that doesn't require any knowledge of math, that's what you could do. Then you wouldn't have to worry about it so much."

"You mean—like art?"

"Damn it, Timothy. You can really be a jerk sometimes."

The following skies had darkened now. A partial moon gave light enough to keep the road sufficiently perceptible to avoid tripping. The cooling night air provided a comforting change from the dust and heat of the afternoon. Night insects announced the twilight with countless flutters and clicks and chirps, although no one could hear them above the rhythmic footfalls of so many men. The insects could be heard again when the men had long passed. The men could hear sounds that did not come from the insects: distant and random, the sounds emanated from beyond the low ridges that rose up ahead before sweeping down to a wide river a little further. The men had heard these sounds before, and they understood what the sounds meant. The men had heard these sounds too many times before. The sounds were of distant rifle and machine gun fire. They were almost there.

"Humphrey. Have you ever thought about how lucky we are?"

Humphrey listened to the crackle of a distant machine gun, and then spotted the brief flash of an artillery piece. He tried to imagine why Timothy thought they were lucky. "Why do you think we're lucky? I don't feel very lucky right now."

Timothy glanced up when another artillery flash burst above Humphrey's helmet. "I mean, in the big scheme of things. I know we aren't exactly lucky right at this moment. That's pretty obvious. But if you stand back and look at the big picture, I think we're kind of lucky."

Humphrey still searched to find Timothy's obscure point. "You're going to have to explain this one to me."

"What I mean is this. I had a friend when I was a kid who could draw like an angel. But even though he could draw a picture of his shoe or anything else that looked like the real thing, I knew he was never going to amount to anything."

"Why not?"

"Because he couldn't control it. No one knew when it was going to happen or what he was going to draw, including him. He might even spend the whole week drawing the same damn thing over and over again. Even if you asked him to draw something special for you, the chances that he'd do it were almost zero."

"Why couldn't he control it? Was there something wrong with him?"

"As a matter of fact, there was. He needed a lot of help just doing easy things, like eating his dinner or taking a pee. He couldn't carry on a conversation, even a really simple one. He couldn't do a lot of things that you and I can do without even thinking about it. But the thing that always bothered me the most—he couldn't look you in the eye. He acted like you didn't exist. And because of that he had no chance of ever going to college, let alone talk about going like you and I are doing right now. I'd be willing to bet that he could draw better than almost anyone, including people who went to college and studied art. That's what I mean by how lucky we are. We can talk about going to college, and maybe even go. My friend never had that chance, and never will."

"What's your friend's name?"

"It's Jonathan. His name's Jonathan."

"Where is he now?"

"I don't know. As a matter of fact, I don't really know if he's even alive. We sort of lost touch after I started high school. If he is still alive, I bet he's drawing like an angel, even if he will never go to college, or even talk about it."

They arrived at the assembly area around 0330. Gunny Talbot ordered everyone to eat something, make sure their gear was in order, and then get some rest. He also told them to change their socks in the morning when they got up. He always reminded them to change their socks, even when it didn't seem all that necessary. They would move out again in less than five hours.

Chapter 8

Attack of the green beans, July 1943

Dinner looked really good tonight: roast beef; mashed potatoes and gravy; a big glass of cold milk; and an enormous, glistening, writhing mound of green beans—this final item the only blemish to an otherwise remarkable meal. He couldn't figure out why mom served green beans so often. Even though he'd made it clear more than once (many times more) that he did not like green beans, they kept showing up on the dinner table. In reality, she served green bean only three or four times a month; his perception had changed this into a nightly event. He loved roast beef and mashed potatoes, and he really loved gravy, but it required unconscionable effort to keep from gagging when he had to force down those green beans. In recent months he had developed a resourceful strategy to cope with the slithery beans: he would chop a couple of the beans into smaller pieces with his knife, mix them up with some mashed potatoes and gravy with his fork, and then, flinging his head back in a theatrical flourish, swallow the entire mess down with a huge gulp of cold milk. This technique had worked a few times—until his dad got tired of the grotesque display and declared it unnatural. Dad immediately demanded that he chew the green beans like a normal person, without gagging them down whole with a mouthful of mashed potatoes and gravy followed by a half-glass of milk.

Now, impaled queasily into the mashed potatoes and slopping onto the top of a thick slice of roast beef, there they were again, the persistent green beans. He stared at the humungous mound for almost a minute and then, as a delaying tactic, began counting them by moving individual beans around with his fork to allow an accurate assessment of his enemy's strength. At the same time he weighed the danger of returning to his old strategy and almost certainly risking his dad's formidable wrath. After considerable thought, he decided that he had no other choice and began cutting the beans up into smaller pieces and mixing them with the mashed potatoes and gravy. He scooped up the consolidated glob with his fork and began moving it toward his mouth. The mashed potatoes were just about to touch his lips—

John, who had been chatting with Martha about something that happened at work, observed this attempted prevarication just within the perimeter of his vision. He stopped mid-sentence and snapped his head around. "Timothy, what are you doing? Are you doing that unnatural mashed potatoes thing with your green beans again?"

Timothy paused, and then acted surprised. "Uh, mashed potatoes thing?"

John scowled. "I think you know what I'm talking about. Are you mixing your green beans with mashed potatoes and gravy, then swallowing the whole thing down with milk without chewing?"

"Uh, no, I don't think so." Timothy set the fork back on the plate and smashed the glob into the mashed potatoes and gravy to conceal the evidence. John watched him do this and noticed two of the beans squirm out.

John's eyes and voice both narrowed. "Let's just eat the beans normally, alright? It's not natural to swallow green beans whole without chewing them. And it's not polite either. I expect you to eat politely. We're not at a damn campfire here. Go ahead and eat the beans properly."

John's angry gaze instantly transfixed Timothy with indecision. Timothy scrunched down in his chair, looking stoically into the center of his unfortunate dinner plate, and felt a sick sensation swell in his stomach and push up to his throat. Swallowing the green beans without mashed potatoes and gravy, followed by some milk of course, would surely be impossible. But chewing them alone would be impossible too. He decided to eat the mashed potatoes and the slab of roast beef first and then worry about the green beans later. Maybe a good idea would pop into his head during the next few minutes. When he had finished the mashed potatoes and gravy, and only a few small chunks of roast beef remained, the green beans were still there, mocking him derisively. He finished the last of the cold milk as slowly as he could to buy a little more time.

John finally noticed that Timothy had finished everything on his plate except for the green beans. "Timothy...what's the deal with the green beans? Why are they still sitting on your plate untouched?"

Timothy sensed John's anger, which didn't take much effort, but still couldn't stop the unfortunate response that popped out of his mouth. "You said not to eat the green beans whole without chewing them, so I didn't."

John accepted this statement as an act of absolute defiance; the anger that had until now remained under his control began to overflow. He paused before responding—usually a very bad sign. "I think you know what I meant. I did not mean that you could skip eating the green beans. I expected you to eat them properly, not like a little heathen." John paused again—a further bad sign. "So get started, right now."

Martha listened quietly, and then decided she should try to smooth things out. "John, maybe he could eat just a few of the green beans. I put an awful lot of them on his plate tonight. I actually didn't mean to give him that many."

John clearly had little interest in any sort of compromise. He saw this entire incident as a serious affront to his authority, as well as a near catastrophic breakdown of traditional family discipline. John did not have to think before responding instantly to Martha's suggestion. "Martha, he needs to eat the green beans like I asked him to. This is no time to coddle him. I don't really care how many green beans are on his plate. I asked him to eat them, and that's what he's going to do."

This fortuitous argument pleased Timothy. He began hoping that his parents would hurl misdirected anger at each other and forget about him and the green beans. He sat in his chair, very still, very quiet, trying to disappear, hoping to fully vanish from their awareness. He focused his mind on this possibility with all his strength. It might have worked too, except for the damnable green beans! They were no longer content to lie passively next to a remnant smear of gravy, and instead had begun a teeming exploration out to the circular rim of the plate. And as they slithered around, they began dividing and multiplying—and rapidly too! And not only that, they soon expanded their territory beyond the modest limits of the plate and swarmed across the table cloth and around the big candle in the middle of the table and over a crumpled serviette—a writhing, squirming mass of slimy green beans, completely out of control, completely unstoppable, completely…completely…oh my God! He covered his eyes when the expanding mass of green beans spilled grotesquely off the edge of the table and surged over the dining room floor into the living room. He wondered if mom and dad could see this ghastly invasion while they argued. The green beans had reached the curved wooden legs of the sofa and were beginning to climb when John finally shattered the horrific vision.

"OK, Timothy, that's it. You're going to sit there until you finish those green beans. And you're going to eat them like a normal person, not with a bunch of mashed potatoes and gravy and milk swallowed whole without chewing. Now get going. You've got homework to do, so don't make a big deal out of this."

Timothy watched with utter astonishment as the green beans hastily imploded back from the living room and the dining room floor and everywhere else into a neat little pile on his plate, back to where they had started. One last bean, a skinny straggler, hurriedly snaked across the table and leaped on the plate with a spring-like flick of its sharp tail. It glared at Timothy with contempt before quietly joining the other beans. Timothy waited for one or two of them to at least squirm around a little, to justify the disturbing vision he had just witnessed, but nothing happened, nothing at all. The green beans just sat there in a disgusting little mound, just like ordinary green beans usually did. Timothy sat too, and stared at the loathsome beans, not knowing what to do, while John and Martha went into the living room to read the paper and do whatever else they did in the living room after dinner.

Almost thirty minutes had passed when John returned to the dining room. Timothy and the green beans still sat where he had left them, staring defiantly at each other. John's gut twisted. "Timothy…when are we going to eat the green beans?" Timothy sat silently, gazing into his plate, refusing to answer the question. "Timothy, when are we going to get going here?" Timothy said nothing. "OK. I think I've had just about enough of this. Start eating the damn green beans right now, or you can spend the rest of the night in your room"—the release Timothy had hoped for. He pushed himself away from the table and took a few steps toward his room, defiantly calling his father's bluff. John heard pounding in his ears. "You wait just one damn minute!" John grabbed Timothy by the arm. "Sit down and eat those damn green beans, right now!"

Timothy tried to yank his arm away from John's grip. "No, I'm not going to eat the damn beans! I'm going to my room, just like you said."

"Sit down!"

"No!"

"I said..." and John started dragging Timothy back to the chair, "...to sit...down!"

"Go to hell!" Timothy swung at John, hitting him hard on the shoulder. John reacted by grabbing both of Timothy's wrists and squeezing while Timothy flailed with his elbows and then his feet. Martha heard the commotion and hurried into the dining room, a flutter of newspaper pages trailing behind.

"Oh my God John! What's going on?" John did not have time to answer. He forced Timothy down to the wood floor and sat on him, straddling him with his legs. Timothy tried repeatedly to twist around and hit his dad again. John responded by holding Timothy's upper arms from behind and then pushing them awkwardly against the floor. Martha covered her mouth with both hands as if trying to hold back a spew of vomit. Timothy squirmed and twisted and pushed to free one of his arms so his could take another swing. He did this for a long time, almost ten minutes, before slumping against the floor in a pose of utter exhaustion. John softened his grip on Timothy's arms, but only a little. Timothy remained still. John relaxed his hands and straightened up. A muscle spasm shot painfully across his lower back.

"What are you going to do John?" Martha, who had watched in disbelief, imagined her tranquil world crumbling while the two people she loved and cared for the most enmeshed themselves in an apparent battle to the death. Normally she would have known just what to say; now her mind emptied itself of any meaningful words.

"I'm going to try to let him up. I think he's calmed down now. Then I'm going to send him to his room for the night." John spoke in panting breaths.

Timothy felt the pressure on his arms and back release. Instinctively, without conscious thought or premeditation, a consuming rage twisted his body around and jerked his left fist up until it struck John flat against his ear. John covered his throbbing ear, then, in self-defense, slammed Timothy back down against the floor. Martha screamed at the moment

Timothy's chin split open against the hard wood floor. Timothy's upper and lower teeth jammed against each other; blood gushed from the jagged tear and squirted onto the floor in splotchy puddles.

"Oh my God John, he's bleeding!" Timothy slumped against the floor, this time without any help from John. The rage inside evaporated after his chin split open, almost as if it had poured out with the blood. John looked down and felt nauseated, not by the blood, but by the injury he had just inflicted on his son. He rolled Timothy over, carefully lifted him off the floor, cradled him gently in his tired arms, and carried him into his bedroom. John laid Timothy gently down on the bed, then stood at the foot of the bed with his hands in his pockets while Martha cleaned the wound and pressed the cut closed with three butterfly bandages. When she had finished, she looked down at Timothy with sadness and confusion. Timothy soon fell asleep. John and Martha went to bed shortly after. They did not speak with each other for the remainder of the evening.

During the night, while everyone slept, the restless green beans again roamed fearlessly through the house, multiplying, expanding, exploring. They poured around the legs of furniture, climbed up window curtains, extruded through cracks under doors, seeped though the open drawers in a kitchen cabinet by the sink, searching for something unknown, something unfound. The next morning, the green beans still waited on Timothy's dinner plate on the dining room table, exactly where they had been left the night before. John stood in front of the plate for several minutes before picking it up, carrying it to the kitchen sink, opening up the cabinet door beneath the sink, and dumping the green beans into a brown paper garbage bag.

♦ ♦ ♦

A steep hill after breakfast, August 1950

A day's supply of C-rations filled an awkward, oblong cardboard box that Marines soon discarded after stuffing the contents into different pockets in their packs. The box contained six cylindrical cans, three with meat and three with fruit or biscuits, as well as a day's supply of toilet paper and a little box containing four cigarettes. The meat cans included delicacies such as hamburgers, chicken with vegetables, ham and lima beans, and sausage patties. The oblong cardboard box also had candy, salt and pepper, and packets of coffee and cocoa. The favorite C-rations among Marines were the hamburger and fruit cans. The least favorite was the wretched sausage patty.

"Anyone want to trade C-rations?" Timothy decided he should eat something before his company moved out, but his only remaining choice had already dampened his appetite.

Don, a young private from a small town in Nevada, responded without hesitation. "Yeah, I'll trade some sausage patties. What'cha got?"

Timothy held the can up and twisted it slowly back and forth to improve its attractiveness. "Chicken and vegetables. Want to trade?"

"Chicken and vegetables—are you kidding? That's one of my favorites. I like that better than a home-cooked dinner." Don grinned sarcastically and wiped his nose with the back of an index finger. "Why're you trading? Something wrong with it?"

Timothy frowned with obvious displeasure. "It's got green beans in it—that's what's wrong with it. I don't eat green beans."

"You don't? Why not?"

"I just don't, that's why."

"Couldn't you just pick them out?"

Timothy responded to this annoying question with growing edginess. "No, I couldn't just pick the damn green beans out. You want to trade or not?"

"Yeah, fine. I'll trade, if that's what you really want. You're sure about this now? I didn't think anyone liked sausage patties."

"Believe me, I'm sure." Timothy snatched the can of sausage patties and shoved the chicken and vegetables against Don's chest. He opened the can and dug the first patty out with his fingers. He didn't much like the sausage patties either, but at least there were no green beans lurking in the can. Pleased to swap his can of sausage patties for something he really liked, Don made a mental note that Timothy would be a good trading partner if he needed to dump more of the patties.

When he had emptied the can, Timothy checked his M-1 to confirm that nothing had broken or jammed since the last time he looked at it. He squeezed the ammo pouches on his belt to verify that each was filled with an eight-round clip, then sat on the back of his boots, his butt wedged against an acceptably smooth rock. He could often sit like this for several minutes before his feet fell asleep.

Holding the can just below his chin, Don scooped out the last of the chicken and vegetables and dumped it into his mouth, carefully licking the spoon clean when he pulled it out. He washed the spoon thoroughly with a little water from his canteen before wrapping it neatly in a piece of cloth and packing it into one of the pockets on the side of his pack. He turned to Timothy to continue the conversation that had begun before the trade of C-rations. "Timothy, are you afraid?"

Timothy closed his eyes and raised his face up to the sky. "Afraid of what, green beans?"

"No, that's not what I meant. Are you afraid of today?"

Timothy did not feel afraid; even if he did, he knew that he wouldn't tell anyone. "You mean, afraid of running through a rice paddy knee-deep in water then across open ground with no cover then up a steep hill with the entire North Korean Army shooting at you with tanks and rifles and machine guns? Is that what you mean?"

Don swallowed hard. Timothy's eyes were still closed. "Uh, yeah, I guess that's what I mean." Don suddenly regretted asking this question. He remembered feeling a lot safer just moments ago—before Timothy's morbid response. "You think they have tanks up there too?"

Timothy lowered his head and smiled, his eyes still closed. "That's what I heard the Gunny say. I wouldn't worry that much about the tanks. It's the machine gunners and snipers who'll get you. Just make sure you don't run in a straight line, and maybe you'll be lucky enough to get all the way to the top. Then someone can run you through with a bayonet. You know, I guess a tank could squash you when you get up there; maybe you should worry about that too."

Don thought this conversation had taken a decidedly unhappy turn, and didn't know if he should try to change the subject or just walk away. He felt a partially digested chunk of chicken and vegetables try to rise up from his stomach. Humphrey had been sitting nearby for most of this conversation and could see that Don had lost some of his color. He decided to interrupt before Don upchucked or fainted.

"Hey Timothy, knock it off. Can't you see you're making Don sick? You don't have to talk like that. I don't think it's very funny either."

Timothy turned his head and opened his eyes. "Just telling Don what to expect up on the ridge. Anyway, he's the one who asked the question in the first place, not me."

"Yeah, right. What you're trying to do is scare the crap out of him because you think it's funny. You're not trying to tell him anything he really needs to know."

Timothy concealed his amusement when he responded to Humphrey's unexpected reproof. "Whatever you say, Humphrey. Next time Don asks me what's going on, I'll just tell him I haven't got a clue, even if I do. Will that make you happy?"

"Yeah, Timothy. That will make me happy."

Gunny Talbot stepped through the rifle company with practiced precision, reminding everyone to get ready to move out soon. His devotion to punctuality verged on fanaticism. Timothy doubted the Gunny had ever arrived late for anything in his entire life, even when he was a little kid. He had probably even completed his mom's pregnancy exactly on time. "Let's get ready to move out, gentlemen. We deploy in forty minutes. Finish your breakfast and pack up your gear. Get everything packed up and ready to go. Check your ammo. Check your weapons. We deploy in thirty-nine minutes. Let's get moving gentlemen. Time to pack up your gear. Change your socks if you need to. We deploy in thirty-eight minutes...."

As Timothy watched Don pack up his gear, he remembered Humphrey's rebuke and began feeling guilty, but only a little. "Tell you what, Don. Why don't you stay close to me and Humphrey, and we'll make sure you get up to the ridge. What do you think?"

Instantly suspicious, Don replied with a vague scowl. "How you going to do that?"

"Easy—I've never told you this before, but Humphrey and I are both invulnerable. Nothing ever touches us—not bullets, not bombs, not nothing." Timothy had actually convinced himself this might be true. He had taken many chances since arriving in Korea, and, as far as he could tell, had never come close to getting shot or blown up. As a matter of fact, he hadn't even stubbed his toe on a rock. He didn't really know if the same was true for Humphrey; he just thought Don would feel better if they were both invulnerable. "Don, you just stick with me, and Humphrey here too of course, and you'll be safe and sound all the way to the top of the ridge. What do you say?"

Toil Under The Sun

Don relaxed his face and licked his upper lip. Maybe Timothy really wanted to help him. "I don't know…I guess, maybe I could…."

Before Don could finish his sentence, several artillery units—probably the same ones brought in by the trucks that should have transported them last night—began blasting the distant ridge. Timothy and Humphrey and Don watched explosions puff across the top of the mountain. Each of them hoped that the North Koreans would be blown off the ridge before they had to run up it. And this is what should have happened. Unfortunately, the artillery units had arrived after dusk the day before; without sufficient daylight to see the ridge clearly, none of them had properly registered any specific targets. Because of this unfortunate occurrence, nearly all of the shells landed harmlessly, leaving most of the North Korean defensive positions undamaged.

Four gull-winged Corsairs screamed overhead to attack the ridge as well, fifteen minutes late. Gunny Talbot noted this failure before quietly cursing to himself. At exactly 0800, his rifle company and one other moved across the line of departure and deployed for attack. They moved into the rice paddies a few minutes after the Corsairs began pounding the ridge. The North Korean machine guns opened up a minute later. Timothy and Don, with Humphrey close behind, began running in slow motion through the water, instinctively zigging and zagging to make themselves more challenging targets. One of the North Korean machine gunners, firing from a fortified trench high up on the ridge, swung his aim in an arc that crossed a few yards in front of their path, missing them, but hitting three Marines to their left. Each of the Marines went down in quick order, splashing hard before bobbing up, blood spreading chaotically across the pulsing surface of murky water.

Timothy watched the three go down in his peripheral vision, his eyes blurred and stinging from sweat. "Shit! Get moving you guys. We've got to get out of this damn water!" The deadly arc of bullets traced a new line in front of them before they reached the far edge of the rice paddy. They splashed out of the water and dived to the ground, almost in perfect unison; tiny puffs of dirt leaped into the air all around them. Timothy rolled, and when his stomach hit the ground he aimed up toward the ridge and fired all eight rounds in rapid succession. He yanked a fresh clip from one of the pouches on his rifle belt and slammed it into his M-1. He jumped up and began running again.

Don and Humphrey quickly followed, staying a little behind him and mimicking his aggressive back and forth pattern that had protected them this far. They charged up the hill, repeating this same pattern over and over again, slowly moving closer and closer to the ridge, looking for cover whenever they could find it, diving to the ground when none existed. They leaped into a fresh crater about a hundred yards from the machine gunner. Two Corsairs split the smoky air just above them. Seconds later, two deafening explosions shattered the ground where the North Korean had dug in and the machine gun went silent.

With this unanticipated opportunity, the Marines who had made it this far now charged straight up the hill, slowing only to fire into the black smoke that hovered along the ridge or to reload. Timothy and Don reached the destroyed machine gun first, with Humphrey and several other Marines somewhere behind. Timothy was pleased that Don had made it. He felt a little smug, now that his arrogant promise had actually fulfilled itself.

"Well Don, what did I tell you? Stick with me and you'll be fine. Here we are, safe and sound, and on the high ground to boot! What more could you ask for?"

Don didn't know whether he should believe in Timothy's invulnerability or not. They had made it to the top of this hill with bullets flying all over the place, untouched while other Marines went down all around them. Maybe Timothy was invulnerable, and Don had somehow benefited from it. Don fell against the mounded earth that had until recently protected the North Korean machine gunner and rested for a moment, contemplating what had just happened. Timothy, too agitated to rest, crawled up to the top of the mound to see the view beyond the ridge. He did not anticipate the scene that unfolded in front of him. Down below, spread across the slopes that rose up from the smoothly curving shores of a wide river, countless North Korean troops supported by dozens of tanks swarmed toward his position. Timothy slid back down the mound until he stopped at Don's side.

Timothy noticed that Humphrey had not yet arrived at the ridge. "Where's Humphrey?"

"I don't know. I haven't seen him for a while."

"We've got a problem. Take a look."

"What kind of problem?"

"Just take a look for yourself."

Don crawled to the top of the mound and looked down upon the spectacular sight below. "Damn, Timothy, there must be thousands of them, and dozens of tanks. What the hell are we supposed to—" He did not quite complete his sentence. When he turned his head to shout to Timothy above the growing noise, a sniper's bullet pierced the back of his neck and shattered his jawbone. The deadly round threw him back. He tumbled down the mound until he rested awkwardly on strangely bent arms. After his body came to a stop, his neck paused, then slowly twisted around until his head rested unnaturally against a sharp stone.

"Don! You son of a bitch! What the hell are you doing?" Timothy rolled Don over by pulling on his damp jacket with both hands. The lower third of his face had disappeared. Timothy stared into the partial face, trying to remember what Don looked liked when he cleaned his spoon after breakfast. He thought he should feel remorse; instead, he felt only the familiar rage. He released Don's blood-soaked jacket, clenched his teeth, and crawled up to the top of the mound again, kicking little avalanches of dirt with each angry step. The forward North Korean soldiers had now moved within range of his M-1 Garand. He could no longer control the rage. Consumed with anger, he began firing, not wildly, but with calculated, lethal aim. He emptied the clip, reloaded, and fired again; slowly; methodically; with the desperate intention of quenching the rage that now dominated him. He killed three men and wounded five more before Gunny Talbot peeled a handful of jacket away from Timothy's shoulder and shook him hard.

"Time to go, private. The company's withdrawing."

Timothy did not look back at the Gunny. He could not leave now—he had not killed enough to sufficiently feed the rage. "I'm not going." He dug his feet deeper into the dirt and lowered his rifle to set up the next shot.

"I said..." the Gunny grabbed Timothy roughly by the bloody sleeve of his jacket, "...that it's time..." and yanked him down, "to go...and that's a damn order." The Gunny added, almost casually, "You've done enough killing for one morning."

As he scrambled down the mountain and waded across the rice paddies before returning to the assembly area—where he had eaten breakfast with Don only three hours earlier—Timothy could not stop thinking about what the Gunny had said. He couldn't figure out what Gunny Talbot meant. Did he mean all the enemy soldiers Timothy had killed, or did he mean Don? But more importantly, where had Humphrey gone?

Also known as the Bent-wing Bird, a prototype of the Chance Vought F4U-1 Corsair was first flown on May 29, 1940. To meet a U.S. Navy specification to develop a shipboard, single-seat monoplane around the most powerful piston engine then available (the still experimental Pratt & Whitney XR-2800 Double Wasp, an 18-cylinder, two-row, air-cooled radial), designer Rex Beisel and his engineering team devised an inverted gull-wing configuration that allowed the use of sturdy, short landing gear, a requirement for punishing aircraft carrier landings, while still accommodating the enormous 13 foot, 4 inch, 3-blade propeller that allowed the Double Wasp to achieve an impressive 2,000 horsepower. Four months later, the Corsair became the first American combat plane to attain over 400 mph in level flight. By the time the Navy received its first production Corsair on July 31, 1942, the prototype had been modified to include six 0.50-caliber Browning machine guns, 155 pounds of armor plating around the cockpit and oil tank, and an improved engine with two-stage supercharger. By autumn 1943, every Marine Corps fighter squadron in the Pacific Theater had been equipped with Corsairs. The Japanese called the Corsair "Whistling Death" because of the plane's robust arsenal of machine guns, cannon, bombs, and rockets. However, Marine Corps use of the Corsair did not end in World War II. A modernized version, the Corsair AU-1, now equipped with four 20 mm cannons and up to four 1,000 pound bombs, saw action again a mere five years later, in the Korean War.

Chapter 9

A desperate foot race, spring 1944

Bleak. Not a wind swept and achingly cold bleakness, rather an emotional bleakness, accentuated with a faintly persistent sadness. Myriad shades of gray blending in moisture-softened edges streaked somber skies to the east to reinforce his perception of bleakness. Yet to the distant west, constantly moving slashes of light flashed radiance and warmth through a copse of gently rustling spruce trees and along the tops of waving grasses sufficient to weaken full-blown weather bleakness. Surprisingly, the day had begun well enough with the early warming glow of a hopeful sun. Now, with the worrisome afternoon task soon approaching, the eastern sky had quietly become the dominant reflection of his feelings, not only of temporary feelings that come and go like the weather, but also of deeper feelings that existed below consciousness and defined his sense of authentic self.

Rain birds chattered away on the adjacent field—at least that's what the school custodian told him the sprinklers were called when he had asked about them. He loved the sounds they made: first the methodical chit…chit…chit…chit as the graceful arc of fluorescent water moved smoothly over the eager grass; then the abrupt machine-gun burst when the pressure of the water returned the rain bird back to the start, ready to begin the chit…chit…chit again. He questioned why he liked these sounds so much. He could think of no similar sounds that evoked the same pleasant sensations. Maybe he liked more than the sounds. Maybe he also liked the rainstorm smell of damp air. Maybe he unknowingly remembered the sounds from a better day, and had since felt the same nostalgia of that day whenever he heard the sounds again, but could not remember why. And maybe the sounds merely distracted him from the concerns at hand to give him a sense of nostalgia that really should never have existed.

As he pulled the laces tight across the top of his track shoe, he could not really justify why he had decided to do this. He had never been a particularly fast runner, a fact accentuated, or more likely caused, by his natural awkwardness; and yet for some reason he had decided to try out, and since Coach Hightower took everyone—even, it appeared, if they were not particularly fast or strong—he made the team. It turned out that Mr. Hightower had this remarkable belief that any kid who tried out and attended practices and worked hard deserved a place on the team. And not only that, they deserved to participate in actual track and field events too. Only a few of Mr. Hightower's colleagues thought this way. Most were interested only in winning and sought out boys with proven natural talent or obvious potential. But Coach Hightower had been a slow kid himself, and had almost given up until a coach finally encouraged him to work hard and to never give up. He ultimately became good enough to run the 880 for a small but respected college track team. Because of this personal experience, and more importantly because it was his nature to believe that anyone who worked hard deserved a chance, he maintained a nearly fanatical optimism about human potential. However, once Timothy made the team and began attending practices, Mr. Hightower struggled to sustain his fanaticism while he tried to figure out what to do with him.

Hoping that Timothy's lack of natural speed might conceal a latent ability to leap, Coach Hightower first asked him to try the high jump. The bar was set about three feet above the ground, a height Coach Hightower thought anyone of Timothy's age and stature could attain without too much effort. After racing down the approach at the highest speed Timothy could muster, he misjudged the take-off point and the angle of ascent at the same time on his way to landing squarely on the bar, straddling it almost perfectly as he crashed face-down into the sawdust pit. Not only did the bar smack him in the face and cut his knee, it also bent into an awkwardly twisted angle when it folded across the edge of the pit, a feat Coach Hightower hadn't imagined possible until he watched it actually happen that afternoon. Refusing to give up, Coach Hightower encouraged Timothy to try it again, this time with the bar set four inches lower, but unwilling to risk injury to his other knee, or worse, Timothy refused.

Timothy agreed to try the shot put next. Unfortunately, he did not even get to the point of making an actual attempt. His knee still throbbing, he stood patiently on the square concrete platform with the circle painted on it, waiting for a big kid with abnormally thick legs and arms to roll the heavy black ball to him. Timothy, who had never done this before, underestimated the weight of the ball as it approached him. He rested his hand on the sharp edge of the concrete to receive the rolling metal sphere, and it smashed three fingers and cut the back of his hand when it whirled up and over his palm. It took Coach Hightower's entire first aid kit to stop the bleeding—and four stitches at the hospital to close the wound—and with that, his shot put career ended before really beginning.

Exasperated, Mr. Hightower sent Timothy to the low hurdles, an event he thought could potentially diminish Timothy's awkwardness, given enough time and effort. At first Timothy practiced with only one hurdle, carefully stepping over it in slow motion, then increasing speed until he could actually jump over the barrier. When he had mastered one low hurdle, he set up two and again practiced in slow motion, increasing his speed cautiously until he could jump over the first hurdle and then the second with relative smoothness. Watching from a distance, Coach Hightower began to believe this might be the right event for Timothy; then…flushed with new confidence after achieving two low hurdles so quickly, Timothy set up a third hurdle and decided to skip the slow motion training. He walked backwards ten steps, took a deep breath, and then plunged forward at full-speed. He made it easily over the first hurdle, had to stretch a little to force his heel to clear the second, then coming up short, he slapped the top bar of the third squarely with the center of his foot before crashing into a heap, tangled irrevocably with the low hurdle's ground supports and vertical stanchions. Two other boys had to help untangle him, and the low hurdles joined the high jump and shot put as failed track and field possibilities.

This unfortunate result left Coach Hightower with very few plausible choices. Thinking, and mumbling to himself, he rubbed his eyes and stroked the front of his neck while looking up at a serenely drifting cloud. *The pole vault might be a possibility. No, the risk of impalement is too great. Then how about the discus? He could probably manage that, couldn't he? No, that wouldn't work either. He'll either drop the damn thing and break his foot or throw it in the wrong direction and kill someone. Hey, there's always the javelin. What, are you insane! Damn, there is just no other choice. Timothy will simply have to run.* Running: this might be the only way to protect Timothy from any obstacles, heavy objects, or sharp projectiles that could cause him harm, and at the same time protect the team's dwindling equipment budget. Sprinting events like the 100-yard dash or the 440 were clearly out of the question: Timothy was just too slow. Even the 880 might be too much of a sprint. That left the mile run. It would be a long race for Timothy, but he wouldn't have to jump over anything, and he would get some exercise if nothing else. Coach Hightower decided that Timothy would run the mile. That afternoon he introduced Timothy to the other four boys who were going to do the same event, all of them legitimate runners with actual talent, and his training began.

As it turned out, Timothy did not exhibit any particular talent for running either, although he did work at it incessantly. He had a loping sort of style with a small upward vector at each step that appeared to truncate any significant forward motion. Coach Hightower had never seen this style before, not that it mattered all that much. The main point to him was that Timothy had made the team. With this momentous achievement, Coach Hightower relentlessly showered Timothy with encouragement and praise, even if he had to stretch the truth from time to time. One particular afternoon, about three weeks after the first practice, and after a painfully unsuccessful run, Timothy became more than a little discouraged and thought about quitting the team. Fortunately, Coach Hightower could sense discouragement, sometimes even before the discouraged person knew of it. Timothy had staggered to a stop by the side of the track. He bent over with his hands on his knees and panted heavily. Coach Hightower approached until he loomed in front of him.

"Hey Timothy—how's it going?" A wide grin stretched across Coach Hightower's face. He adjusted his baseball cap to shade his eyes from the sun, unusually bright for this time of year. He owned a cap for every team in the American League; he wore a different one each day. "It looks like you're making good progress today."

Timothy straightened up and sucked in a ragged breath through flared nostrils. "Oh, yeah, sure." He looked around to make sure none of the other boys could hear him. "Coach, I'm awfully slow." He looked again. "I've been running for almost three weeks, and I think I'm actually getting slower instead of faster. Shouldn't I be getting faster?"

Coach Hightower considered this questions for a few seconds, and knew that he had to give a good answer or risk losing Timothy from the team. "Well Timothy, I just don't think I'd even worry about it. And you know why? Because that's the way it works, that's why. You've got to tear your body down before you can build it up again. Right now, you're in the tearing down phase. But before you know it, you'll run faster than you ever imagined possible. Really fast. Just stay with it. You'll see." The wide grin stretched a little further.

Timothy pressed against his side ache, but it didn't help much. "Really?"

"Yeah, really. Would I lie to you about something this important?"

"No, I guess not."

"There you go. Let's get back on the track and tear that body down some more. Don't forget. You'll be fast as lightning before you know it!"

"OK Coach," and with that, Timothy stepped onto the track and began running again, thinking about how fast he would be before he knew it.

What actually occurred before he knew it was not amazing speed, but the first race. After several weeks of agreeable weather, including several hot, clear days, the smell of rain again saturated the air after a morning initially warmed by the sun. Clouds mostly concealed the sun, except for a few streaks of light that cut through narrow slashes in the melancholy skies to the east. Timothy stood at the starting line, with eight other boys, listening to rain bird sprinklers chit…chit…chit in the next field. Timothy remembered for the first time that he had heard the sound a long time ago when, as a small child, he had not been preoccupied with the burdensome concern of running a race he was ill prepared to run. He glanced down the line of other boys, every one lithe and eager, and felt doomed. All of them looked like they had finished the "tearing down" stage and had progressed into the "faster than you ever imagined possible" stage. Timothy waited for the race to start with an overwhelming sense of bleakness.

Martha and John drove up behind the low bleachers at the edge of the track just as the starter raised his pistol. They hurriedly stepped out of the car when he yelled, "On your mark!" The nine boys moved to the starting line. They began walking briskly toward the track when he announced, "Get set!" All nine boys leaned forward. And they approached the smooth edge of the track as the starter's pistol snapped off a blank round. A puff of white smoke hovered above the track and all nine boys surged forward.

Martha worried that they had arrived too late and missed the race. "I told you we should have left sooner. We might be too late. Can you see Timothy?"

"Sorry, but I couldn't get away from work any earlier. I left as soon as I could." John scanned the nine boys before they reached the first turn. He'd never seen Timothy in a race before and had no idea where to look. After beginning at the front of the line of boys and working back, he finally spotted Timothy's unusual running style in last place. "There he is. He's near the back." John jabbed his finger vigorously to help Martha spot him.

Martha looked about eight inches off the end of John's finger and, after squinting to improve her vision, found Timothy some distance behind the receding pack of boys. "Is that Timothy? Is that him in last place?"

John had not expected Timothy to be the best runner on the team; however, neither had he expected him to be the weakest. He suggested an optimistic possibility. "Well Martha, maybe it's some sort of race strategy. Maybe he's just hanging back so he can see the race better. Maybe he'll move up later after the other boys have burned themselves out and slowed down. I think we should just wait and see what he has in mind." John had no idea of what Timothy might have in mind, but he thought he should say something so Martha didn't worry.

The pack of nine boys spread out a little more after moving into the second lap. Three of the boys began running in a tight clump at the front, with a pair of boys about six strides back, then three boys a little further back, then Timothy even further back. He had never run the first lap this fast before, and a dull ache began throbbing in his side just to the right of his belly button. Even so, he fell a few inches further behind the other boys with each painful stride. The three-boy clump at the front accelerated a little when they entered the turn, and widened the gap a bit more between themselves and the next pair of boys and the threesome and Timothy. The three-boy clump stretched out a little as they raced along the far side of the track, with a gaunt boy from the other team surging a few strides into first pace. The gaunt boy increased his lead to four strides after crossing the starting line for the second time, completing a half-mile. John and Martha waited for what felt like an unreasonably long time for Timothy to arrive at the same point and screamed and waved when he plodded by. Holding his side and breathing heavily, he appeared too preoccupied to notice.

The third lap continued in the same pattern as the second with the gaunt boy increasing his lead to at least a dozen strides. When he crossed the starting line to begin his final lap, he spotted Timothy a mere 100 yards ahead. The gaunt boy decided to lap Timothy and accelerated his pace even more. At the same time, Timothy labored to an increasingly slower pace, the cramp in his side jabbing more aggressively into his stomach with each stride. He pressed his hand against the cramp, which helped a little, but the pain continued to increase until he did not think he could finish the race.

John and Martha watched the race with rapidly diminishing expectations. Martha could see now that Timothy had a side ache and that he had slowed his pace considerably. "John, what's wrong with him. He looks like he's hurt."

John felt a small knot spasm in the middle of his gut. He didn't know whether the knot had formed out of concern for Timothy's demise, or because he felt embarrassed. John answered Martha's questions without emotion to conceal the knot. "I think he has a cramp. He'll be fine, but it looks like he's going to get lapped by the skinny kid."

Timothy's legs burned painfully now, and the cramp had spread across his stomach and turned from a dull throb into a sharp stab. He thought about stepping off the track and ending his misery; then he heard the accelerating footsteps of the gaunt boy coming up fast behind. He glanced back, and realized he was about to be lapped. Finishing the race in last place would be bad enough, but getting lapped would be shameful. At this instant, when the realization of his imminent disgrace jarred his mind, the pain in his legs and stomach evaporated. He then did something he never imagined possible: he willed his legs to run faster. The gaunt boy gained on Timothy for a few more strides until he reached only five yards behind, but by then Timothy had miraculously matched the gaunt boy's pace, even with his awkward, loping steps. Timothy held this pace for the final 100 yards, all the way to the finish line. When he crossed the line safely, the burn in his legs and ache in his side both returned and he could no longer hold speed. Neither did he stop. He completed the final lap, and the race, with the memory of the brilliant hundred yards pushing him to the end. Coach Hightower stood at the edge of the track, waiting for Timothy to cross the finish line.

"That was a hell of a sprint, Timothy. I didn't know you could run that fast."

His voice raw from panting, Timothy managed only a few words. "I just … didn't want to get … to get lapped. That's all."

The wide grin returned instantly to Coach Hightower's face. "That's good. No, that's excellent. Now all we've got to do is figure out a way to put you in constant danger of getting lapped, and you'll run that way for the entire race."

Timothy's side hurt too much, and he felt like he might throw up any moment, so he didn't find this very funny. He nodded weakly and then bent over and swallowed hard to hold back the vomit. John and Martha walked over and stood next to Timothy, waiting for him to straighten up. Coach Hightower slapped Timothy on the shoulder then hustled off to congratulate the other boys.

John thought he should say something instead of just standing there, but he couldn't think of anything clever. "Good job, Timothy."

Timothy heard his dad's voice and straightened up a little. "I finished last."

"I don't see how that matters much. The main thing is, you didn't give up. You did your best and finished the race."

Martha didn't know much about the mile run, or foot racing in general, but she felt honest pride that Timothy had made the track team. She didn't really care that he had finished last. "I'm really proud of you, Timothy. I thought you did a really good job. You kept running, even when you were hurt."

This unwarranted praise annoyed Timothy, especially when it should have been obvious to anyone with average intelligence that he had performed miserably. "I finished last. What's to be proud of?"

John struggled to think of a response to this logical assertion and stood silently. Martha would not give up so easily and spoke quickly. "I don't know, Timothy. I really thought you did a good job and I'm proud of you. I really am." Martha smiled to reinforce her statement. Timothy turned away and glared in the direction of the rain bird sprinklers. He thought he might throw up any time now.

◆ ◆ ◆

Inchon, September 1950

Sharp explosions rolled waves of crackling air across the decks of ships as countless shells and rockets battered the island and its unfortunate defenders. The early morning sun, barely gleaming off the gently swelling seas when the barrage began, had now become fully obscured by thick smoke and dust rising up from the island. Cruisers and destroyers and rocket-firing ships had rained thousands of lethal projectiles down on the island for over five days, creating a hailstorm of desolation. Then, when it seemed the deafening roar would go on forever, it stopped without warning, leaving only the metallic drone of engines and the rhythmic slapping of waves against the sides of the landing craft. The cadenced rising and falling motion of the craft became apparent then too, in disconcerting sympathy with the rhythm of the waves. And then the Corsairs joined the fight.

Inchon, Korea's second largest port after Pusan, rested at the eastern limit of the Yellow Sea. Seoul, the former capital of the Republic of Korea—now controlled by the North Korean People's Army (NKPA)—lay a mere fifteen miles inland to the east. The recapture of Seoul would be a catastrophe for the NKPA; however, because the front had now moved so far south down the peninsula, the North Koreans had no concern for this unthinkable possibility. This ancient city, founded in 1394 by General Yi Song-gye, thrived through the centuries as the most vital road and rail hub in Korea, and, as such, became an essential linkage in the supply line to the NKPA forces now rushing to annihilate the collapsing Pusan Perimeter. Unfortunately, an amphibious landing at Inchon offered perilous opportunities at best. The tides advanced and receded with dramatic swiftness and could suddenly expose up to three miles of dangerous mud flats where once a shallow harbor existed. The channel leading to the landing beaches presented approaching ships with a narrow, snaking puzzle of reefs and shoals. In many areas, twelve-foot high sea walls raised up along the shores. And then there was Wolmi-do Island. Connected to the mainland by a narrow 400-yard causeway, this guardian of Inchon split the two primary waterways leading to the only reasonable landing beaches. Wolmi-do would have to be taken first, then held by the Marines for twelve hours or more until the returning tides allowed the main amphibious landing to occur. Wolmi-do would be the fragile key to an arguably impossible undertaking.

The unexpected silence of the big ship guns shocked Timothy into a revived consciousness. He had almost grown accustomed to the incessant roar. Now it had vanished, leaving only an echo of ocean waves mixed with dull motor noise. His awareness of the smell of saltwater returned at that moment too—he had not noticed the brackish scent since before the guns had started. Somehow the intensity of the bombardment had masked his sense of smell, which he thought curious. Maybe his sense of smell had been overwhelmed by the assault on his hearing, overloading it to the point that it no longer functioned either. Surprisingly, now that the guns had stopped, he imagined that he could smell and hear better than before they had started. He turned to discuss this observation with Humphrey just as a Corsair roared overhead and blanketed the nearby beach with a fierce spray of 20 mm cannon fire. His sense of smell vanished once again.

Timothy felt several sharp pings on his helmet and heard the sound of the pings all around him. "What the hell is that?" He twisted his head left and right to see if someone had thrown a bunch of pebbles at him.

Humphrey studied the curiously warped wings of the passing Corsair before it vanished over the edge of the landing craft's bow. He found the shape of the wings fascinating and hoped to see one of the planes up close some day. "What the hell was what?"

"I think someone's throwing rocks at us. Didn't you feel it? They're landing all over the place. You can hear them too."

"Yeah, I did feel something." Humphrey looked down at his feet and saw several shiny objects rolling around on the deck in little circles. His pack and rifle pushed against the man standing behind him when he crouched down to pick up one of the objects. It felt nearly too hot to hold in his hand.

"Well I'll be damned. Can you imagine that?"

Timothy had looked up at the sky when Humphrey bent down, waiting to spot another plane. "Can I imagine what?"

"It's a shell casing from that Corsair. There must be dozens of them here; and there're still really hot. Can you imagine that?"

The shell casings intrigued Timothy. He had seen other planes fire their guns before, but he had never thought about where the shell casings went. He decided that they had to go somewhere. He reached down and picked one up too. "Damn, they are still hot. That Corsair must have been about twenty feet off the water. Good thing it didn't dip a wing—might have sliced our heads off. Then they'd have to cancel the landing."

"I don't think it was that close. It just sounded like it. I'd guess it was about two hundred feet above us when it flew by." Humphrey rubbed the shell casing between his hands until it cooled, then stuck it in his jacket pocket. He kneeled again and picked up a few more and stuck them in the same pocket. "Wait until I get home and show everyone these shell casings and tell them how I got them. They'll never believe it! I can't wait to see my dad's face when I give him one. I bet he'll be impressed." Humphrey put his hand in his pocket and jingled the shell casings around like valuable coins.

"Are you kidding, Humphrey?" They won't believe hardly anything you've done over here. I'd say there's maybe half a chance they'll believe this one, and that's only because you've got the shell casings to prove it. You should warm one up on the stove before you give it to your dad, to make the story extra realistic." Timothy stuck one of the shell casings in his pocket too. That wasn't such a bad idea. Maybe he would tell the same story to someone. Maybe he would even warm the shell casing up on the stove too.

"You don't think anyone will believe anything I've done over here? What do you mean by that?"

"Well, think about it Humphrey. Tell me one thing you've done in Korea that even sounds like it has the slightest chance of being believable. Tell me one thing. And I'm not talking about eating breakfast or tying up your bootlaces or sleeping in a wet sleeping bag. I'm talking about some of the strange stuff we've done, not all the day-to-day stuff."

Humphrey scrunched his face up. There must be something he had done that qualified as both strange and believable. He had almost thought of a possibility when Timothy abruptly changed the subject.

"Hey Humphrey. I just noticed something wrong. We're at the back of this damn landing craft. Look at all the guys standing in front of us. That really pisses me off."

Humphrey stretched his neck up and looked around. Given that he had no idea of who might be waiting for them when the landing craft arrived and the ramp lowered, it seemed like a pretty good place to him. "What's wrong with being near the back? Seems like a pretty good spot to me."

Timothy shot back impatiently: "Because I don't like being at the back of anything, that's what's wrong. I like the front, not the back. I like finishing first, not last."

"And what are you going to do about it?" It looks to me like we're stuck here. And I don't think we're supposed to move anywhere else. You know the Gunny will get pissed if we move out of line. I think we should stay right where we are."

"Hey, we're not in any line, so the Gunny won't give a shit. Let's move up to the front where we belong. I want to be the first one on the beach, and you're coming with me."

Sliding his hands under his pack and rifle straps, Timothy paused long enough for Humphrey to decide that he would go along with this, and then with sardonic politeness began pushing his way through the ranks of men. "Excuse me gentlemen. Mind if I move forward? Excuse me. Oh, did I step on you foot. I'm so sorry. I promise it won't happen again. Excuse me. Oh, pardon me. C'mon Humphrey. Everyone's moving aside for us. Hurry up before they close up again."

Humphrey mustered his most sarcastic tone of voice. "Why, that just surprises the hell out of me. I can't imagine why everyone's moving aside. Why would anyone want another body in front of them when the ramp goes down? I just can't imagine."

When Timothy neared the front of the landing craft, he became less polite. "Hey, buddy—move aside. Coming through. Let a real Marine up front. Step aside sissy. Hey, next time don't put your damn foot there! Hey asshole, do I have to ask you to get out of the way twice?" With a final push, they both arrived at the very front, only a few inches behind the heavy steel ramp.

Now that he stood at the front, completely exposed to whatever waited beyond the soon to be lowered ramp, Humphrey questioned Timothy's decision to move up. "Are you sure this is a good idea? What if a bunch of North Koreans are waiting on the beach with machine guns and sniper rifles?"

Timothy acted unconcerned. "Are you kidding? Didn't you listen to that naval bombardment? I don't think there's a single living thing left on that island. I'm surprised there's even an island left for us to land on. Why, it'll be like taking a walk on the beach on a summer afternoon back home. There'll be nothing to it"

Humphrey's doubt increased with this explanation. He had studied some military history and thought Timothy might be wrong. "Didn't the Navy blast the hell out of those islands in the Pacific before the Marines landed?"

Timothy brushed off Humphrey's concern. "Well, yeah, but they're a lot better at it now. Trust me, you've got nothing to worry about. And remember, you're with me too—what could go wrong?"

Still apprehensive, Humphrey reached out and touched the ramp and, running his hand along one of the rusty metal bars welded to the back to provide slip resistance, felt its roughness. When he pulled his hand away from the bar, the sharp edge of an unfinished weld sliced cleanly across the first joint on his index finger. He held the finger up close to his face to judge the severity of the cut, and watched a small drop of blood fall indifferently to the deck next to his dampened boot. As the drop dispersed in the salty moisture glistening on the deck, the bow of the landing craft pushed up hard against the beach and the ramp began falling away from him, giving him an increasingly better view of the sea wall beyond. When the ramp slammed against the beach, Timothy bounded down and leaped off the end, landing hard against the steep, rocky slope rising up from the lapping edge of salt water. The first one to step onto the island, he turned and grinned at Humphrey to acknowledge his achievement. Other Marines rushed by him, almost knocking him down.

Chapter 10

Chewcoughski, February 1945

Timothy crossed his arms and frowned with displeasure. No, not with displeasure, with bitter resentment—really...bitter...resentment. He preferred doing most things by himself, especially on Friday nights after enduring a long week of misery at school. He spent much of his school time during the week thinking about Friday night and the weekend that would follow: a whole evening and two days to do whatever he wanted and spend his time however he wanted. Of course, he would have to squander a little of this time doing enough homework and chores to keep his parents off his back, although that usually didn't take too much effort. They were usually busy doing stuff during the weekend too, and often left him mostly to himself. But the loss of his precious Friday night filled him with bitterness, and the manner in which he had lost it added a thick, scummy layer of resentment. His mom had once again volunteered him for a task that he found nearly intolerable. He told her the last time she did it to never ever volunteer him to do this ever ever again. She had ignored his plea and done it anyway, and he could think of no reasonable way to get out of it. Now he sat uncomfortably in the passenger seat of the car, glaring through the window, pretending to enjoy the scenery as it raced by in blurred streaks of gray, squeezing his arms together until his elbows throbbed with resentment too.

What really surprised him though, was that he had been asked to do this again after the absolutely wretched job he thought he'd done the last time. His parents had told him many times that if he did a good job he would get hired again. Therefore, he assumed, if he did a bad job he wouldn't get hired again. He remembered having gone out of his way to achieve this goal. He remembered acting downright unreasonable several times during the evening. He therefore could think of no rational explanation why the other parents had called his mom and given her a sickenly glowing report about the great job he had done.

They had literally gushed with disgusting praise until he thought he might upchuck. They had said he was a really good boy too, but he knew in his heart that this could not be true. With the nearly imminent loss of another Friday night, he understood that he would have to redouble his efforts to show everyone his true character.

Engrossed in this private discussion with himself, Timothy did not realize that the car had stopped several seconds ago. Martha said something to him, but he did not hear it. She set the parking brake and spoke to him again. "Well, we're here, Timothy." Timothy remained still, quietly glaring through the passenger window. Martha spoke to him again, a little louder this time. "Timothy, I said we're here. Time to get out." She had to wait several more seconds before he acknowledged that he had heard her.

"What? You say something?" He had actually heard her the second time. He tried to delay the approaching doom for as long as possible.

"I said we're here. Time to get out of the car."

No—time to make one last-ditch effort to get out of this stupid job. "You know I don't like doing this job. I told you before. Why did you have to volunteer me again?"

Martha sidestepped Timothy's apparent resentment by responding cheerfully. "Oh Timothy, it isn't all that bad. And the Petersons told me what a great job you did before. Remember what dad and I told you. If you do a good job, you'll get hired again. I think it will be fun. Don't act so gloomy."

"You know something mom, that's the funny thing. I don't think I did such a good job last time. As a matter of fact, I think I did a really, really, really crappy job. And I'm probably going to do an even crappier job tonight, so don't count on any more good reports from the Petersons."

"Oh Timothy, don't be such a party pooper. You'll do fine, just like last time."

Timothy sensed that his mom had no intention of backing down. He still opened the car door as slowly as possible and then methodically stepped out in a final demonstration of passive resistance, although he had actually accepted the hopelessness of his position several minutes earlier. They walked together, slowly, and methodically, up to the front porch. Martha knocked on the door with three neat taps. While they waited for someone to answer, she licked her fingertips and tried to flatten one of Timothy's upturned hair tufts; he artfully ducked away: he had no desire to look good for the Petersons. Mrs. Peterson soon opened the door, with Cynthia—or Cindy, as she preferred to be called—at her side. His horrific evening had finally commenced, and he could do nothing to stop it.

"Cindy, look who's here. It's Timothy, your favorite babysitter. Hello Martha. How are you doing this evening?"

"Fine Jane. And how is little Cynthia doing tonight?"

Cindy had just celebrated her sixth birthday on Saturday, which may have been why she sounded especially annoying to Timothy. "My name is Cindy, and I'm not little, I'm six years old now." She turned to Timothy and smiled. "Hi Timothy."

Timothy responded with a flat tone, devoid of enthusiasm. "Hi." He had no desire to engage in a long, probably meaningless conversation with Cindy right now. He made a note to himself that he would not say another word to her tonight, although he knew this would probably be impossible. Maybe he would tell her to "shut up" a couple of times. That would require only a few more words. Yeah, he could do that.

The two moms exchanged more useless bits of information about the day and school and the PTA and Cindy's ballet lessons and who knows what else. When they had finally finished, Martha walked to the car and drove away. The Petersons finished dressing—they looked like they were going some place really fancy—and were heading out the front door when Mrs. Peterson gave Timothy the familiar instructions.

"Timothy, here's a phone number where we can be reached. And there are some cookies on the kitchen counter and a bottle of fresh milk in the refrigerator. We should be back by eleven. I expect Cynthia will be ready for bed by nine. You have a good evening and we'll see you a little later."

Timothy waved a feeble goodbye to the Petersons, and a pervasive cloud of gloom settled in around him. Everyone had left the home and he and Cynthia—no, Cindy—were now stuck with each other for the rest of the night. Not that her name mattered all that much. He didn't really care what she wanted him to call her. He wasn't going to talk to her anyway. He shambled into the living room and plopped heavily onto the couch. The gloom followed him and hung thickly over the couch, seeping into the cushions. Cindy chattered incoherently in her bedroom, rooting around for who knew what and who cared anyway. She skipped into the living room a few minutes later with a wide, obsequious smile stretched across her tiny face. How could anyone be so happy? It just wasn't natural to be that happy.

"Timothy, I brought some books for you to read to me." She jumped up on the couch and sat next to him. He scooted away from her. "I brought *The King's Stilts* and *The 500 Hats of Bartholomew Cubbins*."

Timothy remembered his promise to not say a word to her, but he couldn't pass up the wonderful opportunity that now presented itself. "I think both of those books are really stupid. Whoever heard of a guy wearing 500 hats at the same time? That's impossible."

Undaunted, Cindy quickly pushed back. "They're not stupid. I like these books. Please read them?" Cindy smiled and locked her elbows flat as she held the books out for Timothy to take.

Timothy's hands remained motionless until he thought of a way to get out of this tiresome chore. "I read them to you the last time I was here."

Cindy held the books up a little higher. "I know, but I like these books. Please read them again, Timothy."

After thinking about how much fun he could have telling her to shut-up and go away, Timothy decided it might be easier to read the stupid books than to keep arguing about it. He also found it impossible to continue resisting her request when she had asked him so damn politely. He gave in and read the books to her—again. He really didn't mind the stories. They were actually pretty clever. Because he didn't want Cindy to know this, he occasionally read with a little edge of sarcasm in his voice to remind her that he didn't really want to do this. He tried to skip a few lines on the fourth page of one of the books, but she caught him and made him read the lines anyway. When he had finished the last sentence of *The 500 Hats of Bartholomew Cubbins*, Timothy felt he had done his duty and went into the kitchen to check out the cookies. He found a blue ceramic plate loaded with chocolate chip cookies—his favorite. And they tasted wonderful with a big glass of the fresh milk. He devoured three of the cookies before Cindy found him again. He gave her a couple of the cookies and suggested she eat them someplace else. She insisted on staying in the kitchen with him. He poured her a glass of milk too.

"Timothy, do you know how to do the waltz?"

"How to do the what?" Timothy stammered through a half-swallowed cookie. This did not sound good.

"How to do the waltz. It's a dance." Cindy clasped her little hands behind her back and pushed up on her little toes. Then she giggled.

A dance? And what does that have to do with anything. Can't a fellow just relax here in the kitchen; by himself; alone; eating chocolate chip cookies and drinking milk? And why did he have to be her favorite babysitter, anyway? What heinous blunders had the other babysitters committed to have ended up lower than him on the Peterson babysitter list? And even if the other babysitters did screw up—what of it? They probably actually liked the job. "No, I don't dance."

Cindy giggled again. "Then come into the living room and I'll show you."

This request slammed Timothy into silence. All of a sudden, reading the Dr. Seuss books didn't sound too bad. "Maybe we should read some more books instead?"

Cindy crossed her arms and began tapping her left foot. She had seen her mom do this more than once and could mimic the technique flawlessly. "Timothy..." then she paused for theatric effect, "...I think it's time to do the waltz!"

Timothy could not think of any way to get out of this, and meekly agreed. Cindy skipped into the living room and then veered over to the record player next to the bookshelf by the picture window. She thumbed through a small pile of records. After thoughtfully studying each title, she picked one out. She carefully removed the shiny black disk from its dust jacket, just like her dad had shown her, and placed it on the fat, cylindrical spindle where two retractable plastic prongs held it in place until ready to drop onto the turntable and start spinning under the sharp stylus.

Timothy watched this elaborate process, and realized that Cindy might have just enough knowledge to get the record player to work—and that he might have to dance if she did. "Are you sure you're supposed to be messing with your dad's record player? I don't want to get fired just because you scratched one of his records or broke something." On the

Toil Under The Sun

other hand, maybe scratching the record would not be such a bad idea. If she did, maybe he would never be allowed inside the Peterson home again and this stupid job would be finished for good. Maybe he should have kept his mouth shut.

"It's OK, Timothy. My dad showed me how to do it and put a mark on the records I can play." She twisted a red knob on the side of the record player and the turntable started whirring, slowly at first, then with increasing velocity. "Let's practice first. I'll start the music when we're ready.

Refusing to accept that he might actually have to dance, Timothy stalled. "Who…who taught you how to dance…anyway?"

"My mom's teaching me. She says I'm a natural dancer. The waltz is easy, once you get the hang of it." She walked across the room and grabbed Timothy's sagging hands. "All you've got to remember is one-two-three-one-two-three-one-two-three over and over again. That's all there is to it." She demonstrated the step pattern for him, but his feet did not move. "Timothy, you've got to move. You'll never dance the waltz if you just stand there!" Grudgingly, he attempted to follow the step pattern. His natural clumsiness, and lack of interest, made it more difficult than she had said it would be. "No Timothy! You've got to do the opposite of me." Cindy persisted even though he nearly stepped on her tiny foot several times, and began shouting encouragements at him whenever he made a mistake. After five minutes of this ordeal, he surprised himself when he reproduced the step pattern correctly three times in a row. Cindy stopped and put her hands on her hips. "See, Timothy. It's easy to do the waltz, once you get the hang of it. Let's start the music now." She skipped over to the record player and slid a knurled switch. The record dropped onto the turntable and the arm moved smoothly across before setting gently on the fragile surface. The first sounds were a rhythmic hissing followed by a brief crackle, and then the music began. Cindy ran back across the room and grabbed Timothy's hands again. "Don't start yet. We have to wait for the one-two-three-one-two-three part."

Timothy had never heard this music before. As he listened to each passing measure and line, he became more and more fascinated. He soon had to admit to himself that he really did like it. He risked exposing his interest by asking Cindy a question. "What's the name of this song?"

"It's called Sleeping Beauty Waltz. It's by Chewcoughski. My dad says he's a great composer, but he died." Cindy glanced back to the record player. "Just a little longer and the one-two-three part will start. It's getting close. Closer. It's almost here. Start!" The waltz began, and Timothy liked this part even better than the beginning. Cynthia suddenly yanked at his hands, forcing them to waltz along the front of the sofa. They almost knocked over a lamp when Timothy tripped on the electrical cord. They swung across the living room and nearly collided with the coffee table by the picture window. Timothy struggled to compensate for his awkwardness, but he liked the music so much that he started to get the feel of it. They waltzed back and forth across the living room, and even made it into the dining room at one point, knocking against the chairs when they wound their way around the dining room table and back out again. After the music stopped, Cynthia skipped over to the record player and started it up again. They played the record five more times before they both dropped onto the couch in mock exhaustion.

Cynthia loved dancing the waltz with someone other than her mom, especially with Timothy, her favorite babysitter. "Wow Timothy. You're a good dancer."

Timothy nearly responded positively, but then cautioned himself that he didn't want to do this job again. Unfortunately for his future Friday nights, he couldn't work himself up to a sufficient level of harshness. "No I'm not. I told you I really don't dance. The music was alright, I guess. What did you call it again?"

"The Sleeping Beauty Waltz. It's my favorite music. Well, I think you're a good dancer, even if you don't."

Cynthia stretched out her slender six-year-old arms and yawned. Bedtime was still a half-hour away, even though a long day of activities and dancing had worn her out. They read one more book, played hide-and-go-seek for a few minutes, and then Timothy put her to bed. She fell into a deep sleep in five minutes. Timothy waited by the door and listened to her fall asleep before walking quietly into the living room. He removed the record from its jacket, put it back on the fat spindle, started the record player up again, and listened to the music while sitting quietly on the couch. He leaned back against the softness of the couch and closed his eyes, and imagined himself drifting among the clouds. He listened to the beautiful music three more times, enjoying it more with each listening, then carefully returned the record to its paper sleeve and filed it with the other records. Although he would never admit it to anyone, he had really enjoyed the evening, even the dancing. He had nearly finished the last of the cookies and another glass of milk by the time the Petersons returned home.

♦ ♦ ♦

A city square in Inchon, September 1950

A young Korean, her youthful face awash in panic, pulled her son along a narrow road bordering a city square in Inchon. The road led to a row of five houses lined up neatly along a low ridge that formed a steep wall at the northern boundary of the square. The early afternoon sun, modestly high in the autumn sky and nearly blocked by gathering clouds, cast erratic shadows on the cobblestones that formed the coarse surface of the road. The woman, her eyes fixed only on the first of the five houses, did not look at the square as she advanced up the road. Once crowded with people sitting on benches and students reading beneath trees and old men talking in small groups and mothers watching children play, only the same erratic shadows that marked her path filled the square now, providing welcome cover to an occasional passerby.

The woman stepped over a jagged crater and a gentle rain began. She held her hand above her head and then asked her son the same question she had asked him three times before. "Are you sure you saw your sister leave the house before the bomb hit?"

The boy, only nine a month earlier, struggled to remember when he had seen his sister in relation to the explosion. He knew what his mother wanted to hear. "I think I saw her leave before the bomb."

The mother stopped and turned. She pulled her son's hand close to her breast and squeezed. "Do you think you saw her, or are you sure you saw her?"

The boy felt panic through his mother's hand and heard fear in her voice; he could not say what he did not know. "I'm, I'm pretty sure I saw her."

This answer did not give the woman the relief she sought. Without speaking, she turned and quickened her pace up the narrow road, forcing her son to keep up by jogging. When she neared the house, she saw that the bomb had blown several oddly shaped chunks of roof onto the road, blocking her path. The nearest wall and part of the second floor had collapsed too, providing a grotesque sectional view of the house. The woman walked closer and reached out to touch a shattered remnant of the collapsed wall. At that moment she noticed that a second floor closet had been sheared in half, scattering dresses and shoes and hats across the floor below. She stepped over the collapsed wall, chafing her knee on a sharp stone. She bent down to pick up a charred shoe; her hand touched her daughter's favorite doll instead, its silky hair partially burned and its pink face blackened with smoke. She picked up the doll and held it for a moment as if—but then her knees lost all strength to hold the weight of her sadness and she slumped to the ground.

Her son tried to console her by repeating his earlier answer. "Don't be sad mom. I think I saw her get out of the house before the bomb."

The mother turned her face slowly before speaking in a whispered voice. "Why did you not take her with you?"

"I was frightened when the bombs started and just ran."

The woman pressed the doll against her cheek and looked down to conceal her sorrow. "You should not have left the house without your sister."

The percussive clatter of sporadic rifle and machine gun fire echoed off stone walls and tile roofs and cobble streets a few blocks away, cascading down alleys and roadways until arriving at the city square sounding like muddled fireworks. Occasionally the sharp rumble of a Pershing tank's 90 mm gun joined the clatter, resonating violently around the square before dying below the clatter's normal din. A South Korean mother and her child walked swiftly across the square and then up a narrow road toward a row of damaged houses. They did not appear to notice the widespread damage or rifle fire or the ground-shaking rumble of the heavy tanks. They walked a little faster and covered their heads when a gentle rain began washing the dust covered square and wetting the tile roofs and muting the sounds of the rifles. Another sharp crack rumbled beyond the edge of town and the shallow harbor and mud flats: this time only the sound of thunder.

Lieutenant Meyer decided to give his platoon a rest near the edge of the square, opposite the narrow road and shattered house. His men had fought hard since the landings yesterday, with very little sleep, and needed a break. He gave instructions to Gunny Talbot who promptly ordered the Marines to spread out and take a short rest. He also told them not to get too relaxed because they would be getting back to the house-to-house fighting in a few minutes and he didn't want to have to kick any of their asses to wake them up. They all knew he would do it too.

Meyer had studied mechanical engineering at Iowa State. After graduation he looked around for a job for a few months. After failing to find relevant employment he decided to enlist in the Marine Corps. This impetuous decision had appalled his mother and father, but by the time he told them about it he had already enlisted and refused to change his mind. Unfortunately, at least from his parents' now grim perspective, he always followed through once he made a decision. There was that one time in the fourth grade when he had agreed to sing in the school play. When the curtain opened he stood in petrified silence in front of an audience of baffled parents. Other than this isolated event, he always did what he said he would do. He couldn't exactly explain to his parents why he had enlisted; he did know in part that he yearned for a true test of his courage, and this seemed to him the very best way to find that test. Although his parents had not realized it, Meyer had also grown increasingly weary of his boring, straight-arrow life, barren of exciting or unusual events, bereft of any genuine personal challenges. Recently (within the last few months), he had also felt a desperate urge to get out of Iowa. Not that Iowa was a bad place—if you liked farming and humidity. He just wanted to explore other parts of the country, and maybe even other lands too. Of course then the war started in Korea, and everything changed in an instant.

There weren't a lot of good places to rest at the edge of the square. After searching around for a minute, Humphrey found a level shred of ground to sit on next to a partially knocked-down wall and then figured out how to lean against the wall comfortably enough to doze a little. The amphibious landing had turned out less dangerous than he had thought—Timothy had been right. The Navy really did blast the crap out of Wolmi-do, and with the Corsairs shooting up the ground in front of the advancing Marines there hadn't been much resistance. In fact, not a single Marine had died on the island. There were a few injuries, but nothing really serious. Traversing the causeway leading to the mainland had made him a little nervous; otherwise it hadn't been much of a challenge—quite a difference from the intense combat down by Pusan. And so far the house-to-house fighting in the city had remained tolerable, with tanks leading the way most of the time and blowing up anything that didn't surrender. Maybe things would turn out all right from now on. At least he could hope so.

"Hey Humphrey, mind if I lean against that wall too? It looks like a pretty good spot." Timothy's exuberance certified that it had started raining again.

"Fine with me. I think there's enough room for both of us."

"Thanks. You know, it seems like there's always enough room for both of us." Timothy leaned his M-1 against the wall and slipped his pack off, letting it fall to the ground with a soggy smack.

Humphrey lifted the edge of his helmet and turned his head slightly. "How come you're always so cheerful when it rains?"

"I don't know. I can't really explain it." Timothy lowered himself to the ground and leaned against the wall, tipping the brim of his helmet down against the top of his nose. He could hear the rain inside his helmet, and he liked the sound. He felt momentarily safe with the sound resonating all around his head. "You know Humphrey, I've always liked the rain, even when I was a kid. I don't remember why. It's just the way I am. Why, don't you like the rain?"

A thin stream of cold water poured off the rear of Humphrey's helmet and drooled down his neck. He shivered convulsively before reflexively scrunching his head back. "No, not really. I don't mind the rain when I'm indoors, but it's not my idea of a good time when I'm outside. I guess it's good that at least one of us is happy about it."

Timothy sat up a little bit and lifted his helmet. "You're not happy? Shoot, you're not dead are you? That fact alone should make anyone in this platoon happy."

Humphrey closed his eyes again. "I guess you could look at it that way."

"You're damn right you could look at it that way. What other way is there to look at it?" Timothy, suddenly playing the unusual role of the optimist in counterpoint to Humphrey's momentary pessimism, doubted he could adequately carry on the conversation with this unusual shift in position. He stopped talking and tried to rest a little before the Gunny ordered them all to get moving again. He drifted for almost three minutes before he became aware of a faintly murmured sound. He opened his eyes and lifted the brim of his helmet, turning his head to the side to hear a little better. The sound wafted over the top of the stone wall they were leaning against. Timothy stood up and turned fully toward the sound. He couldn't quite identify it, but knew it could not be far away. A machine gun chattered a few blocks away and obscured the sound; when the echoes faded he could hear it again.

"Humphrey, do you hear something?" Humphrey did not answer or move. Timothy nudged him sharply with the toe of his boot. "Humphrey, do you hear that funny sound on the other side of the wall?"

Humphrey coughed and sat up. "Hear what? I don't hear anything."

"Well then, stand up so you can hear it. What do you think that is?"

Annoyed, but also curious, Humphrey stood up facing the wall and listened. "Yeah, I do hear something. It sounds like…it sounds like…like someone's crying."

Timothy picked up his rifle. "Sounds like crying, huh. Sounds like it could be some sort of enemy trick to me. Let's go check it out."

This suggestion alarmed Humphrey. "Shouldn't we tell the Gunny? I don't think we should go wandering off without permission."

"Relax, Humphrey. It'll be fine. Get your rifle and let's go find out what's going on behind this wall. Maybe we'll even get a medal or something."

"Yeah—or something." Humphrey picked up his M-1, slung it over his shoulder, and followed Timothy around the jagged edge of the wall. Both of them crouched down low just in case the North Koreans were waiting for them.

The wall separated the open city square from a small residential courtyard. Some rubble from the wall had fallen along the edge of the courtyard; otherwise it looked surprisingly clean. The sound, still very soft, grew louder and more intense when they stepped over the rubble.

The sound flowed around the corner of a single story house that formed the opposite side of the courtyard. They listened more closely, and it did sound like crying. No, more than that, it sounded like a small child crying. Timothy and Humphrey stepped slowly and warily across the courtyard toward the sound. They communicated with hand signals after they reached the side of the house. Humphrey stayed back a little, his M-1 now unslung and ready to fire. After pausing to set his feet, Timothy leaped beyond the corner and instantly aimed his rifle at the mysterious sound. Humphrey watched in confusion when Timothy stared down at the ground for a long time, then lowered the aim of his rifle before crouching and sitting comfortably on the back of his boots. He signaled Humphrey to come over with a casual flick of his hand.

"What is it?"

"Come and look for yourself."

With the brim of his helmet scraping along a wood siding board, Humphrey slowly moved his eye past the corner or the house. Instead of a North Korean trap, he saw a little girl, probably six or seven, sitting against the base of the wall of the house, sobbing. She rubbed a tear from her dirt-smudged face with a grimy hand. She looked straight at Timothy, then at Humphrey, then back at Timothy. Timothy smiled and rolled onto his knees to move a little closer to the little girl. She dug her heels into the ground and pressed her shoulders into the wall.

Timothy thought he should say something in Korean to calm her down. He scrolled through his mental list of words and phrases and realized that he could only remember swear words and insults. "Do you remember how to say hello, I'm a friend in Korean?"

"Well, I haven't exactly had a lot of opportunities to socialize with the locals to practice my Korean. No, I don't remember how to say that. As a matter of fact, I don't remember how to say anything at all."

"Then do you have any candy? Mine's all gone."

"Yeah. I think I've got some chocolate left." Humphrey rummaged through his jacket pockets until he found a few disks of chocolate. He set them on Timothy's upturned hand.

Timothy unwrapped one of the pieces of chocolate and took a small bite before offering the rest to the little girl. She hesitated at first; and preparing to dig her heels into the ground again, could not resist her hunger any longer. Apprehensively, she reached out and grabbed the chocolate and stuffed it into her tiny mouth, barely chewing it before swallowing. Timothy unwrapped a second disc and gave it to her. This time the little girl stood up and accepted the candy without hesitation. With the chocolate melting in her hand, she rushed at Timothy and hugged him around the neck, almost knocking him over. Timothy did not have time to think and reacted spontaneously; he hugged the little girl back and stood up with her. She squeezed him tightly around the neck and began sobbing against his jacket, already damp from the rain. Timothy instinctively patted the little girl on her head. He closed his eyes and stood there quietly for several minutes. Her heartbeat pulsed metrically through his jacket; and then he heard that music, the music he had loved years before and had not heard again since that last night he baby-sat for Cynthia. Now; astonishingly; here; in this place; the music began playing again, perfectly in his head, every note and chord and nuance, as if the strings and winds and brass and percussion now performed just beyond the wall at the edge of the city square where his platoon rested in the ruble. Then the dance part started.

At that moment, when the dance part commenced and he forgot about Humphrey and Korea and his platoon and everything else, he began moving with the music, slowly at first, but then with increasing speed: one-two-three-one-two-three-one-two-three, over and over again. He moved smoothly across the courtyard, along the wall, and then back to the house before starting over again. The little girl, surprised at first, smiled when Timothy whirled in smooth waltz circles. She began laughing by the time Timothy made a third tour of the small courtyard, lifting his feet higher with each rotation and splashing wildly in several deep puddles that had expanded with the increasing rain. Then Timothy heard applause. He didn't remember any applause at the end of the music before: it just ended with the rhythmic scritch…scritch…scritch of the stylus. The applause grew louder as more hands joined in, and finally it grew so loud that he could no longer hear the music in his head and he stopped dancing. Timothy turned around. He was astonished at first, and then horrified, to see most of his platoon looking around the end of the wall and leaning over the top of it and standing along the edge of the courtyard—applauding. Thankfully, he immediately understood that they were not mocking him: they were simply applauding. He set the little girl down. She tried to hang on to his collar; he had to pry her little fingers loose before standing up again.

Gunny Talbot stood near Timothy, just a few yards away. He was not applauding; he did not appear angry either. "The party's over, private. Time to saddle-up."

Timothy felt the little girl reach up and grab his hand. "What about the little girl? What's going to happen to her?"

Gunny Talbot had seen this before and he already knew the answer to this question. "I don't know, but there's nothing we can do about it. We've got other business to attend to."

Timothy resisted the idea of leaving her alone. "Do you think her parents are around? Maybe I could take a few minutes and try to find them."

Although sympathetic, Gunny Talbot did not have time for this conversation. He had to get the platoon moving before something bad happened. "Her parents are either dead or she's been abandoned. There's nothing we can do about it. She'll have to stay here and wait for help from someone else. Now let's get going before the enemy realizes that we're just standing around like a bunch of dopes."

"Can I give her some food?"

"Suit yourself, but make it fast. OK gentlemen—time to move out. The dancing lesson is over."

Timothy tightened his fingers around the little girl's miniature hand, smudged with dirt and melted chocolate, led her to the edge of the wall, and lifted her up on top. He pulled a can of fruit from his pack, opened it, and gave it to he. He had been saving his last can of fruit for desert, but he figured she needed it more than he did. She smiled up at him and began eating with her fingers. Humphrey and several other Marines set a few assorted C-rations by her side, not thinking about how she would open them, and then walked away from the courtyard. The platoon moved out efficiently. When it had reached the center of the open square, Timothy stepped out of line to check on the little girl one more time. He turned and looked. There on top of the jagged wall, eating a can of fruit with his fingers, sat a little Caucasian boy dressed in his best Sunday clothes. The little boy looked up for a moment, smiled, and then waved. Timothy blinked hard to clear his eyes, and the little girl sat there again with her dirt smudged face and can of fruit. She smiled at Timothy and then waved with her little hand. He turned and broke into a jog to catch up with the other Marines. He stepped into the line and did not look back again.

Chapter 11

A small boat harbor in Northwest Oregon, May 1946

An intensely new sense of freedom seared his thoughts—in a way he had never known before. Junior high would be over in less than a month, and with its completion the unique freedoms of a new summer would commence with natural expectations of glorious weather and limited responsibilities. This new sense of freedom emerged differently from a perception uniquely implied by finally arriving at the threshold of high school; and though his perception of high school would prove false soon enough, he could at least use it for comparative purposes in the present. No, this new kind of freedom burned unlike the untroubled freedoms of summer, and he liked the way it made him feel. He liked it so much that he did not appreciate the potential consequences of the new freedom, especially the regrettably enduring consequences that could linger for a lifetime. He did not consider any consequences at all. He simply enjoyed how he felt at that moment.

The boat harbor could be quite agreeable in early May, especially when evening still glowed with leftover warmth from the retreating sun. The air would cool with the approaching darkness in a short while. For now, dusky light muted the colors of the water and docks and boats and added pleasantness to the ending day. With dusk also came a heightened sense of hearing. Sounds that had dissipated in the heat and toil of the afternoon were somehow amplified by the diminishing light until they became an essential part of the day's final moments. Birds called to each other a last few times high up in the gently swaying spruce trees across the road. The chirping sounds darted over the road and around the docks like the birds themselves in unseen flight. Waves from a distant trawler, darkened by reflections of a fading sky, gently surged against the sides of moored boats and dock pilings. With the rolling water came an incessant creaking of dock planks, of metal rings and straps against eroded wood, of barnacled wood against smooth wood, and of salt-crusted lines against metal cleats rubbed smooth by years of use.

Three boys peddled furiously along a gravel road bordering the slender fingers of the docks, and, with cool air sizzling noisily over whirring spokes, talked in panting breaths about the end of junior high and the beginning of summer and the things they planned to do. They talked also of high school in words that hinted of a deep longing for the respect and freedom that must certainly come with that institution. One of the boys had never stayed out this late, and spoke of a new sense of freedom he felt at that moment. The other two boys, for whom this unsupervised activity had become commonplace, even boringly expected by their indifferent parents, felt no special sense of freedom at all. They were both surprised and amused that anyone could feel freedom by merely staying out late: they did it all the time and never felt anything in particular. The lead boy stopped his bike abruptly with a violent reversal of pedals; his skidding rear tire scattered gravel in a long arc. The other boys pulled up next to him with less spectacular stops. The last rim of sun rested on the distantly cambered skyline as they rearranged the bikes for easier conversation.

"You've never stayed out this late? Are you sure you won't get in trouble with your mommy?" Raymond, a large boy with coal-black hair and pudgy cheeks, made his best effort to sneer, but his inquiry came across only as a stupid question. Raymond's father worked as a construction laborer, when he could find work—and when not out drinking or shooting pool with his dubious friends. His mom had stayed with the family until his seventh birthday. She left home early one Friday morning after his drunken father had beat her for the last time. She never returned or made any attempt to contact Raymond after that. He had one haunting memory of her departure: he heard the sound of sobbing before the door creaked and quietly latched.

"No, I never have, but I'm sure it's OK. My parents pretty much let me do whatever I like. I can stay out late as I want to."

Raymond got about halfway through the first word of his sentence before the other boy cut him off. "Yeah, that's the same for me. My dad's only rule is that I don't get into trouble, and I figure that I didn't get into trouble if I don't get caught." Wesley looked the opposite of Raymond: sinewy, lean, with sandy blond hair and sharp features. His small size belied a fierce and combative temperament; and although Raymond outweighed him by at least 40 pounds, Wes functioned as the unquestioned leader of the duet, and also the insidious instigator of most of their ultimately shared trouble. "So where do you live?"

"Just up the road a couple of miles. But I come down here a lot."

Wes eyed the new boy suspiciously. He didn't remember seeing him down by the docks before, especially at night. He studied him through mocking eyes before responding. "That's funny. I don't think I've ever seen you down here before. When's the last time you were here?"

The new boy paused to think before answering with noticeable caution. "Well, I usually come down during the day," then he added after a self-conscious hesitation, "—sometimes after skipping school." To bolster his story, he finished with, "This is actually only my first time down here at night."

This sounded plausible to Wes; he relaxed a little. "Yeah, Raymond and I like to skip school too. As far as I'm concerned, school's mostly a bunch of useless crap. I'll tell you what—I'd burn that building down if I thought I could get away with it."

Both Raymond and Wes laughed while the new boy, not knowing what else to do, nodded approvingly. Burning down the school didn't exactly sound funny. Maybe he had missed something only Wes and Raymond understood. Then he wondered for a moment how Wes would go about burning down the school. Although he did not really want to know the answer to this question, he couldn't think of anything else to say to continue the conversation, and he thought he should say something. "Uh…gee…how would you burn down the school? Wouldn't that be dangerous?" The moment the question spilled out of his mouth he regretted having asked it. Wes's assertion that he would burn down the school if he could get away with it had actually shocked him. At the same time, he felt a morbid fascination rising up from an inexplicable dark place in his mind.

Wes leaned back on his bicycle seat and crossed his arms. "Oh, I'd probably never really do it, but then again, if things were right, I think I might." He raised his arms and sucked in a slow, rattling breath for theatric effect. Raymond moved his bike a little closer so he could hear better. "It'd be easy. First I'd get a…." and Wes, not appearing to notice whether the other two boys were actually listening, began a laborious soliloquy outlining his detailed plan to burn down the school. When he finished, almost ten minutes later, Raymond had leaned forward until his bike almost slipped out from under him. He quickly stuck his leg out to prevent an embarrassing fall. The new boy, shocked and fascinated at the same time while listening intently all the way to the end of the morbid plan, sat straight up on his bike. He was still not quite sure if he should have asked the question in the first place. However, he had asked it, and he got an unexpected answer complete with premeditated details.

The sky continued to darken. The three boys leaned their bikes up against a stubby wooden railing and walked down a steep ramp toward the docks. Several streetlights up on the road ignited, projecting a gentle glow down to the harbor that painted soft-edged shadows on the curved sides of darkened boats. Men worked on several of the fishing boats beneath work lights that blazed across the boat sterns and far out to the black waters beyond the rocky breakwater rimming the harbor. As the men worked under the yellow lights, they chatted about broken gear and the weather and the likelihood of catching a lot of fish the next day. One of the men whistled the *Liberty Bell* march over and over again while he mended a torn net. No one knew if he could whistle any other marches because he only whistled the *Liberty Bell*. No—that's not true; once he got halfway through *Three Blind Mice* before he transposed back into the *Liberty Bell*.

"What do you guys do down here on the docks?" Possibly a stupid question, but his query about burning down the school had gone well enough, and the new boy couldn't think of anything else to ask.

"What do we do down here on the docks?" Wes paused before asking Raymond to answer the question for him. He often used this cunning technique to exert subtle control over the larger boy. He also often repeated the same question a second time before asking Raymond to answer it. He did this to add drama to his display of leadership. "What do we do down here on the docks? Why, Raymond, why don't you tell him what we do down here on the docks?"

Raymond felt instantly puffed with vanity—like he always did when Wes asked him to answer a question. He coughed twice to clean a film of mucous out of his windpipe, then swallowed heavily. He wanted to answer Wes's question as clearly and intelligently as possible. "We check out the boats."

This didn't mean anything to the new boy; he gambled that he could ask another question. "You check out the boats? How do you do that?"

Toil Under The Sun

Wes responded, "Go ahead, Raymond. Explain it to him."

Raymond's vanity beamed even louder. "You know. We check out the boats when there's no one around. We climb onto the boats to see if there's something that isn't exactly tied down."

"You mean…you steal stuff?"

Increasingly annoyed with the new boy's pathetic naiveté, Wes broke in and finished Raymond's explanation. "I wouldn't exactly call it that. If it's not attached to anything, then someone must not figure it's worth keeping. That being the case, we borrow it."

"Do you put it back when you're done with it?"

Wes snapped, "Why would we do that?" Although he didn't say it out loud, Wes thought this question verged on downright stupidity. He rolled his eyes before continuing, a furtive signal to Raymond that he should also act exasperated. "When we're done with whatever it is we borrow, we dump it somewhere."

"Like where?"

Wes now concluded that this kid didn't know a damn thing about anything. How could anyone be so dumb? He must have been born under a rock, or something worse. "Like in the forest. Or maybe off the bridge into the river. Or someplace like that. Isn't that right Raymond?" Wes maintained a polished edge of sarcasm in his voice.

After thinking about this question too long, Raymond figured out that Wes expected him to agree. "Uh, yeah, that's right. Out in the forest, or someplace like that."

Wes had already grown bored with this meaningless conversation—meaningless from his perspective of what made sense in the world—before Raymond's words of agreement stumbled out. "Well maybe we should stop flapping our lips and start checking out some boats. What'ya think Raymond? Should we start checking out some boats, or just go home early tonight?"

Raymond knew from experience that when Wes offered him two choices, he should never pick the second one. He answered more quickly this time. "Yeah, we should start checking out some boats."

Wes turned casually to the new boy. "You coming too, or are you going to go home to your mommy?" Wes clearly intended this question, dripping with derision, as a test.

The new boy knew instinctively that he should not go with Wes and Raymond; at the same time, he knew that he would. He answered without pausing to avoid embarrassment. "Yeah, I'm coming. I'm not afraid of checking out some boats."

"Good. Then let's get going. We'll leave the bikes at the top of the ramp. We might need to leave in a hurry later." Wes turned abruptly and trotted toward the nearest float, with Raymond and the new boy following a few steps behind.

Midnight would arrive in less than 20 minutes, and with the new day's approach John's lower back twitched more and more from both exhaustion and anger. After a long and unsettled argument with Martha nearly two hours ago, he had driven around town in an exasperatingly unsuccessful search for Timothy. Because he had no particular idea of where to look, he had resorted to random turns and distances. At first he had stopped occasionally, stepping out of the car to yell Timothy's name through cupped hands while he walked back and forth. When nothing came of this except looking like a damn fool, he stopped yelling and just looked. The cold air had rasped his throat raw anyway. He drove up and down the main street of the town four or five times, watching all of the store lights go off, without spotting Timothy. He even stopped to ask a few acquaintances if they had seen him, although he found this deeply embarrassing. No one had seen Timothy, but they all promised to keep an eye out for him. They must have wondered what kind of father could lose his son in the middle of the night. He also noted cynically that he must have finally reached a point of serious desperation to accept such personal humiliation this effortlessly.

John drove north through the center of town again before turning west at the hardware store, toward the road that ran along the ocean. He reached the coast road in a few minutes and turned right. He hadn't checked out the harbor yet, although he thought it unlikely that Timothy would be there. There was nothing to do there at this time of night and it would be dark and cold near the water. But Timothy hadn't shown up anywhere else, and John didn't want to go home where he would have to finish his argument with Martha and then endure her wrath for failing to find their son. A drive to the harbor seemed like a sensible thing to do. John rolled down the window to get a little fresh air. The air chilled his face so he turned up the heater to warm his legs at the same time. He could see the top rigging of several fishing boats just ahead in the glare of the car's headlights. He turned off at a driveway to the gravel service road and rolled down to the edge of the harbor. He could see work lights reflecting off the deck of one of the fishing boats. They must be getting ready to go out early in the morning.

The three boys were groping around the cluttered stern deck of a fishing boat at the far end of the float when Wes spotted the headlights. He only glimpsed the car for a fraction of a second, but thought he saw a police insignia. He attempted to conceal his panic by slowing down his words. "We have to get out of here. Drop your stuff. We can't take it with us." Raymond flinched and tossed a gaff hook over the gunwale into the dark water. It made a pleasant "floowsh" sound when it sliced in. The new boy set a fillet knife down on the deck next to a partially open hatch. They both followed Wes as he hurdled over a low railing onto the damp dock and began running toward the bikes. They had almost reached the end of the dock when they collided with John.

John heard the rapid approach of pounding footsteps. Surprised by the violence of the collision, he still grabbed two of the boys by furiously clutching their jacket sleeves. The third boy darted around him and escaped up to the gravel road before hopping on a bike and disappearing into the darkness. John tightened his grip on his catch, pulling the two boys a little closer to look into their faces in the dim glow of a distant streetlight.

Raymond shook with terror. His legs shivered and he spoke in a broken voice. "Puh, puh, puhlease don't hurt me mister! I wa, wasn't, da, doing nothing!"

It took Timothy only a momentary glimpse to recognize his father, and even less time to feel intense shame and anger filling his stomach and then forcing its way up his throat. He felt shame because John had come to look for him. He felt anger because of the embarrassment this would surely bring with his new friends. And then he felt something different that he couldn't quite identify: something worse than the shame and anger put together.

◆ ◆ ◆

Wŏnsan, October 1950

After the stunningly successful amphibious landings at Inchon, and the subsequent recapture of the South Korean capital of Seoul, the 1ˢᵗ Marine Division returned to Inchon; not to rest or go home, but to begin loading troopships for another long voyage at sea. Carrying over 30,000 passengers, the ships departed from Inchon on October 15, 1950; and steaming around the far southern tip of the Korean Peninsula then north again, a journey of 830 sea miles, arrived five days later at the east coast port of Wŏnsan, 110 miles north of the 38ᵗʰ parallel. Unfortunately, the ships could not immediately land because the Marines were forced to wait for a channel to be cleared through thousands of Soviet magnetic and contact mines, a small detail that had been overlooked during planning of the operation. To allow time for completion of this dangerous work, the ships were ordered to sail north before returning to the harbor, a maneuver that consumed five days and was dubbed "Operation Yo-Yo" by the skeptical Marines. Before finally landing on October 25ᵗʰ, the Marines learned they had been beaten to Wŏnsan by air maintenance crews and the Republic of Korea Capital and 3ʳᵈ Divisions. But more profoundly crushing than this was the news that they had also missed comedian Bob Hope and actress Marilyn Maxwell in a USO show staged in Wŏnsan only a day before.

Gunnery Sergeant John Talbot had the unusual distinction of being the first born of a large family. His parents, although very young when he came into the world, were also unquestionably devoted to each other. Two sisters, a brother, another sister, and finally a second brother followed him, each less than 15 months apart. He was almost eight years old when his parents decided to end any further propagation; his parents conceived his last brother soon after. His dad lost his job ten months later, and the family moved to Southern California in search of other opportunities just before his newest brother's first birthday. After exploring several different communities, John's father decided that the family should settle in San Diego, in an old neighborhood a few miles from the ocean.

John did not grow as tall as his parents expected, nor did he demonstrate unusual muscularity. He therefore struggled to understand why they so often gave him responsible charge of one or more of his siblings when several of them already outweighed him. When he reached twelve years his parents suddenly expected him to baby-sit all of the siblings at the same time. This irksome responsibility became more and more onerous by the time he reached his middle teens because by then nearly all of the siblings, including his two oldest sisters, outweighed him. Thankfully, John had somehow learned—or more likely received at birth—the mettle of authentic leadership, and his size didn't really seem to matter most of the time. Of course, his natural feistiness, clearly a gift received from his mother at birth, also proved useful whenever a sibling rebellion loomed. With practice, he became skilled at moderating such rebellions, a skill reinforced by his proven willingness to squash any resistance to his leadership with immediate and overwhelming force.

Although John Talbot had reached the respectable height of 5 foot 7 inches and a sufficient weight of one hundred and fifty-two pounds after his final growth spurt, he had grown tired of being thought of as small and weak by everyone, including himself. He had also had enough of taking care of his brothers and sisters, so at the age of 19 he enlisted in the Marine Corps. The year was 1939, and he had achieved the rank of corporal when the Japanese bombed Pearl Harbor. His first opportunity to prove himself occurred a few weeks after the primitive amphibious landings at Guadalcanal. An errant chunk of shrapnel sliced his left thigh during his first real combat, an injury that would give him his first Purple Heart. He continued fighting through the night and into the next morning before a corpsman stopped him and forced him to sit still while he dressed the wound. Sergeant Talbot finished the war on Okinawa, where he received a second Purple Heart. Now he had landed in Korea and, as far as he was concerned, it felt a little too much like baby-sitting his brothers and sisters all over again.

Gunny Talbot felt the year's first pungent chill on his face as he strode quickly away from the ragged edge of town and the dark seas to the east. Winter would arrive soon, and he could already imagine the cold. A small shiver shot up the middle of his spine before erupting at the back of his neck. Maybe he would get used to the cold this time—or maybe he would suffer like he always did. Up ahead, about a hundred feet away, he could see the heads of Marines bobbing up and down as they dug foxholes. They were probably swearing at him too. Although one of the new officers had said this area should be clear of all enemy activity, he had ordered his men to set up a strong defensive perimeter because he had a bad feeling. When he approached the nearest foxhole, he wondered if he should trust the feeling. Maybe the cold had simply altered his perspective, or maybe he just worried too much. When he arrived, he found the two Marines sitting in the bottom of a half-finished hole taking a break and smoking cigarettes. Damn—it *was* just like baby-sitting his brothers and sisters.

With honest enthusiasm, Timothy vaulted into the hole to take his turn and immediately began whacking at the hard earth with the little folding shovel he carried strapped to his pack. Humphrey sat cross-legged a few feet back from the edge of the hole, his elbows resting comfortably on his M-1 rifle, and squinted into the setting sun. Humphrey, who had never been particularly fond of physical labor, marveled that Timothy could make digging a damn hole in the ground look like fun. Then Timothy began whistling too—not a specific tune Humphrey could identify—just…random…whistling. After listening to a few "stanzas," Humphrey finally recognized a slightly modified and out-of-tune rendition of *Amazing Grace*. Before getting to the end of the song, Timothy disappeared into the hole. He reappeared a few seconds later, and with a deep grunt pushed out a large egg-shaped rock. The rock paused briefly, then rolled unevenly down the gentle slope below the foxhole for about twenty yards before stopping in a nearly vertical position. Timothy seemed very pleased with the rock, and especially with the artistic way it had stopped.

"You know, Humphrey, if we find a few more rocks like that one, we could build ourselves a nice little barricade in front of this foxhole. I bet that would finally make the Gunny happy. Yeah—he'd see our little rock wall and probably give us both a damn medal."

Humphrey yawned and rubbed some dried sweat from the corner of his eye. Timothy picked up the shovel and resumed digging. "Yup, when the Gunny sees this foxhole, he'll be so damn proud of us he'll probably start blubbering."

Humphrey thought he heard footsteps. He turned his head just enough to see Gunny Talbot's boots standing a few feet away. He quickly tried to signal Timothy by coughing and grunting at the same time, followed by an exceptionally long throat clearing. Timothy ignored Humphrey's sudden hacking and continued his oration. "You know what I think we should do? I think we should go around to the

Toil Under The Sun

other foxholes and collect everyone's rocks so that we can really do some building here. Why stop at a wall? We could build some steps too. Shit, if we build some nice steps so it's easy to get in and out of this hole, the Gunny would probably shit his pants and…."

Timothy stopped mid-sentence because Humphrey had started coughing again; this time it sounded like he was dying. "Damn it Humphrey! Why don't you go somewhere else if you're going to cough and wheeze like that." Humphrey responded by violently clearing his throat again. Timothy spun around to *really* tell him to knock it off, but instead stood in silence and dropped the shovel into the foxhole. There, standing mere inches behind Humphrey, his face scowling against the setting sun, stood Gunnery Sergeant John Talbot.

Gunny Talbot hooked his thumbs around his belt and surveyed the defensive line with keen interest. He moved his eyes up and down the line from left to right and then back again, carefully studying every detail before fixing his gaze directly on Timothy's eyeballs. A distant memory of Guadalcanal darted abruptly into his consciousness: he recalled the night a similar line was nearly overrun by a terrifying Japanese frontal assault. Then the memory faded away, returning to the enshrouded place it had come from. A new shiver began forming below the small of his back, but he willed it to stop. "I almost fell into your foxhole before you guys even knew I was here. I hope you do better tonight."

Timothy relaxed. The Gunny hadn't heard any of his unfortunate statements. "With all due respect sir, we weren't expecting an attack from the rear."

Another glimpse from that horrific night on Guadalcanal surfaced briefly, then immediately diminished until it floated invisibly below the surface. "Expect an attack from any direction at any time. Do not assume anything. Anticipate everything." Gunny Talbot paused as flashes of rifle and machine gun fire reflected off the low-hanging mist floating around his besieged foxhole and the screams of men echoed against dark jungle walls beyond his sight. "I want one of you on guard at all times tonight. And if you're not on guard duty, don't get all cozy in your sleeping bag. No zippers tonight. And don't take your boots off. I want both of you ready to fight at any moment. I've got a bad feeling about this place."

"Begging your pardon sir, but won't it get a little cold if we don't zip up our bags?" Timothy liked hard work as much as he hated the cold. Freezing while waiting for an improbable attack in a secured area because the Gunny had a bad feeling did not make a lot of sense to him.

"Your comfort is not my concern. Keeping you alive to kill the enemy is. Now get to work and finish this foxhole before it gets dark." Gunny Talbot turned crisply and walked north to check out the next pair of Marines. After a dozen steps he stopped and turned back, looking directly at Timothy. "And don't worry about building those steps. I'm not interested in shitting my pants tonight."

They finished digging the foxhole minutes before the last sliver of light vanished below the western hills. It quickly turned much colder. Timothy squatted against the edge of the hole and aimed his rifle into the spreading darkness. He reached out and tenderly touched the honed edge of the bayonet to remind himself that it had not fallen off. Then he offered to take the first shift. Humphrey wrapped his sleeping bag around his legs and slept fitfully, waking several times to shiver. The temptation to pull the zipper and seal himself in the gentle warmth of the bag occurred more than once. He resisted each time, not because of any legitimate concern about North Korean soldiers slinking around in the darkness, but because he feared the wrath of Gunny Talbot if caught. He didn't know if the Gunny would really come back to check on them or not, but he didn't want to take any chances.

Timothy heard the unzipped sleeping bag chafe against a rock imbedded in the side of the foxhole when Humphrey rolled over in a hapless attempt to find a comfortable position. "Humphrey…are you awake?"

Humphrey still had an hour to go before his turn at guard duty. He didn't want to use this precious time talking, even if he had already spent his first hour shivering. "Not exactly, but I'm trying to get some sleep before my turn. What is it?" When he finished his words, he realized that he should have pretended to be asleep and kept his mouth shut.

Timothy did not believe in Gunny Talbot's bad feeling, and decided his boredom justified keeping Humphrey awake to talk. "Nothing. I was just thinking that I should change my name after we get home, and wanted to know if you think that's a good idea."

Toil Under The Sun

Humphrey had expected something more important, and had already missed his chance to fake unconsciousness. "Why would you want to change your name? What's wrong with Timothy?"

"I don't know. It's just a little too Biblical, I guess. Plus I have this strange feeling that my parents gave me the wrong name. I wouldn't want to change it until I get back home. I don't want to confuse the Gunny. There'd also be a lot of paperwork to get new dog tags." Timothy paused to allow Humphrey a chance to say something, but heard only silence. "I've actually thought of a few possibilities. Would you like to hear them?"

Humphrey knew from past conversations that he was about to hear the possibilities whether he wanted to or not. He therefore decided that his best strategy to get to sleep as quickly as possible would be to listen quietly and respond only when necessary. "Well, I guess I could listen to a few of them."

"Good. Now, I want you to keep an open mind here. That's really important. What do you think of Blenny Rimalderon? I think it has a nice ring to it."

"Blenny what?"

"Rimalderon. Blenny Rimalderon. I just thought it up, sitting here in the dark. What do you think?"

Suddenly wide awake, Humphrey wondered if Timothy had gone mad while on guard duty. He had heard lurid stories of this happening to other Marines, especially in the jungle during World War II. And although he had never confirmed it, a gruesome story had floated around about a Marine blowing his brains out while on guard duty at night back home at Camp Pendleton. "You, uh, made this name up—just now, I mean, tonight?"

"Yeah, I did. That's not the only name I came up with. How about this one? What do you think of Specmal Minsrubick? Sounds kind of scholarly to me. I thought it might be a good name if I go to college."

Humphrey thought about someone with this name trying to get into college. "Uh, believe it or not, I think I actually like the Blenny name better."

"Blenny Minsrubick?"

"No, no, Blenny Rimalderon. I like Blenny Rimalderon better."

"I'll make a note of that. I've got two more if you're still awake."

"You've got two more?" Now utterly wide-awake, Humphrey worried that Timothy had almost certainly cracked, and that he should keep him talking until help arrived.

"Yeah, I do. What do you think of Flen Klensrolf?"

"Flen Kleinsloft?"

"No, no, *Klensrolf*, but that's a pretty good variation. I might try to use that later." Timothy prepared to offer his last name when the rock he had rolled out of the foxhole earlier rolled again. He quietly turned around and gaped into the darkness. "Gunny, is that you?" No answer. Humphrey slid his legs quietly out of the sleeping bag and groped for his rifle. "Gunny, this isn't funny." Timothy raised his rifle and wrapped a gloved index finger around the metallic coolness of the gently curving trigger. He tried the password for the night, and again heard no response. He squinted and looked slightly to the side of the rock, a trick he had learned in the Boy Scouts just before he had left the Troop. Still nothing.

In another foxhole, not far away, a dozing Marine quietly hissed when an NKPA soldier slid a long, sharpened bayonet smoothly through the side of his neck and down into his lung. The man fell back into the hole, gently gurgling blood up from the pierced lung into his gasping mouth. His fellow Marine, awakened by the fall, grabbed franticly at the zipper that entombed him in the warm sleeping bag. The NKPA soldier stepped casually into the foxhole, stood above the struggling man, then pushed the sharpened bayonet through the bag until it penetrated several inches into the soil below. He pressed his foot against the convulsing bag and jerked the blade out with a hard pull.

Timothy tried the password one last time, and then yelled, "I sure hope you're not the Gunny." He fired three times, aiming several feet above the egg-shaped rock. The flashes of light exposed at least seven men with gleaming bayonets mounted on slender rifles creeping toward the foxhole. Two fell awkwardly after Timothy's remaining rounds cut them down. The others began running at the hole, raising their rifles to fire. Humphrey slid up next to the edge of the foxhole and fired into the oncoming soldiers while Timothy reloaded.

Chapter 12

A visit to the police station, June 1946

Of all the days of the week, John liked Friday best, even more so than Saturday. Not that Saturday didn't have its good points too. There were many reasons to regard Saturday as the second best day after Friday. On Saturday, he could get a few chores done without the scheduled encumbrances of a normal workday. On Saturday, he could feel some distance from the incessant grind of work. On Saturday, he could fish or take a hike or play some golf. And on Saturday, he could sleep in to make up for any late nights accumulated during the week. However, Saturday could only be enjoyed for its own sake because it had nothing to anticipate. Friday, on the other hand, could anticipate Saturday, and to John this important distinction made Friday special. He had preferred the anticipation of an event to the actual occurrence of it since the first grade, and, because Saturday could not anticipate itself, he liked Friday best.

John shuffled through some loose papers on his desk and listened to the horn of an outlying train move slowly along the edge of town. Friday again, almost four o'clock, and he felt deep contentment as he thought about the end of the day and several interesting things he might do on Saturday. For no particular reason, he thought back to a Friday at the end of sixth grade and before the beginning of summer. He remembered feeling agitated with the anticipation of summer the entire day. After the final bell rang, he ran home to collect his baseball glove, bat, and a ball, then ran back to school. Excitement vibrated deep in his stomach when he approached the recently abandoned buildings and grassy fields. Now that summer had begun, and he had finished elementary school, everything looked different. The school did not seem as it had only hours ago. He had not expected this, and surprisingly this new perception actually felt strangely pleasant. He remembered standing at the edge of the cool grass, enjoying the feeling for as long as it remained. He remembered too that the feeling amplified his anticipation of summer.

Three school friends waited for him under a cluster of blotchy shadows by a clump of tall, leafy alders. They played catch to warm up and talked excitedly about summer. John walked over and joined them. After a brief discussion they decided to play *over-the-line*, to their minds the best activity ever invented for a small group of boys. A simple game, it charmingly mimicked the magnificence of true baseball, while demanding only four players instead of eighteen. The rules were elegantly simple too, once understood and appreciated. First they established the teams, each with two boys. To increase everyone's enjoyment of the game, they took special care to make sure that the teams were evenly matched. The boys then imagined a straight line between two trees or other convenient objects. It was better, of course, to have a real line, because disputes sometimes erupted about the location of the imagined line: good sportsmanship usually minimized the number and intensity of disputes. One team set up beyond the line with one boy standing a few feet behind the line and the second boy standing much farther back. The second team took their positions at bat, with one boy pitching underhand and the second boy hitting, the pitcher always attempting to lob the ball to the hitter's favorite spot. The precise location of this spot often generated a lot of discussion before an actual pitch could be made, and usually changed more than once as the sun moved across the afternoon sky or the wind shifted direction.

The boys played *over-the-line* with innings and three outs for each team, just like real baseball. Scoring and outs were based on the manner the defensive team fielded—or did not field—a hit ball. A grounder successfully fielded by the first boy, after crossing the imaginary line, counted as an out. A grounder hit past the first boy and fielded by the second boy counted as a single. A line drive hitting the ground behind the first boy but successfully fielded by the second boy scored a double. Any ball, including a grounder, which passed the second boy scored a triple. Any ball caught in the air by either boy was an out. And though nearly impossible to achieve, a ball hit over the head of the second boy scored a home run. None of the boys had ever heard of anyone in their neighborhood hitting a grand slam home run. There were of course a few other rules, but these were relatively subtle and not really important to the basic play of the game, at least as John remembered it sitting at his desk on a Friday afternoon.

The first hit of the game, a sharp ground ball that caromed off a sprinkler head just before crossing the line, darted past the first boy at exactly seven minutes after three. Nearly two hours later, after a long and aggressively contested game, the boys reached the bottom of the ninth inning. By that time, the sun's corona barely glowed over the tops of an evenly spaced row of gently swaying trees rimming the field to the west. Recently mowed grass saturated the air with a pleasant fragrance. John remembered the light and smell and play of the game vividly. It had been a close game with several lead changes. His team trailed by two runs, seventeen to fifteen. He had made two brilliant fielding plays during the middle innings to keep the game that close, including a diving catch of a screaming line drive in the top of the sixth inning that would have driven in two more runs. John walked up to the plate, his bat slung casually across his shoulder, with the bases loaded and two outs. His hitting had been a bit sporadic that afternoon, but somehow he knew this would be a big at-bat for him. His teammate, Charlie Sorensen, a kid he had known since the second grade, pitched him a beautifully floating parabola smack down the middle of the imaginary plate. John coiled like a tempered steel spring as the ball approached, and then, at the perfect moment, uncoiled explosively, his feet twisting cleanly against countless blades of bending grass, his bat cleaving smoothly through the late afternoon air and rushing toward the oncoming ball, his wrists snapping at the—

The telephone rang and jolted John from his pleasant memory. He had planned to leave for home in a few minutes and didn't really want to answer it. He picked up the handset anyway because he couldn't resist his reliable nature. "Hi, this is John."

"John, I'm glad I caught you before you left. This is Chief Tennosrep. I have your son down here at the station."

John felt a small jab in his stomach. "You have Timothy at the police station?"

"I do, John…unless you have more than one son." John and Chief Rich Tennosrep had maintained a casual friendship for years. They had played a round of golf on a pleasant Saturday morning only a few months ago. John certainly never expected to get this kind of call from him.

The small jab grew into dull pain and slid below his stomach, probably somewhere inside the small intestines. John had felt this sensation before, but not with this much intensity. "What did he do?"

The Chief answered John's question with sympathy in his voice. He knew how hard John worked to be a good father. This call could not be easy. "Well John, it appears Timothy had a little problem down at the grocery store. According to the store manager, he stole some candy and a few other things with a couple of other boys. The owner caught them just before they tried to leave the store. I got the call over an hour ago. The other boys got away, but Timothy is here at the station. I'd like you to come down so we can decide what to do."

Although his first instinct shouted at him to walk away from this, to return to that pleasant Friday afternoon at the end of sixth grade when the sun's warmth waned against the ending day, to finish his last turn at bat and smack Charlie Sorensen's pitch into glory, he knew that he could not. That summer had faded long ago, and he had never again played a game of *over-the-line*. He forced himself to return to the present, and to accept responsibility for his son, and then wondered how Friday could ever be the same again. There were no more questions to ask. He said the only thing that made any sense: "I'll be right down."

The drive to the police station filled John with confusion and uncertainty. He did not call Martha before he walked out of the office because he hoped it would not turn out as bad as it sounded on the phone. No reason to get her all upset with imaginary exaggerations, he thought to himself. He rationalized that it would be best to give her an accurate account of what had happened, and this could only be accomplished after talking to the Chief first and thoroughly understanding the details of the event. He drove up to the front of the station and pulled into a parking space next to the Chief's car. When he stepped out onto the dark pavement he realized that he had made the trip from his office to the police station without any recollection of it. He could not remember any scenery along the way, passing cars, people walking by the side of the road, barking dogs, children playing with balls, stop signs, crosswalks—nothing. This unsettled him because it had never happened before. He hoped that he hadn't broken any traffic laws or run over anyone without knowing it. He trudged up the wide concrete steps and through the heavy double doors at the front of the station, his small intestines squirming harder than before. The Chief waived at him from behind an imposing wood counter.

"Afternoon, John. Sorry about this."

"Not your fault Rich." John felt an edge of shame as he greeted his friend for the first time at the police station. "Glad it was you who picked him up instead of someone else."

"I suppose that's a good way to look at it. Timothy's in my office. Why don't we go in and have a chat with him?" John followed the Chief to a modest office with corner windows. The wall behind the Chief's desk had been decorated with numerous recognitions and remembrances, several from the New York City Police Department where he had first served as a patrol officer. Timothy sat slumped into a heavy side chair with an uncomfortably flat wood seat and heavy curved wood arms, his face buried in his hands.

The Chief sat in a leather chair behind his desk and then began speaking in soft, pleasant tones. "Timothy, your dad's here. Why don't you tell him what happened down at the grocery store today?" Timothy remained hunched over and did not move, except for a sadly imperceptible shudder. The Chief waited a few seconds before pressing him further, his voice slightly harder now. "I know this is difficult son, but you've got to tell your dad what happened. The sooner you do, the sooner we can all go home."

At this second prompting, Timothy slowly sat up in the hard wooden chair and rested his hands on the curved wooden arms. The old chair's arms had been rubbed to an oily gloss finish by countless other hands. The seat of the chair had been rubbed smooth too. Smudgy tear tracks streaked Timothy's youthful face. He looked at John briefly, then lowered his head a little. He opened his mouth slightly, but then didn't say anything.

The Chief tried a different tactic, his voice softening again. "Well, Timothy…how about I tell your dad what happened, and then you tell him if I got it right?" Timothy looked up again and nodded slightly. The Chief nodded back and said, "Alright, let's go with that."

Chief Tennosrep explained the events of that unfortunate afternoon in vivid police-like detail. Timothy, and two "friends" named Wes and Raymond, had arrived at the store before the end of the school day and had then proceeded to loiter near the back for nearly an hour.

The storeowner hadn't really taken much notice when the boys walked into the store; he became suspicious when they stayed so long without buying anything. When he stopped them at the door as they tried to leave, Wes and Raymond ran, flinging the door open with enough force to damage one of the hinges. When the owner yelled at them to stop, they kept running. Timothy did not run, and in fact froze in position, making it easy for the storeowner to grab him. It turned out that his pockets were filled with candy, chewing gum, and a small metal whistle. The owner called the police station and spoke directly to the Chief. When he arrived, he found Timothy sitting on the floor next to the checkout counter. He did not try to run, unlike the other boys, and didn't talk back or cause any other problems. When the Chief finished interviewing the storeowner, he drove Timothy to the station and called John at his office. "Well Timothy—is that about it?" Timothy nodded, but only slightly again.

John stared silently at the top of Timothy's head while he listened to the Chief finish his report, and then looked down at the floor in front of his toes. His intestines felt like they were trying to squirm right up to his throat. His voice cracked slightly as he began speaking. "What now, Rich? What's the next step?"

The Chief had done this enough times before to understand that he had to scare Timothy to prevent this from happening again. "Well John, he's too young for prison. And he's too old to just let this go with a slap on the hand. I think maybe he ought to do some work at the grocery store to pay off his debt, including the broken hinge. I don't know what work he might do, but it will probably be hard and take a long time. I think that's the best solution in this case."

John struggled to speak directly to Timothy. "Timothy, is that what you want to do? It sounds like a fair suggestion to me." Timothy looked up a third time and nodded, methodically as before, without any emotion. That nod was a sufficient answer for John—he didn't want to stay in the Chief's office any longer. "Alright Chief, that sounds like the way we're going to go. What do I need to do? Should I call the grocery store right now?"

"No John. I'll give the owner a call first thing in the morning to set something up. You can call him Monday morning to make any final arrangements. I think it would be wise if you and Timothy go to the store together the first day." Timothy returned to his hunched position and began sobbing again.

John nodded his agreement. "I guess that's it. Thanks for your help, Rich. I really appreciate it. OK Timothy, let's head home. You've got some explaining to do to mom." Timothy pushed against the smooth chair arms and stood up. He dreaded the idea of telling his mom what had happened, but could think of no way to avoid it.

Timothy remained silent during the endless drive home. John thought he should say something, but couldn't find any words. About halfway home he stopped thinking about what he should say to Timothy. He realized that he had a much larger worry—what to say to Martha when they arrived this late for dinner without calling.

♦ ♦ ♦

Lieutenant Meyer, November 1950

With Thanksgiving less than three weeks away and autumn paled by the gently tilted earth, each succeeding afternoon cooled more quickly. Not that the afternoons were not already cold enough. Yet today, with the sun drifting lower in the ashen skies and dissolving behind wind-honed mountains closer to midday, the coolness of the afternoon felt more intensely impatient; and the wintry air, thickened by the cooling of the day and emerging as fresh winds, flowed along the valley floor and pressed up the sides of abruptly plunging mountains and eddied over the rocky edges of the narrow road to increase the coolness and warn of prolonged harshness to come.

The narrow road; squeezed at points to a marginal lane by unyielding mountains, a little wider in other places where the same mountains receded; weaved unevenly in sinuous harmony with the push and pull of the valley floor. Because of the geography of the road—sometimes pressed hard against a sharp rock face on one side, sometimes falling off abruptly into a dark chasm on the other—the men walked in a line cautiously aligned with the center; stretched out along its length, footfalls landing in the preceding footfalls of other men, undulating, weaving, at times unaware of the front of the line, or the back, or of the line itself, always ascending inexorably into the ambivalent mountains with each trudging step.

With the end of the day fast approaching and twilight closing in with unforgiving certainty, the narrow road and the men marching upon it fell into the shadows of the mountains and forfeited the sun's reassuring warmth. Sunlight still washed the jagged sides of outlying pinnacles and sometimes peeked over a distant saddle or through a deep crack to tease the steep cuts above the road, but no longer offered warmth directly to the road itself or the line of men. The sun's aloof radiance, when still visible from the road, could be enjoyed by the eyes but not felt by the body, and therefore offered only psychological comfort to those who could imagine it. Many of the men viewed the distant glow of the sun as an ironic taunt, scornfully indifferent to their loss. When the next days shortened even more, and the lethal winter nights fell upon them with unremitting anguish, they would learn to be thankful for view alone of the sun's imagined warmth. For now, at this time, marching along the narrow road in the chill of the shadows and the bite of the wind, they resented the view and longed only for the comforting warmth of direct sunlight.

Stepping out of line and neatly reversing direction, Lieutenant Meyer strolled backwards alongside his advancing platoon until he had looked into the face of every Marine under his command. Only a few of them looked back. Most of them focused instead on the man ahead, or the falling temperature, or the end of the day and the approaching chance to eat and rest. Making eye contact with the lieutenant was one task too many; Meyer understood and appreciated this and did not take the lack of response as an insult. Reaching the end of his own platoon and the beginning of the next, he turned, lengthened his strides to catch up, and fell in next to the last Marine.

"How's it going back here private?" Meyer often talked casually to individual Marines to assess their morale. An experienced officer had suggested this to him before he left for Korea, and he had practiced the idea so many times that it now formed a comfortable habit.

Meyer's question surprised Timothy. He had not noticed the lieutenant walking next to him because he had been thinking about dinner. At least the Gunny hadn't surprised him. The Gunny would have instantly chastised him for his lapse of awareness and then given him the usual lecture about staying alive to kill enemy soldiers. "Uh,

Toil Under The Sun

fine sir. A little cold maybe. My feet especially." Timothy chuckled. "You couldn't ask for a nicer day for a walk."

"I guess you could look at it that way." Meyer squinted and peered across the valley at a pair of icy pinnacles, then down the long line of Marines. The line snaked ahead a few hundred feet before disappearing around a sharp bend in the road. "I'm afraid it might get a lot colder before we're finished." Meyer prepared to quicken his pace so that he could speak with a few of the other Marines when Timothy asked him a question.

"Begging your pardon, sir; do you mind if I ask you a personal question?"

Meyer looked at Timothy suspiciously. "No problem. Shoot."

Timothy turned his head to see the lieutenant's face, but Meyer's upturned collar and the rim of his helmet blocked the view. "I heard from one of the other Marines that you went to college. Is that true?"

"Yes it is. What about it?"

"Did you graduate?"

"I did, although it took a little longer than four years."

"What did you graduate in?"

"Mechanical engineering. I went to school at Iowa State. It's in Ames."

This confirmation puzzled Timothy. It didn't make any sense to him that a young man with a college degree should end up with the Marine Corps in Korea. "With all due respect sir, then what are you doing here?"

"To tell you the truth, I've wondered the same thing myself a few times. I didn't exactly anticipate this war when I enlisted. I guess I shouldn't be too surprised, the way the world is going these days." Meyer thought about this response for a few steps, and then decided that Timothy deserved a better answer. "I got bored with my life, and I wasn't quite ready to get a job and sit all day behind a desk. And this may sound funny, but I also wanted to get the hell out of Iowa. I guess I'm getting all the excitement I could ever have wanted. And you know, this certainly is a lot different than Iowa."

"Yes sir. I guess we all are. I've never been to Iowa. I don't imagine it has much of a chance of looking like this."

"That's for damn sure. I haven't seen a single corn field since we arrived. And I don't think we'll see one this high up in the mountains either."

Timothy smiled. "No sir, I don't suppose we will."

Meyer nodded. "You're right about that. Say, I've got to move up the line, but we can talk about college again sometime, if you like."

"Sure, I'd like to do that." Without saluting, Timothy returned a respectful nod when Meyer moved ahead. He chuckled quietly again—nothing that anyone could hear—loud enough to confirm to himself that he had found this conversation amusing. He perceived college as a faraway goal that would probably remain beyond his reach. Even with Humphrey's numerous pep talks he did not really believe he could achieve it. The lieutenant, who had already graduated from college, had chosen the Marine Corps instead of a desk job and now walked on the same narrow road in North Korea with him. It really didn't make a lot of sense; neither did much else at the moment. It would be something to discuss with Humphrey at a later time. He didn't expect Humphrey to necessarily have any answers, but it might be an amusing way to pass the time in the next foxhole. It might also be a good topic to discuss over a game or two of chess, assuming the little metal chess pieces hadn't frozen together inside the box.

The Marines walked along the road a little further. After reaching a wider plateau, they were ordered to halt. A cluster of small dwellings clung to some meager ground just above the edge of the road, a little beyond where they had stopped. Tile-clad gable roofs, glazed with new frost, protected the weatherworn wood-sheathed walls of the homes and gave comforting shape to the small village. Below the road a thin layer of ice had formed over the surface of rice paddies that fell away in serpentine terraces from the road's edge. A mild breeze, flowing down the mountain from behind the village, spilled between the rustic homes and the disintegrating line of men and over the road to gently ripple the pools of water that had not yet frozen. Reddish light flickered through a small window in the nearest building, projecting a dancing glow across the ancient pavers that formed a pathway to the thick wooden entry door. The door; weatherworn like the siding, tarnished with age, striped with rough-hewn rails and stiles; sat sturdily in a heavy timber frame.

Toil Under The Sun

Gunny Talbot walked briskly to the rear of his platoon. When he arrived, he ordered the last four Marines to check out the village for enemy activity. He also told them to watch out for booby traps. "I don't like the look of this village," he said. "Where in the hell are all the damn people? I want the four of you to get off your butts and to go check things out. Be careful not to shoot any civilians. And don't touch anything that might be booby-trapped. Now get going." He muttered something about a bad feeling as he turned and walked away. Timothy, the last Marine in line, had now lost his opportunity to take a rest and get something to eat. Worse, the Gunny had just stuck him with three guys he hardly ever talked to. Actually, now that he thought about it, he hadn't talked to two of them at all. He remembered saying a few meaningless words to the other one; nothing to adequately justify any sort of relationship. He would probably have to say a lot more to all three of them now, even if he didn't care to.

Timothy made a half-hearted attempt at humor; he did not find a receptive audience. "Well…it looks like we get to have some fun while everyone else is forced to take a break and eat dinner. The Gunny must really like us." The other three men, tired and hungry from the day's march, did not acknowledge this sarcastic joke, and began trudging up a gentle rise toward the apparently abandoned village. Timothy joined the line behind the last man, not quite knowing what to say next. Then he thought of something. "Hey, if you don't mind, I'd like to move up front—unless you guys really like it up there." The three men stopped, each of them looking back at Timothy in turn, each not knowing if this was a serious offer or just another joke. Timothy accepted their expressions of surprise as a positive response to his request and continued walking until he arrived at the front of the formation. After taking a few more strides beyond the three confused men, he stopped and looked back. "Are you guys coming or not? Someone needs to cover me while I check out this first house. Unless of course, you want to do it."

The three men, perfectly content with Timothy in the lead, fanned out in front of the first house, ready to fire their rifles as they checked around the sides and back. One of the men, a husky Marine with massive forearms and thick hands supporting a Browning Automatic Rifle, crouched down in front of and slightly to the side of the heavy wood entry door, ready to cut down any enemy soldiers who might step from the small house into his deadly sights. He nodded to Timothy and, setting his index finger gently against the trigger, anxiously awaited the onslaught. Timothy approached the door from the side, his back sliding against the rough wooden wall. He cradled his M-1 over his forearm and under his armpit and reached backhanded to open the door. Although heavy with age, the door opened easily, creaking a little as the hinges rotated. When the door had swung about 45 degrees, he shifted the rifle to both hands and used his foot to kick the door fully open. Keeping well behind the protective mass of the doorframe, he swung his rifle around in a smooth arc and aimed into the house. He scanned the single room of the home quickly, his eyes adjusting to the small, flickering flame in the center almost instantly. Whoever lived in the home had gone somewhere else. He lowered his rifle and breathed deeply.

"There's no one inside. You can relax." Timothy stepped through the doorway, clicking the heel of his boot on the edge of the stone threshold. The husky Marine lowered his BAR and followed Timothy into the opening, almost filling it with his dark shape. Timothy studied the space and its few simple contents. Someone had set up a small wooden table with three chairs for dinner. A narrow sleeping area stretched along the opposite wall. The flickering flame actually looked like a cooking fire, and the meager dinner it warmed appeared untouched. "Looks like someone left in a hurry. They must have been afraid of us."

The husky Marine stepped into the center of the room, leaned over the cooking fire, and sniffed at the dinner. "Hey, what's for dinner? Maybe we should have some hot chow before we check out the other huts. I'm starving."

Timothy glanced around the room again and observed the smallness of it, the simplicity and paucity of the contents, the care that had been used to construct the small table and chairs, the cleanliness of the ancient surfaces, the meagerness of the abandoned yet carefully prepared evening meal. At that moment he understood something for the first time: the people who lived in this home and worked the rice paddies below the slender road and survived day-to-day in this village were, from his unique perspective, poor; even so, even though it was obvious to him that they had very little compared to what he had back home, he sensed profound appreciation. He sensed it from this simple home and the way it looked and felt, and it made him feel good and confused at the same time. "I don't think that would be a good idea. I think we should just move on and check out the other houses."

This response irritated the husky Marine. He did not like cold C-rations—not that anyone did—and now had an opportunity to eat some hot food. "What, you afraid to eat this because you think it's booby trapped or something?"

Timothy turned slowly, and at first appeared ready to argue with the husky Marine. Instead, he looked down at the cooking fire and spoke in calm words. "No, I'm not afraid it's booby trapped. I doubt it is. We're not going to eat this food because it belongs to some poor family in this village who needs it more than we do. Now let's get out of here and check out the other huts before the Gunny wonders what in the hell happened to us." The husky Marine grunted his disagreement and, reluctantly, turned to leave.

Chapter 13

Marie, October 1946

The tender days of summer gave way to autumn's bite: the bite was not unkind, only a different and sharper sensation to replace the comfortable and lazy warmth of recent months. In an odd way, the sharp coolness of the air blended with the pungent moistures released by countless decaying leaves to refresh the senses. And as dead leaves swirled along the dampened streets and walks in gusty breezes and dying leaves trembled on bending trees to create a wash of autumnal sounds, the musty smell of the leaves merged with the sound of the kinetic leaves to create a melancholy sense of loss, not loss of anything specific or remembered, but loss nonetheless.

The last day of junior high school had ended before the now faded summer, and through its passing had created a pensive sense of loss as well. The innocence of those middle years; amplified by the pleasant summer, sharpened by the cooling autumn that now fell upon the days; soon receded before the exhilarations of a new school and a new year. The power of these exhilarations to replace innocence and hasten the sense of loss was easily underestimated. New possibilities and dangers awaited, once patiently when the innocence had flourished full-blown, now ruthlessly impatient and eager to lure him beyond innocence. The innocence would then become true loss, experienced beyond this point in time and in his remaining life only as a fragile memory, if remembered at all.

Now an experienced sophomore, and therefore no longer a child, Timothy had begun to discover and enjoy the myriad potentials of high school. At the same time he had performed reasonably well in his classes, with one A, a few B's, and a marginal C in a math class that he found a challenge to become interested in. He had joined the school band, a decision influenced by his mother. And encouraged by his noticeable improvement in the mile run since his early attempts in junior high, also thought about trying out for the track and field team.

Unfortunately, he did not have to decide this until much later in the year, and future events would eventually render this decision, and many others, irrelevant.

Although he had played with the band in junior high for two years, this had proven a relatively benign experience—in spite of the manic energy of the music instructor. Regarded by many in the school district as a dedicated teacher, an excessive love of music had unfairly consumed her life. Because of this love, she had developed a nearly pathological aversion to notes played out of tune, a significant and chronic dilemma for a junior high band teacher. However, this same aversion had also produced numerous students with an excellent ear, an attribute that would eventually help several become highly regarded professional musicians. But the day-to-day conflict between her love of music and the mangled variants she often listened to would sometimes overwhelm her. More than once she had thrown her baton across the room and then screamed wildly at her startled students that she would go mad if she had to listen to one more sour note. She eventually did—a mere three years after Timothy graduated from junior high school—but that is an unrelated story.

The high school band director presented a much different temperament. He consistently maintained an attitude of calm and patience, although everyone suspected that he too had an intense passion for music. His latent love of music first revealed itself during a run-through of a simplified version of *The Planets* arranged for high school band, when missed entrances by the snare drum, cymbals, base drum, and timpani finally dissolved his composure. He shattered his baton against the edge of his podium and shouted to the back of the room, "Damn it! I don't want you to be drummers, I want you to be percussionists!" From that point on, this often repeated demand became his obscure way of telling the section that he wanted them to play as musicians, not like wild children pounding haphazardly on cardboard boxes. His name was Mr. Reynolds, and only the principal and a few of the teachers knew that he had a master's degree in conducting from some fancy school back east. None of the students knew why he had ended up at a small high school on the west coast; although there were rumors that floated around from time to time, probably all untrue.

Timothy did not surprise anyone when he decided to play in the "percussion" section. He had also been responsible for the missed cymbal entrance that fateful day when Mr. Reynolds broke his baton. In fairness, he did have a credible excuse for the mistake. Instead of maintaining the intense focus necessary to accurately count several hundred rests leading up to the entrance, his mind had wandered for the briefest moment across the room to one of the flute players, another sophomore with the lovely name of Marie. He had noticed her the very first day of band, and with the semester nearly over, now found it increasingly difficult to pay attention to anything else, especially tricky percussion entrances. This was bad enough, but when he began to think of her outside of the band room, in other classes, at home during dinner, in the morning when he tied his shoes, and while riding his bike to school, he began to worry that something might be desperately wrong.

Still, she became the primary reason that he enjoyed playing in the band. It gave him pleasure to glance over at the flute section every so often to see what clothes she wore or how she had combed her hair—that is, until she looked back one day, straight into his eyes; or more accurately, straight through his head. Her discovery of his peeking so horrified Timothy that it took several seconds for him to break loose, but not before she smiled. He instantly looked down at his music, blushing and pretending to count quarter rests, praying she had smiled at someone else. He forced his eyes to stay there for five or six measures, then…slowly…very slowly…with absurd deliberation…he raised his eyes once more until they barely gazed over the top of the music stand. She smiled again when their eyes connected for the second time, thereby completing his absolute horrification.

Marie began playing the flute while attending elementary school. Neither of her immigrant parents could play a musical instrument; when Marie expressed an interest at the age of 11, they excitedly made a withdrawal from their meager savings account, bought her a good used flute from the local music store, and arranged for private lessons. She became quite good before the end of junior high school, and by that time had taken a serious interest in the instrument and music in general. She even thought of going to college and majoring in instrumental music, although she didn't know how she would pay for it. But something else made Marie even more interesting than her musical talent: although

Timothy did not realize it, she had actually noticed him a year earlier in junior high school, at the back of the room with the other drummers.

Timothy responded to Marie's astonishing smile the only way he could think of—he avoided her. And although it required serious effort, because he still thought about her constantly, he succeeded in no longer looking at her during band because he feared the same electrifying embarrassment if their eyes were to meet again. This strategy worked very well for almost a week, when due to a brief lapse of concentration between periods, Timothy almost spun her around in the hallway as he raced to math class. Although Marie managed to stay on her feet, she did drop one of her books. It fell to the floor with a sharp slap that echoed down the crowded hallway. Timothy, still in a hurry, turned and picked up the book, and as he raised it from the floor and prepared to shove it back into the thick stack of books wedged between Marie's arms, he found himself looking directly into her mesmerizing eyes again, and this time he stood only ten inches away. Although he had read in a biology textbook that they existed, he had never actually seen green eyes before.

"Thanks for picking up my book. You must be in a hurry." Marie smiled and reached out to take the book. Timothy did not speak or move—he just stared into those green eyes. Marie, hearing no reply, decided to try a different tack. "You're in Mr. Reynolds' class, aren't you?" Of course she knew this, but she didn't want him to think that she might be too sure about it. With this question, a new realization shook Timothy. In only seconds he would be exposed as that creepy guy at the back of the room who has been staring at her all semester. He had to immediately change the subject or face unconscionable shame. This could have worked too, except that he had no idea of what to say.

"Uh, yeah. I guess I am in Mr. Reynolds' class. How did you know that?" The moment this question slithered out of his mouth, Timothy knew that he surely sounded like a complete moron. The skin around his neck suddenly burst into flame, and then a rivulet of sweat trickled down his back to prove it.

"Oh, I think I've seen you at the back of the room a few times, in the percussion section—right? Are you a percussionist?" Marie's hand remained cantilevered in the smoldering air between them, still anticipating the errant book.

Timothy's mind swirled chaotically. He groped desperately for something smart to say, but those green eyes had emptied his psyche of all available thought. Then, thankfully, he remembered what Mr. Reynolds had said after the shattered baton incident. "Uh yeah, that's right. I'm not a drummer—I'm a percussionist. At least that's what Mr. Reynolds says." His mind immediately relapsed into a muddled void.

"Do you mind if I take my book? I'm going to be late for class." Marie moved her hand closer to Timothy until it rested just under the edge of the book. She felt the book tremble when she slid her hand further and touched the tip of Timothy's finger. This imperceptible caress ignited an explosion of electricity that crackled up Timothy's arm and scorched the base of his brain stem.

Timothy looked down at the book and realized he had been holding it out like a department store mannequin for the entire conversation. "Oh, the book! Oh sure, you can take the book!" He released his sweaty grip on the book, his arm lifeless from the touch of her hand.

Marie slid the book out of Timothy's damp hand, thanked him for picking it up for her, and turned to walk to her next class. She took a few bouncing steps before stopping suddenly and turning around to look back at Timothy. He still held his now empty hand out. "Maybe we can talk again sometime?" She paused long enough for him to look into the green eyes one last time.

Talk again? Is that what they we were doing—talking? Timothy thought he was mostly making a fool of himself. "Uh, sure. That would be great. Anytime." Anytime? Now he had confirmed his foolishness. Marie smiled, then turned again and walked quickly down the corridor, skillfully weaving her way between several on-coming students. Timothy fixed his eyes on the back of her head until she disappeared through one of the heavy classroom doors. He stood there for most of a minute, his hand still holding the phantom book, until the bell rang and reminded him that he also had a class to go to. He didn't really care if he made it or not.

The next days passed in confusion. By admiring Marie from the back of the band room, and assuming she did not know of his admiration, Timothy had achieved a tolerable sort of emotional equilibrium. Now that she had become aware of him, and had actually talked to him and touched the fingertip of his outstretched hand, his emotions began to fluctuate erratically. To suppress these new and troublesome feelings, he forced himself to avoid looking at the flute section during band class. To his surprise this actually worked, and within a week he had again reached a tolerable existence. Unfortunately, another chance meeting with Marie shattered his tenuous emotional balance. He was innocently leaving the band room when it happened. As he stepped though the door and turned right to head down the hall to his next class, he found Marie standing in his way, blocking any sort of graceful maneuver to get around her.

"Hi Timothy. How are you doing today?" She stood very straight with her white and black saddle shoes pressed neatly together and pointed straight forward. She cradled three books against her chest in her left arm and held the narrow leather strap of a flute case down by her side in her right hand. Her hair looked shorter today.

"Uh, hi. I'm, uh, on my way to class." *Damn—that's not what she asked. She asked how you're doing, not where you're going!* Timothy slid back a quarter step to give himself more space to think. Marie deftly slid a half step forward and pressed the saddle shoes together again. She now stood closer to him than before. He decided not to step back again.

"That's nice. So am I. What's your next class?" Marie looked up at Timothy to compensate for the four-inch height difference. He thought about bending his knees a little to bring their eyes to the same level, then decided this would just make things worse, as well as look pretty stupid.

"I, uh…my next class?"

"Yeah, what's your next class?"

"You mean…right now?"

"Yes silly, right now."

Timothy's right lung began collapsing, starving him of air. "I, uh…" he sucked in a deep breath with his remaining good lung, "…I think…it's…" then his left lung imploded too, "uh…English. Yeah, I'm pretty sure that's it. English."

Marie did not appear to notice his impending suffocation. "Timothy, I talked to my mom last night, and she said you could come over to my house tomorrow after school so we could study together. That is, if you wanted to. She said she could make cookies for us." Marie smiled when she finished her pleasant invitation, and with that smile her eyes transcended any common hue of green he had ever seen before.

Now Timothy felt completely and utterly adrift. The thought of going over to Marie's house and studying with her at the same table spun him around. And meeting her mother—that's pretty damn serious! And she would make cookies for them too! He had to answer her question with unwavering courage: he had no other choice. "Uh, yeah, I guess. Wha, what time?"

Marie smiled a little more energetically and rose up on her toes slightly. "Well, school gets out at 2:15. How about three o'clock. Does that work for you?"

Timothy had no idea if that worked for him or not. He didn't even know what the question meant. His brain had stopped responding to any conscious thought. He thought himself damn lucky to still be breathing. "Yeah. That works."

She handed him a neatly folded square of paper with her address and phone number written on it in No. 2 pencil. "Here's my address and phone number. Give me a call if you get lost. See you tomorrow after school." She turned, took a few steps, then stopped and turned back again. She had practiced this little habit for years, and now had no awareness of it. "And don't forget to bring your homework." With that she pivoted smoothly and walked away, leaving him late for class again. And again, he didn't really care.

Timothy struggled to fall asleep that night. Whenever he came close to drifting off, an imagined blunder at Marie's dining room table snapped him awake to a vaporous chimera of Marie's mom waving a spatula and scowling at him from the foot of his bed. Although he had never seen Marie's house before, and he had never met her mom, he could see the whole thing clearly; and did; about seven times, each time a little different. The fourth time she threw a bowl of raw cookie dough at him. The dreams stopped around five o'clock, and he slept until the alarm went off at seven. The bike ride to school went smoothly. He managed to avoid looking at the flute section during band, and slipped quickly out of the classroom before Marie had finished packing up her flute and putting away her music. The rest of the day blurred into a confused lump until he walked out of his sixth period class. His stomach ached with anticipation as he stepped through the door and into the crowded hallway.

"Hey Timothy, how's it going?" Wes leaned against a concrete pilaster, with Raymond standing right behind him, looking big as usual.

Timothy hadn't run into Wes and Raymond for almost two weeks, and now here they were waiting for him outside of class. "Hi Wes. What are you and Raymond doing here?"

"Well, we have a little proposition for you." Wes grinned his sly grin, something he did when he had a devious plan in mind. "We've got a line on some booze, and we're going to skip the last class and go drink it at Raymond's house. Raymond's dad won't get home until late. We thought you might want to come along and help us."

Timothy felt a small jab behind his ear. "Uh, I'd really like to Wes, but I've got to go somewhere at three. I really shouldn't."

"Where's that. Where do you have to go that's more important than drinking some booze with me and Raymond?"

Timothy considered telling Wes and Raymond about Marie, but then decided not to. "I'm…well…I just gotta be somewhere else, OK?"

Timothy's sudden assertiveness surprised Wes, but only momentarily. He quickly resumed his attack. "No reason to get all upset. Just asking, that's all. If you don't want to tell us where you're going, that's fine with us." Wes grinned slyly again. "So what's it going to be? You coming with us or not? I'll tell you what—I promise we'll be done before three. That way you can drink booze with us and still go wherever else it is you have to go to. You can do both."

Timothy didn't want Wes to interrogate him anymore about Marie. He decided to accept, especially since Wes promised he'd be done before three. They sneaked off the school grounds and arrived at Raymond's house a short time later.

◆ ◆ ◆

Ecclesiastes and Dog Hill, 27 November 1950

A product of the inventive genius of John Cantius Garand and the federal armory in Springfield, Massachusetts, the M-1 Garand Rifle was praised by General George S. Patton, Jr. as "…the greatest battle implement ever devised." Adopted by the U.S. military in 1936, this superb weapon served as the standard combat rifle in both World War II and the Korean War. Loaded with an eight round en bloc internal clip, the gas-operated semiautomatic Garand had a high rate of fire and an effective range of over 400 yards. The M-1 utilized the .30-06 rifle cartridge, and, fully loaded with eight round clip, cleaning kit (stored in the stock), sling, and dense wood stock, weighed a little over 11 pounds. An unusual feature of the Garand was the metallic "ping" produced during automatic ejection of the clip after firing the last round, a distinctive sound that could prove fatal during close combat. There was also no way to top off the clip. To fully load the rifle, the clip and any remaining rounds had to be ejected and a fresh clip inserted. During the bitter Korean winter of 1950, Marines who had been taught at boot camp to keep a thin coat of oil on their weapons found that the congealed oil could freeze the action, rendering the rifle inoperable. They soon learned to wipe the M-1 Garand dry.

    Nearly six months ago, the midday sun traced its highest arc in the southern heavens and warmed the lands and seas of the northern hemisphere. With the passage of summer the autumnal equinox soon came upon the earth, a harbinger of cooler and wetter days to come. As the earth continued its inexorable journey through tenebrous space from the opposite side of the sun and summer's time, its exquisite tilt pushing the northern lands farther from the sun's life-giving energy, the days continued to shorten until the winter solstice, once a distant memory, again became an imminent reality. The temperature of the days, until now heroically resistant to the approaching season's resolve, at last plunged below zero and forced an unforgiving chill over the land and those who lived and traveled upon it. In truth, winter had only just begun.

    Surrounded by several Marines from his platoon, Timothy sat placidly on a small flat-topped boulder off the side of the road. The men lingered in the soundless air of the fading afternoon; waiting for word of their fate, walking in small circles and stomping their feet against the hardened ground and slapping gloved hands together to generate the illusion of warmth. While they waited, two regiments of Marines (nearly 7,000 men) trudged north in long lines up the narrow mountain road before vanishing beyond a sharply ascending curve. Although Timothy and the other men in his platoon did not appreciate this unexpected separation from the main body, they assumed there must be a good reason—at least that is what many of them hoped.

Tired of sitting and waiting, Timothy pulled the cleaning kit out of the butt of his M-1. He cleared the rifle then began disassembling it, taking care not to let the sliding bolt pinch his thumb. Humphrey walked up and joined the small group of men as Timothy separated the barrel and receiver from the stock. Humphrey stood behind him, watching with noticeable interest while Timothy finished taking the rifle apart.

"Timothy, what in the hell are you doing?"

Timothy did not look up. "What does it look like I'm doing?"

"I can't say for sure, because what it looks like you're doing doesn't make any sense, given the situation we're in."

Timothy set the rifle barrel across his legs and lifted the brim of his helmet, then glanced up at Humphrey. "And what exactly is it that I'm doing that doesn't make any sense, given the situation we're in that is?"

"It looks like you're taking your rifle apart. So I've got to ask myself—why would anyone in their right mind do that out here where we could be attacked at any moment?" Humphrey swung his arm around, gesturing toward the many avenues of possible attack.

Timothy's eyes followed Humphrey's hand as it traced a wide arc. "You know, Humphrey, I think I see what you mean. Damn. I just didn't stop to think. I mean, the mountains around this pass could be crawling with North Korean troops, ready to pounce on us at any moment, and here I am, making the platoon completely defenseless by taking apart the only functioning rifle we've got. I can't believe I'm so damn thoughtless." He lowered his head and shoved the cleaning rod down the barrel.

Humphrey did not find any humor in Timothy's bald-faced sarcasm. "Gee, maybe I was a little too hasty. Maybe a bigger danger at the moment is that I might slap you on the side of the head with my rifle butt."

Timothy looked up again. "I don't think you want to do that."

"And why's that?"

"Because if you did, who's going to put the platoon's only functioning rifle back together again? After they finish cleaning it, that is."

Gunny Talbot walked up as Timothy yanked the cleaning rod out of the barrel. "That's what I like to see—someone taking pride in the cleanliness of his weapon. Gather 'round. I've got some news. Our company's staying here for the time being to hold this area. Headquarters has decided that no one will be able to get back through here if the enemy controls this mountain pass. Therefore, it looks like we're going to stay here and take a little vacation while the rest of the regiment moves north to do some real work." This last comment exposed Talbot's profound disappointment. "Any questions?"

To no one's surprise, Timothy had a question for the Gunny. "Does that mean we can get to bed early tonight and get some extra sleep?"

Gunny Talbot grinned approvingly. "Oh, that reminds me. I've got even better news. The captain's getting a little jumpy about possible enemy activity in this area, which means we're going to dig in and prepare a strong defensive perimeter before we do anything else, including eating or sleeping."

Several of the men groaned softly. The thought of digging foxholes in the frozen ground and setting up defensive positions in the dark did not appeal to anyone, especially when the danger appeared imagined rather than real. Humphrey asked the next question. "Where are we going to dig our foxholes?"

Gunny Talbot looked sternly into Humphrey's eyes then turned his gaze down the frost-sparkled road. "See that abandoned hut above the road cut, a couple hundred yards from here? We've been ordered to set up on the steep hill behind that hut. It's called Dog Hill. We scouted it out earlier, and we'll have excellent fields of fire to all likely approaches to this pass from there." Another Marine groaned, loud enough for the Gunny to hear. "I know you're all looking forward to a few hours of hard work so that you can get warm before sleeping in total safety tonight. I know I am. Let's get started. We've got a lot of work to do, and the sun's going down fast." He turned and walked away, heading briskly up the road toward Dog Hill and the abandoned hut, followed by the unconvinced Marines.

On the map, the topographic lines of Dog Hill swirled around above a sharp switchback in the road like a small shapeless lump balanced on the tip of an inverted "V" with the right leg of the vee pointing down to the south and the left leg pointing southwest. Built by the Japanese 20 years ago, the road cut into the base of Dog Hill to form a steep, rocky bank about 10 feet high. The bank diminished in height where it followed the roads away from the deepest cut. The abandoned hut sat about 50 feet above the top of the bank and a little east of the switchback. Two small groves of pine trees, widely separated, sprouted near the top of the hill, and added some visual interest to an otherwise rocky and desolate landscape.

Standing across the road, Captain Matheson scanned the two pine groves and the terrain below. His eyes swept down the hill to the abandoned hut, pausing before darting left to the road then right along the top of the cut. He suppressed an edgy conviction that something bad might happen at any moment—an affliction that had haunted his thoughts since before high school. Although he had convinced himself that this recurrent pessimism had emerged during puberty, in truth he had inherited the temperament from his Prussian-born grandmother. Fortunately for the men under his command, a talent for military tactics had come with the same package of genes, and as he stood on this narrow road in the wintry mountains of North Korea, he integrated both gifts to stunning effect. An extraordinary mirage blended with his conscious sight. Hanging from the two pine groves at the top and resting upon the sharp fulcrum of the switchback at the bottom, a great iron ring, segmented into three equal parts, encircled the facing slopes of the hill. Each iron segment suggested a location and configuration for each of the platoons in his rifle company. The left and right platoons, curving down the sides of the hill and enveloping the abandoned hut, would have commanding fields of fire along the length of both road approaches and over the downward slopes of Dog Hill itself. The third platoon, arcing across the top of the hill between the pine groves, would be held in reserve and could also defend against any attacks from the boulder-strewn slopes on the far side of the hill.

Captain Matheson squeezed his eyes shut and shook his head. When he opened his eyes again the great ring had faded. Without hesitation, he gave orders to each platoon to replicate the segments of the iron ring. When the platoons had finished this work, he personally set every machine gun and mortar position, then assigned defensive sectors and fields of fire—he reset one of the machine gun positions twice before satisfied with the sight angles. By the time he finished, darkness had shrouded the hill for nearly an hour. Captain Matheson designated the abandoned hut as the new company command post. Finally satisfied, as well as exhausted, he retired there for the night, confident that the company could defend Dog Hill and control the mountain pass.

Located at the top of the hill, Lieutenant Meyer's platoon stretched out above the far edge of the western pine grove to just a few yards beyond the eastern grove. Timothy and Humphrey had dug in near the western end of the platoon, about 30 feet from three tall pines. From that position they could see the abandoned hut and the lower ends of the other two platoons near the road. Someone had built a small fire near his foxhole, and Humphrey bent over the flickering light and attempted to read a book. Timothy had stripped down to the waist while digging the foxhole; he pulled on his pile-lined hooded parka as he approached the fire. He walked up behind Humphrey and tried to read the book over his shoulder. He couldn't quite distinguish the tiny words in the poor light.

"Hey Humphrey. What's this you're reading? And how come you're not dead-tired after digging that damn hole in the damn frozen ground. I know I am. But you know something?...thanks to the captain, I'll sleep soundly tonight knowing we're completely invulnerable to enemy attack."

Humphrey looked up from the small black book and sniffed at the cold air. "I'm reading Ecclesiastes."

Timothy squirmed his face. "Ecclesiastes? Why are you reading that?"

Humphrey looked up again. "I guess I just felt like reading by this pathetic little fire before hitting the sack, and I thought it might be interesting."

"I see. Well, if it's that interesting, how about reading it out loud so I can enjoy it too?"

"Read it out loud?"

"Yeah. That's what I said. Oh, I know what's going on. You're afraid of reading it out loud because then I'll find out that you really can't read at all and have been faking it all along, right?"

"If you really want to hear it, I guess I could give it a try. It's pretty hard to see by this fire."

"Yeah, I would."

"OK, but I'm not sure you're going to like it." Humphrey flipped back a few pages and started reading at the beginning. "The words of

Toil Under The Sun

the Teacher, the son of David, king in Jerusalem." Humphrey paused. "I went back to the beginning. That's the way it starts."

"I sort of figured that out already. Keep reading."

Humphrey continued. "Vanity of vanities, says the Teacher, vanity of vanities! All is vanity. What do people gain from all the toil at which they toil under the sun? A generation goes, and a generation comes, but the earth remains forever. The sun rises and the sun goes down, and hurries to the place where it rises."

Timothy interrupted. "Wait a minute. Before we go any further, who wrote this thing?"

"I haven't figured that out yet."

"Does it tell you later who wrote it?"

"Not that I could tell, but I haven't made it to the end yet."

Timothy thought about this for a moment. "You don't think it's this teacher guy?"

"No, I don't think so. I think someone else wrote it. But it's supposed to be the words of the teacher."

"You think someone ghost-wrote it for him?"

"I don't know. Maybe."

"Never mind. Keep reading."

Humphrey tilted the book to see the delicate pages better in the fire's fading light. "The wind blows to the south, and goes around to the north; round and round goes the wind, and on its circuits the wind returns. All streams run to the sea, but the sea is not full; to the place where the streams flow, there they continue to flow."

Timothy poked Humphrey on the shoulder. "This teacher guy seems a little obsessed with the weather. Do you think he was a weatherman?"

"Hey, we're not going to get very far tonight if you keep interrupting me."

"Sure, but do you think he was a weatherman?"

"No. I don't think they had weathermen in those days."

"What days are we talking about?"

Humphrey sighed. "I don't know. We're talking a really, really long time ago."

"Like hundreds of years?"

"No. More than that. Probably thousands."

"Fine. That's all I wanted to know."

Humphrey tilted the book again. "All things are wearisome; more than one can express; the eye is not satisfied with seeing, or the ear filled with hearing. What has been is what will be, and what has been done is what will be done; there is nothing new under the sun. Is there a thing of which it is said, 'See, this is new'? It has already been, in the ages before us. The people of long ago are not remembered, nor will there be any remembrance of people yet to come by those who come after them." Humphrey squinted to read the last words as the fire died in the increasing cold. When he finished, he closed the book with a little thump and slid it into his parka. "I can't see any more. What do you think?"

Timothy could feel the cold now. He had worked up a sweat while digging the foxhole, just as the Gunny had promised. Now he felt like he might shiver. "Gee, Humphrey. That last part is pretty damn depressing. What did he mean when he said there's nothing new under the sun, that it's already happened before? Do you think what's happening to us has happened before? And what's that part about not remembering anybody?"

Humphrey warmed his hands over the cooling embers. "I'm not sure he meant that this exact thing has happened before. He was probably talking about things in general."

"But that's not what he said."

"Yeah, I know that, but I don't see how what we're doing now could have happened exactly like this before. That's all."

Timothy looked down the hill then across the road to the dark mountains beyond. He could still see the edges of the mountains against the sky's vestigial light. He looked at the hut, still visible in the reddish glow of one of the warming fires. "You know, I think the teacher guy might be right."

Humphrey rubbed his hands together. "Right about what?"

Timothy crouched down and held his hands over the embers next to Humphrey's. "I think this *has* happened before. We just don't remember it."

Chapter 14

Mr. McDermott, February 1947

Timothy pulled the ice-crusted flap of his sleeping bag down and squinted into the morning's first light. Blotchy clouds had masked the stars during the night, but with the sun just moving above the mountaintops and a gentle breeze pushing the clouds to the south, the morning air had turned crisp and clear. A few wispy cirrus clouds drifted high in the northern sky; they did not detract from the clarity of the morning. Timothy flipped to his stomach and propped himself up on both elbows, the ground crunching softly under his shifting weight. He felt a surge of warm air on his face when it gushed out from the sleeping bag. He jerked the flap snugly around his neck and shoulders to prevent further heat loss. The dark green pine trees of yesterday, now lightly dusted with milky frost that sparkled in the slanting light, stood perfect and motionless in the cold, still air. He looked around the camp at the dozen or so sleeping bags scattered around him. He appeared to be the first one up.

"Alright you lazy little campers! It's time to get up and stop wasting the day!" Timothy was not the first one up. "C'mon now! Let's get a move on here. Everyone up! Time to get up!" Timothy heard several groans, and noticed that although a few of the sleeping bags had started squirming they moved at the speed of excited starfish. "I'll get the fire started while everyone gets dressed. Lord! What a spectacular morning. You can see forever! You've got to get up and see this morning!" Timothy thought to himself that Mr. McDermott always acted too damn happy in the morning. He usually behaved more somberly at night during the hours before bedtime, but in the morning, especially when the sun shined through clear skies, he acted too damn happy. Mr. McDermott began whistling *Scotland the Brave* while he built the fire, a selection from his prodigious repertoire of military marches, religious hymns, and unfamiliar popular tunes. In a few minutes Timothy could hear dry tinder crackling beneath larger timbers. The fire would begin roaring pleasantly in a few minutes more.

Timothy shoved his hand down into the bag and grabbed his rolled-up clothes. Mr. McDermott had taught all of the scouts to do this so their clothes would be warm when they got up in the morning. While still in the bag, Timothy unrolled the clothes and pulled on his socks and wool pants. He flopped around a few times before he finished. A layer of frost had glazed the zipper during the night, and it unzipped with impressive difficulty. After persistent effort, Timothy threw the bag open and felt a chilly bite of frigid morning air pour across his stomach. He pulled his boots and jacket on and jogged over to the fire. Mr. McDermott propped two more logs against each other on top of the blazing kindling and the fire snarled and hissed. The warmth of the fire felt good on his legs. "What time is it, Mr. McDermott?"

Mr. McDermott peeled back the sleeve of his long underwear and looked at an impressively large gold watch. "Let's see. Why, it's nearly seven-thirty. The day's almost over and we haven't even started breakfast yet. Did you have a good night's sleep, Timothy?"

Timothy yawned, his mouth gaping as he struggled to respond. "I...I...did. Did you have a good night's sleep, Mr. McDermott?"

"I certainly did, Timothy. But you know something? I always sleep good out here in the wilderness, especially when I know I'm going to wake up to a glorious morning like this." He stood up while holding his hands behind his hips, stretched back, and gazed up into the crystalline sky. "My, that feels good. I think it's time to get breakfast started. You ready for some breakfast, Timothy?"

Timothy licked his chapped lips. "I sure am." He hadn't appreciated his hunger until Mr. McDermott asked the question. "What're we having this morning?" Several of the other scouts had now crawled out of their bags and, attracted by the crackling fire and talk of breakfast, began pulling on their clothes.

Mr. McDermott pulled a rumpled piece of paper from his pants pocket and slowly unfolded it. He then opened a small leather case and removed a pair of gold-rimmed reading glasses. After carefully sliding the glasses over his ears and nose, he read the penciled words on the paper. "Let's see. It looks like pancakes and hot chocolate are on the menu this morning. Anyone here like some pancakes?" Mr. McDermott knew the scouts loved his pancakes; he always asked the question anyway. He prepared the batter with Timothy's help, and within minutes the scouts were cooking up pancakes for the morning feast. The smell of wood smoke mixed with the aroma of sizzling cakes persuaded the last of the dozing scouts to leave the warmth of their sleeping bags and step into the cold morning air. The scouts soon devoured the tasty pancakes, eagerly washing them down with hot chocolate. Mr. McDermott brewed himself a pot of cowboy coffee on the fire while the scouts finished breakfast. He drank two cups of the strong coffee before ordering the scouts to break camp.

"OK men, let's pack up our gear and clean this camp up. I don't want anyone to know we were ever here. We've got a long hike ahead of us today. It's time to get moving." While the boys scurried around the campsite rolling up sleeping bags and stuffing clothing and mess kits into overflowing packs, Mr. McDermott skillfully organized and packed his own gear until it looked like a camping display in a hardware store window. After storing the last item in a side pouch, he swung the heavy pack smoothly onto his back and adjusted the straps while he looked around the camp. When he thought the scouts were ready, he yelled, "Time for inspection! Patrol leaders, line up your patrols." The scouts organized themselves neatly into patrols and stood stiffly at attention while Mr. McDermott inspected the campsite, walking methodically back and forth as he studied the ground in front of his feet. After asking the scouts to pick up a few missed articles of clothing and a bit of garbage, he inspected the scouts themselves to assure himself that everyone had dressed properly and that their packs were secure. He asked one of the scouts to adjust his scarf and another to button his shirt, then shouted, "Patrol leaders, move your patrols out! Quickstep, march!" With patrol flags fluttering and the scouts stepping off in single file, not quite together but pretty close, they stepped off to wherever Mr. McDermott had planned to take them. The actual destination for the day really didn't matter: they were confident it would be somewhere good.

It turned out that Mr. McDermott had decided to take them up the side of a mountain. To begin their journey they hiked out of the sparse pine forest where they had camped and into a wide clearing with stunted shrubs, runty trees, low grasses, and a narrow meandering stream. Beginning at the edges of the sharply cut earth and working toward the middle, a sheen of ice had recently begun to form over the pleasantly trickling stream. Several of the scouts filled their canteens with the ice-cold water and enjoyed a refreshing drink. Mr. McDermott dropped to his knees, scooped up some of the clear water in his bare hands, and drank with pleasurable slurps. "You know boys, there's nothing like drinking from a clean mountain stream out here in the wilderness. Yes sir, there's nothing like it." He looked up to the sky and smiled broadly, then wiped his chin with the back of his sleeve. A peregrine falcon soared high above the clearing, its rhythmic song fading hauntingly as it flew toward the mountain that ascended from the thick pine trees beyond the edge of the clearing. The hawk shrank to a small speck in mere seconds. Mr. McDermott identified the hunting bird for the scouts before they moved on.

With the arrival of the great bird, the excited scouts found it more difficult to maintain the single-file discipline of the patrol as they crossed the remainder of the forest clearing. They scattered haphazardly and searched for other animals in the sky and on the ground. Mr. McDermott did not seem to mind, for he too began observing the skies more keenly, hoping to see another peregrine or other interesting bird. He walked more slowly now, stopping occasionally to study a specific sector of the sky. He did this for several minutes before noticing Timothy walking next to him.

"Timothy, my lad, what can I do for you?"

"Nothing Mr. McDermott." Timothy paused. "I was just wondering where we're going, that's all."

Mr. McDermott smiled. "You wonder where we're going? Don't we all, son. Don't we all." He chuckled because he knew that several years would pass before Timothy might understand his private joke. "In answer to your question, we're heading into that pine forest and up the mountain to the snow. If I've read my map correctly, and I'm sure I have, we'll be hiking through the snow before lunch. What do you think of that, Timothy?"

Timothy considered whether or not this question might be trickier than it sounded before answering. "Well, Mr. McDermott, it sounds sort of cold."

"That it does, Timothy, that it does." This time Mr. McDermott, enjoying the innocence of Timothy's answer, laughed wholesomely. "Tell me Timothy, have you ever camped in the snow before?" Although

Mr. McDermott had been the scoutmaster for several years, today would be the first time his scouts would camp in the snow.

"Well, sir, I've played in the snow before. I guess I can't say I've ever camped in it." Timothy tried to remember his snow experience. "I made a snow angel once."

"A snow angel! I did the same when I was a boy, Timothy. Maybe I'll make another one today when we reach the snow. That would be something, wouldn't it?"

"I've never seen an adult make a snow angel."

"You haven't? Then you shall see it today, Timothy."

They quietly strolled across the clearing for several minutes while Mr. McDermott scanned the sky above the mountain for more peregrine falcons. A couple of rowdy crows darted overhead, but they didn't really count. Timothy sniffed in a breath of cold air. "Mr. McDermott, I've been wondering about something."

"You've been wondering about something? And what might that be that you've been wondering about?" Mr. McDermott slowed his pace and turned his head away from the pleasant sky to look down at Timothy.

"I've been wondering about something I heard that's sort of been bothering me." Timothy did not have the courage to ask his question outright; he decided to build up to it.

"And what did you hear, Timothy?"

Timothy hesitated to swallow the gob of spit that had pooled at the back if his tongue. "I, uh, I heard you were in prison once. That's what I've been wondering about."

Mr. McDermott stopped and turned to face Timothy. "Well, Timothy, you can stop wondering now. I *was* in prison once."

"You were?" Mr. McDermott's immediate and direct answer surprised Timothy.

"I was. Why are you surprised? Don't you believe me?" Mr. McDermott smiled.

"Sure I do!" Timothy cringed the moment the words popped out.

"Well I'm so glad to hear you are so sure I was in prison."

Timothy felt curious and shaken at the same time. Now that he knew the rumors were true, he couldn't stop until he heard the entire story. He thought about the possibilities: maybe Mr. McDermott had robbed a bank; or maybe he had been a thief and stolen jewels from a safe hidden behind a picture; or better yet, maybe he had murdered someone in cold blood during a shoot-out. "What did you do? I mean, to get into prison?"

"You know, Timothy, no one's asked me about that for a long time. It's not a very nice story. Are you sure you want to hear about it?" A little somber for the first time on this camping trip, Mr. McDermott did not smile.

"Yeah. I would like to hear it. What'ya do. Rob a bank or something?" Timothy imagined Mr. McDermott, the scoutmaster of his troop, breaking into a bank with his ruthless gang, stealing huge bags of money, and making an escape in a fast getaway car while conducting a raging gun battle with the police.

"Nothing quite that interesting." Mr. McDermott paused to remember the details of his story. He had only told it twice in the last 32 years—the second time to a group of parents before he became the scoutmaster. "It happened in 1916, during the first week of July. I was a young man then."

"How young were you?" Timothy focused on Mr. McDermott's lilting voice, and lost awareness of the other scouts walking nearby.

"I was almost 22—less than a month from my birthday. It's funny I remember that, Timothy. It did not turn out to be a very good birthday."

"Were you home when it happened?"

"No, Timothy. I wasn't. I was in France, far away from home."

"What were you doing in France?"

"I had just been promoted to sergeant in the British Army. My regiment was deployed near the Somme River, in Northern France." Mr. McDermott remained silent for eight or nine steps after saying this, as if the word *Somme* held some special meaning for him. "We were lined up in the trenches, waiting for the order to go over the top. Heavy rains had pounded us all night and into the morning, and we were standing ankle-deep in mud. It seemed like we were always standing in mud. Artillery had bombarded the German positions for days. God, the noise was something awful. I thought some of the men might go mad from the noise. Then, just when I thought we couldn't take it any more, it went suddenly quiet. We listened to that eerie quiet for a long

Toil Under The Sun

time…and then the whistle blew, signaling the start of our attack. We climbed out of the trenches, lined up in ranks in good order, and began marching toward the German lines.

The cadenced song of another peregrine pierced the sky above where they walked. Mr. McDermott glanced up briefly, then quickly returned his gaze to the ground. "A low mist covered the field, making it a little hard to see; a few of the lads slipped in muddy holes or tripped over discarded rifles. Nothing happened at first. We reached the first line of barbed wire and started climbing over it. That's when the German machine guns opened up on us. Men started falling all around me. One of the lads in front of me was thrown back and knocked me over. Men got shot to pieces as they tried to untangle themselves from the barbed wire. I pushed myself up to my knees and looked around. Over half of my men were down. We lost more men as we fell back behind the protection of a small rise in the ground."

Mr. McDermott stopped swinging his arms, slowed his pace, and clasped his hands behind his back. "We laid there in the mud behind that little rise for maybe ten minutes. Bullets still sprayed the air just above our heads. I was thinking about trying to get my men back to our trenches when a captain crawled up next to me and began yelling. He demanded to know why I had stopped the attack. He ordered me to move forward. I looked around at my few remaining men and then told him what he could bloody well do with his bloody insane order. They stripped me of my rank and sent me to prison after that."

Timothy had not expected a story like this. His romantic images of an exciting bank robbery and high-speed getaway evaporated. He stopped walking and turned toward Mr. McDermott. Mr. McDermott stopped and turned too. "Where you there a long time?"

"Long enough, Timothy. I came to America after I got out."

"Gee."

"Gee indeed. That was a sad business, and long ago too. Maybe we should think of happier things now. What do you say?" Mr. McDermott smiled again and his voice brightened. "Maybe we should talk about the pleasant things we're going to do this afternoon after we reach the snow."

"Sure." Timothy said this with mock excitement. He could not stop thinking about Mr. McDermott's astonishing story.

"Gather 'round scouts! Gather 'round!" Boys ran from all directions and soon encircled Mr. McDermott and Timothy. "Who wants to know what we're going to do this afternoon? Raise your hand if you do." Every hand but Timothy's shot up. "Who's ever built a snow cave before?" The scouts stood silently. "Anyone?" Still no answer. "Well that's fine, because that's what we're going to do this afternoon. Does that sound like fun?" Every scout but Timothy cheered. "Alright then. Let's head up the hill to the snow so we can get started! The day's a wasting!" The scouts lined up and followed Mr. McDermott as he marched into the pine trees at the edge of the clearing. Timothy thought about Mr. McDermott's story throughout that afternoon and into the evening. He thought about it too before he drifted off to sleep wedged between two other scouts in a small snow cave. In a month or so the story would begin fading into a distant memory; before that time, it haunted his every thought.

◆ ◆ ◆

The road beyond Dog Hill, 27 November 1950

Stiff and unruly from the plunging temperature, the black phone wire hissed violently as it raced off the whirring reel mounted at the back of the jeep. Louder than the irregular pounding of the hardened tires against the rough surface of the mountain road, and higher pitched than the surging whine of the engine, the sibilant clamor echoed dissonantly in advancing and receding tones when the road moved back and forth between the sharply rising mountains. As the wire emptied itself onto the road in tight slapping loops, the spinning drum accelerated, continually elevating the pitch of the hiss until it replaced any reasonable consciousness of the pounding tires or whining engine. When the spewing phone line reached its tattered end, it yanked off the reel's spindle with a sharp snap that cracked the frozen air like a cowboy whip before falling lifelessly to the frozen surface of the road.

Corporal Russell, hearing the whip-snap of the black wire, forced the jeep to a sliding stop with a brutal jab against the break pedal. He stepped through the open side of the vehicle and walked unhurriedly to the rear of the jeep, then a few yards more before stopping. The two men sitting in the back near the empty reel watched him go by. Russell

Toil Under The Sun

looked up into the clear night sky and focused on the bright moon that floated almost directly overhead. "You know, it wouldn't be such a bad night if it wasn't so damn cold. Look at all the stars! I don't think I've ever seen so many stars before." The two men in the jeep hopped out and walked toward the corporal. Russell turned and griped while they approached. "Don't that beat all. I could've sworn we were going to make it to the end on that reel. The last thing I wanted to do is stand out here in the middle of nowhere freezing my damn fingers off splicing a stupid phone wire."

The shorter of the two men, a PFC named Schmidt, looked up at the myriad stars and wheezed out a vaporous breath. "Good night for snipers too. Nice and clear. You can see everything with that moon!"

Schmidt's jeep companion, a taller PFC blessed with the nearly unpronounceable name of Ustasiewski, did not acknowledge the humor in Schmidt's remark. "You know, I was mostly worried about freezing to death or falling out of the jeep. Now I have to worry about getting my head blown off too."

Schmidt acted unconcerned. He slapped his gloved hands together then rubbed them violently to generate a little warmth. "I wouldn't worry about any snipers. You probably *will* freeze to death before someone shoots you. Besides, there's probably no one within a hundred miles of here." This observation did not appreciably calm Ustasiewski, who did not believe there was no one within a hundred miles. However, the comment did evoke a brief, if admittedly gloomy, chuckle.

Corporal Russell peered down the twisting road until he had located the end of the phone line, then looked back at the jeep. The full length of the road, as far as he could see in either direction, sparkled with reflected moonlight. "I guess the only way to keep from freezing to death or getting shot is to get the last reel mounted and splice the line and then get the hell out of here. Let's go." They had done this many times before, but never at 15 degrees below zero. Russell backed the jeep up and stopped about 12 feet from the wire. Schmidt and Ustasiewski mounted a fresh reel and pulled out enough new phone wire until they could make the splice comfortably. Russell quickly went to work on the splice. "Hey, someone hold a flashlight here. That moon's just not quite bright enough for me to see what the hell I'm doing."

Ustasiewski retrieved a large green flashlight from the back of the jeep and held the weak beam on the impending splice. He shook the flashlight. "Hey, it looks like we need some new batteries. I'll go get some."

Russell could already feel the cold biting his exposed fingers when he twisted the first two phone wires together. "Don't worry about the batteries. Let's just get this done."

Schmidt pulled his sleeve back enough to look at his watch. "You guys know it's almost midnight? I should be in bed by now if I'm going to get my eight hours of sleep."

Corporal Russell chuckled for the first time. "When's the last time you got eight hours of sleep?" Only one more wire to go, and they could wrap this damn job up and get the hell back to regiment where they belonged.

"Wait a minute. Let me think. I know—it happened within the last ten years. It's almost coming to me. Oh yeah. I remember. It was the night before boot camp. That's the last time I got eight hours of sleep. Or maybe it was the night before…you know, I just can't remember for sure." Schmidt felt some unexpected nervousness near the end of his joke. The moon had begun its descent to the rugged horizon, and as it gradually shifted position in the clear sky it cast weirdly changing shadows against the jagged landscape of boulders, hills and crevices that bounded the narrow road. Schmidt walked to the jeep and pulled his rifle out of the back. He took a few cautious steps, then stopped and slowly searched the top of the shadowy mountain across the road. "You know guys, I have to admit that this place is giving me the creeps. Are you finished with that damn splice yet? I'm ready to get out of here."

Corporal Russell could hear the edginess in Schmidt's usually calm voice. He chided Schmidt without looking up. "Dammit Schmidt, I'm doing this as fast as I can. I don't like it out here any more than you do. It'll be done when it's done."

Schmidt complained by sniffing loudly, then quickly ejected the half-empty clip from his rifle. The clip pinged rhythmically when it bounced on the frozen ground. He picked it up before ramming in a fresh eight-round clip.

Ustasiewski smiled. "I thought you said there was no one within a hundred miles."

Toil Under The Sun

Schmidt did not smile. "Yeah, I did. But it's better to be safe than sorry. At least that's what my dad always said."

Ustasiewski did not intend to make a joke, but he did anyway. "Well, I wish your dad was here now. We could use the help."

Colonel Wu Zongxian squinted though his Japanese field binoculars and brought the dark jeep below into the clearest focus the moon's shifting light allowed. These binoculars, taken off a dead Japanese officer during the closing days of the last war, were his most treasured combat tool. Far better than the standard binoculars issued by his own army, and far more reliable, he had used them to enhance the proficiency of his leadership more than once. He used them now to discern the nature of the strange activity that unfolded a few hundred yards away in the middle of the narrow road. When he had snapped the jeep into a clear image, he swung the binoculars smoothly to the left until he could see three shadowy men standing close together. While he watched, one of the men walked to the jeep and pulled a rifle out of the back. The man with the rifle took a few steps before stopping to look up at Wu Zongxian. He quickly shielded the binoculars with his free hand to prevent an errant reflection of moonlight off the polished lenses. The man with the rifle stared directly at him, but then quickly looked away. The colonel removed his hand from the binoculars and continued his observation. The man then did something very odd. He appeared to empty his rifle, then bent down and reloaded before rejoining the other two men.

Captain Lin Wulong fidgeted next to the colonel, uncomfortable from the cold and eager to know what the colonel was looking at so intently. He could see movement down on the road, but no specific details. "Can you tell what they are doing, sir?"

Colonel Wu Zongxian lowered the Japanese binoculars and rubbed his eyes, strained from squinting in the low light. He carefully slid the binoculars into the leather case that hung from a strap over his neck and shoulder and quietly snapped the lid shut. Then, speaking in a soft whisper, he responded to his officer's question. "Three Marines and a jeep. They appear to be repairing a wire. One of them has a fully loaded rifle. One is holding a flashlight. They do not know we are here; however, they are nervous."

Lin Wulong promptly voiced his excitement. "Three Marines? Should I take some men down to the road and kill them, sir?" Weary of hiding during the light of day and waiting in the icy mountain shadows at night—and anxious for real combat—he had grown impatient to prove his courage.

Colonel Wu Zongxian considered this suggestion. He understood Wulong's impatience because he had once felt eager for battle too. His youthful eagerness for immediate action had been tempered into patience and wisdom during too many terrible battles with the Japanese and the following civil war with the Nationalists. "You young officers are both fearless and impatient. If you could kill them quietly without detection, I would not hesitate to give the order. Yet one mistake, even a small one, and the entire regiment will be revealed to the enemy. No. We will let them go. We have an objective of far greater importance."

Captain Lin Wulong listened respectfully to the colonel: he did not agree with the answer. An opportunity to kill Marines had presented itself, and the colonel had decided to do nothing. He understood the need to kill them quietly, but had absolute confidence that he could do it. He tried to conceal his disappointment. "Yes sir, I understand."

Colonel Wu Zongxian sensed Wulong's disapproval, and still remained certain of his decision. He spoke with a considerate but firm tone. "Do not be impatient. You will have many opportunities to kill Marines before we are finished. Now we must return to the regiment and prepare ourselves for battle."

Captain Matheson eyed Russell keenly. The corporal stood neatly at attention in the abandoned hut that now functioned as the company command post. He wasn't quite sure what to think about a jeep racing down the road toward his position after midnight, towing a phone line, and making a lot of unnecessary noise. He questioned the corporal with suspicion. "At ease, corporal. Now explain this to me again, just like you told it to the guard. You're here to install *what* in the middle of the night?"

Corporal Russell relaxed and shifted his feet and released his hands. "A phone line, sir. Regiment wanted a phone line brought to your position as soon as possible. We're here to install the phone."

"I see. A phone. And how long will it take to install it?"

"Not long, sir. We'll be out of your hair in a few minutes."

Matheson relaxed. "Alright then. Install the damn phone and then get the hell out of here. It's late and you've got a long drive back." Captain Matheson had not expected a phone connection to the regiment that had recently disappeared up the road.

"Yes sir. Right away, sir."

"One more thing."

"Yes sir?"

"You guys have got a lot of guts driving out here in the dark to install a damn phone. I appreciate the effort."

"Thank you, sir."

"You're welcome, corporal."

Timothy was taking his turn at guard duty when he heard a jeep racing noisily down the road. He watched two Marines with the forward platoon force it to stop. The jeep sat there for a minute, and then drove on until it stopped again below the abandoned hut with the engine still humming. The driver stepped out of the jeep and ran up the hill and into the hut. Timothy nudged Humphrey's sleeping bag with his rifle butt. "Hey Humphrey. Wake up. There's something funny going on down by the hut."

Humphrey heard Timothy tell him to wake up and felt the nudge of the rifle. The intense cold made it hard to sleep. He pushed himself up on one elbow and yawned. "Wha, what's going on by the hut?"

"A jeep just pulled up, and some guy jumped out and ran into the hut."

Humphrey yawned again. "And how does this concern me?"

"I dunno. I just thought you might be interested."

"Yeah, but it's my turn to sleep. Would you want me to wake *you* up just because a jeep drove up and some guy jumped out?"

Timothy poked Humphrey with the rifle butt again. "You're damn right I would."

"OK OK—I'll try to remember that. Do you mind if I go back to sleep now? I've still got almost an hour left before my turn."

"Sure. I'll just sit here quietly and make sure nothing happens to you while you're sleeping." Timothy leaned against the frozen edge of the foxhole and studied the jeep. Two men stood next to it now, talking to one of the Marines. He could hear that they were talking, but couldn't understand any of the words. The driver came out of the hut and then all three of them went in. After about ten minutes they loaded back into the jeep and drove up the road. Timothy remained quiet for only a few more seconds. "Hey Humphrey."

Humphrey turned his head inside the sleeping bag until his nose poked out of the hooded opening. "What now?"

"The jeep's leaving."

"Great. Thanks for letting me know."

"Humphrey."

"Yeah."

"You ever heard of the Battle of the Somme?"

"The Battle of the what?"

"The Somme. It's a river in Northern France."

"Sounds familiar. I think I might've heard about it in school. What about it?"

"I was thinking that Ecclesiastes might be about the Battle of the Somme, that's all."

"How's that?"

"The part that says *What's been is what will be, and what's been done is what will be done; there's nothing new under the sun.* That's the part I was thinking about."

"How's that about the Battle of the Somme?"

Timothy's voice turned more thoughtful. "There was a small town in Northern England, actually a village, with probably a few thousand people. In late 1915, after the war had already started, all of the young men in this village got together and formed an infantry company. The people in the town were all very proud, and had a big party to celebrate. Before the young men left they had their picture taken together in the town square. They were all smiling and wearing their best clothes. They left right after that. A local photographer developed the picture a few days later. They went to boot camp together, and they loaded onto the train in London together, and they made the trip across the channel to France together. They arrived at the front in June 1916, ready to fight." Timothy paused for a long time.

Humphrey sat up and leaned against the bumpy side of the foxhole, still zipped up to his underarms in the sleeping bag. "Then what happened?"

Toil Under The Sun

"The young men were sent to the front line trenches facing the heavily fortified German positions along the Somme River. They waited there while English artillery pounded the Germans for days. It turned out that the German soldiers just took their machine guns and went underground and waited. When the artillery stopped, they came back up and remounted the machine guns. The company of young men was in the first wave. When the whistle blew the company went over the top and marched across no man's land. When they reached the barbed wire, the German machine guns opened up on them. But you know, this didn't stop them. They just kept on going. The entire company got wiped out in less than two minutes."

Humphrey blinked twice. He hadn't expected the story to end this way. "Every last man? You mean, not a single guy made it?"

"Every man from that small village in Northern England was killed in less than two minutes." Timothy sat silently for a moment, and then added, "Their picture is still hanging on the wall in the town hall. You can see it if you go there."

Chapter 15

The color guard, July 1947

Martha struggled to restrain her lip from curling in delight. Every year John complained he'd never do it again, and every year they asked him to do it again, and every year he said yes anyway. In fairness, part of Martha's amusement derived from her own inability to say no in similar situations. But for the moment she could overlook her comparable weakness and simply enjoy John's—or more accurately, his response to it. With practiced skill, she waited for the perfect moment to tease him. "You know, I can't imagine how you ended up on that committee again, especially when you told them last year you were never going to do it again. Those people just don't listen to a word you say, do they."

John lowered his head and voice at the same time and sighed. "I didn't exactly tell them I wouldn't do it again. I might have been a little vague last year."

"Oh, I can understand that. But since they asked you again this year, and you told them 'no,' I just couldn't imagine how you ended up on the committee again. That's all."

"Uh, well, um, I didn't exactly say 'no' when they asked me this year."

"You didn't? What did you say?"

"I, uh…I sort of said yes."

This time Martha could not resist a pronounced curvature of her upper lip. She swallowed back a chuckle. "Oh—you *sort of* said yes. How did you do that? I mean, *sort of.*"

John knew that he could no longer avoid a full confession. "Alright, dammit! I admit it. I flat out said yes when they asked me. But I'm sure it won't be as bad as last year."

"It won't be? How's that?"

"I just have one job this year—it should be a lot less work than before."

"What job did they give you?"

"I just have to put together the color guard. It should be pretty easy."

Toil Under The Sun

No longer able to conceal her complete glee, Martha grinned openly this time. "The color guard? Oh yeah—that should be pretty easy all right. Let's see, there's four in a color guard, right? And how many veterans live in this town and the surrounding area. Oh, I would guess the number is in the hundreds, maybe even higher. Gee, it should be easy to pick out the four who are going to get to do it."

John felt a wave of heat flow across the back of his neck. Martha's sharp observation suddenly forced the complexity of his dilemma into clear view. What had appeared a reasonably simple task only a few hours ago now loomed as an insoluble predicament. He could see the members of the Fourth of July Committee having a really good laugh right about now. He decided to gag down his last remnant of pride and ask Martha for help. "I was sort of hoping you could give me a hand."

"Is that like *sort of* saying yes?"

John nearly shot off an angry response before deciding that he could not risk losing his only convenient ally. "You know what I mean. Are you going to help me out or not?"

Martha paused to let John sweat a little more. "Sure, I can help you out. But the real question is—what do I get in return?"

John grunted. "We can talk about that later. I don't have a lot of time right now. The parade's in less than two weeks. Do you have any ideas?"

Martha nodded, sympathetic for the first time, and then they sat down together at the dining room table and made a list of possible names. They agreed that it would be good to have individual members from the Army, Navy, Marines, and Army Air Corps; they made four columns and divided the names up. They crossed off anyone who had done it before, which reduced the list quite a bit. Although they easily came up with good candidates for the Navy, Marines, and Army Air Corps, there were too many choices for the Army position. They both stared at the list for a long time. Martha finally made a suggestion.

"I have an idea. What if we tried to pick a decorated war veteran for the Army spot? What do you think?"

John pulled his ear and lifted his chin. "Yeah, that sounds good. The only problem is, how do we figure that out?"

"Well, I had someone specific in mind. What would you think about Zach?"

John felt his gut flinch a little. "Zach?" He tapped a pencil on the table and tried to figure out a tactful way to disagree. "I don't know, Martha. He's pretty young. And he's been a little strange since coming back from the war."

Martha persisted. "He's not that young. He must be at least 26 by now; and didn't he get the Bronze Star, or some other medal?"

"I think that might be right. It was the Bronze Star. He got a Purple Heart too. If I remember correctly, he was a corporal in the 4th Infantry Division. He got the medals during a big battle in the Hurtgen Forest. At least that's what someone told me."

Martha smiled her approval. "Well then, I think we're finished. All you need to do then is contact our four finalists and you're done. That wasn't so bad, was it?"

"Zach's still a little strange. I'm not sure he's the best choice. Maybe we should go with someone more reliable." John scanned the list one more time and found a possibility. "How about Fred? I'm sure he'd be glad to do it."

"Oh John—you know Fred can be a big windbag sometimes. Besides, it would be good for Zach to get out and march in the parade. Just think of all the applause and appreciation he'll get."

John concluded that Martha had no intention of backing down. "I suppose you're right. I guess it wouldn't hurt to ask him. Maybe he'd even agree to do it. That would be something, wouldn't it? And if he says no, we can go with Fred."

"Yes, we can go with Fred if he says no. But you have to ask Zach first. And you have to promise to do a good job of asking him."

"I promise."

A week passed, and John had filled every position on the color guard except for the Army spot. He refused to admit it to himself: even with Martha's encouragement he had avoided driving to Zach's house and talking to him. Martha finally asked him how things were going with the color guard.

"How's the color guard coming along?"

John tried to deflect her question. "Pretty good I think. I'm almost done."

"Almost done? What's left?"

"Well, uh, the, uh, the Army is left. Don't worry—I'm working on it."

"You're working on it? What does that mean?"

"It means I'm working on it."

Martha's eyes narrowed. "Have you even talked to Zach yet?"

"Uh, no, I haven't. But I will."

"I think he's home today. Maybe you should drive over right now and talk to him."

"I thought I might drop by tomorrow sometime—maybe after dinner."

"The parade's less than a week away."

John thought he should stay with his plan to visit Zach tomorrow; then something different came out when he spoke. "I guess I *could* go see him right now. Maybe it would be better to get it over with."

Martha relaxed. "I think that would be good. Dinner won't be ready for at least another hour, and it should only take you a few minutes to drive over there and talk to him."

After a tranquil drive to Zach's house, John felt an unexpected twinge of nerves when he pushed the doorbell. He didn't really know Zach very well, although he knew him well enough to conclude that he sometimes acted a little strange. Surprisingly, he remembered Zach as no different from any other kid before the war. John noticed that the house could use a fresh coat of paint—probably could have used it about five years ago. A dog barked inside and scratched at the wood trim on the other side of the door.

Zach finally appeared and swung the creaking door partway open. He wore a saggy T-shirt and a cigarette drooped from his mouth. He didn't say anything. After a few seconds, John spoke first. "Hi Zach. How are you doing this evening?"

Zach plucked the cigarette out of his mouth, almost spitting it between his fingers. "Fine, John. I'm fine. How are you doing?"

"Fine, Zach. I'm fine too." John prepared himself to ask his question with the right tone of voice. He knew Martha would question him about his tone of voice when he sat down for dinner. "Say, Zach…I'm on the Fourth of July Committee, and I was hoping you'd be willing to march with the color guard this year. What do you think?"

Zach's eyes widened and then blinked twice. He shoved the cigarette back into his mouth and sucked in some smoke then blew it out through his nose. "I…I don't know John. I, uh, I, the fireworks…well, the fireworks make me sort of nervous." Zach inhaled some more smoke, then exhaled through his words. "I usually hole up here during the Fourth so I can't hear them."

Zach had just given John the perfect opportunity to say thanks and drive on to Fred's house, but he knew Martha would chastise him mercilessly if he gave up that easily. It would be important to be able to tell her that he had put up a good fight. "Well Zach, the fireworks aren't until hours after the parade. You'd have plenty of time to march with the color guard and then get back home so you wouldn't have to hear them. Besides, I don't think anyone will mind if you're a little nervous. We're all friends in this town, after all."

Zach removed the cigarette again; his hand shivered this time. "You don't understand, John. I get *really* nervous. Sometimes I can't even think straight any more. I, I wouldn't want to embarrass everyone."

John decided to push a little harder. Martha would be proud of him, even if Fred did end up on the color guard instead of Zach. "Like I said Zach, the only thing you're going to hear is applause and appreciation for what you've done for your country. I think it will be good for you to hear that folks care. However, if you really don't want to do it, I guess I could ask someone else."

Zach thought about this long enough to finish his cigarette. He flicked the smoldering butt through the crack in the door and out onto the front lawn. "There won't be any fireworks until after the parade?"

"That's right. I promise you'll have plenty of time to get home before the fireworks start. I can even give you a ride if you want. Zach, I think you should do this. We're all proud of you, and we'd love to see you march with the color guard."

"O, OK, John. I, I'll do it. When does the parade start?"

"It starts at noon, but staging is at 11:00 am behind the lumber yard. Oh, and don't forget to wear your uniform and your medals. I think folks will want to see those."

"OK John. I can do that." Zach reached through the door to shake John's hand. When John grasped Zach's hand, he felt a discomforting tremble.

Dazzling sunlight blazed beyond the tall slit at the end of the damp alley. Still almost an hour from its zenith, the sun had not yet reached the correct azimuth to fully warm the alley, and instead cast a teasing band of light high up on the mottled brick of the northern wall. Yet the buildings of Main Street, running south and north beyond the western end of the alley, glowed with the pleasantness of the sun's warmth. Later, after the events of the day had played out, the nearly setting sun would fill the alley with radiant light for a few precious minutes, but not enough to drive away the dampness.

"Damn, it's going to be a scorcher. What do you think, Raymond? Do you think it's going to be a scorcher?" Wes did not look up from his work as he spoke. He had arrived at the complicated part and didn't want to make any mistakes.

Raymond looked bigger than ever, almost too big. He gazed around at the moist walls of the dusky alley, then glanced up at the constricted strip of crystal blue sky at the top of the alley. "Yeah, it's going to be a scorcher."

"What do *you* think, Timothy? Do you think it's going to be a scorcher too?"

Timothy felt a little jittery, although he tried his best to appear relaxed and unconcerned. "Yeah Wes, whatever you say."

This listless answer did not satisfy Wes. "You're agreeing with me that it's going to be a scorcher? Is that what you're trying to say?"

Timothy responded with only slightly more fervor. "Yeah, Wes. I agree with you. It's going to be a scorcher."

Wes smiled slyly. "Good. I'm glad you agree with me. Did you hear that, Raymond? Timothy agrees with me."

Raymond held three pudgy fingers over his mouth and sniggered hard until he snorted a string of snot into his cupped hand. He quickly wiped it on the back of his pants so that no one would see. "Yeah, I heard it."

Wes displayed his great pleasure with an arrogant smirk. "Great—since we all agree, let me show you how this works." Wes held up his contraption so Raymond and Timothy could see it clearly. "As you can see, I've twisted the fuses of these cherry bombs into seven groups of three. I ran a single fuse, scavenged from other fireworks, into each group until I have a string of 21 cherry bombs. I then tied the ends of the fuse together to make a ring of cherry bombs." Wes paused to allow time for appropriate admiration of his cleverness. "Now, when I light this end, the fuse will burn in both directions until the first three go off. But then the fuse will keep burning until the next three go off, then the next three, and so on and so on. I expect there will be three cherry bomb explosions every couple of seconds until all 21 go off. It's going to make a hell of a lot of noise and smoke. What do you think?"

Raymond nodded his approval, but then, he never disagreed with anything Wes did or said. "I think it's really great!"

Timothy did not want to repeat the earlier discussion; he answered more passionately this time. "Yeah Wes—it's great, really great."

"Excellent. I'm pleased that both of you recognize my genius. But you know, I don't think it's fair that I should get to throw it just because I made it. Shoot, I had a whole lot of fun making it; why should I be the only one who gets to have fun? I think one of you guys should throw it. What do you think?" Both Raymond and Timothy nodded. "Good. Then here's what we're going to do. I'm going to think of a number between one and ten, and whichever one of you guesses the closest, you get to throw the cherry bomb ring." They both nodded again. "Let's get started then. I'm thinking of a number between one and ten. Raymond, what's your guess?"

"Uh, ten?"

"And Timothy, what do you guess?"

"Three."

Wes acted astonished and then slapped his thigh hard with his free hand. "Damn, Timothy, it was three right on the nose. How did you do that? That's amazing!"

"I just guessed, Wes."

"Then Timothy, because of that amazing guess you're going to get to throw the cherry bomb ring. Now here's the plan. The parade starts in less than an hour, so people should start lining up on Main Street in a few minutes. We'll stay back here until just before the start, then we'll move up to the end of the alley and wait behind the people. Now—and here's the best part—when the color guard passes the end of the alley, we'll light the fuse and throw the ring behind them. When the cherry bombs start going off, you're going to see those stupid old geezers dance like a bunch of idiots." Wes started laughing uncontrollably. "It'll be funny as hell." He fell back against the brick wall and held his stomach while he laughed, almost dropping the cherry bomb ring.

Timothy tasted a gush of bile at the back of his tongue. "Maybe Raymond should throw the ring. He's a lot stronger than I am."

Wes had no intention of letting Raymond throw the ring. "Hell no, Timothy. You won fair and square, and you're going to throw the ring. Now let's get ready. This will be great."

Waiting in a dark alley would normally have been a boring activity, but the next 37 minutes raced by as Timothy stood there holding the cherry bomb ring in his sweaty hand, wishing he hadn't guessed number three. People were lining Main Street, just like Wes had said they would, and before Timothy could think of a way to get out of this the color guard marched by. Wes struck a wooden match against the side of his shoe and ignited the fuse. Timothy just stood there, listening to the dreadful hiss of the fuse, his feet appearing to stick to the damp pavement.

Wes looked down at the burning fuse then screamed into Timothy's ear: "Throw the damn ring before it blows all of us up!"

Without thinking, Timothy ran out of the alley and flung the cherry bomb ring between a little girl and her grandfather. The girl, wearing a white dress trimmed with red and blue ribbons, felt the ring brush her ankle when it whirred by. The ring spun and bounced violently as it skated across the pavement, stopping just behind the color guard. The first three cherry bombs exploded with a deafening roar, bringing screams from the crowd. Then the next three went off, then the next three, and so on and so on, just like Wes had predicted. When the smoke cleared, Timothy saw Zach rolled into a fetal position in the middle of the street, still clutching a white M-1 rifle to his chest while he shivered in the hot sun. Wes and Raymond laughed uncontrollably as they escaped through the other end of the dark alley.

♦ ♦ ♦

Dog Hill parade, 28 November 1950

Born into a large family in the Xinjiang Province in northwestern China, Lin Dehua had fought bravely with the People's Liberation Army in the civil war with the Nationalists throughout the final months of 1949. Now a member of the Chinese People's Volunteer Army, he crossed the Yalu River undetected in late October 1950 during the launch of the *War to Resist U.S. Aggression and Aid Korea*. In the closing weeks of November, as freezing temperatures plunged North Korea into a bitter winter, he moved secretly across the magnificently rugged mountains of the sprawling Changjin Reservoir to a small valley less than three miles from the narrow pass that skirted Dog Hill. Lin Dehua and over 4,000 of his comrades had waited there until tonight, hidden from view by the steep walls of the valley. Now, as the descending moon touched the dark horizon of outlying mountains, his unit moved out again, marching on the same narrow road that had been filled with thousands of Marines earlier in the day.

Tramping vigorously down the road while wedged between two other soldiers, Lin Dehua's fleece-lined cap and quilted uniform provided some comfort from the intense cold for the first time in days. Even so, the toes of his left foot throbbed painfully with each pounding step and the frigid air stung his nose and blistered his lips. A Chinese-made submachine gun, its leather strap taught against his collarbone, bounced metrically, slapping his insulated thigh each time he thrust his leg forward. He could see very little from his position in the column, not because of the fading light of the setting moon, but because men surrounded him on all sides—one to his left, two to his right, and thousands in front and behind. Several times he tried to glimpse the front of the column by comically hopping up and down on his good foot; an annoyed comrade soon discouraged this behavior. He ultimately resolved himself to trudge on bravely without knowing his destination, certain that whatever lay ahead would provide opportunities to prove his courage and serve his country in glory. While he thought of this, he heard a muddled blare of trumpets and the crackling echoes of rifle and submachine gun fire.

"Timothy. It's your turn." Timothy's sleeping bag did not move. Humphrey scraped his knee when he slid a little closer to the dormant bag. "Timothy. It's almost 0400. Time to get up. It's your turn." Still no response. Humphrey moved again until his nose almost touched Timothy's partially exposed ear. When he opened his mouth to speak, Timothy's hands shot forward and grabbed Humphrey around the neck, knocking off his helmet. Humphrey yelped and jerked his head back. Then he swore as he fell back awkwardly against the side of the foxhole. "Gol darn it Timothy! What are you trying to do, scare the crap out of me?"

Timothy chuckled softly, pleased that he had scared the crap out of Humphrey. "No, buddy. Just trying to keep you on your toes, that's all."

Humphrey rolled forward again, and after groping around in the dark for his helmet finally picked it up and pressed it angrily onto his head. "Thanks a lot. I probably won't be able to sleep for the rest of the night because of your stupid joke."

Timothy responded with a measured tone of sarcasm. "Oh, I'm so sorry. Did I really scare you that bad? I mean, did you actually crap your pants?"

"Hell no. You just surprised me, that's all."

"That's good, 'cause the crap would freeze to your butt if you pulled your pants down to clean it up." Timothy peeled the sleeping bag off his legs and fished around in the dark for his shoepacs. He found them crammed behind his pack. When he tried to pull one of them on, the felt innersole had frozen into the shape of a bent sausage patty and prevented his toes from moving beyond the heel. He hissed in frustration. "Hey Humphrey, do you remember what these shoepacs are good for? I think I've forgotten again."

This question puzzled Humphrey, but he made a naive attempt to answer it anyway. "As I remember it, the rubber bottoms are supposed to keep your feet dry and the felt innersoles are supposed to keep your feet warm. Of course, you're supposed to wear wool socks too, and change them everyday. At least that's what the Gunny keeps telling us. I don't know why they have leather tops. Maybe it's to make us look snazzy when we're marching around."

Timothy pried the frozen innersole out of the stiff shoepac with his bayonet and tried to straighten it out by slapping it repeatedly against a rock. "I understand that my feet look really good when I'm wearing these things, but explain to me why my feet are always wet and cold instead of dry and warm?"

"I'm not sure I—" Humphrey heard a faint noise to the northwest that sounded like trumpets and automatic weapon fire. He turned around and peeked over the edge of the foxhole in the direction of the commotion. He could see flashes of light pulse chaotically against the low clouds hovering just above the mountainous horizon. He suddenly stood up in the foxhole and shoved both hands into jacket pockets.

Timothy had finally straightened out the unruly innersole. He complained about the numerous shortcomings of shoepacs as he pulled them on and tied the laces. He thought he could already feel the cold seeping through his wool socks. Humphrey suddenly stood up and moved to the edge of the foxhole. "What is it, Humphrey?"

Humphrey, not quite sure what he was seeing and hearing, hesitated. "I don't know. Looks and sounds like someone's shooting off a bunch of fireworks."

Timothy struggled to his feet and stood next to Humphrey. He squinted into the northern darkness. The trumpet sounds multiplied and the flashes of light grew brighter and more complex. "Damn. It looks like the Fourth of July. Must be something going on up north."

Humphrey sniffed and then wiped his nose on the back of his glove. He studied the flashing lights and listened to the chorus of trumpets. "Yeah, must be."

Lance Corporal Ensley shivered and watched the moon creep behind the mountains. He glanced at his watch for the third time in five minutes—almost 0400. From his position near the bottom of the hill he could still make out the road where it curved out of sight about 400 feet away. The vanishing moonlight would make it challenging to see anything in a short while. He listened for any night sounds and heard nothing. He did hear the hood of his parka when it chafed against the edge of his helmet, but that didn't count. The intense silence reminded him of a particular winter night on his parents' farm back in Caldwell. His dad had given him his first serious responsibility that morning. He remembered carrying a glowing kerosene lamp as he crunched though the brittle snow toward the barn to check on a mare about to foal. Rusty hinges creaked when he swung the heavy door open. He walked into the musty, cavernous barn and the lamp filled the space around him with a gentle glow. When he approached the mare, she jerked her head around to look straight at him and then snorted a foggy cloud. He remembered kneeling cautiously by the mare's side and stroking her gently on the neck. Comforted by his presence and gentle touch, she laid her head back down on the brittle hay. He stayed with her until the foal was born a few hours later. Thinking about this night on the farm warmed him a little, until he heard a strange cadenced shuffling up the road. He squinted in the direction of the sound and could not see a thing. He rubbed his eyes and squinted again, and this time he saw movement.

"Hey Bishop, wake up." Numb from the cold, Bishop groaned a little. "Bishop, wake up. There's something coming down the road."

Bishop opened an eye and coughed. "What?"

"I said, there's something coming down the road."

Both of Bishop's eyes flashed open and he pushed himself up. "What's coming down the road?"

"I don't know. I wanted you to take a look. You've got better night vision than I do."

Bishop hurriedly stripped off the sleeping bag from around his legs and moved to Ensley's side, the toes of his wool socks catching on a smear of frozen gravel. He peered intently down the road, looking a little to the side. "I can't say for sure, but it looks like some sort of parade."

Ensley turned his head and shrugged in the dark. "A parade? Are you joking?"

"No, I'm not joking. It looks like four rows of guys marching down the road. It looks just like a parade, that's all."

Ensley shrugged again. "Can you see if they're ours?"

Bishop squinted, harder than before. "No, can't tell if they're ours, but whoever they are, it looks like they'll arrive here in about two minutes."

"Damn. Go tell the captain. He'll want to know about this." Bishop yanked on his untied shoepacs before stumbling out of the foxhole. He pulled his parka over his head and receded into the darkness. "And don't tell him it's a parade. He'll think you're crazy."

The rhythmic shuffling intensified as it marched closer to Ensley. The first row of men had reached a point less than 200 feet from his position now, and he still could not see who they were. His hand quavered when he pulled back the bolt of his heavy machine gun, loading a .30 caliber round into the waiting chamber with a sharp metallic clack. He braced his toes against the ground and squinted again at the mysterious men, now only 100 feet away. The cadenced shuffling, still muffled by the heavy night air and frozen road, growing in volume with each passing second, became an insistent pounding in Ensley's head when the first row marched to within 50 feet of his line of fire. He could see them now. He could see quilted uniforms and pile-lined caps with silly looking earflaps. He could see burp guns bouncing at men's sides as they bobbed up and down. "Damn, there's a lot of them," he whispered to himself. Ensley swung the front sight of his weapon to the right until it aligned with one of the men in the first row, took a deep breath, and then pressed his gloved finger firmly against the trigger.

Captain Matheson, sleeping peacefully for once and dreaming about something pleasant that happened a few years ago in San Diego, sat up and reached for his rifle when Bishop stumbled into the hut and slammed the ancient wooden door violently against the wall. Bishop panted heavily. "Captain, Captain Matheson, there's, there's a p—, there's a bunch of guys coming down the road, but we can't tell who they are. Ensley thought I should come and tell you about it."

Matheson kicked off the warm sleeping bag. He tumbled to his hands and knees and began crawling around. "Damn it, where are my shoepacs. I thought I put them right here next to my bag." He groped around in the dark hut. "You don't see them anywhere, do you? I'm sure I put them right here."

"No sir, I don't see them anywhere."

"Damn. What's this about a bunch of guys?"

Bishop got down on his hands and knees too and began searching for the missing shoepacs. "I don't know. There's just a bunch of guys marching down the road, but we can't tell who they are. Here they are. I found your shoepacs!"

The sound of Ensley's machine gun erupted outside when Bishop held up the shoepacs. "Bishop! What's going on out there?"

"I told you, sir. There's a bunch of guys marching down the road. Ensley told me not to say this 'cause you'd think I'm crazy, but it looks like a parade."

"A parade?" Matheson sat on the damp floor of the hut and jammed his feet into the shoepacs. When he rolled onto his back to tie the laces, the clatter of Ensley's machine gun was joined by the crackle of rifle fire and burp guns. One of the laces broke off in his hand when he pulled it tight. He sat up, holding the unfortunate remnant in his upturned hand, and then flung it against the wall in disgust. He slammed his helmet on, forced his arm through the right sleeve of his parka, and scooped up his M-1 Carbine with his left hand. He remembered the phone after stepping toward the door.

"Wait a minute, Bishop. I've got to call regiment." He picked up the handset and pressed it against his ear; he held his free hand over his other ear to block out the spreading cacophony outside of the hut, now rising in a frightening crescendo. "Dammit, this thing's freezing cold." He tapped the receiver a few times, then picked up the whole thing and slammed it hard against the table. He listened again, and heard nothing. "Shit and double-shit!"

Bishop stammered with alarm. "Wh, Wha, What's wrong?"

Matheson set the handset down, gently this time, and adjusted his parka. "The phone's dead. I think the line's been cut. Let's get the hell out of here." The loose shoepac flapped on the ground as he ran from the hut. Bishop followed closely behind.

Lin Dehua found it more difficult to see the men to his right and left in the receding moonlight, and consequently more difficult to stay neatly in line. The moon had nearly vanished now behind one of the high mountains encircling the narrow valley. He hoped it would reappear on the other side so that he could see better; he did not know if it would. Although the toes of his left foot had throbbed painfully a few hours ago, they now felt almost fully numb. This both lessened the pain and made it more difficult to march with an even stride. As the numbness overcame his toes he began to notice a pulse of discomfort in his left heel. He remembered the same sensation in his toes. He was speculating whether or not his heel might go numb too when a long burst from a heavy machine gun erupted down the road near the front of the column.

Lin Dehua felt both excitement and confusion until an officer screamed an order for the column to charge forward. Lin Dehua nearly fell to the ground when the man behind him pushed against his back and stepped hard on his throbbing heel. He winced in pain before quickening his pace to a jog as rifle and burp gun fire joined the chattering machine gun. Even though Lin could not see anything, the sounds of the growing battle increased in volume when he approached a curve in the narrow road. After he rounded the sharp curve, the long column of men in front abruptly scattered away to his right and left, leaving him with an unexpectedly complete view of the entire battle. A flare exploded high above him, filling the road with bright light. Flashes of rifle and machine gun fire and exploding hand grenades added to the light. Hundreds of his comrades scattered across the road, running in every direction. Others sprawled awkwardly on the ground, motionless and still.

He continued to move forward, fascinated by the incredible scene unfolding before him. Hindered by his numbed foot, Lin Dehua stumbled. Dozens of faster comrades surged around him, blocking his view again. He tried to increase his stride to catch them, but a mortar round exploded 30 feet ahead, knocking him to the ground. Dazed by the concussion of the explosion, he pushed himself up onto his hands and knees. He could no longer see anyone in front of him. He looked up, and a second flare burst above. Confused, he remained still for a moment—then a stream of machine gun bullets raced up the road toward him. He frantically clawed and kicked at the frozen ground to clumsily propel himself to the edge of the road before leaping off into a ditch. A sharp rock cut his ankle when he hit the bottom. The stream of bullets shrilled by overhead. Lin rolled over to his back against the steep edge of the ditch and reached for his burp gun, but it was no longer there. This concerned him for a moment; then he thought to himself that it should be easy to find another one.

Timothy raised the brim of his helmet a little to see better, but it didn't help. "What do you think it is?"

Humphrey couldn't think of anything better to say, so he simply affirmed Timothy's observation and added his own about the trumpets. "I don't really know, but I think you're right about one thing: it's like the Fourth of July—except for the trumpets. I don't know what that's all about."

"Yeah, I'm stumped about the trumpets too. I'd think the mouthpiece would freeze your lips before you could blow any notes."

"Evidently not."

"Maybe they warm the trumpets up first, I mean before they play."

"How would they do that?"

"I don't know. I was a percussionist, not a trumpet player. Maybe they stick them in a fire or something. Of course, then you'd burn your lips instead of freezing them."

"Yeah, that would be bad. And what's that other sound. I can't quite make it out."

"You mean the gunfire?"

"No, not that. I know what that is. It's another sound, a strange sort of metal sound. But it's too far away and I can't make out what it is."

Timothy turned his head and listened intently for a moment. "Oh, I know what that is. That's an easy one."

"What?"

"It cymbals, a whole bunch of them. I used to play the cymbals."

"Cymbals?"

"Yeah. It's like there's a marching band up north somewhere with only trumpets and cymbals."

"Why would someone be playing cymbals? Doesn't that seem sort of crazy?"

"The only crazy thing is, I still can't figure out how they warm up the trumpets so they don't freeze their lips."

The conversation about trumpets and cymbals and marching bands stalled for almost a minute before Timothy spoke again. "I remember a Fourth of July, a few years ago. It was hot, a real scorcher." He paused to needlessly adjust the position of his helmet and to pull his gloves on a little tighter. "I remember really looking forward to it. There was going to be a parade in the morning and a town picnic at the park in the afternoon and a big fireworks show later that night—big for our town, at least."

"Yeah, they used to have a parade where I lived too. All of the kids used to decorate their bikes and ride in it. I remember tying poker cards on my bike frame with rubber bands so they fluttered on the spokes. It made it sound like you were going really fast, even when you weren't. My dad got pretty mad the next Friday when he played cards with some friends and he was missing a few. Turned out the card he needed during a really important hand was attached to my bike. Why were you looking forward to the Forth of July?"

Timothy stared at the flashing lights and listened intently to the gunfire and trumpets and cymbals before answering. "I, I just remember looking forward to it. I remember thinking it was going to be a good day when I got up in the morning, and just having a good feeling about it." He paused again. "I remember thinking about the parade, and all of the good food at the picnic, and staying up late to watch to fireworks. It should have been a good day."

"And, *was* it a good day?"

Timothy turned his head slightly to look at Humphrey. "Not exactly. It didn't turn out like I expected."

After waiting for Timothy to continue the story, Humphrey asked, "Are you going to tell me about it, or do I have to guess?"

Timothy breathed deeply. A shiver raced down his back, causing him to shake noticeably. He chuckled cynically in his head when he thought about Humphrey trying to guess what had happened. "It's a pretty complicated story, but I—" A long machine gun burst down by the road ripped the tranquil air. Startled, both of them quickly spun around. Humphrey's foot got caught on one of the sleeping bags and he almost fell. They watched in silence until a flare exploded above them, flooding the road below in sharp-colored light and revealing hundreds of soldiers running in every direction.

Timothy finally said something. "Now what do you think this is?"

Humphrey said the first thing that came into his head, although he didn't know what it meant. "I think it's the Fourth of July." Both of them dove instinctively into the foxhole when a stray bullet zinged off a rock a few feet away.

Chapter 16

The Navajo Reservation, August 1947

Despite the fact that it lumbered along the road like a great Sherman Tank, the green station wagon did have one exceptional attribute: the generous amount of space in the back seat, in length, depth, and height. This unusual abundance had proven especially important on previous trips to Iowa. Sitting up in a cramped position with knees jammed into the back of the front seat would have been a desperate exercise at best, especially when crossing the scorched and endlessly monotonous lands of Eastern Oregon, Nevada, Utah, and Arizona. The manufacturer of the vehicle had also provided plenty of storage behind the seat, allowing all of the luggage to fit neatly in the rear and leaving the entire back seat available to stretch out and take a nap—at least some consolation to an otherwise disagreeable situation. At one time, Timothy had fondly anticipated these cross-country trips to visit the relatives in Iowa. For reasons he could not explain, and that his parents refused to understand, he had no desire to go this time. Maybe he did not want to go because he had matured into a young man. Maybe he had lost interest in the countless grandparents and uncles and aunts and cousins who lived from Davenport to Des Moines. Maybe he just didn't care anymore. He told his parents that he wanted to stay home this time. They had listened politely and then ignored his request. So he stretched out in the back seat of the green station wagon one last time and tried not to look at the scorched and endlessly monotonous lands whenever possible.

With effort he probably could have tolerated this last tedious drive to Iowa, but his mom had planned an unfortunate side trip to Arizona to visit a friend he had never heard of. This would divert them several days and hundreds of miles off the traditional route, amplifying his frustration. Although his sense of connection to the Iowa relatives had mysteriously diminished—they seemed more and more unlike him with each passing year—he still found that he could enjoy their numerous eccentricities sufficiently to justify the long trip. In contrast, he had never met his mom's Arizona friend, and could therefore think of no good reason why he should waste his time meeting her now.

"Hey dad, where are we now?" The endless landscape of sagebrush, scrubby plants, and sand gave Timothy no clue as to his location.

John turned his head slightly, cracking the vertebrae in his upper neck after hours of staring down the long, unvarying road. "Ask your mom. She's the navigator."

"Hey mom, where are we now. Are we in Arizona yet?" Timothy thought to himself that they'd damn well better be in Arizona after an eternity of driving.

Martha slowly opened a brittle and faded map, taking care not to tear the already frayed creases. She adjusted her glasses a little further down her nose and looked for the thin red line they were traveling on. "Yes, Timothy. We should be in Arizona now. We crossed the state line a little while ago. At least I'm pretty sure we did."

This imprecise answer did not satisfy Timothy. His boredom had grown almost unbearable, and he needed accurate information to beat it back. "How much longer before we get there? I mean, to your friend's house."

"I don't think she lives in a house, Timothy. I think she lives in a trailer. At least that's what she wrote in her last letter."

Great, she doesn't even live in a house. Where are we supposed to sleep—in the damn station wagon? That would be a joke. "So she doesn't live in a house. How long until we get to the trailer?"

Martha studied the map again. "We're still over a hundred miles from Window Rock, and she lives about 50 miles from there—it'll be awhile."

This annoyed Timothy, and he made little effort to conceal it. "Who is this friend, anyway? Do we really have to see her? It's still not too late to turn back and head straight to Iowa, ya know."

Martha acted surprised by the suggestion that they turn around and head straight to Iowa. "Honestly Timothy! She's a close friend. We grew up together. And she wrote me a letter to invite us to visit her on our way to Iowa. It's a good opportunity to see her again."

On our way to Iowa—you've got to be kidding me. This has got to be hundreds—no, thousands of miles out of our way. And I can't even imagine how much time we're wasting on this ridiculous detour. "This doesn't seem like it's on our way to Iowa. Why didn't you just call her on the phone or something?"

Martha tried to sound sympathetic, although she had no intention of turning around. "I suppose I could have, but that wouldn't be the same as visiting her in person. Besides, this is a special opportunity. I don't think you'll ever get a chance like this again."

Timothy slumped back into the seat and squinted through the side window, discolored by hundreds of miles of dust. He rolled the window down a little more because of the heat, and the wind began a fluttering cadence. He listened to the wind until a juicy bug splattered on the windshield, making a pleasing but inexplicable sound. Scrubby sagebrush and burnt yellow ground continued to race by, endless and boring. *A chance like this again? What was that supposed to mean—a chance to get bored to death maybe?* "What kind of chance are you talking about?"

"A chance to see the Navajo Indian Reservation. That's what I mean. I don't think we'll ever get a chance to see it again, at least not with someone who's been living on it."

A chance to see an Indian reservation? Who the hell cares if we never get a chance like this again? "Is your friend a Navajo?"

"No, silly. She's white, like you and me."

Now that's really stupid. What's she doing living with a bunch of Indians if she's white? "What's she doing on the Navajo Reservation then?"

"She's a teacher. She teaches elementary school to little Indian boys and girls."

Now I've heard everything. She must be crazy to come out here all by herself to the middle of nowhere to teach elementary school to a bunch of Indians. Maybe she couldn't get a job anywhere else. She must be a rotten teacher. Or maybe she's on the run from the law. "Why's she out here? Is she a bad teacher or something?"

"No, Timothy, she's an exceptional teacher. I think that's why she came out here in the first place. I think she wanted to make a difference."

Make a difference—for what? That doesn't make any sense at all. I wonder if she really is out here by herself. "Is she married?"

"No, Timothy. She's single. She never got married."

Never got married? Then she must be really ugly. Maybe she has a hooked nose with a big wart on the end of it. Maybe she's really fat. No one probably wanted to marry her. Maybe that's the real reason she came out here. "Is she pretty?"

Martha smiled. "I would say she is. She's sort of your girl next door."

Aha! I know what that means. Dammit—why did she have to write that stupid letter asking us to see her when she lives in the middle of the desert surrounded by Indians? Why couldn't she just mind her own business? Now it will be days before we get to Iowa, assuming we get out of the reservation alive. "Why did she want you to come and see her? Isn't that sort of strange after all these years?"

"Not really. We've both been busy, and sort of lost track of each other. I don't think it's strange at all that she wrote to me now."

Timothy, already starting to doze a little, did not have the mental vigor to continue the conversation. He grunted impolitely after Martha answered his last question, and, gently swayed by the vibration of the green station wagon, fell asleep in less than five minutes. The lumbering vehicle continued to plod ahead and finally rolled into the small town of Window Rock at the eastern edge of Arizona a couple of hours later. Martha pulled her friend's letter out of her purse, unfolded it, and studied the small map that had been neatly penned on the back of the last page. The asphalt road, unbearably straight and level for the last 300 miles, quickly turned to cracked and bumpy asphalt, then to potholed gravel, then to rolling dirt, then to something else. They arrived at the single-story brick school building just before 5:00 pm. The late Friday afternoon sun would soon slide behind some low clouds that hovered a few miles away. A gentle breeze rustled a cluster of small trees near the edge of a modest playground with slide, swing set, and merry-go-round. The merry-go-round rails and deck were bent out of shape from hard use, but looked like they still worked well enough. The branches of trees scratched metallically against the end of a small silver-sheathed trailer. Someone had improved the entry to the trailer by constructing a wood porch, several wood steps, and a single handrail fabricated from rustic two-by-fours. A shred of sunlight glinted off the polished side of the trailer, then quickly dissolved.

John parked the station wagon near the front entry of the school building, turned off the engine, and set the parking brake. He opened the door and stiffly maneuvered himself out of the vehicle. His left leg tingled unpleasantly after he straightened up. An emerging headache throbbed annoyingly at the base of his skull, but he didn't say anything about it. He rested his hands just above his knees and bent forward to stretch the back of his legs, then moving both hands to his hips, bent backwards, cracking several vertebrae as he exhaled. "Hey Timothy, time to wake up. We're here."

Timothy opened one eye without moving anything else. Then he opened the other eye and yawned as his body stiffened into a comfortable stretch. He sat up sleepily and twisted his head around. "Where are we? Are we still in Arizona?"

"Ask your mom where we are. I'm just the driver." Tired from the long trip, and unhappy with the throbbing headache, John didn't feel like explaining anything right now.

Timothy looked around for Martha; she had already walked over to the wooden porch by the trailer. He pulled the lever on the side door and pushed the door open with both feet, then slid out of the car on his butt. He looked around again after hopping out. "Great, we're in the middle of nowhere."

John had begun stretching sideways and rolling his head around at the same time to ease his headache. "Yeah, it sort of looks like it, doesn't it."

Timothy opened his mouth again to say something unfortunate about being out in the middle of nowhere when Martha and her friend walked up behind him. John quickly signaled him to keep his mouth shut with a familiar scowl. "John and Timothy, I'd like you to meet my friend, Anne. Anne, this is John and Timothy."

Anne quickly stepped forward and stretched out her hand to Timothy. He accepted her hand and then shook it suspiciously. Anne nodded when their hands touched. "Nice to meet you, Timothy." She had a firm handshake. She then walked over to John and repeated the formality. "Nice to meet you, John."

John responded flatly. "Yeah, nice to meet you too."

Martha smiled. "Anne was expecting us. She made enough dinner for all of us."

Timothy glanced over at the tiny silver trailer. He guessed there might be room for two people if they stood during dinner and didn't move their arms. "Dinner? Where're we going to eat it?"

Martha started to shush Timothy when Anne broke in. "I know exactly what you mean, Timothy. It is tiny, isn't it? It's very comfortable for a single person, but there's certainly not enough room for all four of us. We're going to eat in the school, in one of the classrooms. I've set up a table and chairs. I think it will be quite comfortable. You can freshen up in the school, if you want to."

The two friends chatted for a few more minutes, then Anne gave everyone a tour of the local facilities. She showed them her trailer—quite small as Timothy had nearly observed, and extraordinarily clean as well—the playground, and finally the school itself. The single story school building provided enough space for three classrooms, a library, a multi-purpose room that functioned as both gym and cafeteria, a small office, a teacher workroom, and boys and girls toilet rooms. A janitor's closet and storage room nestled in between the girls' toilet room and one of the classrooms. Someone kept the school building clean and tidy just like the trailer. Anne explained that she was the only certified teacher, and that several Navajo women helped her during the day as traditional aids. Her students ranged in age from five to thirteen and grades kindergarten to six. She began teaching on the reservation last year, and planned to teach for at least three more years before moving on to something else.

After the tour they sat down for dinner, with everyone shuttling food from the small trailer's kitchenette to the classroom. They ate roast chicken, corn on the cob, and had apple pie for desert. Timothy secretly thanked God that there were no green beans on the menu because Anne looked like the kind of person who might serve them. After dinner everyone helped shuttle dirty dishes and glasses and silverware back to the trailer. Timothy thought Anne had managed a nice dinner, but eating off a tablecloth and sitting in tiny chairs in the middle of an elementary school classroom felt pretty strange, especially a classroom with such peculiar drawings on the walls. When the dishes were washed and dried, Anne suggested that they all take a walk because she always took one after dinner. She explained that the day had usually cooled enough after dinner to make a walk enjoyable.

They walked through the playground and past the brick school building, and headed northwest over the low rolling hills beyond the school grounds. It had cooled as Anne had predicted, and gray clouds moving in from the north brought a scent of rain. Martha and Anne walked together, talking about memories from earlier lives, current events, and dreams for the future. John lagged a step or two behind

Martha and Anne. Although his headache had diminished to a tolerable level, he still didn't feel much like talking. Timothy held himself back from all of the adults, safely walking a few yards behind John. He could hear his mom and Anne chattering about something, although he only understood an occasional word or two. He dropped back a few steps more until he couldn't understand anything they said.

They had walked over a mile when the women adjusted their pace to allow John and Timothy to catch up. Timothy did not realize until too late that his mom and Anne had slowed down, or he would have taken evasive action. Martha moved next to John and entwined her slender arm with his.

John shoved his hand into his pants pocket. "I've still got a headache. I don't feel much like talking."

Martha squeezed his arm. "That's fine. You don't have to talk. We can just walk and enjoy the evening."

"That's good, because I don't want to have to say anything."

Martha nodded. "You won't have to say anything."

Anne maneuvered next to Timothy. He thought about moving away from her, then decided his mom might scold him for it later. Anne walked with her hands behind her back, and spoke to Timothy in an abnormally pleasant voice. It made him uneasy. "Mind if I join you?"

"Yeah, sure." *What am I supposed to say—hell no, go away? I'd really catch it from mom if I said something like that.*

"Have you been enjoying your trip?"

I guess—except for a really stupid detour thousands of miles out of my way to this Godforsaken wasteland because you had to write a damn letter inviting us to come here. Otherwise, everything has been really swell. "It's been OK, I guess."

"Do you have a lot of family in Iowa?"

Well, that's a hard question, because you see, they aren't really my family. I mean, everyone calls them my family, but they really aren't. I don't know where my real family is, but I don't think they're in Iowa. My mom could be dead for all I know. "I guess. There's quite a few of them, that's for sure. Where are all the Indians? I haven't seen a single one since we got here."

Anne smiled. "Oh, they're around, and they know you're here. I would guess some of them are probably watching us right now."

Timothy quickly scanned the horizon and nearby hills. He didn't see anyone. "Are they hiding then?"

"They're just very private and like to keep to themselves, that's all." They walked for a minute in silence before Anne spoke again. "Timothy, have you noticed that we're walking on something?"

Timothy stopped and glanced down. It looked like the ground was covered with thousands of multicolored flat rocks. He squatted down and shoveled a few of the rocks into his right hand. Anne kneeled next to him. He spread the rocks out on his palm to study them; he couldn't guess what they were. "What are these things, some sort of funny rocks or something?"

"No, Timothy—it's broken pottery."

Timothy held one of the pieces of broken pottery close to his face and rubbed his finger along the fractured edge. "Broken pottery? Damn—it's all over the place. How'd it get here?"

Anne picked up one of the pieces of pottery too; she held it in her closed hand without looking at it. "The Navajos made it, many years ago—some say hundreds of years ago. No one knows exactly how it got here, but for some reason that we can't figure out, the Navajos must have abandoned the pottery and simply walked away."

"They didn't take it with them?"

"No."

"Maybe they took some of it with them."

"Maybe they did."

"How'd it get broken then?"

Anne finally opened her hand and glanced down at the piece of broken pottery. "A lot of cattle drives used to come through here. The pottery simply got stepped on over and over again by the cattle and horses until there were only little pieces left. The rain and sun are eroding what remains."

"Is anyone going to pick it up?"

"No, I don't think so. It'll just stay here until the pieces are too small to find."

"Wow, that's sort of sad. Can I take a piece with me?"

Anne smiled—with a brief glint of sadness. "Sure, Timothy. Take a piece with you. It'll be a souvenir of your visit to the Navajo Indian Reservation."

"Thanks." Timothy picked up a big piece with a faded red slash across it and dropped it into his pocket. He searched the horizon again, but still could not find any Indians.

♦ ♦ ♦

A strange dream, 28 November 1950

Floating peacefully thousands of feet above the ground, Timothy could see the approaching dust particle with intense clarity at the precise moment transparent ice crystals began forming around it. As the crystals clung to the particle and then blossomed out from its jagged surface, a frigid breath of air surged unexpectedly beneath his body, lifting both him and the particle higher before finally relaxing and allowing a continued slow descent through the darkness. Quickening its growth, the delicate crystal began to take more obvious shape: six-sided and platelike, unique in the universe, with myriad reflective surfaces giving the icy transparency a milky tinge. Fascinated by the crystal, Timothy moved closer by pulling his arms through the thick air and frog-kicking his legs. During his approach, the constantly changing crystal mysteriously expanded until it dwarfed him in size. He skillfully maneuvered himself around the crystal with a few simple strokes and a twist of his torso, and then landed softly on one of the longer edges with surprising ease.

He could rest now, safely clinging to the lambent crystal while it descended with an easy flutter. He searched the dark skies around him. For the first time he noticed thousands of other crystals, each different from his, each growing and expanding, each dazzlingly reflective. As he studied the crystals in awe, the swirling air forced them to bump into each other and then cling together, turning them into snowflakes. Excited by the forming flakes and eager to join them, he dug his toes into the partially melted surface of his crystal and pulled hard on an edge until the crystal changed direction. The easy maneuverability of the crystal surprised him. He guided it toward the nearest snowflake; then, with jarring violence, his crystal crashed into the flake and abruptly flung him into the air. He tumbled erratically before landing with a soft thump on the opposite face of the snowflake.

Pushed by a soft gust of wind, the snowflake gradually rotated until Timothy peered straight down to the vacant ground below. At first he expected to fall, but inexplicably he clung easily to the surface of the flake by digging his fingers into the crusty surface. He gazed across the magnificent scene below, clearly visible now, an endlessly frozen landscape covered in brilliant new snow. To the east he could see the Sea of Japan—gray, foreboding, the distant curved edge of the earth blazing with morning sun. To the west, endless mountain ranges, deeply scoured valleys, and steeply cut mountain passes, all sparkling with fresh snow. To the north a broad, sprawling, multi-fingered lake bounded by rugged hills and snow-crusted shorelines. And directly below, a narrow mountain pass filled with foreboding shadows. He studied the shadows, straining to understand them, to penetrate them, to determine their purpose. He thought for a moment that he could see movement, but then explosions of light and a cacophony of trumpets and cymbals to the north distracted him. He turned his head and the snowflake unexpectedly turned with him as if guided by his shifting gaze. The entire lake, calm and dark a few seconds ago, was suddenly engulfed in raging flames with frenzied pillars of light shooting into the dark sky above. He thought it looked beautiful and terrifying at the same time.

As he watched with restive fascination, the flaming lake began expanding and then overflowing its shores. A bright trickle of flaming water found its way to the southwest finger of the lake before entering a steep mountain pass. He slowly turned his head and watched the trickle move southeast, illuminating the sides of mountains with soaring licks of flame. The trickle expanded to a river as it approached, and with the snowflake descending more rapidly now he realized that the flame had reached the ground beneath him. He stared down into the river of flame swirling and crackling below. His snowflake suddenly plunged into the river, but he felt no heat, only the presence of the light. He soon became aware of countless bodies below him, lifeless and unmoving at the bottom of the narrow mountain pass. The body of a young man, still and motionless like the others, lay with upturned face and mouth grotesquely frozen open. In shock, Timothy realized that his snowflake had changed direction and now flew toward the open mouth. He tried to steer the flake, but it no longer responded. He tried to push himself away from the flake so that he could fly as he had done before; the flake would not release him. Then, gasping for air, he could no longer find a breath to comfort his burning lungs. He closed his eyes and shuddered uncontrollably when he entered the frozen mouth.

Annoyed, Gunny Talbot kicked Timothy hard in the side. "Time to wake up, sleeping beauty. You're supposed to be on guard-duty, not sawing logs."

Timothy jerked himself up and rubbed his eyes. The sun had just crested the mountains to the east, bathing the top of Dog Hill in light and warmth. A glaze of fresh snow covered the hillside and the road below. "Where am I?"

"Why, that's a hell of a question for someone who's supposed to be guarding my butt. You're in North Korea son, right where you're supposed to be. Now don't let me catch you sleeping on the job again. If you're going to get your head blown off, it better be while killing the enemy, not while you're sound asleep." Gunny Talbot turned and stepped out of the foxhole.

"Damn Gunny, I just had a hell of a dream. I thought I was floating on a snow flake."

The Gunny stopped and turned around. "Floating on a snowflake? Maybe you shouldn't go to sleep any more if you're going to dream shit like that." He moved on down the line of foxholes to check other Marines, shaking his head in disgust.

Timothy brushed a fine crust of snow off his legs and arms. He removed his helmet and pounded it on the edge of the foxhole to loosen the accumulated snow, then scraped the loose chunks off with his gloved hand. He glanced over at Humphrey's empty sleeping bag. Humphrey arrived a minute later with two cups of warm coffee.

"Want some coffee? It's as hot as I could get it. Better drink it before it freezes."

Timothy accepted the cup of coffee with a nod and then slurped some of it down. The coffee's modest warmth comforted his tongue. "Why didn't you wake me up? I just got my ass chewed by the Gunny for sleeping on guard duty. I was also having a really weird nightmare, and I didn't need to find out how it ended."

"I thought you were awake when I got up. You must have dozed off after I left to make the coffee. You couldn't have slept for more than five or six minutes." Humphrey raised his cup and poured some of the lukewarm coffee into the back of his throat. "Hey, it's still warm. I thought it might be frozen solid by the time I got back."

Timothy stood up to stretch, and as he bent over he spotted a peculiar sight down on the road. "What's with all the lumps on the road? I'm almost sure those weren't there last night."

Humphrey stood up too and moved next to Timothy to get a better view. He wedged his knees against the side of the foxhole and leaned forward. Smooth and gleaming with a thick layer of fresh snow, dozens of oddly shaped lumps now dotted the road. A couple of the lumps close to the foot of the hill actually looked more like mounds, almost the height of a man and the width of four or five men. Humphrey pulled at the skin below his chin. "I'm not sure what's going on. I've never seen snow do that before." He finished his coffee and pounded the cup against a rock to knock out the loose grounds. "Maybe one of us should go down and check it out."

The abandoned hut, once a neatly organized command post, had been rearranged into a chaotic scene. A grenade had blown the front door off the heavy wood frame, taking all of the hinges and a chunk of the wall with it and scattering fragments of splintered wood around the room. Hundreds of bullets had punched holes in the walls and roof, spraying dust and misshapen globs of lead everywhere. The telephone and part of the table had been scattered into sharp chunks against the far wall. All of the furniture, except for a small stool that had managed to stay upright on three legs, looked like someone had smashed it with a sledgehammer in a violent rage. Captain Matheson walked over, picked up the telephone handset, and, with the broken and frayed cord dangling from the end, held it to his ear. In a rare display of humor, he spoke into the mouthpiece. "Hello? No, sorry, you've got the wrong number. And don't ever call me here again." He chuckled sarcastically. "We've got quite a mess here. How many men did we lose?"

Lieutenant Meyer inhaled a deep breath before speaking. "We're double checking right now. It looks like we have 84 casualties, including 27 dead and two missing. Most of the casualties occurred when they overran a machine gun position near the base of the hill. We lost quite a few men throwing them back. It would have been a lot worse if we hadn't dug in last night. We can be thankful for that."

This optimistic observation did not cheer Captain Matheson. "Damn it, Meyer. We're lucky they didn't overrun the whole damn company this morning." Matheson pushed the three-legged stool over with his foot. "There sure were a lot of them. And I have a feeling we haven't seen the end of them yet."

"I don't think so either." Lieutenant Meyer sucked in another deep breath. "There's something else."

"Yeah, what's that?"

"We're low on ammunition."

Matheson thought about this before responding. "I don't know when we're going to get re-supplied." He paused again. "Tell the men to check every dead or wounded Marine for ammunition."

"Yes sir."

Matheson threw the telephone handset across the room into a small pile of rubble. "Where's that damn radioman. Has he gotten ahold of the colonel yet?"

"He's waiting outside. I think he has."

"Well get him in here then. Too bad about that phone. At least the radio's working."

The radioman limped noticeably when he entered the hut. He called regimental headquarters and handed the handset to Captain Matheson. "Good morning colonel, this is Matheson…yes sir, we got hit early this morning…I'd say at least a thousand, maybe…no, we held, but we damn near got over…well, we could use some reinforcements…yes sir, I understand, but we're heavily outnumbered and…no sir, I understand, but…OK, yes sir, I understand…OK…yes sir…I understand…yes sir… no, I really do appreciate the situation…yes, we'll do our best…good luck to you too, sir." Matheson gazed passively through the empty door frame and handed the handset back to the radioman. He appeared to study something beyond the far edge of the road.

Lieutenant Meyer quietly dismissed the radioman. "What did the colonel say? Are we getting reinforcements?"

Matheson continued to stare across the road. After some time had passed, he looked sadly down at his feet. "I've got to get another lace for my shoepac. Almost tripped on the damn thing twice this morning."

Lieutenant Meyer quickly followed the change in subject. "I can probably find you another one."

"Thanks, Lieutenant. That would be helpful. See if you can find a new pair. I might as well replace both of them while I'm at it. Are the tents up yet?"

"Yes sir. We set up a warming tent in the west pine grove and a medical tent in the east grove. We finished over an hour ago."

"Where are you putting the dead?"

"We're lining them up behind the medical tent. Most of the bodies are already frozen."

"That's probably good. No, we aren't getting any reinforcements. The colonel says they're in a hell of a fight up north by the reservoir. He isn't sure when they're going to make it back." Matheson continued staring through the empty door opening. "But that's not the good news. The good news is that if they do make it back, this mountain pass is the only escape route, so we've been ordered to hold it at all costs." Matheson finally broke his gaze away from the doorway and looked directly into Meyer's eyes. "And you know something Meyer—that's exactly what we're damn well going to do."

Even though the last swallow of coffee had nearly reached the point of freezing, Timothy gulped it down anyway, smacking his lips as he savored the last droplets of pungent liquid. He thanked Humphrey for the coffee with a backhanded comment. "You were right about the coffee. You have to drink it fast. Of course, when ya do that, you don't have a lot of time to strain the grounds out through your teeth."

Humphrey's lips twitched in a momentary smile. "You strain out the grounds with your teeth? I thought the grounds were breakfast."

Timothy closed his eyes and raised his chin as morning sun flooded across the foxhole for the first time. The sun warmed his face. "Damn, that feels good. The only problem is, it won't last long enough to make any difference. In a few hours, the sun will move behind that mountain and we'll start freezing our butts off again."

"Yeah, that's for sure. Better enjoy it while we can."

Timothy sat on the edge of the foxhole, still enjoying the sun on his face. "How's Ecclesiastes going? Read any more lately?"

"Yeah, sure. I read a couple of chapters this morning by the light of the flares and exploding hand grenades." Humphrey waited for Timothy to laugh but nothing happened. "No, of course not. Why?"

"I sort of enjoyed it when you read last night. Do you want to read some more while the sun's still out?"

"I guess I could. I suppose it might be a good way to pass the time." Humphrey fished out the dog-eared Bible from inside his parka. With his gloves still on, he fumbled with the delicate pages until he found the place where he had stopped before. He began reading. Timothy, his eyes still closed, listened passively until Humphrey got to chapter three.

"For everything there is a season, and a time for every matter under heaven: a time to be born, and a time to die; a time to plant, and a time to pluck up what is planted; a time to kill, and a time to heal; a time to break down, and a time to build up; a time to weep, and a time to laugh; a time to mourn, and a time to dance; a time to throw away stones, and a time to gather stones together; a time to embrace, and a time to refrain from embracing; a time to seek, and a time to lose; a time to keep, and a time to throw away; a time to tear, and a time to sew; a time to keep silence, and a time to speak; a time to love, and a time to hate; a time for war, and a time for peace."

Timothy opened his eyes and squinted against the sun-brightened snow. "You know Humphrey, every time you read that Ecclesiastes stuff, things seem to get more and more confusing."

Humphrey looked up from his Bible. "How's that?"

"I don't know. It just doesn't make a lot of sense, that's all."

"It doesn't?"

"No, not really. What you just read sounded like a bunch of contradictions."

"You're going to have to be more specific."

"Well, for example, this teacher guy says there's a time for everything. If that's true, what time would you say it is now?"

Humphrey didn't exactly understand Timothy's point. "What time is it now? You mean, according to Ecclesiastes?"

Timothy shot back impatiently. "Yeah. That's exactly what I mean. What time is it now according to Ecclesiastes?"

Humphrey responded with the first reasonable thing that popped into his head. "I would guess it's up to us to decide what time it is."

"It's up to us to decide what time it is? What do you mean by that?"

Using his hand to shade his eyes from the sun, Humphrey glanced up at the snow-dusted mountains to the east. "I think Ecclesiastes is just giving us all of the possibilities, but it's up to us to decide which one applies, and therefore what time it is."

Timothy slumped back into his original position and closed his eyes. "Damn; how is anyone supposed to figure that out?"

"I don't really know for sure. I suppose you could—"

A pair of gull-winged Corsairs darted over the mountain and into Humphrey's view. With engines screaming in a deafening crescendo, they began a steep, coordinated dive after flying directly over the crest of the hill. The shadows of the planes flashed across the foxhole. Moments later, after the pair had pulled out of the dive, several massive explosions echoed up and down the narrow pass, shattering the frozen stillness of the sun-warmed morning.

Chapter 17

Mister Tong, May 1948

Lushly green; painstakingly rimmed with ancient oak trees gnarled from lashing autumn rains and hissing winter winds; deliberately manicured by the furrowed hands of an old caretaker, the town cemetery sloped gently up from the road to a whitewashed wood cross planted at the crest of a modest hill. If you stood next to the tall cross with your hand resting on its weathered surface, you could see the entire graveyard, and—if you cared to—parts of the town beyond the trees growing down by the road. You could also see most of the grave markers—hundreds of them, maybe thousands if you actually had time to count them. Many of the markers were simple flat stones set flush with the underlying soil: some polished with intricate letters and elaborately carved designs, some not. Others rose up from freshly mowed grass as headstones or crosses or actual monuments: a few ornate with complex carvings and dozens of words, many simple and rough-hewn with few words, and almost everything in between. If you strolled through the cemetery and wound your way between the stones, you might find a married couple, or a brother and sister buried together. And near the highest corner of the cemetery, not far from the whitewashed cross, a small marble monument marked an entire family, cremated together during a 1924 hotel fire.

Mister Tong, the newest caretaker, had worked the cemetery grounds for the last three decades of his life. The town gave him the job a few years after he arrived in America when it became evident to the mayor and the city council and almost everyone else that his gift of meticulous gardening made him the perfect choice. The previous caretaker, a withered man near retirement, had also died unexpectedly while trying to move a large headstone during a humid summer day. And since no one came forward to ask for the job, the mayor offered it to Mister Tong. A young man then, Mister Tong decided that he could not pass up the opportunity to work for a reasonable wage. He accepted the job with a glad heart, and soon transformed the cemetery into a stunning garden sanctuary.

Mister Tong worked steadily year after year to improve the cemetery. By the time all of the oak trees were planted and sufficiently rooted into the earth, he had saved enough money to make a down payment on a house just beyond the edge of the town. The local banker had told Mister Tong about the home, and in gratitude for his contribution to the town had also arranged for a loan within his means. A humble single-story dwelling with shingle roofing, a small covered porch, and a carport that leaned a little, the small home nonetheless competed with the cemetery for Mister Tong's love and attention. Only a few seasons passed before new trees, shrubs, and flowers of all varieties and sizes surrounded the little house, creating a smaller but equally stunning garden sanctuary. Mister Tong could often be seen in the late afternoon watering the flowerbed that rimmed the front of the little house, usually after a long day of work at the cemetery.

Today began no differently than most days. After a simple but filling breakfast of boiled rice and green tea, and before the sun had shined more than an hour, Mister Tong walked briskly along the familiar road to the cemetery grounds, arriving at the main entry around 7:30 am. He pulled the wrought iron gates open and walked straight to the little gable-roofed storage shed he had built partway up the hill 20 years earlier. After opening the wood-staved double doors of the shed and setting out the gardening implements and tools he would need for the morning, he trimmed the grass around many of the stones, sawed off some dead branches from one of the oldest oak trees, and oiled the lawn mower wheels and blade gears in preparation for an afternoon's cutting. He walked back to his beloved home a little before noon to eat a quick lunch and to dig up some flowers that he wanted to replant near the whitewashed cross at the top of the hill. He carefully transferred the flowers into sturdy clay pots, and then arranged them neatly in the bed of a small hand-pulled wagon. Before the hour hand reached one, and as a gentle breeze began pushing gray clouds in from the west, Mister Tong pulled the wagon down the walk in front of his home and headed back to the cemetery. He studied the clouds while he walked, and thought it might rain before the end of his workday. This cheered him, because the rain would water the freshly planted flowers. He moved his gaze back to the road and quickened his pace as a wagon wheel bounced over a loose stone.

Sitting quietly at an empty table near the far corner of the cafeteria, Timothy stared indifferently at his tray of food. He studied the typical Friday menu: corn, applesauce, peach cobbler, a glass of milk, and the school cook's cherished tuna casserole. He noted with great amusement that his tray had been very lucky today—each food item fit its respective section exactly, with none of the usual disgusting overflows. Even the applesauce, a food highly prone to tray migration, had behaved itself this time. Timothy used his fork to play with the applesauce before eating two bites of the casserole and then drinking the whole glass of milk in a series of smoothly connected gulps. He began digging into the cobbler when Wes and Raymond approached the table and sat down across from him.

Predictably, Wes sounded annoyed. "Can you believe it? This is the same crap they fed me last Friday. They must think I can't remember more than a week back. And look at this. The applesauce is slopped all over my tuna casserole. How am I supposed to eat this mess?" He angrily slurped at his glass of milk. "Of course, that might be the case for Raymond here, but not for you or me, right Timothy?"

Timothy swallowed a bite of cobbler before he finished chewing it and almost gagged on a peach string. It had been over a month since Wes and Raymond had last eaten lunch with him. "The cook likes to make tuna casserole on Friday. I think it's some sort of school tradition." He wished he hadn't drunk all of his milk. He could have used some now to clear his throat. "What might be the case with Raymond?"

Wes rolled his eyes flamboyantly. "That he can't remember further than a week back. Right, Raymond?" Wes took another drink of milk and eyed Raymond sideways. Raymond only sniggered, trying hard not to make a snorting sound.

Timothy felt a little depressed today and did not find any humor in Wes's habitual teasing of Raymond. With this gloominess also came a little irritability. "You sure Raymond likes it when you talk about him like that?"

Wes acted surprised that Timothy had questioned him. He carefully maintained a fundamental understanding that anything he said or did must, by definition, be right. "Are you kidding? He loves it when I talk to him like that. Right Raymond?"

Raymond realized that he had to do something other than snigger or Wes might lose his temper; he decided to actually speak this time. "Uh, yeah, right Wes." Then he sniggered anyway, followed by a big snort that fluttered the roof of his mouth.

Wes responded impatiently. He had not sat down at Timothy's lunch table to participate in this increasingly silly discussion. "Enough of this useless bullshit. I didn't sit here to talk about tuna casserole. There's going to be a big fight in about 20 minutes and Ray and I are going. How 'bout you? Interested?"

Timothy felt a small squirm near the bottom of his stomach. The squirm intensified for a few seconds and then suddenly diminished. "A fight? What kind of fight?"

Wes smiled broadly and leaned back a little. "Oh, nothing special—just a couple of seniors who have a score to settle. I heard it was something about a freshman girl."

Timothy spooned another chunk of peach cobbler into his mouth, thinking while he chewed and swallowed, taking special care not to gag this time. "Where's the fight going to be?"

Wes leaned forward and lowered his voice. "Behind the graveyard. We don't have a lot of time to ask a bunch of questions here. You need to decide right now if you're going or not."

Timothy hesitated. "Well, I—"

Wes deftly interrupted before Timothy could get any more words out. "I mean, if you're not up to it, that's fine with me. Raymond and I will go by ourselves. Right, Raymond?"

The squirming returned, but Timothy ignored it. "OK, I'll go. How long do you think we'll be gone?"

Wes leaned back and grinned again. "Shoot, I'd say the fight will be over in less than five minutes. Maybe even sooner. We'll be back before the fourth period bell rings."

Timothy no longer felt hungry, so he didn't eat any more of his lunch, including the tuna casserole. The three of them dumped their uneaten food in a nearby garbage can and then tossed the dirty trays through the stainless steel window at the end of the serving line. A young man, probably in his middle twenties, washed the trays and silverware in a huge stainless steel sink. Timothy noticed that he wore a really silly looking white paper hat.

Running part of the way, with Raymond lagging far behind in third place, Wes and Timothy arrived at the main entry to the cemetery in a little over 10 minutes. The gates were wide open, and they raced through and headed up the hill toward the whitewashed wood cross. Wes slapped the front of the cross as they ran by and drove a whitewashed splinter into the side of his thumb, right at the joint. He wouldn't feel it for several minutes because of his growing excitement about the looming fight. Timothy and Wes reached the crest of the hill first, with Raymond arriving a minute later, breathing heavily and almost ready to throw up. Down the other side of the hill, beyond a row of tall oaks, dozens of high school students formed a lumpy mass against the mottled shadows of the swaying trees.

The strange scene surprised Timothy. "What's going on? I thought this was supposed to be a fight between two seniors."

Wes acted surprised too, although he understood exactly what was going on. "Looks like there's a few other people who knew about the fight too. This is going to be a lot more fun than I expected."

Wes trotted down the hill's easy slope, almost bouncing with each thrusting stride. Timothy did not chase after him immediately, but eventually followed. Raymond, still trying to hold the tuna casserole down, waited as long as he could before lumbering down the hill. He stumbled on an exposed root when he reached the line of oak trees, and then hastily regained his balance before Wes turned around. Timothy would have turned around too, but after passing through the trees and stepping out into the dappled light beyond, he became transfixed by the remarkable scene before him. What had appeared from the top of the hill to be a simple group of people casually bumping into each other, had suddenly transformed itself into a swarming mob with two boys, one thin and one stocky, enclosed in a small, roughly circular open space in the middle. Wes led Timothy and Raymond right up to the outside edge of the mob, and then pulled them both into the swarm until they reached a line of bodies close to the circular space.

Exhilarated by the mob and uncharacteristically agitated, Wes could not conceal the extraordinarily malevolent anticipation in his voice. "Isn't this the greatest thing you ever saw? I can't believe I'm here!

This is going to be great. I'd bet money that someone get's hurt really bad before this is over with."

Raymond sniggered as he attempted to mimic his superior, but instead managed only a pathetic semblance. "Yeah, this is going to be great!"

Timothy started to say something to Wes when the two boys in the center, encouraged by the mob, began pushing each other. The pushing turned to shoving, and then *thin* reached back and flung his clenched fist in a wide horizontal arc, landing it solidly on *stocky's* left ear. This unexpected blow enraged *stocky*, and, screaming savagely, he charged straight into *thin's* midriff and tackled him to the ground. The two of them rolled around on the grass a few times, swinging wildly at each other but mostly missing, until *stocky* ended up on top. He paused for a moment to appreciate his unanticipated advantage, then without remorse began pounding *thin* in the face and chest, breaking his nose and nearly cracking his collarbone. Although this event had been advertised as a fair fight, two of *thin's* friends immediately took action, and launched themselves into the little circle of space and dragged *stocky* backwards until a ligament stretched just above his right knee. *Stocky* screamed in agony, involuntarily inviting his own friends into the conflict. One of *Stocky's* friends accidentally knocked a girl to the ground and stepped on her arm as the fight swiftly exploded beyond the original circle. The girl tried to stand up but someone else quickly and violently knocked her down again.

Timothy shook after watching the slender girl fall to the ground a second time. Without thinking, he pushed between several boys to help her up. Wes began backing away when he saw Timothy move toward the girl. When he had reached her, Timothy kneeled down and touched her arm—then someone knocked him over too. He forced himself up, and a large boy with dark hair jumped on his back and hugged him tightly around the chest and arms. Timothy squirmed and twisted, but his feet started floating above the grass. Another boy hit Timothy in the gut, knocking the air out of his lungs. Collapsing to the ground, Timothy made brief eye contact with Wes just before he ran up the hill, followed by the always loyal Raymond. Timothy turned and looked over at the girl again before a black leather boot smashed hard against his side, almost cracking a rib. Timothy tasted a flood of bile at the back of his tongue and his eyes fluttered uncontrollably. The boot prepared to smash into his side again.

Mister Tong reached out a strong hand tempered by years of hard work and, clutching a handful of jacket just below the collar, yanked the boy with the black leather boot backwards before he could land a second kick. He forced the boy's face close to his; in an ominously calm voice filled with tangible threat, he said, "No kick man when they down." The boy, considerably larger than Mister Tong, struggled to pull away from his grip but could not. Timothy watched Wes and Raymond vanish over the top of the gentle hill as the mob scattered around him. He pushed himself up to his elbows and, grimacing from the pain in his side, looked for the slender girl where she had fallen. She was no longer there.

♦ ♦ ♦

Dog Hill, 29 November 1950

After years of guerrilla warfare, China's new communist leaders were concerned about the readiness of the Red Army to field large units in a conventional war. Mao Zedong nonetheless ordered a massive buildup of troops on the Korean border in early July 1950. Initially named the Northeast Border Defense Army; and consisting primarily of the Thirty-eighth, Thirty-ninth, Fortieth, and Forty-second Field Armies, as well as supporting artillery and air defense units; Mao renamed it the Chinese People's Volunteers on October 8, 1950 to allow China to go to war with the United States without an official declaration. By late July over 255,000 troops were in position along the North Korean border.

Originally activated in 1944 and placed under the command of General Douglas MacArthur during the war in the Southwest Pacific, the Eighth U.S. Army was the only active field army from 1946 to 1950. Based in Japan at the outbreak of the Korean War, it became the primary unit for the United Nations Command. Initially consisting of only U.S. forces and the Republic of Korea Army (ROKA), it grew to include units from Australia, Belgium, Canada, Columbia, Ethiopia, France, Greece, Luxembourg, the Netherlands, New Zealand, Turkey, and the United Kingdom, with medical units provided by India, Italy, Norway, and Sweden. Commanded by Lieutenant General

Walton H. Walker, the Eighth U.S. Army in Korea (EUSAK) became the largest and most diverse field army ever led by a U.S. General.

A separate United Nations command was activated on August 26, 1950 expressly for the Inchon landings. Originally designated Force X and placed under the command of Major General Edward M. Almond, MacArthur's loyal chief of staff, it was soon upgraded to X Corps to allow it complete autonomy from EUSAK. In essence, it became a self-sustaining army with two reinforced infantry divisions (The 1st Marine Division and the U.S. 7th Infantry Division), a tactical air-command, an artillery group, engineer and signal units, as well as ordinance, maintenance, medical, and transportation units. The separation of X Corps from EUSAK, and the resultant end of a single command structure for U.N. forces, created serious concern among the Joint Chiefs of Staff: some believed that MacArthur had avoided placing Almond under the command of General Walker because of past disagreements between the two.

The X Corps landing at Inchon, led by the 7th Marine Regiment, began on September 15, 1950, a day before the Eighth Army commenced the soon to be successful breakout of the Pusan Perimeter. EUSAK drove the retreating North Korean People's Army (NKPA) north during the following weeks, eventually linking with units of X Corps on September 27th. With the Inchon landings complete, EUSAK pleaded with MacArthur to restore a single command for U.N. forces. However, General Almond—overcome by arrogance— resisted any such reunification, leading MacArthur instead to order the amphibious landing of X Corps at Wonsan on the east coast of the peninsula. General Walker's Eighth Army crossed the 38th parallel on October 9, 1950, and captured the North Korean capital of Pyonyang near the Yellow Sea ten days later. With EUSAK racing up the west coast of Korea and threatening to arrive at the Yalu River first, General Almond ordered X Corps on November 11th to advance to the Yalu at once. His misguided resolve to win a race with the Eighth Army resulted in the perilously uncoordinated scattering of X Corps along a narrow mountain road in the rugged mountains of North Korea.

The Chinese People's Volunteer Army (CPVA) responded on November 25, 1950 by pouring approximately 300,000 troops into a massive attack. Completely isolated from X Corps by the Taebaek Mountain range, EUSAK retreated in stunned disarray. Within a few days the three divisions of the ROKA 2nd Corps had completely disintegrated, and more than a third of the U.S. 2nd Infantry Division had been lost—including nearly all of its weapons and equipment. What began as a retreat quickly turned into a catastrophic rout. At the same time, Chinese troops drove X Corps back to Hungnam, with the 1st Marine Division 5th and 7th Regiments completely cut off near the Changjin Reservoir. Pushing east of the Changjin Reservoir, Elements of the 7th Infantry Division were quickly overrun by Chinese troops—of 2,500 men, a little over 1,000 made it out. Less than a month later, a few days before Christmas, General Walton H. Walker died in a jeep accident. X Corps was immediately reincorporated into the Eighth U.S. Army in Korea and remained a third corps of EUSAK until the end of the war.

Thanksgiving Day began and ended as a somber affair for John and Martha. Instead of the traditional turkey dinner with friends, they stayed home and ate a simple meal of meatloaf and baked potatoes left over from the night before. That evening they took a long walk in the cool night air. They hardly talked to each other during the two-mile hike. After they returned home, John used wadded-up newspaper and dry kindling to ignite a hot fire in the brick fireplace, and they sat in their favorite chairs in the living room. Martha read a romance novel and John pawed aimlessly through yesterday's newspaper. Martha occasionally asked John a question about the news or how things were going at work; he didn't say more than a few words in response. The clock sitting on the polished wood mantle above the fireplace had reached 11:05 pm when Martha decided to go to bed.

"It's getting late John. I think I'll head off to bed. Are you coming to bed soon?" Martha slid a paper bookmark into her novel and set the book on the floor next to her chair.

John raised the paper off his legs and rustled it flamboyantly to give the impression that he had just finished reading one of the articles. "Yeah, I'll be along in a few minutes. I'm just going to read a little more."

Martha responded to John without turning her head as she shuffled toward the bedroom. "Don't stay up too late. You've got to get up for work in the morning."

This admonition might have provoked John on a different night— this time he didn't care. "Yeah, I know. I'll be along in a bit." After Martha disappeared into the bedroom, John folded the newspaper and dropped it on the floor by the side of his chair. He rested in the chair and studied an envelope that he'd propped up against a candle next to the clock on the mantle. He pushed himself out of the chair and walked to the mantle, keeping his eyes on the envelope. The fire, reduced to a few smoldering embers but still warm, felt good on the front of his legs. He picked up the envelope and removed a folded piece of paper, holding the edges as if afraid to open it. He finally unfolded the single sheet and read the meager words that had been hurriedly scrawled on it with a blunt No. 2 pencil.

Dear mom and dad,
I'm sorry I didn't write you sooner, but I've been kinda busy. I joined the Marine Corps a while back. We ship out to Korea in a few days. Not even sure where it is. Don't worry, I'll be alright. See you later.
Timothy

John read the letter four or five times, hoping to find some bit of hidden information that he might have missed before. Instead, with each new reading his despair amplified as the true meaning of the words became increasingly simple. When he finally slid into bed next to Martha, she had been asleep for over half an hour. John turned over and put his arm around her waist. He did not fall asleep for a long time.

A week later, the first day of December, Martha woke up early to make breakfast. Still tired from another restless night, John rolled out of bed a little later than he should have and then shaved, dressed, and ate breakfast a lot faster than he wanted too. He thought about staying home because a throbbing headache had started squeezing the back of his head, then decided he might feel better after he got to work. He apologized to Martha for leaving two pieces of toast and part of a fried egg on his plate, and swallowed a last gulp of hot coffee before rushing out of the house through the front door. He almost tripped on the morning paper. He thought about looking at it later when he got home, then picked it up right there on the front porch. He opened it up to the front page. The headline, smeared across the top of the paper in large black letters, read:

MARINES TRAPPED BY CHINESE
NEAR RESERVOIR – FEARED LOST

John stared at the headline for several seconds before his hand began shaking. After thinking about taking the newspaper into the kitchen and showing it to Martha, he decided to wait until after work—no reason to ruin her morning too. He refolded the paper with care and shoved it under his arm before walking down the wood porch steps and along the stone path that led to the carport. Timothy had helped him lay these stones. His hand had just touched the car door when he felt a sharp pain shoot down his left arm. The newspaper unfolded and fluttered down into a puddle near his foot. The letters of the headline swelled with moisture and then ran together as black ink bled across the surface of the puddle.

The snow returned not long after the last iridescence of afternoon sun had ebbed behind the western peaks. The delicate gray-blue light of the swiftly transforming sky, surprisingly reminiscent of a more enjoyable time, soon faded from pleasant memory to deep purple then to blue-black and finally to ordinary black. With the loss of sun, the resultant void—deepened by an emergent canopy of starless snow—amplified a renewed sensation of numbing cold. As time lingered, prolonged by the cold and stretched by the dark void that had settled into the narrow mountain pass, perception warped until no sense of normality or purpose remained. The cold and darkness might have been tolerable under ordinary circumstances, but with the pressing void and freezing night air also came a surreptitious threat: dreamlike, abstract, and at the same time chillingly real. Waiting became the only way to pass the time.

Gunnery Sergeant Talbot appeared above their foxhole again, probably with some new and inexplicable reason to chew them out. Timothy could never figure out how the Gunny moved around in the dark without falling into a crater or tripping over a big rock. He never complained about the cold either. Maybe he didn't feel the cold because he spent most of his time walking around chewing guys out. "You need any more ammunition? A lot of men are running low on ammo. I've got a couple of ammo belts I can give you guys, if you need them."

Timothy relaxed. "Dammit Gunny, I haven't even fired a shot yet. Humphrey and I sat up here all night waiting for the company to get attacked from the rear. We should've taken a nap. It would have been more interesting."

Humphrey ignored Timothy's morbid gibe. The fading screams of Chinese soldiers, slowly freezing to death in the void, still haunted his thoughts. "I've got plenty of ammo. Thanks for the offer anyway."

The Gunny tossed a couple of ammo belts into the foxhole anyway. "Your squad has a special assignment tonight. If anyone who even looks like they might be Chinese gets through the front line, you kill 'em and plug the hole. You're going to need the extra rounds."

Timothy lowered his voice. "You think they're going to attack us again like last night?"

"No, I don't. Last night they just walked into us by accident. Tonight they know we're here." Gunny Talbot stepped away from the hole to hand out his remaining ammo belts. He thought about saving one for himself.

The snow thickened and Timothy and Humphrey worked to keep warm in their hole. The evening stretched out into night, gloomy and monotonous, as one tried to sleep while the other shivered on guard duty. They continued this wearisome pattern until after midnight when both of them sat up for over half an hour, neither able to sleep.

Humphrey noticed that he couldn't feel anything in one of his big toes. "Damn, have you ever been this cold in your life?" He thought he should take his shoepacs off and change his socks, but the cold made him lazy.

"Why, I think I have."

"When was that?" Without awareness of it, Humphrey began rocking in a hopeless effort to warm his feet.

Not intending to make a joke, Timothy responded, "It was last night, right here on the side of this worthless hill, out here in the middle of nowhere."

Humphrey rocked for a long time before speaking again. "I wonder if they're going to attack again tonight. It's almost one and nothing's happened yet. Maybe we'll get a break and they'll leave us alone."

"I don't know." Timothy paused for a long time too. He could hear Humphrey rocking. "The Gunny seems to think so."

"Whose turn is it to sleep? I've lost track."

"I think my brain must be frozen. I can't remember either. We could draw straws if we had any—or if we could see them. Why don't you go ahead and take the next turn. I can't sleep anyway. I'll wake you at 0300."

"I will if you promise to wake me at three. I don't want to sleep any longer than my fair share, even if you are having trouble sleeping. You still should get a break." Humphrey pulled off his shoepacs, brushed some of the fresh snow off his bag, and slid in clumsily. Although he squirmed around for a while because of the pain in his toe, he finally managed to fall into an unsettled sleep.

Taking care not to step on Humphrey's foot, Timothy stood and stretched out his arms. He pushed his M-1 high above his head and twisted it from side to side. He swung back and forth until his spine cracked below his neck and then bent forward to stretch the backs of his legs and crack his spine again in a different place. He sat on the frozen ground and looked up at the dark sky. He opened his mouth to let several snow flakes settle on his tongue. He enjoyed the coolness of the flakes melting in his mouth until he shuddered convulsively from the cold. With nothing to see in the blackness all around him, and nothing to think about but his gelid misery, he became aware of murmuring voices on the hill below. He could hear the sounds of men whispering, yet could not understand what the men were saying. He focused more intensely on the nearest voice, and still could not recognize any words or phrases or who the voice belonged to. Intrigued by the sounds and longing to discern the words, he moved to the downhill edge of the foxhole and leaned forward a little; he heard only meaningless whispers. He thought he heard someone chuckle over by one of the pine groves, but when he turned his head the laughter vanished. A muffled groan emerged from the medical tent before quickly fading away. Other whispers floated up the hill from around the bombed-out hut and echoed incoherently against the pine trees, rattling around until absorbed into a gusty swirl of snowflakes. He tilted his head slightly and bent forward more until his elbows rested against a cushion of snow, but the whispers only became more confused and erratic, now appearing to swirl all around him. Suddenly frightened, he jumped up and swung around, pointing his rifle toward the sprawling boulder field beyond the crest of the hill. And then behind him again, down the hill toward the narrow road, he imagined footsteps, barely audible at first, then growing in intensity as other feet joined in. His eyes strained to pierce the darkness hanging beneath the canopy of snow, but he could see nothing. He sucked in a full breath of searing winter air and blew it out before sitting down again. He rubbed the back of his neck, and then reminded himself to wake Humphrey in about an hour.

Metal whistles screamed at the Marines from the ditch across the narrow road. The piercing whistle sounds were joined and then overcome by dozens of fiercely blaring trumpets, hostile and menacing. An explosion glazed the road in shuddering yellow light, exposing hundreds of Chinese soldiers running toward the hill armed with burp guns and satchel charges. A machine gun erupted near the lowest end of the Marine position, spraying the road with hundreds of bullets. Other automatic weapons and rifles began firing into the oncoming soldiers. Dozens of Chinese fell as dozens more stepped over them to sustain the charge. The first wave of men reached the foot of the hill and crouched behind the temporary protection of the rocky bank below the hut. Leaning against the steep bank, they showered the closest Marines with grenades, silencing one of the machine guns. Hundreds of comrades joined them and then surged over the top of the bank.

Responding to Timothy's agitated shouts and screams, Humphrey squirmed out of his sleeping bag. He slammed his helmet down on his head and yanked on the unruly shoepacs. Gunnery Sergeant Talbot appeared out of the darkness. He spoke to them without discernable emotion. "Time to earn your room and board. The squad's moving down to kick these yellow assholes off our hill. Let's go."

Timothy and Humphrey scrambled out of their shallow foxhole and stumbled down the hill with their squad. They slipped on several snow-slicked rocks. When they approached the center of the slope, they could finally see the forward platoon in the glare of a flare—engulfed in a swarm of Chinese infantry. Gunny Talbot ordered them to attack a group of enemy soldiers that had driven into the center of the platoon and split it apart. With his M-1 rifle pressed against his hip and firing every few strides, Timothy charged directly into the advancing mob. He pounced on top of one of the attackers and drove his bayonet into the surprised man. After he yanked the blade out of the man's gasping chest and began searching for a new target, enemy soldiers surged around him and pushed his platoon back up the hill. He spun around

Toil Under The Sun

in a wild search for the Gunny or Humphrey or anyone else from his platoon, but saw only Chinese.

Timothy spoke out loud to himself, "Shit, I'm dead." He quickly kneeled low to the ground, slammed a fresh eight-round clip into his rifle, and prepared to take as many enemy soldiers down with him as he could. He raised the rifle and pressed his finger against the trigger.

A brawny hand clutched the back of Timothy's jacket and yanked him down against the frozen ground. Another pair of hands latched onto his leg. The hands jerked him across the slippery snow until he dropped into a foxhole. A burp gun flashed overhead, brightly illuminating two Marines from the forward platoon. One of the men, his arm covered with blood, nodded and picked up a Browning Automatic Rifle. The other Marine, a lieutenant in his late twenties, lifted an M-1 carbine to his shoulder. He spoke to Timothy without looking at him. "Time to give these guys a big surprise."

Moments ago, Timothy thought his life had ended. Now, crammed into this miserable little hole in the frozen ground with two other Marines and completely overrun by a human swarm of Chinese infantry, he believed he might survive. He nodded to the lieutenant, and then fired down the hill as the BAR sprayed two 10-round bursts into the confused enemy soldiers. Timothy continued to pull the trigger as the Marine with the bloody arm reloaded his BAR and fired again.

Chapter 18

A visit to the old tree fort, July 1948

His last visit to this place drifted beyond his remembrance of it. He struggled to envision the day he first walked here, and doubted the quality of his memory. Vague images of a hot, nearly cloudless day, cool green underbrush that yielded easily underfoot, and lofty spruce trees bending against a tranquil breeze all floated serenely beyond a strangely diaphanous veil. In his mind he reached out to grasp the veil and pull it aside so that he could see more clearly; the veil simply flitted beyond his translucent fingertips, further obscuring the images. With effort he calmed himself and, resting uneasily in the ethereal darkness that enveloped him, carefully studied the shrouded images, straining to bring them into clearer view but seeing only formless and indistinct details. He persistently tried to focus beyond the shroud, and a dark shape with four legs and a flashing tail bounded unexpectedly across the uneven ground at the base of the veil. Another dark shape quickly followed, slower and taller, and also moving with haste. The larger shape appeared to pull something that looked like a wagon piled high with a mound of indistinct yet obviously important possessions. The wagon bounced wildly beyond the veil until it suddenly turned on its side, spilling its precious contents over the cool ground next to three magnificent trees, each tall and powerful. As the larger dark shape bent down and studied the overturned wagon, a flash of trembling light, softly magnified by the shroud, briefly illuminated the distant sky before quickly fading away. A muffled crack of thickly surreal sound followed the light, and as the thunder died away into eerie silence he heard the first raindrops splatter through the branches and leaves above. More flashes of light erupted along the distant horizon, and he waited for the approaching thunder.

He opened his eyes and the veil and hazy images beyond his vision dimmed and then vanished. He pushed himself forward with his hands and tilted his head back against the rough trunk of a tree, sighting up along its impressive length until he thought he could see the very top. The transparent night sky above the tall spruce trees swarmed with stars and, though he could not see it directly, the moon's reflected sunlight bathed the highest branches and leaves in a cool, bluish light. Nearly imperceptible, a fragrant breeze moved through the trees, creating a pleasant leaf-rustling sound. The cool air washed over his face and neck and felt good.

He glanced down and thought to himself that this platform had looked much higher off the ground when he built it. He remembered the day he first came here to build—and the moment he fell off the platform, soon after thunder rumbled across the darkening skies and rain drummed chaotically on the deck boards. For the first time since that day he could clearly see the rapidly approaching ground before he struck it so violently that his mind had instantly collapsed into darkness. He remembered too his dad standing stiffly above him, emotionless and stoic. And when his dad spoke to him in a soft, controlled voice, he remembered looking past him and seeing the glorious spruce trio heroically swaying high above in the rising storm. Timothy lifted the bottle to his lips and poured another swallow into his mouth. He noted to himself that he felt better with each pungent drink. Then he did something he had never done before: he talked to the spruce trio.

"You know…you three guys have been here a long time, haven't you?" The spruce trio listened passively in the moonlit darkness. Nearby leaves flickered delicately in a cool breeze. "I bet you've seen just about everything, at least everything that's been going on in this forest. Maybe you've even seen beyond the forest—maybe all the way to town and even to the ocean? I don't know for sure, but I sure wouldn't be surprised if you had."

Timothy took another sip from the bottle. He swished the clear liquid around in his mouth to taste the full bitterness of it and swallowed it quickly. He spoke unhurriedly with several hesitations and pauses as he continued his unusual dialogue. "Have you ever thought about how… useless everything is? Just think about it. You work hard all your life trying to make things…better for yourself, and it doesn't seem to mean a damn thing. I mean, look at my mom and dad. Seems like all they do is work, and what's it gotten them? Even when they go on vacation it still seems a lot like work. I really can't see where they have much fun in life. Seems like they mostly worry about stuff too, especially about me—if you can believe that. And you know something—it really pisses me off when they do that, I mean…worry about me. They should stop fussing so much about what I'm doing and just try to enjoy life."

He relaxed the back of his head against the tree again and waited patiently for a response. The spruce trio, clearly interested only in listening, remained silent. "And something else I've noticed—everything just goes on about its business no matter what I'm doing. It's almost like it doesn't really matter if I'm around or not. You know, the sun comes up every morning and sets every night all by itself. It's been doing this just about forever and will go on doing it a long time after I'm dead and gone. It doesn't need any help from me, or anyone else for that matter. And the wind blows in from the ocean in summer and freezes your damn ass off in winter whether I like it or not. Even if I complain about it, it's just going to keep on blowing. Think of all the other stuff that just happens that I can't do a damn thing about. For example…I can always count on a swim in the river north of town in the summer. I mean, maybe the river will dry up some day, but the point is, it'll probably keep flowing even if I'm not around to enjoy it. When you get right down to it, it's damn exhausting just to think about how really pointless everything is."

Tired of rasping the back of his head against the rough bark of the giant spruce, he grabbed his knees with both hands and pulled himself forward, taking care not to drop the bottle and its precious liquid. He stared at the spruce directly across the deck from him. An owl sitting casually on a slender spruce branch hooted somewhere behind him. He listened to the owl hoot a second time before continuing. "And another thing that really bugs me—have you ever noticed that when you finally get ahold of something you really wanted, maybe something you were hoping to get for a really long time, that it doesn't make things any better when you finally get it?" Timothy lifted the bottle, pressed the rounded brim to his lips, and took another sip. The acrid drink had numbed his tongue and tasted smoother now. "Remember the time I wanted that wagon with the wooden sides that folded down? That wagon was all I could think about. I thought about it constantly for weeks—maybe even months. And then I finally got it. I remember being really excited about it for a while. But you know something?

After a few weeks it didn't seem like such a big deal any more. Do you remember that? Seems like even if you get a whole bunch of things you really thought you had to have, it's never enough to make things right. Seems like you always want more, or something else after you get tired of it, no matter what it is or how much of it you have. Makes me angry just to talk about it. Makes me really angry."

As Timothy's ephemeral rage swelled and then fleetingly receded back into the bottle, a waning gibbous moon patiently moved across the transparent sky, peaking around edges of the open canopy at the top of the spruce trio and painting him with a pleasantly bluish light. The light surprised him: he shaded his eyes from the moon's intense brilliance with his empty hand and imagined the mysterious presence of the spruce trio. A shiver crawled down the back of his neck and rumbled out across his shoulder blades; he thought a cool breeze had caused it. He began speaking to the spruce trio again, this time almost believing that the lofty trees could hear his words and understand his thoughts.

"It's bad enough that nothing is ever enough to make you happy, but there's something worse as far as I'm concerned—much worse." Timothy breathed deeply a few times, then stood up to stretch his legs and back. He raised the bottle one last time and drained it until only a few drops clung to the glass mouth. Then, using a sidearm motion, he flung the empty bottle into the dark forest with all of his strength, almost slipping on the damp surface of the wood deck. The bottle spun sideways like a flat top and vanished into the darkness. He heard the glass shatter against something hard a few seconds later. The sound echoed against the trees two or three times in diminishing waves before fading into silence. Finished with the bottle and momentarily bored, he studied the myriad details on the surface of the moon before returning his gaze to the spruce trio. He studied them one at a time, each in turn, and then began speaking again. "Have you ever noticed that we're so stupid that we keep on making the same stupid mistakes over and over again?" He waited again for some sort of response. "I mean...even if something has happened before, and things turned out really bad, we go ahead and do the same darn thing again—even if we know it's going to turn out bad again. I just don't get it. Do you?"

He strolled to the edge of the deck and sat down again, his legs dangling comfortably over the side. It felt good to sway his feet back and forth. As he relaxed, a distant memory flared and abruptly faded to nothing before he could remember where it had come from. Then, placing each hand behind his head and intertwining his fingers, he tightened his stomach muscles and slowly sunk back until he felt the moist wood of the deck against his shoulder blades. He tilted his head a little to see the moon clearly again. It seemed brighter than before, but he did not shield his eyes from it this time. He spoke in a mumbled whisper, now confident that the spruce trio *could* hear his thoughts.

"Just think about it for a moment, and I think you'll see that I'm right about this one. Even when you screw something up bad and it makes you feel really sick inside, it seems like you never remember it when you need to. It's like this: when you're about to screw the same thing up again, that's when you forget all about how bad it was before. It's like it never happened. But the funny thing is, you always remember it after you screw up, especially when it's too late." A burst of sadness flowed into his mind when he thought about this. He didn't know why at first; when the sadness thickened, he understood. A new memory flared, and this time did not fade away. "I remember something I really screwed up once. It wasn't too long ago either." The new sadness interrupted him, cutting off his words. He inhaled deeply and rubbed his eyes. "You never met her—she was something really special. I never imagined she'd want to talk to me, but one day she did. I think she wanted to be my girlfriend. I have no idea why; I guess she just did. I was supposed to go over to her house to study homework one day. I remember something about milk and cookies too. I was so scared that I didn't go through with it. Or maybe I just couldn't believe she wanted to have anything to do with me. I have to tell you—that's gotta be the biggest and downright stupidest mistake I ever made. But then…you probably already knew that—right?"

The dampness of the deck had soaked through the back of his jacket and shirt; he pushed himself up to a comfortable sitting position and began swinging his legs again. He didn't mind the dampness soaking through his pants. He realized that he hadn't thought about Marie for a long time. As the sadness of his lost opportunity washed over him, he decided that he didn't have much more to talk about with the patiently listening spruce trio; however, he did want to finish everything he had to say before leaving the grove. He glanced at his watch—almost two in the morning. He hoped his mom and dad hadn't discovered his empty bed. He didn't need to go through that again—especially tonight. "I've got just one more thing to say...then I'm done. It wouldn't be so bad if something good could come out of it, but I'm not sure what that would be. Even if someone else could learn from my mistakes, that would be something worthwhile, but no one will ever know or remember that I screwed up or why, let alone do anything about it. Hell...no one will even remember that I was alive. When you get right down to it, life doesn't seem to mean a damn thing, and that's just the way it's always been and the way it's always going to be." He smiled before finishing, surprising himself. "But then, you already knew that too, didn't you?"

Timothy yawned, slid gracefully off the slick edge of the wood deck, and glided down to the moist ground. He stopped at Phijit's grave for a few minutes before leaving the grove and, standing silently, felt a new and poignantly different sadness. When he passed the outer edges of the grove and walked into the clear moonlight washing the hill, a sour taste emerged at the back of his tongue. The intensity of the taste sharpened with each step until a startling eruption of foul vomit forced him down to his hands and knees. His head pounded when he stood up and continued walking down the hill. Although he didn't know it at the time, he would not feel this good in the morning.

◆ ◆ ◆

The search for Humphrey, 29 November 1950

Timothy paused outside the snow-crusted medical tent and watched the morning sunlight push the night's dark rim across the narrow road to finally warm the fragile hill's ragged edge. In a short while the light would reach the foxhole where he had survived the night. Soon after that, it would warm the steeply slanting canvas sides of the medical tent as well. Although empty now, the foxhole had provided a precarious refuge in the eye of a malevolent storm. The storm had swirled around him and his two companions until pushed back by an equally relentless wind—only minutes before certain annihilation. As Timothy thought of this, he casually played with a fresh bullet hole at the elbow of his parka sleeve and marveled at his apparent immortality. His foxhole companions had not been so lucky. A jagged piece of shrapnel from an errant grenade killed the lieutenant only moments before the Chinese were driven back. The BAR man was shot through the shoulder early in the storm, yet continued firing his weapon until he ran out of ammunition. He had slumped to the bottom of the hole in a pool of frozen blood when a corpsman finally arrived. Timothy assumed that someone had moved the BAR man to the medical tent, although he did not know this with any certainty. But he had really come here to look for Humphrey, so it didn't matter very much.

Timothy had just about decided to enter the tent when a corpsman named Nathaniel flung the stiff canvas flap open and staggered out. An angular chunk of snow slid off the tent roof and slammed into the ground. Nathaniel bent over in apparent exhaustion and gasped in the stinging morning air. Timothy could hear someone groaning inside the tent. He didn't know what he should say. He finally began with a fatuous question. "Hi. How's it going in there?"

Nathaniel unbent himself, slowly, after hearing the question. "As well as can be expected I guess. I lost two more during the last hour. Expect I'll lose a few more before the day's out. Hope I do better than yesterday."

This prediction, filled with doubt, alarmed Timothy. Surprisingly, he had come this far without ever having been alarmed about anything. He decided to stop asking stupid questions and get to the point. "Is Humphrey in there?" He held down any emotion and tried to appear unruffled.

Nathaniel strained to think clearly. He desperately needed a few hours of sleep, but believed that someone might die if he did sleep. He tried to remember if someone had carried Humphrey into the tent during the night. "Yeah, I think he is in there. I think he might be on the left side, near the front. I'm not really sure."

Afraid to enter the tent, Timothy waited for an invitation. Nathaniel bent over again. "Can I go in and see how he's doing? He's a friend of mine." Fighting back the urge to sleep, Nathaniel did not answer the question. Timothy added further justification to his request. "We've been together since the beginning. We were even on the same train together on the way to boot camp. We came over to Korea on the same ship too."

Nathaniel stood up again and peered into Timothy's eyes. He chuckled when he realized that Timothy had asked him for permission to enter the tent. "Yeah, you can go see him. Just don't step on anyone. I've got enough stuff to take care of as it is."

Timothy signaled his thanks by smiling, and then surprised Nathaniel by shaking his hand vigorously before entering the tent. Once inside, Timothy waited for his eyes to adjust from the bright morning sun to the dingy light of two hanging lanterns. At first he could see only fuzzy lumps spread out around his feet. As his pupils dilated, and the low light of the lanterns came into clear focus, he could see misshapen sleeping bags covering the entire floor of the tent. He stepped carefully over two of them and worked his way to the left side. He kneeled down and pulled back the flap of a sleeping bag; it was not Humphrey. He moved over to the next bag. The Marine had rolled onto his side and faced the wall of the tent. Timothy bent over him until his helmet nearly fell off. It sort of looked like Humphrey, but he couldn't see enough of the man's face. "Humphrey, is that you?" The Marine did not respond. Timothy pushed against the man's back with his knee and asked again. "Humphrey, is that you?" The man cringed when Timothy's knee touched his wound.

"Dammit Timothy! What're you trying to do, finish me off?"

Timothy grinned. "Humphrey! You're alive!"

"Of course I'm alive, and I was trying to get some sleep until you showed up and kicked me in the back."

"What happened? I didn't see you again after we charged into the Chinese."

"I don't know. Things got confused. I got spun around, and then someone shot me in the butt. I don't know if it was one of theirs or one of ours. Whoever shot me, I went down and then someone stepped on me. I don't remember much after that."

Timothy relaxed a little. "Are you alright?"

"I think so. It hurts like hell, and I'm feeling a little dizzy, but I think so."

"Can I get you anything?"

"No. I'll be fine. I'm just really tired. I'll be good after I get some sleep."

"That's great news. You just stay here and get a little rest. I've got to get back to the platoon before the Gunny chews my ass. You know how he gets sometimes. I'll come back and check on you again later, when I get a chance. You just take it easy and get some rest."

"Thanks. See you later."

"Yeah, see you later."
"Timothy."
"What?"
"Be careful out there."
"I will. You just get some rest now. Don't worry. You're going to be fine."

The icy air's temperature sank to 20 degrees below zero, and a dull numbness spread throughout Lin Dehua's left foot. The pain had begun as an innocent reddening across the tips of his toes. The redness spread around the nails and down into the crevices between the toes before swelling into painful blisters—and then his toes gradually went numb. Even though the numbness relieved some of the pain, soon after his heel went through the same process. The pain slowly crept from both directions across the bottom of his foot until joining agonizingly in the middle. All of his toes and most of his heel had since turned black, with ice crystals forming in the deeper tissues and the redness and blisters moving up the sides and over the top of his foot. Now Lin began to feel the ominous tingling in the toes and heel of his right foot. As Lin considered the possibility of losing his toes, he wrapped several torn strips of quilted material, taken off the body of a dead comrade, around his damaged foot.

Captain Lin Wulong, his bullet-pierced arm pressed tightly against his body in a makeshift sling, moved methodically down the crooked line of resting soldiers to assess the condition of his men. Today he commanded the remnants of two rifle companies, both badly depleted during the first night of fighting. The fingers of his injured arm ached from the cold; he did not say anything because he knew that many of his men had suffered even more serious injuries. He did not stop until he noticed Lin Dehua wrapping his foot. He knelt down, close to the ground. "What are you doing, comrade?"

Lin Dehua continued wrapping and did not look up. "Nothing sir."
"Is something wrong with your foot?"
"It's just a little cold, sir. I'm trying to warm it up a little. I will be better when I finish wrapping it, sir."
"What's your name, comrade?"
"My name is Lin Dehua, from Xinjiang Province."

This cheered the captain, although he took care not to reveal it. Chatting with a soldier about a cold foot could be viewed as strange by his superiors. To also admit that he found the conversation enjoyable would be too much for anyone to believe. "My surname is Lin too. I'm Lin Wulong. Tell me, is this your first battle?"

Lin Dehua, taught by his stern parents to never boast or speak highly of himself, answered the question as directly and honestly as possible. "No sir. I fought with the People's Liberation Army against the Nationalists…in 1949."

Although this impressed Captain Lin Wulong, he again took care not to reveal any emotion. "That is good. We will need experienced and dedicated soldiers like you when we destroy the enemy tonight. Take care of the foot, comrade. It has been good to speak with you."

"Thank you, sir."

Lin Dehua finished wrapping his foot after the captain walked away. He tucked the end of the strip under one of the underlying loops and then pulled it snug. Although the foot did not really feel any better at this point, it comforted Lin to have at least done something. He turned to speak with the soldier next to him, but the man had slumped into a gawky pose and sat motionless. Lin Dehua studied the man's lifelessly open eyes. He had recently frozen to death; Lin cut off a long strip of quilted material from the base of the man's jacket. He rolled the strip into a compact cylinder and shoved it into his pocket. He would probably need it for his other foot before the end of the day.

Gunny Talbot, too busy talking with Lieutenant Meyer down near the base of the hill when Timothy finally hustled back to his platoon, did not have the opportunity to do any ass chewing. Normally calm and reasonable, the lieutenant waved his arms expansively out across the narrow road before pointing with several agitated jabs toward the remnants of the destroyed hut and former command post. This appeared to signal an end to the conversation. The Lieutenant turned and walked away from the Gunny without any formality, shaking his head almost too slightly to notice. Gunny Talbot paused briefly, looked down at the frozen ground, and then walked stiffly up to his platoon where the men rested near the crest of the hill.

"Good news Marines. Seeing how our platoon is now the largest in the company, we get the pleasure of rotating down to the road today. However, before you get too excited, it gets even better. The captain thinks the Chinese are going to throw everything they've got at us tonight in an effort to wipe us off the face of this damn little hill and take control of the pass. That means you worthless bums are going to finally get to do some real work instead of all the recreating you've been engaged in thus far." Anticipating a humorous sarcasm, the Gunny glanced at Timothy; Timothy stared at the ground and said nothing. "As such, we've been ordered to stack the frozen bodies of dead Chinese soldiers into defensive battlements. As you may be aware, there's a handy supply of them down on the road, as well as all over this hill. The captain told me he would have used sandbags, but his order got delayed in Japan by a recent labor strike." The Gunny hoped this small joke would evoke a few chuckles from the platoon and release some of the tension out of this grim assignment; instead, the men remained silent. He had nothing more to say at this point, and simply asked, "Any questions?" Again, no one in the platoon asked any questions. "OK then. Get your gear together and let's get started. The sun's going down fast. We don't have a lot of time to screw around. Let's go."

Colonel Wu Zongxian kneeled against a frost-glazed rock and studied the swirling contour lines and faded symbols scattered across the tattered map. He traced his finger along the blurred convergence of two lines above and to the north of the hill, and then carefully followed the lines where they spread and swept around the boulder field he had failed to fully appreciate before. When his finger had finished its travels, he lifted the Japanese field glasses to his sun-sore eyes and compared the symbolism of the map to the reality of the terrain that spread out before him. He could see the boulder field clearly, and, to his surprise, a large group of Marines moving down from the crest of the hill, apparently leaving it exposed and vulnerable. Satisfied with his plan, he lowered the glasses and turned slowly to Captain Lin Wulong. "I am giving you new orders. You will not attack the base of the hill as originally planned."

This apparent loss of confidence flustered Captain Lin Wulong. "Sir, we are prepared to attack and destroy the Marines. I promise we will not fail you."

Toil Under The Sun

The colonel sensed Lin's profound disappointment, and this pleased him. "I have not lost confidence in your leadership, captain. You will be a key part of the final battle. You will instead attack at the crest of the hill, across a boulder field to the north."

"The crest of the hill? Is that possible?"

"Yes. I have just determined a workable route. It will be difficult, but not impossible. You will begin moving your men immediately. However, there is something you must understand—it is crucial that you move in complete secrecy. The Marines must not know what we are doing."

"I understand, sir. We will do what you ask. When shall we attack?"

"I will send three fresh rifle companies in an all-out frontal assault against the base of the hill. This will surely engage the Marines in a desperate defense and draw in their forces. You will attack the weakened crest of the hill 15 minutes after you hear the first trumpets, and you will not cease the attack until you have achieved total victory." Colonel Wu lifted the field glasses once more and watched the last of the Marines move down the hill, away from the boulder field. Then, speaking in a solemn voice, he said: "Tonight we will defeat the Marines and take control of this mountain pass. When we have accomplished this, the Marines to the north will be doomed."

"Yes sir, we will not fail." Without standing, Captain Lin Wulong nodded to the unresponsive colonel, still peering intently through the field glasses. Then he waited patiently for the colonel to show him the route to the boulder field.

Timothy reassembled his M-1 Garand after cleaning it, stowed the cleaning kit inside the wood stock, and deftly pushed in a fresh clip. He checked his extra ammunition twice, and then recounted the four grenades Gunny Talbot had given him after the platoon had finished stacking dozens of frozen bodies into an improvised defensive position. With these tasks completed, he rested his rifle across the icy lumbar of a dead Chinese soldier and studied the field of fire across his assigned segment of the narrow road. Other Marines to his left and right did the same. Not expecting any significant forewarning before the Chinese attack, he adjusted his sights to about 100 feet.

Darkness arrived far too early that afternoon, or so it seemed with the unrelenting expectation of a massive assault by an inexorable enemy. With the setting of the sun also came the familiar shadow of intense cold: endless, cruel, and potentially lethal. The evening also arrived crisp and clear, without the obscuring snow flurries of the previous night, and as the nearly full moon rose again above the distant mountains, the narrow road and its many silent burial mounds glittered with infinite crystalline reflections. The mounds would both protect and hinder the oncoming enemy soldiers before completion of the night's combat.

Not wanting to magnify the slowly suffering minutes, Timothy attempted a conversation with the Marine to his right, a man he had never spoken to before. He began with an absurdity. "Cold, isn't it?"

The Marine twisted his face in confusion and turned to see who had asked him such a stupid question. "You talking to me?"

"Yeah, I am. I said it's cold."

The Marine looked away, frowning in disbelief. "That's a pretty big understatement."

Timothy's conversations with Humphrey were always easy and free. This conversation might actually require a serious effort. He attempted a different tactic. "You ever read Ecclesiastes?"

The Marine turned again. First a stupid question about the cold, and now a weird question about who knows what. "Icleesy what?"

"Ecclesiastes. It's one of the books in the Bible."

"A book in the Bible? No, can't say that I have. What about it?" The Marine turned away again, focusing instead on the menacing crevices beyond the narrow road.

Timothy reached out and polished the front sight on his rifle with his thumb. "I was just thinking that it's wrong about something, that's all."

"Wrong about something? Wrong about what?"

"Well, it says in Ecclesiastes that there's nothing new under the sun—that everything has been done before. I was just thinking that must be wrong."

This observation puzzled the Marine; he decided to stay with the conversation anyway. After all, he didn't have much else to do at the moment. Maybe a little talk would distract him from his frozen misery. "Why's that?"

Timothy rolled over to face the Marine. "Because I don't think it's possible that anyone has done this before."

"What, freeze their asses off?"

Timothy paused before responding, "No—use dead soldiers to build a defensive barricade. I just can't believe this has happened before." The perversion of this observation could have ended the conversation, except that Timothy still had a few more things to say. "Do *you* think anyone has ever done this before?"

The Marine thought about this question briefly and, looking back at Timothy again, said the only reasonable thing he could think of. "I certainly hope not."

"Then have you ever *heard* of anything like this before?"

"No…can't say that I have."

Timothy rolled back to his stomach and aimed his rifle across the road. "Then Ecclesiastes must be wrong."

"I suppose so."

Timothy lowered his rifle. "What if it did happen before, and we just don't remember it? What if we've forgotten?"

"I don't know about that. I'll tell you what, though—if it did happen before, I sure hope it worked."

Timothy's chin slumped against the top of his hand. "Yeah, me too friend. Me too."

Chapter 19

The ancient waterfall, August 1948

The morning did not dawn unpleasantly, for the first truly cool air of summer had recently washed over the mountains and flowed through the tall pines in anticipation of approaching autumn. Yet neither did the air feel excessively cool, because the sun, only a few hours distant from dawn and still rising fresh above the eastern horizon, had begun to evaporate the night's dew from infinite pine needles and gently warm the ruggedly plunging land. Moving through the deep valley, the cool air easily pushed against the dense trees in an exuberant declaration of growing power, bending them in intricate unison until windward tensile stresses increased in strength beyond the power of the breeze to hold them; and with a smooth and imperceptible pause and then accelerating reversal, the trees swung back against the flowing air; again in intricate unison, over swinging the vertical before yielding once again to the insistent air.

A soothing blend of multifarious sounds reverberated noisily across the green forest and echoed quietly against undulating mountainsides as gnarled branches sliced through the persistently moving air. The sounds increased with the pulsing breezes and resisting pine trees, only to momentarily diminish when the air slowed and the trees relaxed. And the morning sun, in abiding harmony with the scattered sonance of gently bending trees, still rising in a precisely arcing path from the east, intensifying with each fading minute of the new day, covered the forest floor in a wash of sympathetically dappled light, blending with the forest sounds until sound and light appeared irrevocably linked.

An ancient waterfall, plunging in blurred sheets over 132 feet to an explosively boiling pool at the river's continuation below, toiled beyond the noise of the wind and gently swaying trees. Clouds of transparent mist lingered soundlessly above the noisy water and jagged rocks rimming the pool, sparkling occasional shots of sunlight and mixing the clean smell of the waterfall into the swaying air. But the coolness of the waterfall could also be felt from minuscule droplets that, pressed by the waterfall's gentle wind, floated beyond the edges of pool and stream and caressed the waiting skin. And if one's tongue extended beyond the lips to receive the swirling droplets, too small to comprehend individually, the distant waterfall could be tasted as well.

The ancient waterfall waited patiently—as it had before for thousands of years and countless days—for Timothy's arrival. Moving swiftly, he had by now hiked halfway down the mountain and would soon arrive. Striding deftly over the many exposed roots and rocks and crevices along the primitively uneven trail, walking deeper into the cool valley with each quickening step, his first view of the magnificent falls, and his first smell of it, neared to within an hour. A blister had swelled hotly on the heel of his left foot; he willed himself to ignore the throbbing pain, focusing instead on his imagined vision of the falls. John followed a few steps behind him, struggling a little to keep pace, but managing well enough. Martha lagged farther behind, and, sitting on a flat rock back up the trail beyond John's sight or sound, took time to enjoy the coolness of the morning and the pleasant bird songs of the ambient forest.

An imposing forest spider glinted momentarily in a speckled ray of sun when Timothy rushed by, catching his eye and inviting him to stop. Timothy turned and slowly approached the spider's artistically spreading web, newly constructed and still glistening with remnants of evaporating morning dew. The spider appeared unconcerned, his four pairs of eyes watching Timothy move close to the web until his face stopped only inches away from the spider's fat abdomen and slender thorax. John quietly stopped next to Timothy, glad for the chance to rest. He waited until his breathing had slowed before asking a question about the spider. "What's this you're looking at, Timothy?"

Timothy, fascinated by the size and color of the spider, did not answer immediately. He secretly hoped that a winged insect might land on one of the web's sticky strands of silk so that he could watch the miniature drama that would certainly follow. "A spider—a really big spider. Do you know what kind it is?"

John moved a little closer; not as close as Timothy. A shiny black spider, with fangs dripping lethal venom, had pierced the tender skin behind his left knee on the night of his eighth birthday. He had since developed an unnatural fear of the tiny creatures that had persevered beyond the maturity or logic of adulthood. "Don't you think you're getting a little close to that spider? What if it jumps at you?"

At first Timothy thought his dad's remark was a joke, then realizing the deadly seriousness of the comment felt surprised and amused at the same time. Until now, he had convinced himself that John had absolutely no significant weaknesses, at least none that he could discern or understand through observation. He never would have guessed a fear of spiders. "It's not going to jump at me. I don't think it's that kind of spider. Anyway, have you ever seen a spider jump?"

"No, I've never seen a spider jump, but that's not the point. I've read about jumping spiders in *National Geographic*, and I still wouldn't get any closer." John could feel his calves stiffening up a little from the long hike down the mountain trail. He stepped away from the spider with his left foot and leaned forward to stretch out the calf muscles. "And no, I don't know what kind of spider it is. I'm not exactly fond of spiders, and I haven't spent a lot of time studying the different varieties. I can tell you one thing: I have squashed quite a few."

Timothy thought about this comment for a few enjoyable seconds before the corners of his mouth raised imperceptively in a mischievous curl. "You squash spiders? Why would you want to do something like that for?"

John had squashed spiders his entire life, beginning shortly after that nasty black one bit him, and no one had ever asked him to explain why. This unexpected attack of his childhood fear filled him with unease. He groped for a reasonable explanation. "Well…yeah. I mean…I squash them…if they're in the house…or the garage. I probably wouldn't squash a spider that was…outside. That is, as long as it minded its own damn business."

Timothy had begun to enjoy himself and decided to press the issue a little further. "You only squash them inside the house? I thought spiders were supposed to be good, because they eat a lot of insects."

John felt unusually defensive, and stuttered a little as he struggled to mask his fear. "I, uh, yeah…they are good, uh…because, as you say, they eat insects. But, but there are so many of them…spiders I mean—probably millions—and because of that it doesn't really matter if you squash a few of them from time to time, especially when they get into your house I mean. After all, they really shouldn't be in the house in the first place."

Timothy could not prevent a noticeable edge of sarcasm from creeping into his voice. "I assume this spider is safe then…because it's outside?"

Realizing his downhill slide had accelerated, John calmed himself before choosing his next words. "Oh, yeah, I would never kill *this* spider. I mean, it's out here in the middle of a forest—right? There'd be no reason to squash it." Then John thought to himself—*unless the damn thing started to jump at you. Then I'd stomp on the venomous little killer with both feet.*

Although still filled with unresolved sarcasm, Timothy decided to end the discussion by pretending relief. "That's good. Maybe we should move along then…before something bad happens." He stepped back from the web and turned down the trail, holding his first step for a moment as he looked back at the spider, still sitting patiently in the center of the web. The spider peered back at him through four pairs of eyes, without moving.

John had grown tired of this useless exploration of his childhood fear—and the proximity of the murderous little spider—so he quickly agreed. "Yeah, I think we should. We're probably keeping this little guy from his dinner anyway by scaring away all the insects."

Timothy resumed hiking down the trail. "Yeah dad, I'm sure we are." The spider glanced at them one last time—but still did not appear concerned—and they walked on toward the waiting waterfall.

The ruggedness of the trail did not lessen when they approached the stream at the valley floor. Timothy hopped over several deep cracks in the trail, and, stretching out his strides more aggressively, reached a point several hundred feet ahead of John when he first heard the waterfall, audible above the wind and restless trees for the first time. He continued ahead, walking more briskly as the sound of the waterfall intensified. He jogged another hundred feet and then stopped to smell the sudden moistness of the air and feel its coolness on his face and arms, warm with perspiration from the hike. The smell of the air reminded him of the precious time before an autumn rain.

John did not stop to rest, and moving consistently down the trail soon arrived at Timothy's side. He pointed toward the sound of the crashing falls. "You can really hear the waterfall now. It must be just beyond that switchback."

Timothy continued sniffing the moist air and enjoying the familiar smell. "It smells just like it does before it's going to rain. And I can feel it on my face too."

John sniffed the air, tilting his head back a little as he breathed the damp fragrance in deeply. "Yeah, you're right. It does smell like rain, and it feels good too—nice and cool." Timothy did not respond, so John assumed the conversation had ended. "Ready to move on to the falls? We should be almost there."

"Yeah, I'm ready."

They walked more slowly over the last part of the trail, side by side, together for a moment, each eagerly anticipating the first sight of the waterfall. The rain smell amplified before they reached the last switchback, and the air became more intensely humid after the trail twisted a final time and turned sharply along the rocky edge of the sparkling stream. And then the first view of the waterfall broke full upon them. John and Timothy halted in near unison while their eyes traced from the violently crashing water of the nearby pool and then up its slender length to the smooth curve of gushing water at the top of the falls. Hypnotized by the diaphanous sheets of falling water, they stood quietly for a long time before John suggested that they walk on. "Let's see if we can get in a little closer."

Awestruck by the beauty and power of the waterfall, Timothy eagerly agreed. "Sounds good to me. Maybe we can even stand under it."

"I don't know about that, but we can try to get as close as possible."

With Timothy leading the way, they separated again and navigated a safe route over the slippery rocks and pulverized soil holding back the undulating sides of the rushing stream. The water in the stream flowed icy and crystal clear, obscured only by an occasional swirl of bubbles or the gush of an unexpected eddy. Within minutes they reached three massive boulders at the edge of the pool below the falls, each boulder glistening with cool spray, each inviting them to rest for a while. They both leaned against the impressive stones and resumed their hypnotic study of the waterfall. The coolness of the spray felt good after the long, hot walk from the top of the mountain.

Timothy watched the perpetually cascading water in silence for almost five minutes before asking John a question. He didn't know what had prompted him to ask it because it had nothing to do with the hike or the waterfall—or anything else that he could think of at the moment. The question had surfaced nonetheless, and it must have been important to him or he wouldn't have thought about it in the first place. "Dad, there's something I've been thinking about. Can I ask you a question?"

This inquiry surprised John. Timothy had not asked for his advice in a long time, especially in a setting like this. "Sure. What's the question?"

Timothy poked at the ground with a damp stick he had found near one of the big boulders. "How do you know when someone's your friend?"

When John heard this question, he thought there might be any number of simple answers. When he thought about it more, he realized that this particular question did not have an easy answer. He decided to stall. "Why do you ask? One of your friends giving you some sort of trouble or something?"

Timothy lifted the damp stick up close to his face and studied a lump of mud smeared onto the pointed tip. "No. That's not the problem. The problem is, I'm not really sure if I have any friends." He flicked the stick and sent the lump of mud spinning toward the stream. "I was hoping you could tell me how to figure out if I do or not."

With this explanation, Timothy's original question became uncomfortably serious. A casual answer would not be appropriate or wise. Although John had not realized it at the time, the discussion back at the spider web had been rather simple compared to this. Still stalling for time to think of a decent answer, John stretched back and looked up to the top of the waterfall, then back down to the pool, and finally to the trio of boulders. As he watched a rivulet of condensation stream down the face of the nearest boulder, a uniquely relevant inspiration burst unexpectedly into his mind. Not sure where the idea had come from, but relieved that it had finally arrived, he smiled and began speaking easily. "You know...I was talking to the Ranger back at the lodge before we came here to see the waterfall. Did you hear any of that?"

When they had met the Ranger, Timothy had instantly classified him as a stuffy and boring adult before daydreaming through the entire conversation. "No, not exactly."

"He told me all about how this waterfall got formed. It's really quite amazing when you think about it. Seems that thousands of years ago, maybe even millions, the river we're standing next to flowed way up there in the air—where the waterfall is now. But the ground we're standing on was softer than the streambed at the top of the falls and wore away over time. As a matter of fact, the streambed at the top is hard bedrock, and will always be there. As the river cut into the weaker ground below, where we're standing, the valley got deeper and wider and the waterfall got taller until it's what you and I are looking at right now—over 132 feet up in the air. The point is, the bedrock at the top of the falls will always be there to support the waterfall, no matter what happens." John relaxed, pleased that he had answered Timothy's difficult question so cleverly.

Timothy, however, had no idea how John's story about bedrock and soft ground and millions of years related to his question. "What's that got to do with knowing whether or not someone is your friend?"

Although John had assumed his parable—to him as crystal clear as the water that swirled around the pool and lapped against the trio of boulders and rushed down the ancient river—had surely answered Timothy's question, he didn't mind offering a few more details. "Let me put it this way. As you go through life, you're going to meet a lot of people—in school, at work, at the store, all kinds of places. Most of them will not be willing or able to stick around, and will wear away like the soft ground we're standing on. But a few of them will never wear away, like the bedrock at the top of the waterfall, and will be there to support and help you no matter what happens. Those are your friends."

Timothy thought about this solemnly. Even though he refused to accept the eloquence of John's analogy, he did appreciate the simplicity of the answer. He knew that he would need some time to think about this, but then, time was something he had plenty of. "Thanks dad."

John reached down and picked up a smooth stone and said, "You're sure welcome son," and flung the stone at the churning base of the waterfall.

Toil Under The Sun

♦ ♦ ♦

Lin Dehua's comrades try again, 30 November 1950

Nathaniel felt the temperature drop a little. He studied the limply hanging canvas flap beyond the lumpy bags of wounded Marines and realized that the day's advancing shadow had fully covered the tent. The entire hill would be shrouded in darkness in less than an hour. He finished adjusting a bloody dressing on a 19-year-old Marine from California then stood up stiffly, his knees crackling from too much crawling around on the frozen ground. It felt good to stand and feel the stretch in his legs; until an unpleasant tingling spread across his toes when blood refilled his numbed feet. He had nearly collapsed with exhaustion a few hours earlier; yet at this moment, for no good reason he could think of, he felt only a little tired. He also felt something else. When the exhaustion had crushed down on him, a constant sense of reality had pounded inside his head. Now that he had reached this unfamiliar existence beyond exhaustion, the incessant pounding had disappeared, leaving in its formless vacuum a bleary dreaminess. He thought to himself that this might be a good thing, because his work would not be finished for a long time and he could not yet afford to drift into sleep.

Captain Matheson yanked the tent flap back and stepped from the shadows of the hill into the gloominess of the medical tent. His eyes adjusted quickly to the low light of the lanterns. He studied each bag, some moving, some still, and then focused on the Navy Corpsman standing across from him in the opposite corner of the tent. He could see the vacant look of fatigue in Nathaniel's face. He stepped over several sleeping bags to position himself closer to the center of the tent and prepared to give his speech. He did not like what he was about to say, yet knew implicitly that he had no choice but to say it.

"Marines…listen carefully to what I am about to say." Matheson paused while he reconsidered his first words, then proceeded as he had originally planned. "I believe the Chinese are going to launch a major attack tonight in a final effort to finish us off. We've done the best we can to reinforce our defensive positions; however, as you know, we've suffered a lot of casualties. I'm not afraid to tell you that things are looking pretty bad. We're spread out real thin all around this hill, and

I don't think we can hold them back this time without your help. For that reason, I'm asking for volunteers among the wounded to return to the lines to help defend this hill tonight." He paused a second time before finishing his plea. "I want you to know that I won't think you're a coward if you stay here in the medical tent. After all, you've already proven your courage. That's all I have to say. Good luck to all of you." Matheson turned and walked out without waiting for a response. He had to make the same unpleasant speech in the other tent, also filled with wounded, and he wanted to get it over with.

Although weary beyond what he thought possible, Humphrey slept poorly because of the throbbing pain in his hip and lower back. Nathaniel had given him some morphine, which helped, but the drug also made him a little nauseous, which contributed to his sleeplessness. Unable to rest, he watched Captain Matheson burst into the tent. He listened circumspectly to the captain's little speech. The carefully measured words alarmed him, and then filled him with deep concern for Timothy who could be on the front line right now. Humphrey knew that he had to get up to help Timothy. He groped for the zipper pull along the side of his bag. After finding it, he struggled to pull it down as far as he could before the pain prevented him from reaching any farther. He twisted to his stomach and forced himself up onto his hands and knees. With a final agonizing effort, he dragged his left foot forward and pushed himself up until he could stand. A wave of dizziness hit him after he took a first step, and nearly overwhelmed him when he took a second.

Nathaniel watched Humphrey crawl out of his sleeping bag and stand up. When Humphrey began to sway from dizziness, Nathaniel quickly hopped over the bodies of several wounded Marines and grabbed him around the waist. Nathaniel chided Humphrey for getting up. "Hey! Where in the hell do you think you're going?"

Humphrey stiffened. "I'm volunteering, just like the captain asked."

Nathaniel squinted his eyes. "I don't think so. When he asked for volunteers, he meant guys who still have at least half their blood. You don't qualify."

"I'll be fine."

"Bullshit. You can't even stand up."

"I can if you let go of me."

"Suit yourself." Nathaniel released his grip. After wavering for a few seconds, Humphrey collapsed into a clump next to his bag.

"OK, you're right. Maybe I can't stand up right this moment. Maybe I just need a little rest. I'm sure I can if I get some sleep."

Nathaniel decided to play along, although he didn't really think Humphrey could remain upright long enough to walk out of the tent. "Yeah, that's a really good idea. Why don't you just rest for a few minutes? Then I'm sure you'll be able to go out." Humphrey rolled back onto the open sleeping bag and slid his legs in. He turned over to his side to ease the pain. Nathaniel pulled the flap over and quickly zipped up the bag. "Tell you what—I'll let you rest for 30 minutes, then I'll come and wake you up so you can go out and find the captain and see what he wants you to do."

After the physical exertion, Humphrey finally felt sleepy. "Yeah, that would be great. Let me rest for a bit, then come and wake me up. You promise to do that? I can't stay here. I've got to get up and help defend the hill tonight."

Nathaniel's dreaminess turned more and more surrealistic with each spoken word. He swallowed hard before answering, "I promise."

Badly depleted by two frontal assaults on the hill, Lin Dehua's rifle company had been combined with another to form a nearly full-strength unit. When he first learned of this unusual reorganization, he thought that he had no right to be alive—and that it would take magnificently absurd luck to survive a third such onslaught. Although this fundamental concern troubled him, it pleased him to learn that his new leader would be Captain Lin Wulong, the officer who had stopped to ask about his frozen foot. It pleased him more when the captain explained that they would not be involved in the primary assault on the hill. Three fresh companies would have the honor of charging across the narrow road to engage the Marines frontally. His unit would instead attack the crest of the hill after secretly negotiating a path to the north and then crossing a boulder field. Even better, they would not attack until after the main assault had commenced, further increasing the possibility of survival.

Captain Lin Wulong finished announcing his final orders only minutes before the afternoon sun ebbed behind the western mountains.

He spoke in carefully measured sentences. "I must again state two important instructions. First, it is crucial that we maintain absolute silence while we move up the side of the hill to the boulder field. We can only achieve success if the Marines do not detect us. Take every step with care. Second, we will not attack until 15 minutes after the first trumpet sounds. Do not be fooled by the sounds of the battle. First you will hear the trumpet, then you will wait for my signal to attack. You will advance only when I blow the whistle. Until that time, you will remain still."

Lin Dehua listened to these instructions with great interest. At the same time, he completed wrapping his right foot with the strip of quilted jacket he had cut from the dead soldier earlier in the day. He began by laying the thick fabric lengthwise along the top of his foot and over the front of his toes. He then folded the quilted strip back on itself and wound it neatly around his foot and heel and then partway up his ankle, where he secured it with a bulky knot. He had not originally planned to bind his foot this soon, but the pain in his toes and heel had become more serious, and he hoped the additional insulation would help. He did not understand that the fragile tissues of his toes and heel had already begun to freeze, and that he should have wrapped his foot many hours ago.

With only a remnant glow diffusing across the jagged western horizon, darkness soon enveloped Captain Lin and the men of his newly formed command. Finished with his meticulously delivered speech, and eager to begin the task the colonel had given him, he impatiently studied the retreating sky above the luminous glow as it gracefully dimmed to dark blue, then purple, and finally to endless black. At that moment, when he could no longer distinguish the faces of his men, he gave the command to move out. The company arranged itself in a loose single file and, with the captain in the lead, began an arduous walk up the steep incline west of the enemy hill. At first the men found it difficult to see the path in front of their feet; several fell noisily to the frozen ground after slipping on snow-covered rocks. One time a tiny avalanche of sharp stones and loose snow cascaded a short distance along the trail of men, creating a terrifying noise. Convinced of instant discovery, the entire company stopped. But nothing happened, and within 200

Toil Under The Sun

yards the first edge of moon broke through the darkness to provide a welcomed light. The company had trudged over half the distance to the boulder field when the moon reached its full luminance.

Captain Matheson slouched near the crest of the hill close to one of the battle-damaged pine groves, one shoepac resting on a split-open and blackened tree stump. He glanced down, and, seeing that the splintered stump still smoldered, watched a slender wisp of white smoke curl up around his boot before evaporating into the dense winter air above his knee. He lifted his eyes and resumed his study of the boulder field that spread out before him. Not surprisingly, he noticed that edgy feeling again that often preceded an inevitably bad event. He pulled his eyes off the boulders as the edgy feeling continued to grow, turned, and studied the nine men standing behind him. All of them had volunteered to leave the tents. He noted each injury or wound, and thought to himself that they probably should have stayed in the tents. One Marine stood with the help of a makeshift crutch, both feet wrapped in gauze strips caked with frozen blood. A second had squashed his helmet over a heavily bandaged head wound, his left eye covered by a drooping strand of tape. The other seven men, although wounded in different ways, appeared no less damaged.

Matheson coughed twice to clear his throat. He did not want to begin with a cracking voice. "Is this everyone?" The Marine with the head wound nodded slowly. "Good. I'm forming the nine of you into a provisional squad to defend the hill from an attack from the boulder field." Matheson looked down at one of the now abandoned foxholes that stretched out in a row between the two pine groves. A .30 caliber machine gun had been set up between two piles of rocks. "You'll have this .30 caliber, a couple of BARs, and all the M-1 rifles you want. I even scared up a dozen hand grenades for you." He looked at each one of the nine men in turn. He had expected to see exhaustion and desperation in their faces; instead he found nine determined Marines ready to follow whatever ridiculous order he might dish out. Matheson questioned his own readiness for such responsibility. "I've also ordered one of the mortars to target the ground in front of the boulders. They can lay in a few rounds if you need it. Any questions?"

The man with the makeshift crutch shuffled. A Marine with his left arm cradled in a sling tied back against his body finally spoke. "So what's the order?"

Captain Matheson sucked in a deep breath of the searingly cold air as quietly as possible, then exhaled in a slowly billowing plume of foggy breath. He knew that his newly formed squad could expect little help from the rest of the company tonight. As he thought of this, he realized the simplicity of his order. He looked away from the men, back up to the boulder field, and then turned to gaze directly into the eyes of the Marine who had asked the question. "Hold this position. Do not retreat. Any more questions?"

The Marine with the sling thought about asking what they were supposed to do when they ran out of ammunition, then realized that everyone already knew the answer. He simply shook his head. Captain Matheson saluted the men to thank them for volunteering, then turned and walked down the hill to check on the defenses near the road. As he approached the narrow road, a receding shadow began moving across the hill, cast by the moon rising brilliantly beyond the distant mountains.

Timothy stretched out comfortably on his back, loosely covered by his unzipped sleeping bag, and watched the first clouds of a new morning float in front of a pleasantly iridescent moon. When he studied the moon more closely, he noticed for the first time how easily he could discern the myriad craters and ridges and valleys on the surface. He had never before experienced such awareness of lunar geography. But the shifting sky soon obscured this new revelation. The tattered clouds had floated overhead at an unhurried pace before. He felt a gentle breeze touch the exposed skin of his face, and the tempo of the clouds quickened until little uncertainty remained that they would soon smother the moon's light and cast a murky shadow over the hill. Until now his body had felt too agitated to sleep; when the clouds thickened and drifted to cover the stars with a mottled gray veil, he too drifted away until no longer aware of the clouds or the moon or the intense cold that pressed against his body. His awareness of the passing time diminished as well, and nearly two hours vanished into the early morning gloom before the rising clouds gave up their first snow flurries.

Toil Under The Sun

He slept for a few precious minutes, at peace for the moment, thankfully unmindful of the desperation that closed in all around him. He dreamt, although he would not remember the dream when he awoke. And while he rested, his peaceful face upturned to the darkening sky, a snowflake that had formed thousands of feet above floated down through the uneven layers of increasingly frozen air and gently fell into his open mouth. The snowflake melted on his tongue, and he closed his mouth and shifted to his side.

Captain Lin Wulong peeked to the side of one of the huge rocks that cluttered the edge of the boulder field. The crest of the hill looked abandoned. He thanked his good fortune that his rifle company had not arrived any later—the moonlight that had guided them so well had now faded behind a thick cloudbank. Soon it would turn very dark, and that might be good fortune too, for the coming darkness would further conceal them while they waited before beginning their attack. He looked once more, straining to glimpse some activity beyond the two pine groves: he could only see darkness. No matter—they had achieved total surprise. They would now wait in silence for the sound of the trumpets.

Lin Dehua massaged the sides of his right foot and rested against a frozen boulder. The hike up the mountain had turned out far more difficult than expected. It cheered him that the intense pain had diminished—even if the loss of any feeling in both feet did make him clumsy. He had stumbled seven times because of the lifeless stumps that now pretended to be his feet. The rubbing did not help, so he stopped. He considered cutting off strips of quilted material from his own jacket to add another layer to his feet. After realizing the absurdity of this idea, he decided to wait until he found another dead comrade. He pulled his knees tight against his chest and rocked a little. He did not know if this helped his feet any more than the useless rubbing, but he preferred this to doing nothing.

Returning from his reconnaissance of the hill, Captain Lin Wulong paused by Lin Dehua, attracted by the rocking motion. He kneeled down on one knee and whispered quietly, "Lin Dehua, is that you?"

This inquiry surprised Lin Dehua. No officer had ever spoken to him in this tone before. "Yes sir. It is me."

"Why are you rocking so? Are you alright?"

"Yes sir—just a little cold."

"How is your foot? Is it doing any better?"

"Yes sir, much better. I think the march up the hill helped warm it a little."

Captain Lin Wulong looked back toward the crest of the hill then returned his gaze to Lin Dehua. "Good. I am glad your foot is feeling better." He stood rigidly, and walked into the boulder field until consumed by shadows.

Jolted awake by an explosion and intense light of an illumination round fired from one of the mortars, Timothy sat up with an impulsive jerk. A second round burst high above the narrow road as he twisted around and repositioned his rifle across the grim barricade of frozen men. It had begun snowing again and, enveloped by floating crystals sparkling in the flare light, hundreds of murky shapes glided across the road just south of his position. Moments after the second flare, five or six widely separated trumpets pierced the air with shrill and insistent battle calls; and the murky shapes began running. He pressed his finger firmly against the waiting trigger, not sure that he should fire. A machine gun to his left suddenly sprayed a line of .30 caliber rounds along the narrow road, prompting him to inadvertently flinch off an inaccurate round above the heads of oncoming men.

A third flare exploded above, and then a fourth. The entire road was now bathed in a brightly snow-dappled light, revealing an uncountable swarm of enemy soldiers charging headlong toward his position. The agitated machine gun burst aroused exhausted Marines all over the hill, and within seconds M-1 rifles and BARs and mortars and carbines began firing hundreds of rounds into the oncoming Chinese soldiers. Many fell: some individually, some in small groups, others in growing mounds of twisted bodies. The impressive firepower of the hill did not repress the insistent attack, and with each spent round of ammunition the massive assault moved inexorably closer to the base of the hill.

A scattered group of seven Chinese worked their way through the growing carnage until they found temporary refuge together in the shadow of the rocky bank that cut into the hill at the edge of the narrow road. Armed with burp guns, rifles, and explosive satchel charges, they

Toil Under The Sun

prepared themselves to climb laterally up the bank until they could attack the forward Marine defensive position in a deadly frontal assault. The seven hesitated at the base of the hill until a young lieutenant waved his hand, and then they moved forward.

Captain Lin Wulong watched the second hand pause at each number and line as it ticked down from 15 minutes. Time had passed slowly since his company first arrived at the boulder field; now that the trumpets had signaled the beginning of battle the moments raced by. His eyes jerked away from his watch and strained to see through the thickening snow flurries. The hollow thump of a flare echoed above him. The distant glow of the flare persisted and the sound faded to a hushed rumble, then another flare burst a little farther away and more to his right—probably to better illuminate the narrow road. He turned his eyes away from the light and resumed his timekeeping. A nauseating excitement warmed his stomach during the final two minutes.

A forgotten memory of his family burst into Lin Dehua's mind after the trumpets hissed their defiant response to the exploding flares. The ghostly light of the flares shuddered behind the swirling snow, quickly followed by a low, explosive rumble. He counted the months since he had last seen his wife and son. With a tangled mixture of nostalgia and regret, he realized that nearly two years had passed since he had caressed their tender faces. His son would be almost four now. With a successful completion to this battle, he might return home before his son turned five. Lin comforted himself with this thought as a stray bullet from a Chinese rifle glanced off a boulder just above his head. His legs jerked stiffly in response to the ricochet, jamming his right foot against a sharp rock and sending a spasm of convulsive pain up his leg.

Captain Lin warmed the metal whistle inside the armpit of his quilted jacket before raising it to his painfully blistered lips. He looked down at his watch: the second hand swept quickly over the few remaining lines and then crossed the numeral 12. He inhaled a gulp of freezing air and blew it violently through the whistle, signaling the attack to his men. He lifted his pistol into the air and ran out from the protection of the boulder field. Soldiers with burp guns and rifles poured out from between the huge rocks to his left and right. Others followed behind him. He jogged into the waiting darkness and stumbled on a loose rock.

The faraway light of the flares cast a fading glow on the snow-covered ground before him. Captain Lin Wulong squinted to see beyond the shadows between the two pine groves: it appeared that the crest of the hill had been left undefended. As he continued his advance, he noticed the outline of two tents and a tattered stand of pine trees. A torrid rush of exhilaration raced through his mind when he thought about the stunning surprise his attack would soon bring to the unsuspecting Marines. He quickened his pace and prepared to shoot his pistol moments before a .30 caliber machine gun fired a sudden burst across his chest, throwing him backwards into the soft snow. At first the snow chilled the back of his head; then, as he watched snowflakes float playfully above his extended hand, he felt a pleasant warmth spread over his chest and dribble down the sides of his neck.

The mortar thumped again and sent another illumination round on a steeply arcing flight toward the road. The round burst accurately above the centerline of the road moments later, showering light down on hundreds of advancing Chinese soldiers. Two Marines quickly prepared to load another round as Captain Matheson struggled up the hill to give them new orders. A shower of bullets whistled all around him when he arrived, forcing him to dive to the ground. Another round thumped, and he pushed himself up from the snow and crawled the last few yards to the mortar unit.

He waved a gloved hand in front of the face of one of the Marines and then screamed into his ear through cupped hands, his rasping voice barely audible above the crackling machine guns and rifles and exploding grenades. "Fire an illumination round above the top of the hill, beyond the tents. Something's going on up there and I need to see what it is. Give me two minutes to get up there before you fire." The Marine signaled his understanding by shoving a blackened thumb into the air. Captain Matheson returned the same signal before resuming his journey up the hill, crouching down lower to force himself into a smaller target, collapsing into the snow several times when the bullets got too close.

He had reached the pine groves when the flare exploded above the boulder field. To his horror, the light of the flare revealed dozens of enemy soldiers pouring out from between the boulders and nearly on top of his squad of wounded volunteers. Matheson quickly lifted his M-1 Carbine to an offhand position and fired repeatedly into the oncoming soldiers, emptying the magazine. He began running toward the crest. Without slowing his pace, he fished a new magazine out of his pocket and snapped it into his rifle. Before he could fire again, a stray Chinese bullet tore through his right thigh, just below his crotch, spinning him face down to the ground. With no awareness of pain, he raised up to his knee before forcing himself to a standing position again. He steadied himself as much as he could, and taking careful aim, continued firing into the attackers. Blood flowed down his leg and soaked the inside of his shoepac. Another flare burst high above the crest of the hill. Enemy bullets tore the air all around him, and then the darkness returned.

Timothy and the other Marines around him were rolling hand grenades down on the Chinese soldiers hiding below the cut in the road when a machine gun and rifle fire crackled at the top of the hill behind them. Timothy yanked the pin out of his last grenade and tossed it over the barricade of stacked bodies before turning around to look up the hill. The irises of his eyes had narrowed to control the bright flare light on the road, and he could see only darkness when he squinted in the direction of Humphrey's medical tent.

Just below him, only a few yards away, the seven Chinese soldiers who had made it across the road prepared to move laterally up the cut. One of the men crawled low to the ground until near the top of the slope before flinging a satchel charge into the barricade of frozen comrades. Timothy jerked his head forward and watched the deadly package of explosives float through a sudden eddy of snow. The satchel charge bounced off the back of a dead soldier in front of him before tumbling to the opposite side of the barricade. He instinctively buried his face into the ground and held his helmet tight against his head before the charge boomed a few yards away, blowing a jagged hole in the barricade and spraying the air above him with frozen body parts.

Timothy lifted his head groggily. A persistent buzzing had replaced the sounds of rifles and burp guns and explosions. He attempted to focus his eyes on the ruptured barricade, but could see only blurred images of backlit men running through the jagged hole and fighting hand-to-hand. He shook his head and tried to refocus, and the images became even more obscure. He rolled over and groped for his rifle, but could not find it in the thick snow. He pushed himself up and began crawling around, looking for a rifle. When he moved toward the barricade, a Chinese soldier with a bayonet-tipped rifle appeared above him. The soldier kicked Timothy down to the ground, forcing him to his back. Timothy shook his head again to clear his sight and began desperately reaching for a rifle; the enemy soldier stepped down on Timothy's arm and prepared to drive the bayonet into his chest.

Timothy looked up one last time as the deadly blade began its approach. He closed his eyes and tightened his stomach muscles when the bayonet accelerated and then—nothing happened. A shoepac bumped his head and the soldier's boot lifted off his arm. Timothy opened his eyes. For the first time since the satchel charge had blown him to the ground he could see clearly. There, hovering above him, clothed in a white tunic and gleaming chain mail armor and wielding a magnificent broadsword, a shimmering paladin blocked the deadly bayonet and then slew the astonished enemy with a wide sweep of the honed double blade. The shimmering paladin destroyed two more attackers before a Chinese soldier raised his burp gun and fired into it. Timothy felt a shower of chain mail scales hit his face as the paladin shattered and crumpled down on top of him. One of the metal scales landed in Timothy's upturned hand; he closed his hand and tightened his fingers around it, and the buzzing slowly faded into a pleasant unconsciousness. Although the battle swirled around him for two more hours, the dying paladin concealed him from the light of the flares and protected him from harm.

Chapter 20

Coach Hightower, August 1948

Timothy shambled along the uneven shoulder of the road, the clarity of his mind gloomed by alcohol and lack of sleep, each step requiring conspicuous effort to avoid a catastrophic fall. He could feel the edgy beginnings of a fresh headache squirming around behind his eye sockets. He rubbed each eye in a pointless attempt to press the pain back, and the headache began a familiar throbbing. The throbbing always started quietly—hardly noticeable really—yet he knew that within an hour it would transform itself into a genuinely irksome pounding. With his eyes momentarily closed to the moonlight, he stumbled on a clump of weeds hidden inside the jagged shadow of a wooden fence post, gnarled from years of harsh weather. He stopped himself from falling by quickly flinging his unencumbered foot out beyond the clump and bending over. This sudden movement sent a blast of dull pain through his head that died away slowly like an unpleasant echo. He straightened himself up and looked at the moon in time to see it mock his fleeting clumsiness with a condescending sneer. The bright reflection of the hidden sun hurt his eyes and increased the pounding in his head; he looked away from the light and instead focused on the rhythmic fence post shadows marching down the road and disappearing over the crest of the hill. Beyond the shadows and the glowing rim of the hill he could see a spreading haze of mottled fog resting pleasantly on the horizon. He would have to walk through the fog to find his way home.

It seemed very late, although the exact time of day eluded him. He thought it might be past one in the morning. He couldn't remember when he had left the party and started walking along the road. He didn't even remember arriving at the party. Now that he thought about it, he didn't actually remember much of anything. He raised his right hand up close to his eyes so he could look at his wristwatch in the moonlight, then remembered that the strap had broken during the fight. He felt a twinge of nostalgia: his mom and dad had given him that watch for Christmas last year, probably after scrimping for weeks. His dad had asked him two months earlier if he wanted anything special for Christmas, and he had said that he really wanted a watch. He remembered his parents' happy display when he tore open the last present and revealed the watch. He prayed that someone would find it and return it to him at school. He knew he would feel bad if it never showed up again. The loss of the watch might really piss off his parents too. He didn't know which would be worse. Maybe he could figure it out tomorrow when he felt better and this incessant pounding had weakened.

Probably to deflect attention from the headache, or more likely to conceal his growing melancholy, Timothy began counting the fence post shadows as he resumed walking along the road. Not only did he count them, he also stretched out his stride so that every fifth footfall landed squarely on one of the twisted shadows. To avoid any needless confusion, he counted the shadows only when his foot actually landed on them. One, two, three…twenty-seven, twenty-eight, twenty-nine… forty-six, forty-seven…. He asked himself: *I wonder who the poor bastard was who had to pound all of these damn posts into the ground? Probably some piss-poor dirt farmer who didn't have anything better to do with his time. Maybe he died of a heart attack before he finished.* His secret discussion about the poor bastard and the fence posts ended when a pair of headlights glared unexpectedly over the top of the hill and seared his tender retinas. He covered his eyes with his hand, spreading the fingers slightly so he could see comfortably through the slits. The car slowed and pulled up next to him, and then the window slowly cranked down. He looked inside the open window, but couldn't make out the shadowy driver.

"Timothy, is that you?" Timothy lowered his hand and leaned forward. "It is you! What in sam hill are you doing out here in the middle of nowhere at one in the morning?" Coach Hightower's resonant words boomed out of the car. Even though Timothy still couldn't see him clearly, he recognized the distinctive voice.

Timothy started to ask Coach Hightower what in sam hill he was doing out here at one in the morning too, but then decided, out of respect, to avoid the subject altogether. "I don't know, coach—just taking a walk, I guess."

Toil Under The Sun

Coach Hightower narrowed his eyes a little. "Just taking a walk—you guess? Well, Timothy…that surely does explain everything." He shifted into neutral and set the parking break so that he could relax his foot, then leaned through the window until the cool light of the moon glanced off his forehead. "I assume you're on your way home. Would I be correct in that assumption?"

Timothy moved his hands behind his back and weaved his fingers together. He thought about telling the truth about counting the fence post shadows, then decided this would be too unbelievable, even for Coach Hightower. "I guess you could say I am on my way home. At least I'm heading in that general direction."

Coach Hightower grunted and pushed his face a little further through the open car window. The moonlight flashed off the top of his head. "Do you want a ride home? Or do you want to keep wandering around out here in the dark until some stinking drunk son-of-a-gun runs you over?"

Timothy didn't know if he should accept the ride or not, especially if it meant going straight home. On the other hand, it might sound really suspicious if he turned down a ride when he really shouldn't be out here in the first place. He decided that he had no choice but to accept Coach Hightower's offer and hope that he still had time to make up a good story before arriving home. "Yeah, I could use a ride. I guess it is getting pretty late."

"You're damn right it's getting late. Hop in and let's get the hell out of here. I should be getting home too."

Timothy walked around the front of the car, opened the passenger door, and slid onto the seat. He pulled the door shut with a gentle click, just like his dad had taught him. It actually felt good to sit down and rest in the warmth of the car. Mr. Hightower moved the shifter into first gear, released the parking break with an annoying squeal, executed a masterful three-point turn, and drove toward the crest of the hill and the distant haze. Timothy noticed that the bright headlights obliterated the fence post shadows, rendering them pretty much uncountable. They drove in silence for a few minutes before Mr. Hightower said anything again.

Mr. Hightower thought he smelled alcohol. He wanted to lean a little closer to Timothy and sniff the air around the front of his face, but decided this would quickly end any meaningful conversation. "Tell me Timothy; why aren't you at home at this time of the night. Do your parents know you're out here wandering around in the dark?"

Timothy felt overtaken by exhaustion, and the pounding headache dulled any chance of pretense. He answered the question directly, without calculation, because he did not have enough stamina to do otherwise. "They're not really my parents. I'm adopted."

This response surprised Coach Hightower. He had known John and Martha for years, and had never thought of them as anything other than Timothy's parents. He decided to respond simply and decisively. "Why Timothy, of course they're your parents. They've raised you since you were a tiny baby. How could they not be your parents?"

Timothy realized at that moment that Coach Hightower, hopelessly ignorant about his parents, did not understand anything. Although he had no interest in continuing this conversation, he didn't think he had much choice about it. "My real mom gave me away. She was really young I guess. I don't have a clue who my father was. Probably some drunk."

This sequence of assertions transformed Coach Hightower from surprise to stunned silence. He had thought a simple declaration of what he perceived as the truth would set the issue straight. Instead, he had rapidly sunk into emotional quicksand—and with no one around to throw him a vine. He coughed to clear a suddenly forming layer of mucus from his throat before continuing. "I don't think you should think of it that way, Timothy." He paused while his mind groped for something more convincing. "Your parents are your parents. They've raised you since you were born." He cleared his throat again before backing himself into a philosophical corner. "And anyway, Timothy, they love you like their own. I'm sure of it." He cringed the moment this assumption slobbered out of his mouth.

Timothy quickly pounced on the subtlety of this last assertion. He had never made his next statement to himself or anyone else; all of a sudden the truth had become painfully clear for the first time in his life. "That's the problem, isn't it? I don't belong to them. I don't belong to my real mom either. I don't belong to anyone. So how can you say they love me? I just don't see how it's possible."

Mr. Hightower began thinking that it might have been better to have driven by Timothy and left him roaming around in the darkness. He

Toil Under The Sun

had stopped the car because of his inborn concern for others, especially for Timothy. Unfortunately, this conversation had quickly turned into an ugly mess. Even so, he decided that Timothy needed to hear what he had to say, despite his apparent inability to carry the argument to a winning conclusion. He decided to try a different approach. "Think of this, Timothy…haven't your parents done all kinds of neat stuff with you? Your mom was a den leader when you were in the Cub Scouts. Your dad coached your Little League Team for three years. Shoot, I don't think either one of them ever missed one of your races, even when you were finishing in last place every time. How can you think they don't love you when they've always been there for you? It just doesn't make any sense, if you ask me."

It didn't take Timothy long to figure out an answer to this one. "That's not the point. It doesn't make any difference if they did stuff with me or not. It doesn't make any difference what you think either. The point is, my real mom gave me away. And it doesn't matter what anyone does or says. That fact is never ever going to change."

Mr. Hightower didn't know what else to say. He had reached a point far beyond any reasonable understanding of the complex perceptions that smoldered deep inside Timothy's psyche. He sat helplessly as Timothy's house appeared a few hundred feet up the road. When he arrived at the top of the dirt driveway, he stopped the car next to the mailbox, shifted into neutral, and set the parking brake. Something in his head told him he should make a simple plea for reasonableness, without getting bogged down into any more abstract debates. "You know Timothy, I really don't know a lot about who gave you away or who thinks this or that. Maybe you're right, and then again, maybe you're not. I guess you're just going to have to figure that out for yourself. All I can tell you is that I know in my heart that your parents love you. It's as simple as that. You can debate it all you want, but I'm certain that's the honest truth."

Timothy sat very still. He stared through the dusty windshield and thought about what Coach Hightower had just said. The words twisted around inside his mind because he knew without hesitation that they couldn't possibly be true. "Sorry Coach. I guess I just don't believe you."

Coach Hightower cleared his throat one last time but did not say anything. He put the car back in gear, released the parking break with an annoying squeal, and drove down the bumpy driveway. He stopped the car at the bottom, the headlights shining directly into the big picture window at the front of the house. He could see John standing there, staring out at them. "Do you want me to go in with you, Timothy? I can go inside with you, if you'd like."

Timothy thought about this offer briefly, and then admitted to himself that Coach Hightower's presence would do nothing more than delay the natural consequences he would inevitably have to face. It would be far better to just get it over with so he could go to bed and try to sleep off his headache. "No thanks. I'll be alright." He opened the door, slid across the seat, and stepped out of the car into the cool night air. His hand started to push the door closed, and then he paused. "Thanks for the ride."

Coach Hightower flicked his hand to wave goodbye. "My pleasure, Timothy. Let me know how things turn out when you get a chance."

"I will." Timothy closed the car door gently, and without looking back, walked toward the front porch. Coach Hightower released the parking brake and shifted into reverse as Timothy disappeared behind the entry door.

◆ ◆ ◆

A fleeting vision, Dog Hill, 30 November 1950

Although the snow flurries had gradually decreased, and then stopped altogether sometime early in the morning, Lin Dehua could not recall this important event. He watched the darkness withdraw before the ascent of a new sun and shivered, uncontrollably at times, and waited patiently for the sun's warmth. He remembered running through turbid currents of roiling snow, barely able to see the man in front of him, sharp flakes stinging his blistered face, before bright flashes of light erupted somewhere off to his left. He remembered running in a different direction and then tripping over an unseen body and tumbling to the ground, smashing his chin against a jagged chunk of ice. He remembered tasting a gush of blood in his mouth before it oozed out and froze into a dark mass on the side of his face. He remembered crawling through a thick mat of snow over the frozen ground, pushing his tattered body forward with lifeless feet, as a deadly stream of bullets shrieked above his head. And although he struggled to think clearly, the bitter cold diminished any remaining clarity of thought and he could not remember when it had stopped snowing.

He looked down at his dead feet, pressed together at the soles, and impulsively rocked back and forth to generate warmth. The feet had seemed so important to him when he had first wrapped them with strips of quilted fabric a day ago. He recalled cutting a long strip off the coat of a dead comrade. He noticed that the wrapping on his left foot had somehow unraveled during the night and now trailed away from him in a tangled line. They had once seemed so important, but now he could not understand or remember why. He considered reeling in the unraveled fabric and wrapping his foot again, but could not convince himself that his foot would care. This amused him a little; when he smiled, he could not remember why.

A sharp pain ached in his side: he did not know when the pain had started or what had caused it. He pulled his right hand from inside the limited warmth of his left sleeve and explored the pain. He touched a shredded rip in his jacket, almost even with his limply dangling elbow. The edges of the torn fabric, stiff and frozen, chafed his hand when he rubbed against them. He pushed his fingers into the tear and felt a crusty mass of ice crystals. He tried to probe into the mass, but it had frozen hard and unyielding. He returned his hand to the negligible warmth of the sleeve before resuming the persistent rocking motion.

While he struggled to maintain his dimming vision in the emergent morning light, he noticed two snow-covered tents less than a hundred feet away. He did not recall seeing the tents before, and could not be sure if he had or not because his memories of the night continued to mingle and erode. He watched with interest when a young man stepped out from one of the tents and looked up at the sun. He could see the man standing in the sun and enjoying its warmth. This cheered him a little, because he knew that he too would feel the sun's warmth in a short while.

As he waited for the sunlight to fall upon him, he thought of his wife and son. He could see them standing in the light of the sun like the young man by the tent. No, they weren't standing—they were walking together, down a winding country road through the beautifully glowing fields of a late summer afternoon. A gentle breeze rustled across the yellow grasses that flowed away from both sides of the road and then into an endless horizon. His wife carried a large basket on her head. He could not see inside of it. His young son jumped and skipped and laughed as he tried to keep up with his mother. Strolling and jumping and laughing in the warmth of the pleasant sunlight, his wife and son came closer to him. He could almost see their faces. They were very near now. He could almost touch them. He reached out his good hand to caress their gentle faces as exhaustion and the relentless cold plunged his fading mind deeper into disarray. And then he realized that he could not remember what they looked like. This alarmed him at first, then his thoughts quickly lapsed into an icy complacency.

Lieutenant Meyer leaned against one of the collapsed walls next to the demolished hut and watched Gunny Talbot trudge relentlessly down the hill. Near the end of the battle, before the darkness of night had lifted, a stray round from a Chinese burp gun had cut through the bottom of his shoepac and sliced his heel open. The bullet had created a clean wound, and had not hurt too badly at first; now his foot ached enough to provoke a serious limp. The Gunny completed his last few steps with typical precision before stopping in front of the new company commander. Lieutenant Meyer studied the gunnery sergeant's eyes before asking the question he had been thinking about for several minutes. "How bad is it, Gunny?"

Gunny Talbot pulled at his gloves and organized his thoughts. "Not good, sir. The captain's lost a lot of blood. The corpsman doesn't think he'll make it through the night. We lost the last working radio too. Found it over there by that foxhole, full of holes. It didn't work very good anyway. I think the battery was pretty much dead from the cold. I made a count of everyone I could find, including everyone in the tents. I think I can scrape together maybe 80 men for tonight—if we're lucky. The rest are either dead or too wounded to help. A few are missing, but I don't have any idea where they are. That's about it."

Meyer lifted his bad foot off the ground and winced. "That's not a lot to work with. I wonder how many more Chinese are out there?"

"Good question, sir. We've killed a bunch of them. I don't think we've killed enough to make them lose interest."

"Neither do I. Any suggestions?"

Gunny Talbot looked around the hill before answering. He couldn't remember anything this bad on Okinawa; he remained calmly professional nonetheless. "I would guess they'll attack from above and below again. It's easier for them to attack in force across the road. I'd concentrate most of the men there. I'd say maybe 70 for the road and the remaining 10 on top. But it's your call, sir."

"Thanks, Gunny. That sounds good to me. Let's get the men moving."

"Yes sir." Gunny Talbot turned to begin his work, then hesitated and turned back to face Lieutenant Meyer again. "And sir…"

"Yes?"

"You should see the corpsman about that foot, before it gets any worse."

Lieutenant Meyer glanced down at his damaged foot. The pain had started to really annoy him now. "Thanks Gunny. I'll take a walk up there in a few minutes."

Timothy opened his eyes to the subdued light and smudgy canvas roof of the medical tent. A pounding headache ached inside his head; he could hear a pulsating buzz in both ears. When he tried to turn around, his legs got tangled up because some asshole had stuffed him into a sleeping bag and zipped it up tight around his face. He swore before sliding his arm up the inside of the bag and forcing it through the tight opening around his face. He quickly found the zipper. The damn thing had frozen and resisted his first attempts to move it. He grabbed the zipper from the inside with his other hand too, and after working at it for a minute from both sides, broke it loose and peeled the bag down to his crotch. His swearing and thrashing attracted the corpsman.

Nathaniel stepped over a neatly arranged row of four Marines and knelt down next to Timothy, who had by that time started pulling his legs out of the bag. "What do you think you're doing?"

Timothy answered Nathaniel's question in a very loud voice to overcome the buzzing in his ears. "What do you *think* I'm doing? I'm getting the hell out of this sleeping bag and then I'm getting the hell out of this tent. You got a problem with that?"

Nathaniel had experienced this behavior before and knew exactly how to respond. "No, I don't have a problem with that. Whatever you say."

Timothy flung the sleeping bag open, pulled his legs completely out, and carefully stood up. He felt a little woozy, but not bad enough to keep him from leaving. "See, what did I tell you. I'm fine."

Maybe Nathaniel had underestimated this one. "Yeah, I can see that. What do you plan to do, now that you're up?"

"Which way do I go to get out of this damn tent?"

Nathaniel waved his arm in the direction of the tent flap. "Over there, where you can see the light pouring in. Just be careful not to step on anyone when you leave. I've got enough going on as it is."

"And a rifle. I need a rifle. You know where I can get one?"

"Yeah. Just look around outside. They're all over the place. You shouldn't have any trouble finding one."

"Thanks. I'll be going now."

"Hey, before you leave, I've got a question for you."

Timothy focused on the ground in front of him so that he wouldn't trip on anything. "Yeah? What's that?"

"You had something in your hand when they brought you in here this morning. Took some effort to pry it out of your clenched fingers. I was wondering if you knew anything about it—and how it got there?"

"I did? What did it look like?"

"It looked like a little metal horse. I think it was probably a chess piece, but I'm not sure. You have any idea where it came from?"

Timothy felt a shiver squirm around inside his gut. Then his heart fluttered and skipped a beat. Even though the temperature in the tent had plunged far below freezing, he suddenly felt very warm and began sweating. A fragment of a long forgotten memory darted into his thoughts, distracting him from Nathaniel's question. *What did that old guy say again? Something about greater love. No, that's not quite right—something about no one has greater love than this. But what's the rest of it? I know there's more to it than that; I just can't remember. Shit. Maybe I shouldn't have slept through all of those Sunday school classes after all.* "Yeah, I know exactly where it came from. Do you still have it?"

"Yeah, I do." Nathaniel groped around in his jacket pocket and pulled out the little metal horse, stuck to a dirty roll of medical tape. He held the roll out in front of Timothy. "Now I remember. It *is* a chess piece. It's called a knight."

Timothy raised his hand to remove the little metal horse from the roll of tape; he stopped when Nathaniel announced the common name. "Most people call it a knight, but that's not what it really is."

Nathaniel pulled the roll of tape back a little. "It's not? What do you call it then?"

Timothy swallowed with difficulty before speaking. "It's called a Paladin. Thanks for keeping it safe." Timothy reached out and retrieved the Paladin. He tumbled it around in his upturned palm a few times before dropping it into his pocket and turning to leave the tent. His hand began shaking after his fingers released the metal horse. He quickly wiped away a jagged tear from his cheek before Nathaniel could see it.

"You're welcome."

Timothy did not respond. He stepped over sleeping bags and worked his way across the tent. When he reached the canvas flap, he paused when his fingers touched it. He thought about staying in the tent a few minutes longer, then changed his mind and stepped out into the fresh morning light.

Lin Dehua had grown increasingly weary while straining to see the faces of his wife and son. Finally exhausted, he decided to rest before trying again. The sun would find him in a few minutes. Maybe the sun's warmth would clear his mind and release him from his increasingly muddled thought. The young man standing by the tent started walking toward him. At first the young man did not appear to notice Lin, but then came closer and looked directly at him. The young man stood there, still and unmoving, for what seemed to Lin like a very long time. Lin thought that maybe the young man's feet had frozen to the ground and could not move, but then he began looking down and walking around in circles. Although Lin watched this curious behavior with intense interest, he did not have the energy to guess what it meant.

After tracing an expanding spiral of concentric circles, the young man bent down and picked something up. Lin could not identify it at first; when the young man turned, he could see the silhouette of a rifle. The young man stopped about 20 feet in front of Lin, and after making several clacking sounds, raised the rifle and aimed it at Lin's chest. Too tired to care, Lin worried that he would never feel the sun's warmth again. He still could not see the faces of his wife and son, and for the first time since he had left home, he felt a piercing shame.

Timothy pushed through the tent flap, stiff from the frozen breath of wounded Marines, and stepped outside into the clean air. A ragged slab of snow slid off the tent roof when the flap slapped back and fell harmlessly to the ground behind him. He closed both eyes and raised his face up to the morning sun to feel its pleasant warmth on his blistered cheeks and nose. The incessant buzzing increased when he closed his eyes, so he opened them again and focused straight ahead on a man sitting cross-legged about a hundred feet away. He squinted to improve his vision and could see the man rocking back and forth. This reminded him of a small child he had once seen rocking in a small crib. Curious, Timothy walked toward the man until he reached a rise in the ground about 50 feet away and then stopped. He could see now that the man wore the quilted uniform of a Chinese Soldier.

Timothy began walking in loosely growing circles as he searched the snow-covered ground for a rifle. Even though Nathaniel had said they were lying around all over the place, he couldn't see a single one. He continued walking until his circle expanded to nearly 20 feet in diameter. Crunching through the crusty surface of the snow near a large protruding rock, he walked a few more steps until his foot kicked something heavy. He scraped his shoepac across the top of a long ridge of snow and exposed the familiar wood stock of an M-1 Garand. He bent down and pried the rifle out of the snow; he felt a little woozy when he stood up again. He steadied himself, and then brushed crusted snow off the sides and top of the rifle as he approached the Chinese soldier. He stopped about 20 feet from the rocking man and then cradled the rifle in both arms. He waited a long time before moving again.

Lin Dehua paused his rocking when Timothy stopped in front of him, and looking at him through eyes blurred with tears, tried desperately to remember the faces of his wife and son in the few seconds that remained. Timothy pulled back the bolt slightly to inspect the rifle's readiness and then released it with a sharp clack. Lin shuddered imperceptibly when he heard the familiar sound. Timothy raised the rifle up to his right eye and sighted down the barrel's length until he could imagine an image of Lin's heart filling the circle of his rear sight.

He held the rifle steady, impatiently waiting for the familiar rage. The rage would pull the trigger for him and instantly cleanse him of his overwhelming grief. He waited. The rage would avenge the death of the friend who had really loved him—a true friend who's love he could now accept. He waited. He waited, and the rage did not come. He tried to coax the rage by remembering how it felt: still it did not come. Timothy ceased his waiting—the rage had left him.

Timothy lowered the rifle and tossed it to the ground. The slowly advancing edge of sunshine moved across Lin's chest and warmed his face. Timothy walked toward Lin until he stood next to him. He knelt down, unscrewed the lid of his canteen, and offered Lin a drink. Dehydrated from loss of blood and a long night without water, Lin nodded to signal his acceptance. Timothy touched the mouth of the canteen against Lin's cracked lips and tilted it until a small sip of water poured out.

When the water flowed into his parched mouth, Lin realized the intensity of his thirst. He swallowed the water with difficulty and some pain, yet did not regret the pain. The soothing warmth of the sun and the refreshing drink cleared his mind for a brief moment. Lin looked up into Timothy's sad eyes, and as he smiled his thanks without speaking, the splendid faces of his wife and son appeared one last time before he slumped over into the soft snow.

Chapter 21

A town in Northwest Oregon, August 1948

    He recalled a recent promise to never do this; and still he stood here, his hands clamped together behind his back, his head drooped in disbelief, about to do exactly what he had imagined impossible. And yet, when he thought about it, this looming failure should not have surprised him. With only a little effort he remembered numerous other times when he had fallen short in the same way—that is, made a promise to himself and then broken it. Sometimes he broke the promise within a few days, just like tonight. Sometimes it took much longer. Once a promise fell shattered to the ground in less than a minute. And although this resilient pattern had never really concerned him before tonight, it did at this moment for reasons his wearied mind refused to clarify. He did not know if normal people suffered from this same affliction or not—whatever *normal* meant. He thought that he might be the only person he knew who did this, and then chuckled cynically. Maybe someone else in his world ignored their own promises too, but he couldn't think of who they were or where they lived, assuming they even existed. Tonight he didn't much care if they existed or not. He had more urgent problems to resolve.

    Hunger presented his newest peril. As he stood in the shadows of the narrow alley, he began to understand for the first time how stupidly unappreciative he had been about the meals his mom had prepared for him, including the weekend lunches he almost always complained about—privately, if not loud enough for anyone to hear. Once he had even conjured up the audacity to complain about the special sack lunches she made for him when he spent all day Saturday in the spruce grove working on his tree fort. Every day she prepared breakfast before he went to school, gave him lunch money, and then had dinner ready every night by 6:00 pm. She even threw in occasional snacks like chocolate chip cookies or brownies or ice cream with chocolate syrup. Where the food came from or who paid for it or how she prepared it or how it ended up on the dining room table all cooked and organized never seemed appreciably relevant to his life. It just, somehow…happened—everyday, week after week, month after month, year after year, without deviation or failure, and without any appreciable recognition from him. The food just always appeared, whether he thought about it or not, whether he said thank you or not, whether he cared or not. Damn, he thought to himself—he'd even devour a big plate of those slimy green beans to chase away the intensity of this hunger, and without any mashed potatoes or milk to help gulp them down either. Well, maybe his circumstances had not yet become quite *that* serious, but he knew with absolute certainty that they soon would.

The warped metal lid no longer sealed the top of the dumpster, and he could smell the contents through the crooked gap. He stood nearly motionless in front of the big steel box, contemplating whether or not he should raise the lid. He still had time to turn and walk away, thereby keeping his promise that he would starve to death before eating garbage out of a dumpster. On the other hand, if he did choose to walk away, then what would he do? He couldn't go home, and without money he couldn't buy any food. He could possibly try to steal some—and if the storeowner caught him he would end up back at home, and under worse circumstances than he currently faced at this unfortunate moment. So he stood there with his hands fumbling behind his back, trying to convince himself to walk away from the dumpster and to open the lid at the same time. He might have stood there all night. His indecisiveness was suspended by an old man wearing a greasy apron and wielding a large black flashlight.

The conical flashlight beam jumped along the uneven alley floor and then darted up his leg until it blinded his fully-exposed retinas. He moved a hand from behind his back to cover his eyes, but instead let it hang passively at his side. His irises quickly fanned to form tiny openings, and the intensity of the light diminished. The light stayed on his face for several seconds before the old man said anything.

"Hey kid. What're you doing back here?"

Not wanting to admit that he was thinking about fishing dinner out of the dumpster, he responded evasively. "Nothing, sir. Just standing here."

The old man did not lower the flashlight. "Doesn't look like nothing to me, kid. Looks like you're getting ready to open the lid on that dumpster."

A true statement; he still did not want to admit it. "Do you mind lowering that flashlight mister? It's really hurting my eyes."

The old man responded by holding the light steady. "Do I know you? You look awfully familiar."

"How about that flashlight?"

The old man finally lowered the flashlight until it shined down his leg and spilled a glowing puddle around his feet. "Yeah, sure. Sorry. I didn't mean to blind you. Do I know you?"

This seemed an odd question. He couldn't possibly have met this old man before. "I don't think so. I'm pretty sure we've never met."

The old man persisted. "You ever passed through this town before?"

"No, not that I know of."

"You sure?"

"Yeah I'm sure; unless my parents took me here when I was a baby or something. And then I wouldn't remember anyway."

The old man paused and tried to remember where he'd met this young man before—nothing came to mind. "No, that's not it. I wouldn't have remembered you as a baby. It's something else. You're sure we didn't meet when you were older, maybe a couple of years ago or something?"

"Yeah, I'm sure. I would've remembered you if we had."

The old man studied the young man's trim silhouette, backlit by a streetlight beyond the end of the alley, before making an extraordinary offer. "You know, I have some leftover food that will just go to waste if someone doesn't eat it. Would you mind coming into the restaurant for a few minutes and having a little dinner before you go? I hate wasting food. You'd be helping me out if you did." The young man did not respond. "Of course, if you've already had dinner, you don't have to come in."

The young man squinted suspiciously. Why would anyone just give him something to eat when he didn't have any money to pay for it, or more importantly, when he didn't deserve it? He hadn't considered this possibility a few minutes ago when he had struggled to decide whether or not to lift the filthy dumpster lid and paw around inside. He had convinced himself that he would have to either eat garbage or steal to survive. He had not imagined the possibility that someone would just give him food. "Uh, no, I haven't had any dinner tonight. I guess I could come in and have a bite. But I'm sort of in a hurry, and I can't stay very long."

The old man smiled. "That's fine. It won't take long to rustle something up. After all, it'll just go to waste anyway. You'd be helping me out if you ate some of it. You can leave when you're finished. No problem at all."

He followed the old man down the narrow alley, through a creaking screen door, and into a storage room adjacent to the kitchen. He thought he would get something to eat there, but the old man continued through the kitchen and pushed through a pair of big swinging doors and walked into the main sitting area of the restaurant. The only customers in the room, a young couple, held hands and drank hot coffee in a booth near the main entry doors. The old man finally stopped at a small square table, next to a window off the main street, and motioned the young man to sit. A yellow candle burned in a glazed ceramic dish in the middle of the table.

"How's this spot? It's the best in the house. This is where I always sit when I'm having dinner. You can watch the cars and people go by from here. Well, maybe not this late at night. You can for sure watch them go by earlier in the day."

It surprised the young man to hear that someone thought his opinion about the location of a table mattered. "Thanks. This spot is fine." He sat on one of the sturdy wooden chairs ringing the table and slid forward. One of the chair legs made a woody squeak when it glided across the floor.

"Would you like to start with a salad? I've got lots of lettuce that I'm just going to have to throw out if you don't eat some of it. I've got a few leftover carrots and tomatoes too. Do you want some tomatoes on your salad?"

"Sure. That sounds great."

"What kind of dressing you want?"

Damn. Now this guy was offering him salad dressing. He had originally visualized a simple cheese sandwich, or something even less elaborate, when the old man first invited him to dinner. Now he had to choose the dressing for his salad. This reminded him of eating in a real restaurant with his mom and dad. "Thousand Island, if you have any. But anything you've got will be fine."

"I've got gallons of it. Thousand Island it is." The old man turned and, after stopping at the only other occupied table to chat with the young couple, disappeared into the kitchen beyond the pair of big swinging doors. He returned within minutes carrying a salad and a small basket covered with a white cloth.

"I thought you might like some dinner rolls too. I like to eat rolls with my salad. Butter's on the table. You want some pepper on your salad?"

"Sure."

"I was thinking that you might like a steak and a baked potato. Maybe a big glass of milk too. Does that sound alright?"

Less than an hour ago, he had stood out in the dark alley, hungry and cold, nearly resolved to eat garbage out of a dumpster. Now he prepared to munch on a salad, with a steak, baked potato, and big glass of cold milk soon to follow. The young man stammered, "Ah, gee, sure…that would, would be really great." He paused, suddenly concerned the old man could get fired for giving away food like this. "Are you sure you should be doing this, mister? I don't want to get you in trouble or anything."

The old man smiled and then chuckled. "Oh yeah, no trouble at all. It's fine. Like I told you, all this food will just go to waste anyways. You're doing me a big favor by eating it. As a matter of fact, I'm really lucky you stopped by. By the way—medium rare all right with you?"

"Yeah, that's the way I like it."

"What do you know—that's the way I like it too."

The young man finished his salad, including the sliced tomatoes garnishing the edge of the plate, and then ate a steak and baked potato, with the old man checking on him every few minutes. He even had butter and salt for the potato. He washed the final bite of potato down with the last of the cold milk.

The old man watched him finish the milk from across the room, then quickly walked over. "Everything alright?"

"Yeah, it was great. Thanks for everything."

"You're welcome. Thanks for helping out. As I said…."

In his eagerness, the young man interrupted. Although he did not intend to sound impolite, he had an important question to ask. "I was

Toil Under The Sun

just thinking, mister. Is there something I could do to pay you for the meal? I don't want to be a freeloader."

The old man grinned broadly and squeezed his pudgy chin between a thumb and finger. "Why sure. I think I could use some help. How would you like to sweep up the sitting area? That hasn't been done yet, and it would really be a big help to me if you did it."

The young man answered quickly. "Sure, I can do that. How do I start?"

"It's pretty easy. You just pull all of the chairs aside, then use a big push broom to sweep out beneath the tables, and a dustpan to collect all the interesting stuff you're going to find. You need to sweep under the booths too—that's not too hard, 'cause you don't have to move any chairs. Think you can handle that?"

"Yeah, I think I can. Just show me where the broom and dustpan are, and I'll get started."

The young man worked diligently for nearly an hour, pulling chairs out and sweeping under tables. He carefully returned the chairs to their original positions before starting on the booths. The booths turned out to be easier, just as the old man had predicted, and he finished twenty minutes later. After tossing the last of the debris into a metal garbage can by the big swinging doors, he found the old man scrubbing countertops in the kitchen.

"I'm all done now. I guess I'll be leaving. I just wanted to thank you for the dinner. It was really great, especially the steak. Thanks."

"Why, you're welcome young man. Say, I was thinking—if you wanted to come back again tomorrow night, I could trade you a meal for sweeping up again. What do you think?"

The young man considered this, but knew that it wouldn't work. "That's really swell of you mister, except I'm just passing through. I probably won't be here tomorrow night. Thanks anyway. I really appreciate it."

"Too bad. I could really use some help with the sweeping. Sure you won't reconsider?"

"Yeah, I'm sure. I should be going now. Thanks again." The young man turned to leave the restaurant. The old man reached out and touched his arm.

"Say, I don't even know your name. I can't say a proper goodbye if I don't even know your name."

The young man hesitated in response to the touch. "It's Timothy."

"Timothy. That's a good name, just like in the Bible. My name's Jake, and you can come back to help with the floor sweeping and get a meal anytime you like, Timothy."

"Thanks, mister. I'll keep that in mind."

"It's Jake. You can call me Jake."

"Thanks, Jake."

"You're welcome Timothy. You be careful now; and take care of yourself out there; and don't forget my offer. You come back anytime you want."

"I won't forget. Well…I guess it's time for me to get moving, so goodbye. Thanks again for the dinner. I really enjoyed it."

"Goodbye, Timothy. It's been a pleasure meeting you."

"You too, Jake." Timothy walked through the front door of the restaurant and stepped out into the cool night air. He looked left for traffic before stepping off the curb; the street was empty of cars. When he reached the far side of the street, he veered right and disappeared into the gloom beyond a flickering streetlight.

◆ ◆ ◆

C-rations with Lieutenant Meyer, 1 December 1950

Timothy dumped a couple of C-rations into the water soon after it erupted into an impressive boil. The two cylindrical cans jumped around erratically in the seething liquid, buffeted by countless bubbles exploding off the bottom of the dented metal bucket. He had never attempted this particular technique. A few weeks ago he tried cooking a C-ration on top of a pile of coarse dirt soaked with about a gallon of stolen gasoline. This unusual technique had been suggested to him by a lance corporal from another company. It did create a spectacular visual display of whooshing flames, but turned out less satisfactory in terms of culinary success. When he pried open the hot can to enjoy a purportedly cooked meal, he discovered that the meat closest to the metal sides of the can had been thoroughly scorched, while the meat in the center remained frozen as hard as an ice cube. After nearly gagging on a chunk of half burnt and half frozen pork, he decided to never repeat the experiment again.

This boiling technique looked more promising, and had only recently been made possible by the availability of several shattered trees that had been strewn haphazardly around the upper slopes of the hill by a few dozen Chinese mortar rounds. Timothy had discovered a wide range of timber to choose from: slender kindling, perfect for starting the fire; larger log-like chunks, good for keeping it going; and just about every other size and shape in between. Timothy had collected the wood and then stacked it into a neat, pyramid-shaped pile a few feet from the cooking bucket. He was poking another stick into the edge of the fire and stirring it around when he noticed the long afternoon shadow of Lieutenant Meyer approaching from below. "Damn," he whispered out loud to himself. "Now the lieutenant's going to make me put out this fire before I get to see if it really works. Damn."

Lieutenant Meyer limped up to the edge of the cooking fire and peered down on it. He leaned precariously on a makeshift cane he had fabricated from a reasonably straight tree branch. "What have we got here?" he finally asked. Timothy could see that a chunk of the lieutenant's shoepac had been shot off.

"It's a cooking fire, sir. I just got it started up a few minutes ago." Timothy hoped this hint about just getting the fire started a few minutes ago would buy him enough time to finish cooking the C-rations.

Lieutenant Meyer studied the boiling water and the bobbing C-rations with intense curiosity. Timothy waited for a stern order to put the fire out. "Say, do you mind if I stick a can in there too? Now that I think about it, I haven't eaten anything since yesterday morning. A hot meal sounds good."

This question caught Timothy off-guard. "Uh, sure, I guess." He paused while thinking of something more intelligent to say. "I can fish my cans out in a couple of minutes, and then we can stick yours in. That should work just fine."

"Great. I'll be back in a few minutes. I've got to find my C-rations." Lieutenant Meyer almost slipped as he turned to head down the hill.

Over his initial surprise, Timothy responded instantly. "Oh, don't go looking for your C-rations, sir. You can have some of mine for now. When you find yours, we can trade. We'll even things up later." Timothy started digging through his pack. "Let's see—I've got ham and lima beans, chicken with vegetables, and I've got hamb…sorry, false alarm, I'm all out of hamburger. I think I finished off the hamburger last week. Hey, I've got two chicken and vegetables, if you're really hungry."

"That's OK. I think I finished off my hamburger too. I'll take the ham and lima beans, if you don't mind. I've never been especially fond of lima beans, but for some strange reason, they sound pretty damn good right now. Maybe it's the cold or something."

"Yeah, I know what you mean. I've never been fond of any kind of beans, including lima beans, but they don't sound too bad to me either."

Timothy let the first cans cook for another minute, then pulled them out with two flat sticks he had readied for the task. The cooked C-rations hissed and steamed when he tossed them into the snow by his foot. He picked up the can of ham and lima beams and dropped it into the water, now boiling more dangerously as the fire licked high up the sides of the metal bucket. He looked up at the lieutenant and said, "This is going to take a few minutes, sir. Maybe you should have a seat and make yourself comfortable."

Lieutenant Meyer needed to sit town. His ankle and knee had stiffened up considerably after his walk up the hill, and the pressure of standing had started to feel very unpleasant. His heel throbbed ominously when he shifted off his good foot. "Thanks. Don't mind if I do."

Timothy jumped up and pushed the large chunk of wood he had been sitting on toward the lieutenant. "Here, sir. You can sit on this."

"I can't take your seat. I'll find another."

"No sir. I mean, begging your pardon, sir. I'll find another. They're lying all over the place. You go ahead and sit on this one."

"Thanks." Lieutenant Meyer eased himself down with the help of the makeshift cane until he sat comfortably on the stump. He leaned back a little and straightened his leg out. "Ahhh…that feels good. I guess I've been standing up too long."

Timothy looked down at the shredded shoepac again. He could see the remnant edges of a bullet hole slightly above the missing heel. "Are you OK, sir?"

Lieutenant Meyer turned his foot and looked at it too. "Oh yeah, I'm fine. Just a little unlucky." He straightened his ankle out again. "I was running across the hill to check on the platoon's flank when a bullet caught me in the foot. I thought it missed me at first. Later I realized the damn thing had sliced open the bottom of my heel. I guess I'm lucky the shot wasn't an inch higher. That would have made a real mess."

Timothy grimaced after the lieutenant finished this narrative. "Yeah, I guess so. Have you seen the corpsman?"

"Not yet. I was on my way when I ran into your little cooking setup here. I'll go up and see him after I'm finished with my hot meal."

"I think your ham and lima beans should be done in a few minutes. Do you mind if I go ahead and eat before it gets cold?"

"No, of course not. We're not exactly in a fancy restaurant with tables and candles. Go ahead and start eating."

Timothy opened the first can and stuck a fork into the contents. The fork plunged easily down to the bottom of the can. He pulled out a chunk of chicken and popped it into his mouth. It burned the tip of his tongue. "Damn, it worked." He quickly finished off the rest of the can. The last bite had just started to cool down as it touched his lips. "That was pretty good. Hot at the beginning, and just starting to cool down when I got to the last bite. Possibly the best meal I've ever had—at least since I arrived in Korea. For sure since I've been stuck on this hill. Let's see how yours is coming along." Steam billowed up from the surface of the boiling water and washed over Timothy's chest and face when he leaned over the bucket to check the lieutenant's ham and lima beans. Partially hidden by the steam, Timothy furtively slid a small hand-shaped branch up his right sleeve and held the stem inside the cuff of his jacket with his now concealed hand. He bent down to get a better look at the C-ration and casually stuck his "hand" into the fire. He held it there until it had fully ignited.

"Careful there Timothy. You're getting awfully close to the fire. I wouldn't want you to burn yourself."

Timothy glanced down at his hand, and then suddenly raised the flaming member up into the air. "Hey look, lieutenant—my hand's on fire!" Lieutenant Meyer stared at the burning "fingers" in speechless disbelief. Timothy continued talking as if nothing had happened, gesturing nonchalantly with the flaming hand at the end of his sleeve when he made each point. "You know lieutenant, this actually feels pretty good. No, it feels really good. As a matter of fact, I think this has got to be the first time I've felt really warm since we left Wonsan." Lieutenant Meyer suddenly squirmed with agitation, and began pushing himself up frantically with the makeshift cane to put the fire out. He had almost straightened his leg out when Timothy dropped the burning branch into the snow and punched his real hand out of the sleeve. "Hey lieutenant, I was just joking. See, my hand's not on fire. It was just a branch."

Lieutenant Meyer slumped back onto the chunk of wood and listened to Timothy's fake hand sizzle in the snow. "Darn it Timothy! You just about gave me a heart attack. First I thought your hand was on fire. And then when you started talking about it being warm and feeling really good, I thought you were going crazy. I didn't know whether I should put out the fire or just pull my Colt and put you out of your misery."

"Yeah, pretty funny, huh?"

Lieutenant Meyer maintained his normally stoic expression for nearly five seconds before exploding into laughter. "Yeah…Timothy…that was…pretty damn…funny." For a few precious moments he forgot about Dog Hill and the thousands of Chinese troops waiting beyond the road. "Yeah, pretty damn funny. It surely was. Thanks."

"Do you think Gunny Talbot would like the flaming hand trick?"

Lieutenant Meyer tried to imagine how Gunny Talbot would react to this joke. "I wouldn't push your luck."

"Yeah, maybe you're right. I don't think he has a sense of humor."

"Oh, he does. He just doesn't show it when he's got a lot of things to think about and take care of."

Timothy gathered up the two flat sticks again and used them to remove the lieutenant's C-ration from the boiling bucket. "Yeah, you're probably right. Maybe some other time." He opened the can, dug a spoon out of his pack, cleaned it in the snow, and then handed both to the lieutenant. Lieutenant Meyer accepted the can with a nod, and sat quietly and ate his hot dinner. He bent his knee slightly and dug his injured heel into the snow. The cold felt good for a few minutes, but then the bottom of his foot began to ache again. Timothy sat quietly too, and contented himself with studying the burning hand as it extinguished itself in the melting snow. The last of the day's sun faded as the flame went out. The air would soon turn much colder.

"Thanks, Timothy. That really hit the spot. I wish I had a good cigar to finish off this delicious meal. You wouldn't happen to have any, would you?"

"No sir. I smoked my last one last night."

"It's just as well. As much as I'd like to sit by this fire for a little longer, I'd better head up to the medical tent before it gets completely dark." Lieutenant Meyer pushed himself up with the makeshift cane and faced up the hill.

"Sir?"

Lieutenant Meyer turned partway back without moving his feet. "Yes?"

Timothy stood and took a half step toward the lieutenant before asking his question. "Do you think we're going to make it out of here?"

Surprised by this question, Lieutenant Meyer did not have a prepared answer. No one else had asked him this before. He thought carefully about what he wanted to say. He understood that he had to maintain as much morale as possible; at the same time he didn't want to tell an obvious lie. "Well Timothy, I certainly hope so. I think we have a chance. It depends on what the Chinese do tonight. What made you ask that question, anyway?"

Timothy's voice quivered for the first time. "Because…I've got some things I need to do, and some people I have to talk to. It's really important. I can't end up buried out here on some no-name hill in North Korea with things the way they are. I just can't."

Lieutenant Meyer paused before speaking. "Well then—let's do everything we possibly can to get you out of here."

"And everyone else too?"

Lieutenant Meyer did not respond. He turned as if he had not heard the question and began limping up the hill toward the tents. When he finally reached the medical tent, he chuckled out loud about Timothy's flaming hand trick.

Chapter 22
Timothy and Seth, August 1948

Seth pinched the flat body of the shiny metal lure between the thumb and first two fingers of his weak hand, then attached a brass snap swivel with his good hand. He tugged gently on the nylon line tied to a tiny metal ring at the rear of the swivel to lock it into place, taking special care not to pull the sharpened treble hook into his hand or fingers. He had no desire to begin this Saturday evening's fishing adventure by removing a barbed hook from his own flesh—assuming he could even extract the damn thing by himself. He had impaled himself in this manner once before, and forcing the razor-edged hook through the heel of his hand until it emerged near his wrist, so a friend could cut the barbed tip off with a pair of rusty pliers, had become a memorable event he did not care to repeat. After he had properly secured the lure, he tossed it over the top of the weathered wood railing at the far end of the pier and swung the rod out smoothly behind it. He jiggled the lure at the end of the looping line before allowing it to come to rest. He reeled the lure in until it hung about a foot below the tip of the rod, and then waited. The sun had just begun its descent behind the distant horizon's tenuous arc, and the lure flashed in the slanting afternoon light after rotating in the easy sea breeze flowing in from the west.

Seth waited patiently until the last edge of sun dropped beyond his sight and only a pale blue light refracted across the lower sky. When the sun's afterglow faded away, he reached back with the supple rod and then whipped it forward, slicing the air violently and sending the gleaming lure zinging out over the gently swelling waters of the Pacific Ocean. The reel fed out the rapidly uncoiling line and whirred pleasantly until the lure dived into the briny water with a familiar "plunk," almost too far away to hear. Seth grasped the rod firmly with his good hand, and with his weak hand reached down and snapped the steel bail over to arrest the unraveling line. As he reeled in line, his weak hand struggling to push smoothly through each turn, he jerked the rod from time to time to improve the attractiveness of the lure to any fish that might be feeding in the waters off the end of the pier. A cramp twitched his hand before he finally glimpsed the flashing lure below the surface of the water, moments before it jumped into the cool evening air. He sighed. Not a single fish had attacked the sharpened hooks during the lure's first trip back to the pier. He positioned the lure near the tip of the rod again, and, with the same violent snap, flung it out again over the smooth water and into the dusky sky.

The westerly breeze quickened, and as the pale blue sky thinned above the faraway ocean rim and transposed to dark blue and then to purple, a few precocious stars twinkled near the edges of scattered clouds. Three electric lights, mounted high up on evenly-spaced wood poles, flashed on a few minutes later and instantly bathed the damp boards of the pier in an iridescent glow. Seth had positioned himself directly below one of the lights; when he glanced up at the glowing bulb and listened to its buzz, he felt a small tug on the rod. He counted out loud to three, and then jerked the rod hard to set the hook. At first nothing happened, but then the line began pouring out of the reel and chattering violently against the lightly set drag. Seth squeezed the rod firmly in his good hand and rested his weak hand against the vibrating reel. When the speed of the clicking drag had slowed a little, he raised the rod to pull the fish closer and then smoothly reeled in line as he dipped the tip back down. He did this five times before the fish exploded away from him again, pulling at least 20 feet of line back into the sea. Seth waited again until the line slowed, and again he pulled the fish closer. He had retrieved the 20 feet, plus a little more, when the fish raced away again. While Seth focused on his battle with the fish, he did not notice that a small boy had walked down the dock and now stood near his side. The boy stepped up onto the lowest rail so that he could see better.

The boy looked down at the dark water and up at the back of Seth's head. He leaned out over the top rail as far as he could before asking the only question that mattered. "Catch anything, Pastor?"

Seth reeled in some more line before turning to look down at the small boy. He smiled before speaking. "Oh, it's you. You gave me a start. What are you doing out here by yourself on a Saturday evening?"

The boy grinned widely. "My parents are taking a walk down by the boats. I asked them if I could go to the end of the pier to see if you were here. I can only stay a few minutes or else they might get worried."

Seth nodded. "I see. Can you stay long enough to help me net this fish? I think it's a pretty big one—at least big for me. The net's over by the tackle box."

The boy nodded and hopped down from the rail to retrieve the net. He returned to Seth's side a few seconds later. The fish had finally tired, and Seth managed to reel it in until it swam in erratic circles just below the edge of the pier. He prepared to pull the rod back one more time to retrieve a little more line when the fish jumped out of the water and flashed its tail in the embracing glow of electric lights. Seth eased up on the rod, and the fish twisted into the water again.

"Alright, Andy. Are you ready to net this fish? I think it's time to bring it in."

"Yes sir. I'm ready." Andy held the net out over the top railing as far as he could, his little arms shaking with strain.

"Hey Andy, you might want to hop down and stick the net below the railing. I don't think I can lift the fish up that high."

"OK, Pastor." Andy hopped off the lower railing, and sliding quickly to his knees, shoved the net below the bottom rail. He gripped the handle with both hands, squeezing it so hard that his eyes started to squint.

"Ready, Andy…here it comes…I'm bringing it up now." Seth reeled with all the strength his weak hand could muster as he pulled the fish out of the dark water and lifted it up to the waiting net. His weak hand began to lose its grip on the damp rod handle when Andy reached out with the net and scooped the fish in. The fish, a beautiful Coho salmon, sparkled in the electric lamp light when Andy dragged it across the deck.

The colorful salmon thrilled Andy. "Wow! It's a really nice one."

Seth rested his weak hand in his jacket pocket and inspected the exhausted fish. His hand wouldn't have lasted much longer. He felt thankful for Andy's help. "Yeah, it is. Must be at least 10 pounds. What do you think?"

"I think it must be at least 12. It's a big one."

"Could be. It is a big one. Can you stay and have some. I'm going to walk down to the beach and make a fire to cook this fish up. Since you helped bring it in, you can stay and have some, if you want. You can even invite your parents."

This offer tempted Andy; sadly, he knew that too much time had already passed and he should return to his parents. "I'd like to stay and eat some of this big fish, but I've got to get going. Maybe some other time."

"Sure. Maybe some other time. I'll tell you how it tasted when I see you in church tomorrow. Oh, and thanks for your help. I don't think I could have brought this monster in without your expert assistance. I really appreciate it."

"You're welcome. See you tomorrow." Andy spun around and waved before skipping briskly down the long pier and disappearing into the misty shadows beyond the reach of the electric lights.

Two nights had passed since Jake served dinner to the mysterious young man, and still he struggled to remember where they had met before. Even though the young man had insisted that they did not know each other, Jake remained certain that they had met—he just couldn't remember when, or where for that matter. He sat quietly at the table by the window, the same one the young man had used to eat dinner, and struggled to remember. Maybe Jake's aging brain had blurred the past too much. In truth, the young man's face had also started to blur a little, and after only two days. Jake sat there at the table, trying to reconstruct a past event that didn't appear to exist, and after a half-hour of futility, decided he should move on to something else. He rubbed his eyes and tried not to think about the young man.

"Hi Jake. How are you doing tonight?" A slender woman in her early thirties stood primly by the table with her polished black shoes pressed neatly together. She wore a cream-colored dress and held a brown leather handbag at her side.

Jake lowered his hands and looked up at the young woman's face. He almost knocked the chair over when he stood up. "Why, it's you! I'd recognize that pretty little face anywhere. What are you doing in town? I don't think I've seen you for at least ten years. How long's it been, anyway?"

The young woman smiled. "I think it's been 15 years, Jake. At least 14."

"I guess you must be right about that. My memory isn't so good these days. As a matter of fact, I've been trying to remember something for two days, and can't come up with a darn thing. I'll be damned—15 years. That's a long time. How are you doing, anyway?"

"Things are going fine. I'm living in Portland now. I have a good job at a big department store downtown, and I live in a really nice apartment too. It's only a short walk from where I work. I think you'd approve of it."

"I bet I would. Did you ever get married, if you don't mind me asking? Just tell me if I'm getting too nosey. You know how I am."

"I don't mind, Jake. No, I never did. I guess I just never felt like I met the right man. Maybe I will someday."

After an uneasy lull, Jake failed to conceal his disappointment. "That's nothing to be ashamed of, you know. Lot's of folks don't get married. As a matter of fact, there are a lot of folks who get married who shouldn't, if you want my opinion. Anyway, can you stay for some dinner? It's on the house."

The young woman smiled again. "Thanks, Jake, but no. I really can't spare the time. I'm just passing through on my way to visit some friends, and I have to get going. I'm already late. I just wanted to stop in and say hello and see how things are going for you."

"Well that's swell. I'm really glad you did. It's been a long time."

"Yes it has."

"You have a safe trip then, and stop in again when you get the chance and have more time. I'll give you a rain check on that dinner."

The young woman stepped forward and hugged Jake. A tear squeezed out of her eye and streaked the makeup on her cheek. "I will Jake. I might try to stop by on my way back, if I get the chance."

Jake returned the hug, patting her on the back with both hands. "Sure, you do that. We can have that dinner when you come back through town, or whenever you want."

"That sounds great. I have to get going now. I'll see you later." The young woman soaked the tear up with a white handkerchief and turned to leave.

"Good-by Sarah. It was awfully good to see you again. Don't stay away so long next time. I really enjoyed talking to you."

"Good-by Jake. It was good to see you too."

Seth listened to the big salmon sizzle over the crackling fire. The fire had burned long enough for him to collect an impressive mound of glowing embers. He had spread the embers out neatly before setting a small metal grill with folding legs above them. The thin metal bars heated up quickly, and the fish sizzled when its succulent flesh touched the grille. With the fish cooking nicely, he decided to brew a pot of coffee. He usually didn't drink much coffee, especially this late in the evening; he did like a cup or two when resting on the beach near the pier after a good afternoon of fishing. He retrieved a dented metal coffee pot from deep inside a green canvas bag, threw in a handful of coffee grounds, filled the pot about halfway with fresh water from an old canteen, and snapped on a tarnished lid. He wedged the base of the pot into the edge of glowing embers and twisted it level.

A cool breeze still moved in over the water, bringing with it a memorable scent of salt spray. He listened to sea waves churn and then break softly against the beach. A faraway gull chirped as it hovered on the breeze. He laced his fingers behind his head and leaned back far enough to look up at the evening sky. The clouds had cleared a little, and he could see the moon surrounded by numerous stars. He had never thought of himself as an expert stargazer, although he had learned a few of the important constellations years ago from his mom's father. He remembered fondly the nights his grandfather had led him out into the field behind the house to point out constellations with a crooked, arthritic finger. He quickly found Orion with his telltale belt. He rolled his head until he spotted the Little Dipper, then moved his eyes along the curved handle until they arrived at Polaris. He had nearly located Cassiopeia when he heard someone stumble on a rock down the beach. Seth jerked his eyes down from the stars to see who or what had made the sound, but could see nothing in the darkness. He heard footsteps clearly now, and then another stumble when the unseen person slipped again on one of the numerous slime-covered rocks that covered the beach. Seth squinted into the darkness and focused a few feet to the side of the noise, and then blinked when a young man stepped into his view. The young man stood without moving or saying anything. Seth decided that the young man looked cold and hungry. No—not only cold and hungry, but downright miserable too; and not only miserable—harmless as well.

Seth could see that the young man might stand there a long time unless something caused him to move, so he invited him to dinner. "Would you like something to eat? I was lucky enough to catch this big salmon today and there's more here than I could possibly finish tonight." The young man remained silent and motionless. "I've got some hot coffee too. I'm not sure it's very good. I *am* sure it'll warm you up a little. Why don't you come over and sit by the fire and have a bite."

The young man shivered and clasped his arms around himself. He hesitated, then decided that Seth sounded like a decent man who intended no harm, and started walking toward the fire. "Thanks mister. I am pretty hungry. The last time I had anything decent to eat was over two days ago."

Seth found another metal plate in his bag, and also pulled a metal fork with a bent handle out of a small canvas pouch. He held the plate close to the edge of the grille and flaked off a big chunk of salmon. The young man eagerly reached for the plate when Seth offered it to him. The young man devoured the salmon, and Seth gave him a few more chunks to eat. After the young man had finished his meal and relieved his hunger, he noticed that Seth's left hand appeared much smaller than his right.

Seth refilled his cup from the metal coffee pot. "Would you like some coffee? It's good and hot now."

The young man had sipped coffee a few times before, during breakfast with his dad. He remembered his surprise when he first tasted the bitter darkness of it. He wondered why his dad drank more than one cup during breakfast. His surprised continued, and increased, when he saw his dad drinking more of the nasty stuff at his office. Right now it sounded damn good. "Sure. I'm pretty cold. Maybe it'll help warm me up a little."

Seth poured some of the hot coffee into a metal cup, and reached out over the fire to hand it to the young man. "Be careful not to burn your lips. That pot's been sitting on the fire for quite a while. The coffee may not be any good, but at least it's hot."

The young man glanced at Seth's left hand again when he took the cup, and realized that it was not smaller than the other hand, but thinner, almost as if the skin had shrunk tightly around the fingers and thumb and squeezed all the blood out. A sudden meal after two days of starvation had diminished his sense of tact; he asked Seth what happened outright. "What happened to your hand? It looks thinner than your other hand."

After a long pause, Seth told the young man a story about the South Pacific and an Island called Tarawa. The horrific story filled the young man with terror…and with fascination. When Seth had finished telling the story, he sat quietly and stared into the center of the fire. The young man sat quietly too.

Seth returned his thoughts to the present and lifted his eyes from the fire until they focused on the young man again. "It's really none of my business, but I'm curious. Why are you wandering around down here by the pier at night? And why haven't you eaten in over two days?"

At first the young man considered telling a lie. He finally decided that he should trust this stranger with the withered hand. "I left home. I had a big fight with my parents, and I just walked out."

"What kind of fight?"

"A big one."

"Yeah, you said that. It must have been a really big one for you to leave home for so long." Seth poked the glowing coals under the grille with a stick. "Are you going to head back after you wander around starving for a few more weeks?"

The young man did not smile. "No, I'm never going home again. That's the end of it."

Seth drew in a heavy breath and slowly exhaled before speaking again. He could still smell salt in the air and hear the rhythmic ocean waves. "*Never* is a really long time. Are you sure that's what you really mean?"

The young man sipped the last of his coffee and then stared into the empty metal cup as he rolled it around in his hands. "Yeah, I think it is."

"Do your parents love you?"

This seemed a pointless question to the young man. He answered it anyway. "Yeah, I'm sure they do, but what does that have to do with anything?"

"Well, if they love you, you should go back home. They're probably going crazy with worry right now. I bet they're looking all over for you."

"No, I can't do that."

"Can't do what?"

"I can't go home."

"You said your parents love you. Doesn't it make sense that if you go home, they will welcome you back with love? If you want, I can even drive you there tonight. I'd be glad to go into the house with you too, if you thought it would help. We can leave any time you want. We could even wait until tomorrow, if that suits you better. I've got some friends you could stay with tonight. What do you think?"

This idea tempted the young man. He considered it briefly before responding. "No, it just wouldn't work."

"It wouldn't work? You know, I can't tell you what to do, but from everything I've just heard, I believe it would."

"No, you don't understand."

"Understand what?"

"I don't deserve my parents' love. That's why I'm never going back again."

This unanticipated statement startled Seth. He now realized that he faced a dilemma much deeper and more complex than a simple fugitive from home. He struggled to think of the right thing to say when something he had learned several years ago flared unexpectedly into his consciousness. He recited it in his mind a few times, and then said it out loud, slowly with a soft voice: "…a time to embrace, and a time to refrain from embracing; a time to seek, and a time to lose; a time to keep, and a time to throw away…"

The young man listened to Seth recite the verses. He did not understand what they meant, or why Seth had recited them. "What are you talking about?"

"I believe I'm talking about you, Timothy."

This didn't make any sense. "Talking about me? How's that?"

"Because whatever you decide to do now, you will have to do in your own time. You will have to find your own way on your own terms. I can't force you to do anything or make any decisions for you. There is a time and place for everything under the sun, and I believe with all my heart that the time will come when you are ready to accept your parents' love. That time has not come yet, but I truly believe that one day it will."

Timothy lowered his eyes and stared into the metal cup again. "You know, I thought I was understanding what you were talking about until now."

Seth smiled; Timothy did not see the smile. "I know. How 'bout I wrap the rest of this fish for you to take with you? There's probably enough here for a couple more meals."

Timothy looked up again. "Yeah, I would really appreciate that."

◆ ◆ ◆

Waiting for the Chinese, Dog Hill, 2 December 1950

Subdued by the fleeting warmth of an inexorably declining sun, the fading day's bitter cold seemed nearly tolerable. This illusory comfort did not last, nor did it heal Timothy's cold-damaged flesh. His fingers still ached when he squeezed them together inside his thinly insulated gloves, and he could no longer feel most of his toes. He paused from the grim work of rebuilding the barricade at the base of the hill, and attempted to squirm the toes inside his right shoepac. Surely his brain had sent the proper electrical impulses to persuade the toes to move, yet he could feel nothing inside the brittle boot. He wondered if the unfortunate toes had withered and disappeared. More than two days had passed since he last changed his socks, and when he thought about it, he hadn't really checked to confirm that the toes were still there before pulling the dry socks on. This thought concerned him briefly, and he decided to go on with his work without further worry. He thought to himself that he might try to find the toes later, assuming he still cared or thought it made any difference when the time came.

The dying sun vanished behind broken mountains to the west as Timothy and a fellow Marine swung and dropped the last frozen body needed to renovate the barricade. The Marine shoved the body with his foot until it locked into place like a lumpy keystone. The loss of the sun's remedial light plunged the fragile hill into a deeply imagined sense of desperation. A narrow sliver of faded blue chased the sun beyond the jagged horizon. A few early stars flickered through the endless black above before a quickly moving mass of low clouds obscured the emerging moon. Timothy looked up at the advancing clouds and settled into an uncomfortable position behind the barricade. He strained to see a faintly dispersed glow of pulsing moonlight, but could not make out any of the moon's surface details. The relentless clouds continued flowing into the valley and across the moon, veiling more and more of the remnant light above. A few of the stars that had earlier flickered so promisingly vanished behind edges of the spreading clouds. The darkness would soon emerge full-blown.

Timothy breathed deeply from the intense activity of reconstructing the barricade. Still visible in the fading light of dusk, his breath surged into billows of frigid mist. As he leaned his M-1 Garand against the top of the barricade, an errant breath condensed over the rear sight of the rifle, covering it instantly with a hard glaze of milky frost. The frost glinted in a last remnant of the day's light. At first Timothy thought his aim might be hindered by the annoying frost, but when he imagined the approaching battle, he realized that the obscuring rime would likely be of little concern: so many of them would soon charge across the narrow road and up the base of the hill that exact aim would be unimportant. He could simply shoot anywhere into the approaching mob to be assured of a kill. He would do this over and over again until he had used the last of his ammunition. Then, unstoppable, they would rush over him. He held this thought beyond his vision, and darkness enveloped the hill.

Martha held her breath before speaking, a clear sign of annoyance. She hurriedly pushed herself out of the chair and skipped to the side of the bed. "Now John, what do you think you're doing. You know the doctor said you have to stay in bed at least one more day."

John frowned with equivalent annoyance; at the same time he knew from practiced experience that it didn't work for them to both be annoyed at the same time. Although he spoke of it, he carefully concealed any real display of frustration. "What does it look like I'm doing. I'm getting myself out of this damn hospital bed so that I can go for a walk. I'll go crazy if I lie here one more minute, let alone a whole damn day."

Martha touched his arm to tenderly persuade him to stay in bed. When he continued pressing forward against her touch, she grabbed him above the wrist and squeezed down on his arm. "The doctor said you have to stay in bed for at least one more day, and that's what you're going to do. Let's not be foolish."

John chuckled when he felt Martha squeeze his forearm. "It's not the first time I've been a fool, or the last I expect." He relaxed at Martha's persistent urging and slumped back against the imposing mound of pillows the nurse had constructed earlier. He gazed up at the whitewashed ceiling and sighed deeply. "I don't see how it could hurt to take a little walk. I'm feeling just fine. Seems like it might be a good idea to get up and move around a little."

Martha relaxed, but did not sit down. She stayed by the bed and prepared herself for the next attempt. "It'll be a good idea when the doctor says it's a good idea. Until then, you need to stay in this bed and rest for at least one more day. Then we'll see what the doctor has to say about taking walks or doing anything else."

"I'm still feeling fine."

"You may feel fine right now, but you're lucky to even be here complaining, let alone going for a little walk, as you put it."

"Is that so? Well I disagree."

"Yes, that's so. How could you possibly think otherwise?"

John smiled, although not enough for Martha to see. He smiled because he understood something that no one else ever would, including Martha. "I don't want you to laugh at me, or think I'm crazy."

Martha leaned over the cold metal bed rail, and then turned her face to look into John's eyes. "Why would I laugh at you about something like this?"

"I don't know. I just thought you might." John clasped his fingers together and rested his joined hands against his chest, just above his beating heart. He could feel each reassuring thump in the tips of his entwined fingers.

John's remark intrigued Martha, and she did not want to let it go. "What is it?"

John hesitated, then decided he had already said too much. Now Martha would pester him forever until he spilled the entire story. "Nothing much. I had a sort of dream while I was lying there next to the car. Actually, maybe you'd call it more of a vision."

John did not immediately continue, so Martha prompted him, her curiosity growing with each word. "A vision? What kind of vision?"

"A very strange vision. I saw myself living again, sometime in the future. I was walking in the sun, down a beautiful country road. It looked like a road I walked on many times when I was a boy in Iowa. A cool breeze flowed across the road and made the leaves in the trees rustle. I really liked that sound when I was a boy. It made me happy." John turned and looked out through the open window. A pleasant wisp of air fluttered the curtains.

"Are you going to tell me what you were doing walking down this road?"

"I'm not sure. The main thing I remember is that after awhile, I could see a young man walking toward me. He was a long ways away, but coming closer and closer as we continued to walk toward each other. I couldn't tell who he was at first; then I suddenly recognized him."

Martha fidgeted her foot impatiently, accidentally tapping it against the bed several times—a clear signal to John that she wanted him to stop elaborating and just get to the point. "So...who was it?"

John stared down at his hands to delay answering the question. He still believed that Martha would probably laugh at him. He hated it when she laughed at him. "Well, it was Timothy."

This surprised Martha. She put her hand against her mouth, muffling her voice as she spoke. "Timothy? You saw Timothy in your dream?"

"Yeah, and then I realized something really strange. I knew at that very moment with absolute certainly, that if I could find some way to make it—to live through this awful heart attack—then he would make it too." John lifted his eyes from his hands and looked at Martha. "I know it sounds pretty silly. You're not going to laugh at me, are you?"

Martha sniffed and wiped both eyes with the sleeve of her sweater. "No, John. I'm not going to laugh at you."

Yesterday had ended in frozen darkness nearly an hour ago. The veiled glow of the moon, visible for a brief period after dusk, had departed from the frightfully black sky that now pressed down upon the hill. Timothy remembered looking up at that subtle glow several times before the clouds spread above him and flowed against the distant horizons. He looked up, and the moon glowed cheerfully. When he looked again, the moon had disappeared. It didn't seem possible, but it had. He thought it likely that he would never see the moon again.

Timothy's brooding thoughts were interrupted by the sounds of irregular footsteps accompanied by a rhythmic click. The click stopped behind him. Lieutenant Meyer leaned precariously on his makeshift cane. He kneeled down and spoke in a low voice. "Damned hard to see where you're going when it's this dark. Almost slipped a few times; still managed to stay up somehow. Everything down here under control?"

Timothy responded with a friendly, yet clearly cynical tone. "Yes sir. Everything's just dandy here."

Toil Under The Sun

"Timothy, is that you?"

"Yes sir."

Lieutenant Meyer chuckled. "You know, I still laugh about that burning hand trick. You really got me with that one. That's the best damn laugh I've had in months. Thanks."

"You're welcome." Timothy rolled over. He could almost see the Lieutenant's silhouette when he squinted and looked to the side. "How's your foot?"

"Oh, I'm pretty sure I'll survive. The corpsman put something on it that hurt like hell and then wrapped it up. It took both of us to get the damn shoepac back on."

"Yeah, I bet. At least you can get around."

"Yeah, I guess I can be thankful for that."

"Mind if I ask you a question?"

"Shoot."

"Are you afraid of dying?"

Lieutenant Meyer's eyes widened. And then he coughed. Of course he was afraid of dying. "Afraid of dying? What made you ask a question like that?"

"Because something funny happened this morning."

"Something funny?"

"Yeah. Until yesterday, I didn't give a shit whether I died or not. But now I do. What do you make of that?"

This puzzled Lieutenant Meyer. He had never heard of anything like this. "I don't know that I make anything of it. I've never heard anything like that before."

Timothy responded quickly and then changed the subject. "Yeah, neither have I. When do you think the Chinese will attack tonight?"

This somber question reminded Meyer of a few tasks he still had to take care of. Although he wanted to stay and talk longer, he knew that he could not afford the time. "I don't know. I suppose it could happen any time now. As a matter of fact, I need to check the other platoon before the Chinese do show up. I'll see you in the morning." He straightened himself up with difficulty and walked away, each pair of muffled footsteps accompanied by the familiar click from the frozen tip of the makeshift cane.

Timothy rolled back over and touched the wooden stock of his rifle to confirm it had not shriveled up. He lifted his eyes above the top of the barricade and peered into the darkness engulfing the narrow road. An hour passed and it remained peaceful. He heard a sporadic cough or sneeze to the side or behind, but nothing from the narrow road or the shadowy crevices beyond. Another hour passed, the seconds and minutes moving methodically by and vanishing into the night; still no evidence of activity beyond the road or above the hill. He checked his rifle and counted his clips to pass the time, expecting the onslaught to begin at any moment. Another hour passed, and with its passing his hope for a new morning's sun did not improve. Then, Timothy heard voices far to his right, about fifty yards away.

He turned to the man next to him, the one who had helped him rebuild the barricade earlier, and whispered, "Did you hear something?"

"I don't know. I might have. Did you?"

Timothy pulled back the hood of his parka and lifted the edge of his helmet. He cocked his head and then heard the voices again. "There it is—did you hear it?"

"Yeah, I did. Those damn Chinese bastards are sneaking up on us again. Get ready."

Timothy lowered his helmet and pulled the hood back into place. He squirmed up to the edge of the barricade and slid his index finger in front of the trigger. He swung the rifle to the right a little until it angled in the direction of the voices. And then, without thinking, he pulled back the bolt and ejected an unspent round. The bolt made a loud click when it slammed forward. He realized his mistake instantly, but it probably didn't matter. They would be coming now. He waited for a flare to burst overhead and signal the beginning of his final night on Dog Hill. He waited....

An agitated voice with a distinctly Southern accent shouted out, "Don't shoot. Don't shoot. We're Marines. Who are you?"

Someone behind Timothy quickly yelled a response. "We're Marines too. Identify yourselves."

"Hey asshole, I just did. We're returning from up north, and we've got two damn Marine regiments right on our tail. Who'd y'all *think* we were—the damn Chinese Army?"

Epilogue

Goodbye to Hungnam, December 1950

The 5th and 7th Marine Regiments began a fighting withdrawal from Yudam-ni near the western arm of the Changjin Reservoir on December 1, 1950. In spite of sub-freezing temperatures, persistent Chinese resistance, and narrow snow-covered mountain roads, they reached the Toktong Pass in only two days. The route became easier from the pass down to Hagaru-ri, near the southernmost tip of the Changjin Reservoir, where the Marines arrived in orderly fashion and mostly intact with almost all of their equipment and around 1,500 casualties. After reuniting with elements of the 1st Marine Regiment and other Army and Marine troops at Hagaru-ri, the withdrawal resumed on December 6th. A day and a half more passed during the march south to Koto-ri, a journey of 11 miles through snow flurries and constant attack by Chinese troops. From Koto-ri, the advance continued on December 8th to Chinhung-ni, 10 miles further south and now held by advance units of the U.S. Army 3rd Division. However, the march to Chinhung-ni was temporarily interrupted by the earlier destruction of the bridge over the 2,900-foot deep Hwangch'oryong Pass. Special prefabricated bridge sections, each weighing over 2,500 pounds, were parachuted into Koto-ri and then trucked to the pass for installation. The bridge sections were quickly installed by the U.S. Army 58th Treadway Bridge Company, allowing the Marines to cross the pass on December 9th. The last Marines passed though the safety of the U.S. Army 3rd Division's defensive perimeter north of Hamhung during the afternoon of December 11th, arriving in the port city of Hungnam shortly thereafter.

The evacuation of Wonsan, approximately 50 miles to the south, had actually taken place a day earlier on December 10th. The survivors of the 1st Marine Division departed Hungnam harbor five days later on December 15th. In all, more than 100 ships were required to evacuate over 87,000 U.S. and ROKA troops, as well as nearly 90,000 Korean refugees who preferred not to remain behind to greet the approaching Chinese Army. As the last of the ships departed Hungnam, Navy demolition experts destroyed *the waterfront facilities with explosive charges, leaving a devastated port to the Communists.*

Secretary of State Dean Acheson called the incursion into North Korea, and subsequent retreat, the greatest defeat suffered by Americans since the Battle of Bull Run. Newsweek magazine called it America's worst licking since Pearl Harbor. Yet the U.S. Marine fighting withdrawal from the Changjin Reservoir to Hungnam, a journey of nearly 80 miles completed in a mere 13 days against overwhelming odds, must be considered one of the greatest maneuvers of its kind in military history. However, this heroic action came at high cost. It is estimated that the Chinese Ninth Army Group lost 25,000 killed in action and 12,500 wounded during the campaign, rendering it all but ineffective. Marine losses are estimated at over 700 killed, 200 missing in action, and 3,500 wounded.

Possibly a more eloquent description of the battle was made by Frank E. Low, a retired Army major sent to Korea by President Truman to assess the situation. He reported the following in a memorandum to the president: "The close cooperation and coordination existing between officers and enlisted men exemplified the true "Esprit de Corps" that is so easily recognizable in a Marine unit. At no time did the Marines retreat or withdraw during this operation. They continually fought their way out of the trap, and effectively destroyed the combat effectiveness of two Chinese armies. Their casualty toll was heavy, primarily due to frostbite; but they succeeded in carrying their dead and wounded with them, and did not lose any of their equipment. Indeed, a magnificent performance."

Timothy slid his palms along the round steel deck railing and felt the enduring edges of dozens of long forgotten paint jobs chafe the skin of his tender hands, still healing from frostbite. The slanting side of the massive troop ship had appeared smooth and consistent when he first glimpsed it over a mile away. He remembered thinking this while the remnants of his platoon weaved along the crowded dock toward the drooping gangway. When he leaned over the railing and sighted down the uneven hull to the swelling steel-gray water below, he could see hundreds of imperfections. Many of the bumps and divots had been almost smoothed over by the same multiple layers of paint that coated the railing—but he could still see them. A small oil slick glistened and swirled at the waterline before spreading out unevenly against the dock pilings, reflecting the gray light of the overcast sky. Timothy felt the rhythmic rumblings of the ship's engines through the thick steel deck beneath his feet. The vibration of the massive engines fluttered the oil slick, giving him a sign that the ship would soon depart.

Raising his weary eyes from the shadowed water, Timothy looked out over the long dock, swarming with countless troops and refugees—all eager to board one of the many ships that waited in the harbor. After scanning several faces without much interest, he unexpectedly focused on a young Korean mother with a small child attached securely to each hand. The dirty-faced children revealed no emotion; he could see an intense expression of worry on the mother's face as she forced a path through the expanding crowds of strangers. He watched the three of them for almost a minute before they vanished between two dark buildings beyond the bow of the ship. He felt fortunate to stand again on the deck of one of the ships. Soon he would leave North Korea. He hoped that the mother and her children would find safety too, but because they were walking away from the ships he worried that they might not.

Timothy heard an awkward gait accompanied by the familiar cane tapping that signaled the approach of Lieutenant Meyer. He looked up from the dock when the lieutenant had reached about five steps away. Timothy looked down at the cane and smiled. "I see they gave you a better cane."

Lieutenant Meyer smiled too. He stopped next to Timothy and hung the handle of his new cane over the railing. "Yeah, they did. I was starting to get used to the other one. This one just doesn't quite have the same feel to it."

"I know what you mean. It seems like a lot of things don't have the same feel any more." Timothy turned his head and resumed his study of the people on the dock.

Lieutenant Meyer continued the conversation. "Are you going to be alright?"

Timothy thought about the Chinese soldier who had shot off a chunk of the lieutenant's heel, and wondered if he and his buddies were marching down the road toward Hungnam at that very moment. "Yeah, I'll be alright. I'm just a little tired. That's all."

"I could use some rest myself. As a matter of fact, I could probably sleep for about three days if no one wakes me up." He lifted the cane off the rail and supported some of his weight on it. "First I need to get something decent to eat, and it's not going to be a damn C-ration, I can tell you that much." Meyer chuckled. "By the way, how's your hand?"

"My hand? It's fine. Why?"

"I was just thinking about that burning hand trick. I still laugh when I think about it."

"Oh yeah, the burning hand. It's fine—just a little frostbitten, that's all."

"Good. Glad to hear you're doing OK. I'll probably be seeing you around. You take it easy now."

"Yeah, thanks. You take it easy too."

Lieutenant Meyer limped and tapped his way along the gray steel deck before disappearing through an open hatch. Timothy stared at the hatch expectantly, waiting for someone else to come out, but they never did. He rubbed his eyes and thought about sleep. He was not a little tired as he had told the lieutenant—he was absurdly exhausted. He thought back over the last three weeks and remembered having achieved somewhere between 40 and 50 hours of credible sleep. A little nap sounded like a good idea. He pushed himself away from the painted railing and began searching for a comfortable place to lie down. He found several big coils of rope out of the weather under a steel overhang near the stern. He nestled himself into the largest coil and closed his eyes. A few minutes later, the ship shuddered noisily and began moving away from the dock—he did not feel it.

At first he cannot see where he is. Although his eyes are open and focused, a formless, silent gloom shrouds his vision. The intense stillness of the gloom flows all around him and lifts him above an unseen ground, filling his stomach with a familiar queasy sensation of aimless floating. His awareness of the gloom is severed when a hazy blue light unexpectedly appears and then dances far beyond his vision. He squints at the light, and, although it does not become clearer or more focused, it begins moving toward him, slowly at first, then with rising acceleration. And as the intensity of the light increases enough to hurt his eyes, he realizes that the light is not moving toward him—he is moving toward the light.

The blue light grows beyond the edges of his vision and begins to envelop him. The spherical edges of the light pass around him. When the light has closed in behind, he can for the first time hear a gentle swooshing sound and feel a vague coolness against his skin. The intensity of the sound amplifies when he pushes deeper into the light, and he soon recognizes it as the swirl of a distant wind. With each passing moment the light grows more intense as well, rising sympathetically with the advancing wind. Accelerating, moving faster into the light, no longer floating, flying with ever-increasing speed, no longer in control of himself, he realizes for the first time that it is not the sound of wind he can hear, but the ominous sound of an approaching storm. He looks down and recognizes the snow-covered floor of a dark forest racing below. And then, in a sudden explosion of light and wind and furious sound, he dissolves into a small boy sitting high up in a tree.

Squeezing his slender arms around the rough trunk of the tree, he struggles to hold his position against the raging storm. Flashes of lightning sear the dark sky high above him. Leafless branches whip against his face and arms, cutting his ashen skin. Snow crystals, sharp and unforgiving, swirl around him, blinding his eyes and freezing his ears and nose and fingertips. Buffeted by the unrelenting wind, the usually reliable branch he is sitting on unexpectedly heaves up and then collapses back down, almost tossing him off. Terrified and surprised, he pulls himself even tighter against the trunk, cutting his hands and wrists against the sharp bark of the tree. A drop of blood trickles down his arm and splashes against his thigh. He prepares to close his eyes for the last time and to surrender to the storm when he hears familiar voices below.

He leans over the branch and looks down—he remembers doing this before—and easily recognizes his parents. They are speaking to him, but the rage of the storm's wind and the rumble of crackling thunder cover them up. He leans further out, and still cannot hear what they are saying. He looks into their eyes, first his mother's and then his father's, and sees the gleaming reflection of the menacing forest. It is a familiar sight, a vision he has witnessed many times before. But then he looks deeper, and the fearful image fades a little. The darkness of the forest is gradually overcome by the gleam of a tranquil sunrise. He watches a warm edge of sun break across the horizon, and then beholds a clement golden light spread across the halcyon sky.

He does not believe what he is seeing at first, and gazes up through the gnarled branches of the old tree to the clearing sky above. He is surprised to find that the lightning and dark clouds and swirling storm winds have all vanished, giving way to puffy cumulus clouds now floating pleasantly against an increasingly azure sky. He listens again for the rushing wind, and hears that the once raging storm has receded, replaced by the sounds of a trickling brook and the singing of birds. He feels for the stinging ice crystals and whipping branches; instead a gentle breeze wafts through calmly swaying trees as light from the rising sun warms his skin. He sniffs the air for the scent of decay and finds only the pleasant odor of evergreens and flowers and the mist of the trickling stream.

He looks down again to see if his parents are still standing near the base of the old tree. He is pleased to see that they are, but now, unlike before, they are not alone. Dozens, no, hundreds of other people are standing around them. He cannot tell who any of them are at first, but as bright shafts of sunlight break through the thick trees and illuminate the forest floor, he begins to recognize each one. There's old Jake, who gave him dinner and a few kind words, standing behind his dad. And the man with the dirty raincoat who shared his fish and told him there would be a time to accept love. And look, there's coach Hightower, standing behind his mom. And Phijit's here too, barking and leaping all over the place like usual. And Jonathan—sitting on the ground with his drawing paper and pencils, getting ready to draw another picture of his shoe. And there's his old teacher, Miss Hennessey, probably still teaching kids to read. And his scoutmaster, Mr. McDermott, whistling *Scotland the Brave* and making pancakes. And Lieutenant Meyer, trying to figure out the burning hand trick. And, and…there's Humphrey…in gleaming chain mail, wielding a magnificent broadsword and smiling like everything is just fine. What's he doing here?

Martha cups her hands around her mouth and yells up at the small boy. "Timothy, it's time to come down from the tree. You don't need to stay up there any more. You can come down now." Timothy looks down at his mom and does not move.

John beckons to Timothy with a quick wave of his right hand, his left hand occupied with a fly rod. "That's right son. Time to come down from there. Look—I brought my fly rod so we can go fishing. The sooner you come down, the sooner we can go catch a fish."

Humphrey presses the tip of his broadsword into the fragrant ground and kneels down to pet Phijit. "Yeah Timothy. What are you waiting for? Time to come down from the tree—no reason to stay up there any more."

Others in the crowd join in, waving and shouting and clapping at Timothy to come down and join them. Timothy watches this for a long time, then slowly releases his grip from the old tree and looks at his hands and wrists: they are smooth and clean. He looks at his leg, and the blood is gone. He looks down at his mom and dad one more time before sliding off the gnarled branch and gracefully swinging to the ground.

Resources

The following resources were used during the writing of portions of this novel. I am deeply indebted to the authors, editors, collaborators, and their excellent work.

Ambrose, Stephen E. *Citizen Soldiers*, published by Simon and Schuster, Copyright 1997 by Ambrose-Tubbs, Inc.

Cain, Charles W., in collaboration with Mike Jerram, *Fighters of World War II*, published by Exeter Books, 1979, Copyright 1979 by Profile Publications Ltd.

Laymon, Charles M., Editor, *The Interpreter's One-Volume Commentary on the Bible*, published by Abingdon Press, Copyright 1971 by Abingdon Press.

Manchester, William. *Goodbye, Darkness – A Memoir of the Pacific War*, published by Dell, Copyright 1980 by William Manchester.

Manza, John D. *The 1st Provisional Marine Brigade in Korea: Part II*, Marine Corps Gazette, Quantico, August 2000.

Russ, Martin. *Breakout – The Chosin Reservoir Campaign, Korea 1950*, published by Fromm International, Copyright 1999 by Martin Russ.

Simmons, Bgen Edwin Howard. "Coping with the Cold at Chosin," Leatherneck Magazine, December 2001.

Tucker, Spencer C., Editor, *Encyclopedia of the Korean War – A Political, Social, and Military History*, published by Checkmark Books, Copyright 2002 by Spencer C. Tucker.

About The Author

R. Phillip Ritter is the son of a father who served as a first lieutenant with the U.S. Army in the Korean War and a mother who taught first grade for nearly three decades. Born in Des Moines, Iowa in January 1952, his family moved to Southern California before he began the first grade. He attended second grade through high school in Anaheim, and then California Polytechnic State University in San Luis Obispo. He graduated with a bachelor of architecture degree in 1975. He completed his thesis year in Denmark, and while there met Kristine (born in Alaska, she was completing her second year of architecture through the University of Idaho) in the balcony of the Royal Danish Ballet in Copenhagen during a performance of Prokofiev's *Romeo and Juliet*. He moved to Alaska and married Kris a few years later (she would say it took longer than a few years), and has lived there ever since. Both continue to practice architecture. The author and his wife have two adopted sons, one who served as a U.S. Marine in Iraq, and one who is a gifted artist. Although the author has written seriously since the age of 15, this is his first novel. He already has plans to write a second, and, given the time it took to complete the first, it should be available for publication in about four years. The author dedicated this book to his father, a member of the "Greatest Generation," two days before his death in January 2002.

Printed in the United States
65535LVS00003B/76